Dear Michael ~

Thank you for speaking with
Jeff as he put this together —
think you'll be pleased with the result.

But most of all, I'm grateful for your
support and love of this place over decades —
We wouldn't be nearly as strong without it.

Yours,
Presto

MW00445197

O'the Neill

O'the Neill

The Transformation *of*
Modern American Theater

Jeffrey Sweet

Photographs edited by
Preston Whiteway

Forewords by
Michael Douglas and Meryl Streep

Yale UNIVERSITY PRESS
New Haven and London

Copyright © 2014 by The Eugene O'Neill Theater Center.

All rights reserved.

This book may not be reproduced, in whole or in part, including illustrations, in any form (beyond that copying permitted by Sections 107 and 108 of the U.S. Copyright Law and except by reviewers for the public press), without written permission from the publishers.

Yale University Press books may be purchased in quantity for educational, business, or promotional use. For information, please e-mail sales.press@yale.edu (U.S. office) or sales@yaleup.co.uk (U.K. office).

All illustrations, unless otherwise credited, are from the Eugene O'Neill Theater Center.

Designed by Sonia Shannon.
Set in Electra by Princeton Editorial Associates Inc., Scottsdale, Arizona.
Printed in Canada by Friesens.

Library of Congress Cataloging-in-Publication Data

Sweet, Jeffrey, 1950–

The O'Neill : the transformation of modern American theater / Jeffrey Sweet ; photographs edited by Preston Whiteway ; forewords by Michael Douglas and Meryl Streep.

    pages   cm

Includes bibliographical references and index.

ISBN 978-0-300-19557-6 (cloth : alk. paper)

1. Eugene O'Neill Theater Center—History.   2. Theaters—Connecticut—Waterford—History—20th century.   3. Theaters—Connecticut—Waterford—History—21st century.   I. Title.

PN2277.W4742S94   2014

792.09746'9—dc23   2013044553

A catalogue record for this book is available from the British Library.

This paper meets the requirements of ANSI/NISO Z39.48–1992 (Permanence of Paper).

10 9 8 7 6 5 4 3 2 1

For Kristine

Contents

Foreword

IN 1966, I ARRIVED AT a brand new theater on the shore of Connecticut as an intern, responsible for lawn mowing and facilities maintenance. In between carving out a new amphitheater next to an old barn, I began working with the incredible playwrights, directors, and actors who were also spending their summer at the Eugene O'Neill Theater Center, with work so inspiring that I spent the next two summers there too.

Since its founding, the O'Neill has pioneered the discovery and development of new playwrights, actors, and artists for the stage—hosting some of the biggest names in American playwriting, including August Wilson, Wendy Wasserstein, John Guare, Adam Rapp, John Patrick Shanley, Sam Hunter, and hundreds more. The musicals *Avenue Q*, *In the Heights*, and *Nine* all got their start at the O'Neill.

I would not be who or where I am today without the O'Neill. It is a magical place, one of the most important influences on my life and career, and why I've served on the O'Neill's Board of Trustees since 1980. Danny DeVito and I met there as teenagers, and there are a few stories around of the trouble we got into.

In 2010, I had the honor of introducing the O'Neill's Tony Award for Regional Theatre on the CBS telecast, the second Tony the O'Neill has received for its contributions to the American theater. It was an incredibly proud moment for me, to be able to share with millions of viewers the story and impact of the O'Neill on my life and on the lives of thousands of other artists.

The year 2014 marks an important moment—the fiftieth anniversary of the O'Neill's founding and, with it, the founding of play development. The O'Neill "model" is one that has inspired thousands of artists, and one that has spawned or inspired hundreds of similar programs—including the Sundance Institute, the Humana Festival, and the Ojai Playwrights Festival. American theater is fed by the O'Neill's output and is stronger because of its work.

This book traces that history and demonstrates that the O'Neill's artistic vibrancy, innovative spirit, and sense of fun continue boldly into the future. I look forward to what comes next.

Michael Douglas

Michael Douglas with James Broderick in Lanford Wilson's *Lemon Sky*, National Playwrights Conference, 1968.

Foreword

THE MAIN THING I REMEMBER about that summer at the O'Neill after graduating from drama school is all the characters: the actors, dramaturgs, directors, and administrators, dreamers all; such a motley, idiosyncratic bunch.

I think of Arthur Ballet and Martin Esslin, distinguished essayist and translator/adaptor of plays, respectively (Martin Esslin's books were required reading at Vassar), and I think of two men in the teeniest, tiniest bathing suits I had ever seen in my life, Arthur particularly deepening his tan with expensive suntan oil (from France!).

The elegant Charles Fuller, author of *The Brownsville Raid*, and his magnificent cast. Tall and dreamy, intellectual Jamie Hammerstein; wild and animated Lynne Meadow, a gorgeous whirlwind full of ideas and energy. And Edith Oliver, at that time a theater critic for the *New Yorker*, sitting in the baking sun, a little old lady with a smile as big as the beach, benignly helping to midwife at the birth of so many plays . . . can you imagine a critic of today, of any performance art, paying such devotion to the art form for which he claims expertise?

Ed Zang, an actor whose tangy, cigarette-stained voice cracked wise in service of his raspy wit; Joel Brooks, an actor at whom I could not look on stage because I would break down in tears of laughter (I did have focus and concentration problems). Jill Eikenberry, whose ethereal beauty and true sweetness as a person drew a circle of friends like honeysuckle for the bees. Christopher Lloyd, with whom I had performed *A Midsummer Night's Dream* and Andrzej Wajda's *The Possessed* at Yale, pulling up in a little red Triumph convertible, the only actor with a car, and what a car! He'd always played such intense, fierce, scary characters, and here was this little rakish fun side of him!

And the person I have retained most closely from those days is my buddy Joe Grifasi, who, as I recall it, was the one responsible for my going to the O'Neill. He's the one who told me about it and, I thought, got me in. One of the funniest actors in the world, known to everyone in the theater community for forty years, and the embodiment of the "just get up and do it" school of acting. A champ.

Meryl Streep with Joel Brooks, National Playwrights Conference, 1975. Upon her graduation from the Yale School of Drama, the O'Neill's Conference was among Streep's first professional engagements. In the spring of 2014, she received the O'Neill's Monte Cristo Award, an honor presented annually to an artist who has had a significant impact on the American stage.

I remember Lloyd Richards, always in dark clothes, and George White, always in a white linen suit, presiding happily over the suppers, which spilled out onto the lawn overlooking the water, the conversations intense and exuberant and exciting . . . the lights from the amusement park flickering across the water from the other side of the harbor, the other fun house no one had any time to visit because we were lighting up the sky from our own side as well.

We were all engaged with full-hearted passion in sometimes the silliest of exercises, and all in service of finding that wiggly, elusive creature, a new play. When I look down the list of plays and participants, each face swims up indelibly, but the plays? Ah, the plays flew by, for the actors, at least, in a blur of instant prep and even faster production. I think five plays in four weeks?

One I do remember, *Isadora Duncan Sleeps with the Russian Navy*, for a few reasons: first, obviously it had the best title at the Conference, and second (naturally), because I was Isadora. I do recall having as my only prop a twelve foot (twenty foot ?) length of scarf that I employed in all manner of ways—for sheets in which to ensnare lovers, tie them up, and then embalm them, whipping them, cradling them, and ultimately, of course, strangling on it as I rode in a motorcar. . . . Since we mounted the plays in less than five days and the script was huge, I realized I couldn't manipulate the scarf and read from the script, so I lost the script: that is, I memorized it, which Joel Brooks thought was amazing, and I thought: anybody can MEMORIZE, what a dull achievement! (This was something I was able to do in those days fairly quickly BECAUSE I WAS YOUNG. Those days are gone.)

That summer the process was so condensed that I learned a sort of invaluable swiftness of decision making, out of necessity. The "choices" could not be labored over, and that, for certain types of thinking actors, is a gift of exigency. You had to, like your fifth-grade teacher said, in multiple-choice questions, just go with your first instinct, don't worry it to death. That's what actors did at the O'Neill, and with full-blown commitment. Like jumping off the platform onto the swinging trapeze . . . don't hesitate. It's a good lesson. One I've carried with me my whole life.

Meryl Streep

Preface

I HAVE HAD A LONG if sporadic history with the Eugene O'Neill Theater Center. I first made the trip to Waterford, Connecticut, to attend the National Critics Institute in 1970 and have been brought back to work in various functions—running workshops in improvisation for the Critics Institute; teaching for the National Theater Institute and its summer extension, Theatermakers; and offering various presentations and seminars at summer conferences. I have also had the luck to be present at a handful of signature moments—seeing *Fences* and *The History of the American Film* in their National Playwrights Conference incarnations, catching an early Meryl Streep performance the summer after she finished at Yale, scattering the ashes of veteran actor John Seitz around the stage of the Edith, and attending the memorial for Lloyd Richards.

Something Wonderful Right Away, my first book, was published in 1978. It concerned the origins of America's improvisational theater movement, culminating in the creation of Chicago's Second City troupe. Not long ago, a publisher in the process of reissuing that book asked me if I wanted to write a book about another theater institution, and I instantly proposed the Eugene O'Neill Theater Center as a topic. Though Second City trades mostly in spontaneously created comedy and the O'Neill first gained its reputation as a home for the development of new written work, there are parallels. Both are institutions that resemble little of what came before them. Both arose in response to the needs of their times, and, after fifty years, both manage the considerable trick of staying relevant.

What's more, the innovations created at both helped shape innumerable other institutions. An uncountable number of improvisational companies have been inspired by or created in reaction to Second City, and scores of programs and institutions that help writers refine works-in-progress inevitably can trace most of their methods back to the O'Neill.

One more key similarity: both were created by visionaries (Paul Sills and George C. White) who didn't quite know what they were creating even as they took up the work that would define their lives. By coincidence, in 2012, Sills and White were simultaneously inducted into the Theater Hall of Fame (Sills posthumously). (Oh, and Sills was once a guest teacher at the National Theater Institute.)

I contacted executive director Preston Whiteway to find out if he and his staff would be willing to give me the necessary cooperation to undertake the book. Preston's response was, "Funny you should ask." He told me that the O'Neill and Yale University Press were planning a volume in celebration of the O'Neill's fiftieth anniversary, and he wondered if that might interest me.

Though my impulse to write this sprang from my admiration for the Center, I knew I would have to include—along with the breakthroughs and discoveries—something of the tensions and controversies. There are accounts of some fierce arguments in here, including conflicts that to this day have not been resolved. To not relate the most important of these would be to falsify important aspects of the story. An institution grows not only because of its successes but also from what it learns when it stumbles.

A word about methodology: the bulk of what follows is the product of more than a hundred interviews recorded between September 2012 and September 2013 with the knowledge and cooperation of those interviewed. In almost all cases, I can provide exact dates. (A few dates escaped recording.) All participants were informed that I was interviewing them for this book and that the interview was being recorded. Though I had a few questions in mind beforehand, inevitably responses prompted new areas of exploration. The recordings were transcribed (usually by valued volunteers), and then I reviewed the transcriptions to correct names and other errors, frequently checking them against the recordings. When someone is quoted, he or she is identified. What appears between quotation marks is a direct quote. On one or two occasions, when I felt I had to rephrase something to make a coherent sentence, I contacted the subject and asked if the new sentence was something he or she would affirm or if it required rephrasing. Most often I got a modest further rephrasing. Without the generosity of the O'Neill community and veterans, this book could not have been completed.

I cannot claim that what follows is comprehensive. You will not find here a list of all the scripts developed at the National Playwrights Conference, all the musicals and operas workshopped at the National Music Theater Conference, all the artists who worked at the National Puppetry Conference, all the productions of the National Theatre of the Deaf, all the performers who participated in the Cabaret and Performance Conference, all the journalists who sharpened their skills at the National Critics

Institute, or all the young artists who trained at the National Theater Institute. To include every name and date between these covers would exhaust the space available to tell stories that need to be told, and the book would be out-of-date within months of publication.

Inevitably, some readers (particularly alumni) will feel that important tales and voices are missing. They will be right. This is necessarily an introductory effort. Each of the programs surveyed could and should be the subject of a substantial individual volume. I will be happy if this book loosens the soil.

Instead, my intention is to tell how one young man's enthusiasm—sparked by an observation by his father one afternoon in a sailboat—changed the course of the American stage.

The Eugene O'Neill Theater Center campus, formerly the Hammond Estate, ca. 1965. Long Island Sound and the Atlantic Ocean are at the top of the photo, with the Hammond Mansion (offices, bedrooms, and cafeteria) in the center and the Barn Theater to its left.

1. Beginnings

 It's a truism that nobody who came of age after *Citizen Kane* was released can truly appreciate it. The films made in its wake swiftly appropriated the devices director Orson Welles and his team invented, and those devices entered the common grammar of film and became familiar to the point of invisibility to later audiences. Only those who attended the movies regularly before Welles went to Hollywood could register the scope of *Kane*'s numerous technical and structural innovations.

Similarly, nobody who has come into the theater since the Eugene O'Neill Theater Center was founded can appreciate how thoroughly the American way of making theater has changed in the past fifty years. And few younger than fifty can appreciate how big a part of that transformation can be traced to the O'Neill.

Though best known for the National Playwrights Conference, the Center pioneered programs in puppetry, musical theater, cabaret, international exchanges, media, and criticism, as well as founded the National Theatre of the Deaf and the National Theater Institute. Each of these initiatives in turn has had a ripple effect. Indeed, much of what we now take for granted in contemporary theater contains DNA that can be traced back to a green patch of land overlooking Long Island Sound in Waterford, Connecticut.

Left to right, Richard Barr, O'Neill founder George C. White, and playwright Edward Albee on a panel in the Sunken Garden, National Playwrights Conference, 1967. Albee was an early proponent of the O'Neill Center and its mission. Photo by William Auwood.

To appreciate the changes the O'Neill has wrought, we need to look at what prevailed before.

Fashionable as it is to bash Broadway as a redoubt of crassness—a place where pursuit of profit invariably trumps art—it once worked pretty well. For many years, commercial producers managed to regularly introduce works of consequence—from *Beyond the Horizon, The Front Page,* and *The Adding Machine* in the twenties, through the introduction of Clifford Odets and Sidney Kingsley by the Group Theatre during the Depression, and the stretch when Arthur Miller, Tennessee Williams, William Inge, and Robert Anderson teamed with director Elia Kazan for a string of landmark productions, until the sixties, when the comedy of Neil Simon and his colleagues dominated. (And let's not forget the parade of musicals whose overtures immediately play in the mind's ear when the name "Broadway" is spoken.)

Central to the Broadway method of producing was a system for revising material—the pre-Broadway tryout. Plays were tested on audiences in a series of cities before being subjected to the mercies of New York critics. Works composed in isolation must prove themselves by being played in front of human beings—and human beings are what these tours provided. Producers sent their companies on a circuit of mostly eastern engagements, commonly including Philadelphia; Boston; Washington, D.C.; and the traditional penultimate stop, New Haven, Connecticut. The audiences, through their reactions (or lack of), would tell the company what grabbed them, what confused them, when their attention strayed, and what might bear more exploration. Over the course of a production's progress from the first out-of-town performance through the tryout gauntlet and finally to New York, it was common to see running times shortened, characters cut, parts recast, themes redefined, and opening numbers and final curtains reconceived.

The stories of projects saved or transformed on the road are the stuff of Broadway lore. *A Funny Thing Happened on the Way to the Forum* opened in 1962 to disastrous reviews in Washington, only to have its fortunes turned around by a new opening number called "Comedy Tonight!" composed by Stephen Sondheim on orders from consulting director-choreographer Jerome Robbins. Neil Simon realized

During the first National Playwrights Conference in 1965, panels (which often became heated) were held on the state of American theater under the "Conference Tree." Here, left to right, Roger Stevens (chairman, National Endowment for the Arts), Sigmund Koch (Ford Foundation), Robert Crawford (Rockefeller Foundation), and Tony Keller (State of Connecticut Arts Council) speak about funding for the American theater. At the time, all these organizations were funding start-up regional theater companies.

how to solve problems in *The Odd Couple* when Boston critic Elliot Norton said that he was sorry not to see more of the Pigeon sisters; Simon hammered out a revision in which he incorporated them into a satisfying resolution.

This system started to go by the wayside as pre-Broadway tryouts became too expensive to justify. Rather than taking a show on the road, producers increasingly began productions with previews in New York. For example, the 1962 Broadway premiere of Edward Albee's *Who's Afraid of Virginia Woolf?* was notable for not touring but instead opening after five previews on Broadway. As pre-Broadway tours fell from favor, it was time to come up with other ways to test and revise new material.

Edward Albee believes that the tradition of the pre-Broadway tour had ceased to be of much value long before the business model of premiering plays in commercial productions started to falter. Even the best of what that system produced, Albee thinks, was dismissible as "high middle-brow commercialism." From his travels, he was convinced that much of what was lacking had to do with the insularity of American theatrical culture. "I think the most important period of my learning about being a playwright was what was going on in Europe in the forties and fifties and sixties. I read and saw a lot of stuff. And I spent some time in Europe, mostly in Paris. I don't know where any of us would have been without Beckett, without Pirandello, without Ionesco and all those amazing people. How did we pretend to have a culture without knowing what was going on in Europe?"

In the sixties, some European work found its way to Broadway, including Jean Anouilh's *Becket* (New York premiere, 1960), Rolf Hochhuth's *The Deputy* (1964), and Peter Weiss's *The Persecution and Assassination of Jean-Paul Marat as Performed by the Inmates of the Asylum of Charenton under the Direction of the Marquis de Sade* (usually referred to as *Marat/Sade*) (1965). In addition, producers like Alex Cohen and David Merrick brought over many key efforts from the new wave of postwar British theater, including John Osborne's *Look Back in Anger* (opened in London in 1956 and on Broadway in 1957), Shelagh Delaney's *A Taste of Honey* (1958, 1960), Joan Littlewood's signature production of Charles Chilton's *Oh! What a Lovely War* (1963, 1964), Harold Pinter's *The Homecoming* (1965, 1967), and the groundbreaking satiric revue *Beyond the Fringe* (1960, 1962). Many of these were provocative, but it

Lin-Manuel Miranda, cocreator and composer/lyricist (and later lead actor) of *In the Heights*, walks across the O'Neill campus with his keyboard in 2005, when *In the Heights* was part of the National Music Theater Conference. The musical would go on to win the 2008 Best Musical Tony Award. Photo by A. Vincent Scarano.

was galling for American writers that New York stages were so often occupied by the work of non-American dramatists. And it was doubly galling that the imports tended to be more adventurous than the American work producers did choose to premiere on Broadway. Clive Barnes, then the critic of the *New York Times*, wrote in 1968, "at the moment Broadway is only for Establishment playwrights such as Neil Simon, Tennessee Williams, Arthur Miller or Robert Anderson, fine fellows all, but hardly the most interesting playwrights in the United States."

Such new American plays as did premiere on Broadway were the result of individual relationships between producers and playwrights. As director Lloyd Richards once observed, "There were certain individuals who had the means, and housed a talented playwright, and would help him or her develop. . . . During the 1960s, many of the old producers who supported playwrights were dying out. These were really guys who knew theater, knew the development of plays. New works were not happening on Broadway and . . . in this entire country, there were maybe five places that were interested in developing new writers."

One of the first of these places had its genesis some years earlier in a 1949 letter that aspiring dramatist Michaela O'Harra wrote to Howard Lindsay (coauthor of *Life*

Elizabeth Olsen in class at the O'Neill's Moscow Art Theatre semester program, 2009. The program is a division of the O'Neill's National Theater Institute and is the only undergraduate program of its kind. Harvard/American Repertory Theater created a graduate program based on the O'Neill's curriculum there. Photo by Anastasia Korotich.

Judith Light during rehearsals for *Uncommon Women and Others*, by Wendy Wasserstein, National Playwrights Conference, 1977. The play launched Wasserstein's career as a playwright. Photo by Roger S. Christiansen.

with Father and *The Sound of Music*). She expressed her dismay at "working alone with no adequate or stimulating exchange of craft information possible." Lindsay responded by rallying a group of fellow Broadway playwrights to found New Dramatists. The new organization offered seminars, readings, free tickets to plays, and even rooms where out-of-town members could lodge without incurring the expense of a New York hotel. As its current artistic director Todd London notes, "When New Dramatists was founded, Broadway was still everything. There were no MFA [master of fine arts] training programs for playwrights and nothing you would call new play development. It was a kind of Catch-22: you had to write the Broadway play in order to become a Broadway playwright in order to do production so you could learn your craft." Through New Dramatists, developing playwrights could hold Broadway apprenticeships without having to be produced on Broadway. As valuable as New Dramatists was (and continues to be in its home in a former church on West 44th Street), it catered to a handful of writers admitted for a limited term of membership. More support was needed for the many writers who did not have the good fortune to be welcomed into New Dramatists.

Stirred by the desire to offer works that didn't have to appeal to a mass audience to survive, in the fifties producers began to put on more adventurous offerings in smaller venues, many downtown in Greenwich Village. The event commonly cited as kicking off sustained interest in off-Broadway was the 1954 American premiere of Kurt Weill and Bertolt Brecht's *Threepenny Opera*, which opened for a long run in an adaptation by Marc Blitzstein at the Theater de Lys (now the Lucille Lortel Theatre). Off-Broadway also became the place for second chances for works that had flopped in the commercial arena: Eugene O'Neill's *The Iceman Cometh* (1956) and *A Moon for the Misbegotten* (1968), Tennessee Williams's *Summer and Smoke* (1952), and Jules Feiffer's *Little Murders* (1969) all found favor after being rejected in bigger houses in mid-town.

These smaller venues began to host new works as well. Before Albee's uptown success with *Who's Afraid of Virginia Woolf?*, his one-act plays had been featured at the Cherry Lane Theatre and the Provincetown Playhouse. Off-Broadway also introduced world or American premieres of plays by Beckett, Ionesco, Pinter, Amiri Baraka, Athol Fugard, Murray Schisgal, and Thornton Wilder, among many others.

But these productions resembled Broadway in that they existed because of support from commercial interests and played under contracts that Actors' Equity—the union guarding actors' interests—approved. Writers who hadn't developed to the point where commercial producers would gamble on them yearned to find opportunities to develop their skills. And then there were writers who either were indifferent

HRH Sarah, Duchess of York (right), arrives with George C. White at the O'Neill for a ribbon-cutting ceremony, 1988. Photo by A. Vincent Scarano.

Kevin Spacey accepts the 2009 Monte Cristo Award in New York City. The award is given every year by the O'Neill, in honor of its namesake's "pioneering spirit," to an individual who has had a positive impact on the American stage. Photo by A. Vincent Scarano.

to commercial success or believed that their subject matter would never be welcomed by a general audience but nevertheless were driven to find ways to engage people ready to hear what they had to say.

The stage, being a social medium, necessarily reflects what is happening in the community. The unrest that bubbled under much of American life in the fifties began erupting as that decade came to a close, and open conflict came to characterize the sixties. Many institutions and assumptions that had long gone unchallenged were now being confronted by those who came of age during the years following World War II. Increasingly, these confrontations informed new playwriting, though such plays were slow to secure commercial support.

Racial issues had occasionally been addressed in American drama before this time. O'Neill's *All God's Chillun Got Wings* (1924) concerns an interracial marriage, a major subplot of the musical *Show Boat* (1927) concerns the ostracism of Julie on racial grounds, and Richard Rodgers, Oscar Hammerstein II, and Joshua Logan courted controversy with a song in *South Pacific* (1949) called "You've Got to Be Carefully Taught." It wasn't until 1959, however, that the first serious play on the subject by an African-American writer achieved popular attention; Lorraine Hansberry's *A Raisin in the Sun* was the surprise hit of the season.

Notwithstanding the success of *Raisin*, its production was not immediately followed by a stream of commercial productions of works by other black writers, though there were such plays that merited staging.

Works dealing with gay and feminist themes were also not much in evidence. Though gay concerns occasionally were referenced in mainstream plays (e.g., Lillian Hellman's *The Children's Hour* [1934], and via offstage characters in Gore Vidal's *The Best Man* [1960], and Tennessee Williams's *A Streetcar Named Desire* [1947], and *Cat on a Hot Tin Roof* [1955]), it wouldn't be until 1968 that a commercial production featuring unambiguously gay Americans as principal characters met with success—Mart Crowley's *The Boys in the Band* (1968). Feminist concerns had little representation on Broadway (apart from *A Raisin in the Sun,* in which the character of Beneatha clearly anticipates the generation of women who would come of age in the sixties); this is not surprising, given the paucity of productions of plays by women writers at that time.

Apart from the lack of representation of black, gay, and female perspectives, the commercial stage reflected little of the rise of the counterculture. American involvement in the war in Vietnam—a war that would divide the country to the point of violence—had begun during the Kennedy administration. It wasn't until 1966, with *Viet Rock,* a musical by Megan Terry, that the existence of the war would be acknowledged in a commercial production (albeit one that had a brief run). Significantly, *Viet Rock* was moved to a commercial run after an initial production at the La MaMa Experimental Theatre Club.

It was at La MaMa, the Caffé Cino, and other shoestring operations that those writers who had little chance in the conventional theater found their first homes and champions. It is not accidental that La MaMa was founded by a black woman (Ellen Stewart) and Cino by a gay man (Joe Cino). Nor is it accidental that neither Stewart nor Cino had had any prior experience in the professional theater. John Guare, in

Lucy the Slut makes an entrance in the musical *Avenue Q,* developed at the O'Neill's National Music Theater Conference, 2002. Shown, left to right, are John Tartaglia and Rick Lyon. Photo by A. Vincent Scarano.

Angela Lansbury attends the first O'Neill Center fundraiser, 1966. Shown, left to right, are Doug Lawrence, Lansbury, George C. White, and Delbert Mann.

an interview with the *Paris Review*, illustrates: "I brought two plays to Cino. He said, 'Sorry we're only doing plays by Aquarians.' I sputtered that I was an Aquarius! He looked at my driver's license. February 5. He weighed my plays in his beefy hands, then checked his astrological charts, and said, 'You go into rehearsal in two weeks, run for two weeks with a possibility of an extension for a third.' I don't know what would have happened to me if I had been a Gemini."

The Cino was the first of the storied venues linked to the birth of off-off-Broadway. It opened in 1958, and plays became a regular feature in its tiny space on Cornelia Street in 1960. La MaMa opened its doors in 1967, and other companies, such as Theatre Genesis and the Judson Poets' Theater, were launched at about the same time. Projects were commonly put up on budgets in the hundreds of dollars (or less).

Few could have anticipated that the next major development would occur 125 miles from the streets of Greenwich Village. It began with the twenty-six-year-old George C. White and his wife Betsy sailing in Long Island Sound with George's father. Betsy remembers, "His father said, 'See that mansion up there? Remember the Hammonds used to live there?'" He pointed to a large, dilapidated structure at the top of a hill. Betsy remembers her father-in-law explaining, "The Hammonds had given the property to the town of Waterford. The town was really only interested in the beach. They didn't know what to do with the rest of it. A lot of kids thought it was a good place to hang out and smoke pot." White asked his father whether the town had any particular plans for the house and the other buildings on the property (including a barn). The leading idea? To set them on fire to give practical experience to the local fire department.

Founder George C. White (age twenty-nine) in front of the Barn (later renamed the Rufus & Margo Rose Theater Barn) in 1965, a year after taking possession of the dilapidated property on the Connecticut shoreline, the former Hammond Estate.

White, a native of Waterford, thought there had to be a better use for the place.

American playwriting icon Eugene O'Neill had spent much of his young life in the area. O'Neill biographers and married writing team Arthur and Barbara Gelb devote several paragraphs in their book, *O'Neill: Life with Monte Cristo*, to the young O'Neill romancing girlfriend Barbara Ashe on the very property White sailed past, mentioning that the long-gone railroad millionaire who owned it—Edward Crowninshield Hammond—had had them chased off the grounds. White was a recent graduate of the Yale School of Drama, and it occurred to him that a link between the legacy of O'Neill and one of America's leading drama schools would be a natural. He proposed that the site be used as a summer adjunct of the school. The Yale Corporation, however, refused to approve the idea.

James Bundy, dean of the Yale School of Drama and artistic director of the Yale Repertory Theatre (Yale Rep), believes that this was ultimately a stroke of luck. "I think if he had been embraced by Yale, it would have been seen as a continuation of what he experienced here while he was a student. At that time, Yale didn't have a professional theater. That was before the founding of Yale Rep. I think the O'Neill would have been more of the academy and less of the profession."

White had to adjust his goals. In the meantime, in 1963, along with others in Waterford interested in the theater, he did the paperwork to incorporate an organization called the Waterford Foundation for the Performing Arts as a not-for-profit. The Foundation negotiated a 30-year lease at one dollar a year for the area of the park on which the buildings stood and started to raise money to begin operation, as well as figure out what that operation should be.

Initially the idea was to open a new theater. But the funding wasn't available to do that. "It was probably a blessing," White comments. "The obvious thing, if we had a lot of money, would be to try to do an O'Neill play. But we didn't, so we had to come up with something that would get us started."

Volunteers staff an O'Neill membership table outside the Sunken Garden in 1964, shortly after securing permission to use Eugene O'Neill's name from his widow. To this day, the O'Neill uses a membership rather than a subscription model.

Carlton House,
680 Madison Avenue,
New York 21, N.Y.

August 3, 1964.

Mr. George C. White,
Waterford Foundation For The Performing Arts,
Post Office Box 174,
Waterford, Connecticut.

Dear Mr. White,

        I beg of you to excuse this
more than tardy reply to your letter of June 23.
I have not been very well which made a great
deal of work pile up, and my time was really not
my own.

        This is to tell you that I am de-
lighted that you wish to name your Foundation
for a theatre project in the name of Eugene O'Neill;
could he know this, he would be more than pleased.
Also, I hope that some day I will be able to visit
the Foundation.

        May you have even greater success
than you expect.

                    Very sincerely yours,

                    Carlotta Monterey O'Neill

Letter from Carlotta O'Neill giving permission to use her husband's name in the name of the Center.

Robert Redford attends a reception at the Monte Cristo Cottage (Eugene O'Neill's childhood home, owned by the O'Neill Center), 1980. Redford was visiting the O'Neill to use it as a model for his newly launched Sundance Institute with its similar mission: to discover and nurture new screenwriters for film. Redford also created a theater lab as part of Sundance. Photo by A. Vincent Scarano.

Then history repeated itself. Michaela O'Harra's letter to Howard Lindsay had resulted in the founding of New Dramatists. Similarly, another young playwright, Marc Smith, approached White as he was trying to define a direction for his new organization. White remembers, "He said, 'Why don't you have a playwrights conference?' And the reason that that sounded good to me was it was cheap." So White decided he would invite playwrights to Waterford. But how to find the playwrights?

He recruited initial participants primarily from two organizations. One was New Dramatists. The other organization brought White into contact with Edward

Albee. Albee and Richard Barr and Clinton Wilder (the co-producers of *Who's Afraid of Virginia Woolf?*) had channeled some of the profits from their hit into the Barr-Wilder-Albee Playwrights Unit, a group the three of them had founded in 1961. Based at off-off-Broadway's Vandam Theater, the Unit put up short runs of new plays that were rehearsed for two weeks and were not open for review. (One of the plays it would present a few years later was the aforementioned *The Boys in the Band*.)

Drawing on people affiliated with these groups, as well as some White knew from his connections with the Yale School of Drama, the Waterford Foundation invited twenty writers to attempt a realization of Smith's conference concept. White also turned to David Pressman, a director he knew from working for producer David Susskind. Pressman introduced White to David Hays, who had designed the two landmark productions that in 1956 sparked the revival of interest in O'Neill, *The Iceman Cometh* off-Broadway and the American premiere on Broadway of *Long Day's Journey into Night*. Both had been directed by José Quintero. One night in 1963, White and his wife Betsy invited Pressman, Hays, and Quintero to their New York apartment on East 90th Street for dinner. White started to articulate some of his ideas for Waterford. White recalls, "Quintero didn't know who the hell I was. Understandably. And he probably was bombed. He said, 'Okay, who's going to be artistic director?' I hadn't even gotten that far. And I said, 'Gee, José, I don't know.' And he said, 'It's obviously Pressman! It's Pressman. Pressman!' And he gets up to storm out, and opens the door and . . . it's the wrong door. It's the door to the kitchen, and there's Betsy standing there with this plate of spaghetti." Of the three dinner guests, it would be Hays who would have the enduring connection with the new enterprise.

In the meantime, the Foundation had been blessed with a psychological boost. In a letter dated August 3, 1964, Eugene O'Neill's widow, Carlotta, wrote, "This is to tell you that I am delighted that you wish to name your Foundation for a theatre project in the name of Eugene O'Neill; could he know this, he would be more than pleased." She ended by writing, "May you have even greater success than you expect." Her wish would come to pass beyond anyone's expectations.

The Foundation was renamed the Eugene O'Neill Memorial Theater Foundation on November 19, 1964, and received its tax-exempt status on November 23, 1964. And on August 4, 1965, "the O'Neill" welcomed twenty playwrights to the grounds at Waterford for the birth of the National Playwrights Conference.

It was not an easy birth.

2. Finding the Way

Lucy Rosenthal's playwriting professor at Yale was critic and anthologist John Gassner. "He advised me to transfer to the education school so I could be home at three o'clock to give the children milk and cookies. And then he said—if you want to know what the culture was like— 'There aren't any women playwrights, except Lillian Hellman, and she's really a man.' This was said to me in private. I think Gassner knew, even then, that this shouldn't be put on the P.A. system."

George C. White, who was familiar with Rosenthal from Yale, apparently had a different opinion about the possibility of a woman succeeding as a dramatist. Rosenthal recalls, "He took me and Oliver Hailey to lunch one spring day at the Yale Club and began to talk about this idea he had. He was kind of spellbinding." White was describing the conference he planned and sounding them out about their interest in being part of it. Rosenthal was able to attend that first summer; Hailey came to Waterford later.

The first John Guare heard of the inaugural National Playwrights Conference in 1965 was in a letter from White. "Would I be interested in coming to Waterford, Connecticut, to discuss the beginning of a new possible theater?" The idea appealed; he had yet to find a way to establish himself in the theater scene that existed. "The abyss between Broadway and off-Broadway and then between off-Broadway and off-off-Broadway was immense." He remembers that there was the beginning of a sense of community among the young writers in New York, particularly the significant number of them based in Greenwich Village. "We were all *living*. Just hanging out. And feeling that downtown was a different world. I lived in a fourth floor walk-up with a twenty-foot ceiling and a skylight and a wood-burning fireplace and an eat-in kitchen and a bathroom that looked down on a garden. Thirty-two dollars a month. Terrence McNally lived over here and Lanford Wilson lived over there. It was being young and fun and fucking around. You'd go to the theater every weekend. You'd go to La MaMa and Theatre Genesis and Cino and Barr-Wilder. You didn't go to see something specific, you went to see what was there."

As the first day of the conference approached, invitee Frank Gagliano got a call from White. "George would rent a station wagon for me if I could bring up some playwrights who didn't drive. I think Sam Shepard might've been in the car, but I know that Lanford Wilson was."

Most of the others invited, Guare remembers, boarded a bus that left from Times Square "to take us Fresh Air Fund kids to the country." The "Fresh Air Fund" reference suggests a theme Guare often refers to about the attitude then toward helping young writers. "That new playwrights were sort of like a disease. Charity. Polio was taken, you know."

And so the playwrights arrived in Waterford. Among the others in that first cohort were Charles Frink, John Glennon, Israel Horovitz, Joe Julian, Tobi Louis, Leonard Melfi, Joel Oliansky, Tom Oliver, Sally Ordway, Emanuel Peluso, Doris Schwerin, Sam Shepard, Douglas Taylor, and the writer who suggested the conference in the first place, Marc Smith. Lucy Rosenthal recalls, "They housed us that first year with townspeople, and the houses were quite grand, or so I thought then. I remember a very luxurious bed and I think either floral wallpaper or sheets." Their lodgings arranged, the writers began to look warily at what was being offered by a host many of them had never met.

Playwright Lewis John Carlino, who arrived at the conference late, wrote about his apprehensions in the September 12, 1965, *New York Times*. "What's to be gained by such a meeting?" he thought as he approached Waterford. "What can possibly be exchanged between me, us, and the panelists (top people in the fields of design, directing, producing, acting, agenting and writing) that hasn't already been discussed endlessly before and shaped into all the neat, seemingly significant and wholly inane generalities usually found in Sunday supplements entitled, 'What's Wrong with the American Theater?' I don't know about these other guys, but I've got misgivings."

Playwright Lanford Wilson and actress Angela Wood on the back porch of the Hammond Mansion, National Playwrights Conference, 1965. Long Island Sound and the Atlantic Ocean are in the background.

Playwrights Joe Scott, Lanford Wilson (seated, left), Barbara Calley, Sam Shepard (seated at back), and Harvey Perr gathered in the Hammond Mansion living room, first National Playwrights Conference, 1965. Photo by Barnes Studio.

Hammond Mansion under renovation in 1964, immediately after the Eugene O'Neill Theater Center secured a lease for the property from the Town of Waterford, Connecticut. The property was in need of extensive repairs.

The playwrights entered the drive of the Hammond Estate, a dozen acres sloping up a broad lawn from the Long Island Sound to the twenty-four-room mansion White's father had pointed out. The Mansion cut a noble figure, but it was run down to the point of being dangerous. The nearby barn was in better shape; at least the roof wasn't likely to collapse. Given the condition of the buildings, White thought it best to hold many of the gatherings in a sunken garden to the east of the Mansion, underneath a huge old copper beech tree.

Poet Odell Shepard offered the opening remarks of the conference, telling of a time in colonial days when townspeople raced down to the waterfront of New London to catch a view of a caged lion on display on an anchored ship. He suggested this might have been the area's first example of an entertainment attraction.

Later in the conference, the playwrights heard from Audrey Wood, a literary agent famous for spotting and encouraging playwriting talent. The story of how she discovered and sustained Tennessee Williams through hard times until his breakthrough was legend. She had also had an active hand in advancing the fortunes of Robert Anderson, William Inge, Arthur Kopit, Carson McCullers, Murray Schisgal, and Guare, among many other writers. A brochure published by the O'Neill Center in the wake of the conference quotes some of her remarks, including her concern about the effect of the commercial marketplace on contemporary playwriting. "Plays

Audrey Wood (center right) with Sally Pavetti, Bill Liebling (second from left), and George C. White, ca. 1970. Wood was the agent for Tennessee Williams (among others) and a major proponent of the O'Neill Center. She left her papers to the O'Neill.

with film potential get the best production breaks," she is reported to have said. "Nine out of ten serious scripts are brushed aside in favor of comedies."

As the conference got under way, White became aware of rumbling among the writers. They were angry, particularly the unproduced (and underproduced) ones. "I was totally horrified at all these crazies that came up," he recalls. Guare believes that some of the anger had its roots in the suspicion that the Conference assumed that the writers wanted careers on Broadway. It was an assumption that he also encountered later, when he became a member of New Dramatists. "People would come to New Dramatists like in 1968 to tell us how to write a hit Broadway comedy. You got the sense that the old status theater was trying to hold on desperately by its fingernails. It was [also] in the air at the O'Neill. So when we had a chance to speak, we said, 'We don't want to be part of this.' We were interested in the new theater."

This anger bubbled up even during what White had assumed would be an uncontroversial panel. "I thought, who's going to get angry at scenery?" So he scheduled as one of the early sessions a conversation featuring set designer David Hays and costume designer Patricia Zipprodt. But the dialogue soon moved to confrontation. Frank Gagliano says, "I guess it must have been David Hays who said something about never reading stage directions. Just reading the script. I remember seeing red at that. Not reading a writer's stage directions!"

Hays's version of that encounter is a little more complicated. "I said, 'Many designers—and I sometimes found myself in this position—want to just read the play, see what they come up with in their mind, and maybe, *then maybe*, read the playwright's directions.' So Sam [Shepard] blew up, said, 'When I want such

David Hays and Patricia Zipprodt before the Design Panel, first National Playwrights Conference, 1965.

and such a set, and when I want such and such a costume, that's what I want!' Pat Zipprodt spoke up and said, 'You know, Sam, if you say that the heroine is in a black dress and she looks like shit in a black dress, I'm not going to put her in a black dress.' And then I said, 'I just designed *All the Way Home* for Arthur Penn. The playwright [Tad Mosel] suggested six settings, and I said you can do it in one without a turntable, nothing. No change. Look at what you save in construction.'" (Hays was nominated for the 1961 Tony Award for the design.)

A meeting with some established producers—Lyn Austin, David Black, T. Edward Hambleton, and Judy Rutherford Marechal—also triggered resentment. Carlino's account confirms Guare's theory: "Mr. Black suggests we write comedy for our first Broadway effort. Then the next plays can be *serious*. From the back of the barn comes a sharp retort, 'Nuts!'"

The most dramatic confrontation came during a panel on criticism, which featured Henry Hewes (of the *Saturday Review*), Norman Nadel (from the Scripps-Howard newspaper chain), Leonard Probst (of NBC), and Boston eminence Elliot Norton. Guare had a very particular quarrel with Norton.

Guare relates, "I'd been working for William Inge. He opened a play called *Family Things, Etc.* in Boston." Norton was featured on a local Boston television program, to which he invited people associated with the plays he covered. Inge was booked to appear on the broadcast before Norton's review was released. The playwright arrived at the studio unprepared for what the critic had in mind. Guare remembers, "Norton said, 'I think it would be very interesting today on the broadcast to read the review, and then discuss the review. Do you mind this, Mr. Inge?' Inge said, 'No.'

"The review was devastating. Something like, 'What was at best a mediocre talent stretched beyond all limits.' Embarrassing him so publicly that he never wrote again. And so, at the criticism panel, I had to ask Norton what he felt his obligations towards playwrights were when he felt so free to destroy one by catching him off guard and reading a devastatingly destructive review while the camera was on his face."

Guare wasn't the only one who confronted the Boston critic. Says Gagliano, "I seem to remember Elliot Norton bringing up Shakespeare and Sam Shepard getting up and saying, 'Fuck Shakespeare! It's not about him anymore!'"

Shepard left Waterford midway through the conference. White shrugs at the memory. "Lanford tried to get him to stay. But we served a great purpose for Sam: he needed some place to walk out of. I mean he really did. To make a statement. He was nineteen."

According to White, what rescued that first conference were two playwrights, one living and one dead.

The living one was Edward Albee. White arranged for Albee and one of his producing partners, Richard Barr, to meet with the young writers. Albee had a unique status. On the one hand, he was a famously uncompromising figure in the playwriting world whom the invited writers saw as a colleague and ally. (As Carlino wrote,

George C. White (right) introduces the Criticism Panel, first National Playwrights Conference, 1965. The panel quickly became tense. Shown, left to right, are Norman Nadel (Scripps-Howard), Elliot Norton (*Boston Globe*), and Leonard Probst. Photo by Barnes Studio.

"I mean, he's one of us. He understands.") On the other hand, he was commercially successful, having authored *Who's Afraid of Virginia Woolf?*, the most notable new play of the past decade. "Edward was a hero because he had given his royalties to start Barr-Wilder [Albarwild Theatre Arts]," Guare says. He and the others were pleased to see Albee but did not quite understand what the latter was there *for*. "We loved Edward, but we didn't know what we were supposed to do."

Without particularly intending it, Albee found himself bridging the gap between the would-be insurgents and what they perceived as the establishment. Not exactly famous in those days for being a peacemaker, Albee nonetheless kept stressing to his fellow playwrights that the O'Neill organization was worth taking a chance on. Albee explains his support of White was based on a simple fact: "If nobody's giving you anything, and then somebody decides to give you something useful, you're enthusiastic. I was impressed by the fact that he seemed to know something about what he wanted."

White says, "I told him, 'I owe you a lot.' He really helped make order out of chaos."

Edward Albee and Richard Barr (both seated at the table, Albee on the left) listen to a question, first National Playwrights Conference, 1965. Given the ramshackle state of the buildings at that time, the outdoor Sunken Garden was the meeting place of choice. Photo by William Auwood.

Albee's support for the O'Neill is all the more notable because it ultimately evolved into a place with a method that he does not find personally useful. Albee famously composes his plays in his head, puts them on paper in a rush when he feels they are ready, goes into production, and doesn't revise much. He doesn't hesitate to state that the idea of staged readings and workshops of his own work holds no appeal for him but acknowledges they may be of value to those who don't write the way he does. With characteristic mischief, he says, "I tell playwrights: don't write first drafts. Write the finished piece."

As for the dead playwright who eased the tensions—that was Eugene O'Neill himself.

The drunken spaghetti dinner at the Whites' apartment forgotten or forgiven, José Quintero arrived in Waterford with actors Barbara Colby and Robert Viharo and gathered the conference participants for a presentation in the barn. As White wrote, "it was necessary to surround the [barn] with fire engines, as there was still dry hay beneath the floor (which sagged in the middle). The lighting was provided by a line of 75-watt bulbs strung down the center. The audience sat in folding chairs provided by the local firehouse."

The presentation was of a rehearsed reading of a scene from *A Moon for the Misbegotten*, featuring the character of Jamie Tyrone, the alcoholic older brother familiar to audiences from *Long Day's Journey into Night*. *Moon* focuses on the relationship between Jamie and Josie Hogan, a young woman who lives with her father on a farm Jamie has inherited. Josie is described by O'Neill as being "so oversized for a woman that she is almost a freak." In one of the most poignant encounters in dramatic literature, one night Josie expresses her feelings for him. But it is too late for Jamie to be redeemed. Eaten up with self-disgust and guilt, he now wants nothing more than to greet permanent oblivion. All that Josie can offer him is the temporary relief he gets from confiding in her. Exhausted, Jamie falls asleep on her breast. When he wakes, he remembers little of the evening before and affects a jauntiness before leaving her for what she knows will be the last time.

The conference participants watched Quintero and his actors explore this extraordinary material, aware that a supporting character named T. Stedman Harder (who ends up covered in mud) was a fictionalized version of Edward Crowninshield Hammond, on whose estate the conference was being held, and that O'Neill pictured the location of the Hogan farm near the Harkness Pond, a stone's throw from where they were sitting.

Barbara Colby and Robert Viharo perform a staged reading of a scene from Eugene O'Neill's *A Moon for the Misbegotten* in the Barn under José Quintero's direction, closing night, first National Playwrights Conference, 1965. The night galvanized the playwriting and local communities, who could now envision the potential success of the Conference. Photo by Barnes Studio.

Gagliano remembers, "The woman playing Josie wasn't a big girl. She said, 'How do you act big?' And he said, 'By acting small. A big person wants to be small, like a drunken person wants to look sober.' And she did it and it worked." Carlino was struck by "the rapt faces caught by the crazy magic of the creative process."

The balm Josie offers Jamie reportedly conferred a kind of balm on the contentious playwrights at Waterford. White sensed that the anger that had simmered throughout the conference had dissipated. The warmth of Josie's pure love brought the first conference to a close as if it were a benediction. White wrote, "It was an eloquent expression of talent, theater, and O'Neill and served to bond the conference together; it changed the negative attitudes into an overall feeling of enthusiasm and optimism."

The playwrights returned home. Carlino described his thoughts as he drove back. "A whole town said, 'We feel the future of the theater rests in the hands of the

Director José Quintero (right) and Joe Anthony during a panel discussion immediately following the performance of an excerpt from Eugene's O'Neill's *A Moon for the Misbegotten* in the Barn Theater, National Playwrights Conference, 1965. Photo by Barnes Studio.

playwright and we want to do something about it.' O.K. So they open their homes to a bunch of strangers. . . . And guess what? They want us back. And they are going to spend the next year trying to get the money to bring us. . . . Nothing like this has ever been done before with us or for us."

Guare was more skeptical. "I thought I would never hear from them again," he says of the conference organizers.

As White undertook the challenge of raising money for the O'Neill Center, he started to think about what changes he should make. Having sailed since he was a boy, the strategy he employed now was not unlike tacking, recognizing the direction of the wind and shifting the sail in relation to it to modify his course. The wind necessarily came from what he learned from the playwrights when he queried them after the conference. "I asked them, 'What do you really want?' And they basically said, 'We want Broadway productions,' but what they really meant was that they wanted professionals to work on their plays. In those days, 'professional' translated to 'Broadway.'"

Critic John Lahr observes that, for all the legend that surrounds the early days of off-off-Broadway, something has been generally overlooked: "The level of technical expertise in Caffé Cino and La MaMa was never, ever very good. It was pretty [much] amateur night. Some of it turned out to be very influential and had some verve and some personality, but a lot of the work was shocking. What the O'Neill had was a higher level. They had real directors and really confident actors."

Harold Clurman, co-founder of the Group Theatre, lectures in the O'Neill's Sunken Garden, National Playwrights Conference, 1966.

For the second Conference, in the summer of 1966, White decided to assign a couple of those real directors and a company of really confident actors to full productions of two new plays. In addition to the writers of the two plays he chose, White invited back the veterans of the first conference.

Guare was surprised to receive an invitation to return and was pleased that the comments he and the other writers had made had been heeded. "The shock was, when we went back next year, what we asked for was there," says Guare. "We came back and found that it was no longer the ghost of Broadway. The next year it was people from the Group Theatre. Bobby Lewis was there, Harold Clurman was there. Phenomenal. And Franchot Tone—very glamorous. [Their presence] anchored it in a way that it had not been anchored in the first year."

Tone's arrival at the O'Neill had a special resonance—he had played Jamie Tyrone opposite Wendy Hiller in the short-lived Broadway premiere of *A Moon for the Misbegotten* in 1957. He was in Waterford to act the lead (under the direction of Fred Rolfe) in one of the two plays White had selected for full production, *The Bird, the Bear and the Actress* by John Glennon. The play was a dramatization of the later life of Edward Gordon Craig, the revolutionary British figure who pioneered much modern theatrical theory, developing new techniques in scenic design still influential today. Tone was a great admirer of Craig and was delighted to be cast as him. He was also excited to be part of the O'Neill. As he told reporter Janet Roach in an August 5, 1966, interview for the *New London Day* (now *The Day*), "If this place can retain its purity of intent, escape the commercialism, it can be one of the landmarks of culture in the country, perhaps in the world."

Tone had some basis for his comments. As Guare noted, he was a veteran of the Group Theatre, the company that Harold Clurman, Cheryl Crawford, and Lee Strasberg founded in 1931 that was active for about ten years. In 1945, Clurman wrote a vivid memoir called *The Fervent Years*, describing the Group's mission and history. Though it produced plays on Broadway, the Group was created to challenge the prevailing star-focused ethos of Broadway by generating productions based on an ensemble consciousness. It was notable for premiering works by Clifford Odets and Sidney Kingsley and introducing to America an approach to acting informed by the theories of Constantin Stanislavski (an introduction that would later be reinforced by the founding of the Actors Studio, which Strasberg led for decades). The Conference playwrights saw members of the Group as early fighters in the same struggle in which they were engaged—to create vital theater uncorrupted by the conventional practices of commercial management.

The other script White chose to give full production was Joel Oliansky's *Bedford Forrest*. The play is a somewhat overstuffed epic, in which the likes of Abraham Lincoln, James Buchanan, and Robert E. Lee make cameo appearances, but there is a strong central story about the title character—a slave master turned Confederate general—and a black man he used to own named Brewster, who, after escaping, is determined to kill Forrest. It was Oliansky's idea to hire Lloyd Richards to stage it.

Constructing the Amphitheater, 1966. The future Barn-El (later renamed the Dina Merrill Theater) is in the background. The Barn Theater is to the left.

"I didn't even know Joel Oliansky," Richards told N. Graham Nesmith in the *African-American Review*. "They asked him who he wanted to direct his play, and he said me. He had been a Yale graduate student and had seen some of my plays that had come through there. I got a call from a man I never heard of, named George White, asking me to come to a place I had never heard of, to direct a play I had never heard of . . . in a theater that was yet to be built."

As part of a speech he gave introducing a play at the Conference in 1994, Richards described his first visit to Waterford in greater detail. "I was met at the train. . . . They brought me to the Mohican Hotel in town and told me all about that's where O'Neill used to sit with the cracker barrel and then get drunk and go home. I said, 'Great, but where's the theater?' . . . [They] drove me up to the Mansion. The 'Mansion' we call it now, because that's what it is now and that's what it may have been some hundreds of years ago, but we went in and the water was coming through the roof. It was being caught in cans. And I said, 'Fine, but where's the theater?' And [George C. White] said, 'Oh,' and we took our umbrellas and we walked down the path, and he pointed to a hole in the ground with about four feet of water and he said, 'That's the theater.' 'And I start rehearsal when?' 'Two weeks.' And I said, 'Fuck.'"

The pit White showed Richards was dug in part by playwrights. Guare remembers, "We had shovels. When we got up there, we started digging out what became the Amphitheater." Opening night for Oliansky's play was August 5, 1966. Designed by David Hays and Fred Grimsey, who also supervised the construction, the 130-seat Amphitheater wasn't quite ready as scheduled, though. Says White, "We had to hold the curtain. The asphalt was still cooling. We had to hose it down." Even with that step taken, Hays remembers, "The chairs were sinking into the flat top."

Bedford Forrest was a huge undertaking. Richards remembered: "We had about sixty people in the cast. We had armies, battles, and the Ku Klux Klan." For those with an eye for the intersection of history and politics, the casting of James Edwards as the defiant Brewster had particular overtones. Edwards had made a splash with a leading role in the film *Home of the Brave*, a movie about prejudice in the Army. A paucity of opportunities for African-American actors in film in those days and the suspicion that he held leftist sympathies combined to keep him from the career his peers believe he should have enjoyed. (Some believe his disappointment contributed to his early death at fifty-one.) Black writers weren't represented at first at the O'Neill, but the participation of two major black artists—Richards and Edwards—announced the intention of the Conference to be part of a movement to enlarge the scope of American theater.

(*above*) Lloyd Richards (center, hand raised) speaks
during a break in Amphitheater construction, National
Playwrights Conference, 1966. (*right*) Overhead view
of the finished Amphitheater during a rehearsal, 1967.

A scene from Joel Oliansky's *Bedford Forrest*, the Civil War epic that was fully costumed with production values for the National Playwrights Conference, 1966. Michael Douglas stands front right with a sword. The chaos of mounting a full production in so short a time meant the focus was pulled away from serving the playwright and resulted in the birth of the "O'Neill method"—staged readings.

Bedford Forrest was also notable for providing an early stage credit to a young man connected to one of the Center's earliest supporters. One of the founders of the Center, William Darrid, was a New York producer who also had credits as an agent, writer, and actor. In 1956, he had married Diana Dill, the ex-wife of film actor-producer Kirk Douglas, and in so doing, he gained a stepson named Michael. Darrid suggested to White that Michael—now 21—might be of use in Waterford.

Douglas remembers, "I was in my sophomore year in college [at University of California, Santa Barbara], and I'd just started getting interested in acting. My stepfather, whom I adored, suggested that I work on the construction crew at the O'Neill, focus on building the Amphitheater, with the hope that I might get a couple of small parts in some of the plays that they were trying out at the playwrights conference." He speaks of the exhilaration of those days, particularly "being hoisted up this 60-foot ship pole to adjust the follow-spots."

This early experience working with developing writers on new scripts turned out to be of importance to Douglas's later career as actor and producer. "I wasn't aware of it that moment, but it was an incredible time for playwrights. Israel Horovitz, Lanford Wilson, and John Guare—a lot of great writers. Since this was a *playwrights* conference, the actor's responsibility was to serve the playwright. You started learning [about what distinguishes] good writing from bad writing, and you learned a lot about structure. Analyzing text. I've always been an old-fashioned structuralist, you know, in terms of three acts. That experience has carried me through my entire career in terms of realizing that the material is the only thing that matters. My acting career—everything has pretty much been based on what the material was.

"It was my first experience in summer theater. It was like an adult summer camp—a balance between working on original material and the promiscuity of young actresses and actors hanging out together. I had some wonderful romances over those summers."

Many writers from the first conference—including Guare and Rosenthal—were there for the second summer. Says White, "I sensed that the last thing those playwrights wanted was to sit around and watch another play that wasn't theirs being worked on. They said, 'Can we bring up plays and read them?' And I said, 'Yeah, sure.'"

Thus began the so-called backyard readings. In addition to Guare and Rosenthal, the playwrights whose works were performed in this series were Rolf Fjelde, Paul Foster, Israel Horovitz, Joe Julian, Tobi Louis, Sally Ordway, Edward Peluso, Doris Schwerin, and Douglas Taylor. The most prolific director was Melvin Bernhardt, who put up five of them, including the first act of a play that would come to be viewed as one of the key works of the new wave of playwriting, a dark comedy about

The former ship's mast that was placed directly behind the Amphitheater for use as a lighting platform and flagpole. Photo from *The New London Day.*

Lloyd Richards (left) discusses a scene with Michael Douglas on the O'Neill lawn, National Playwrights Conference, 1966.

a desperate would-be songwriter named Artie Shaughnessy plotting to escape the borough of Queens on the day in 1965 when the Pope visited New York.

As Guare recalls it, "*Bedford Forrest* was the play that was supposed to make the place. *The House of Blue Leaves* was also being put up. The first act of it. (I knew what the second act was going to be, but I had only had time to finish the first act.) I had trouble casting *Blue Leaves*. I couldn't find a man to play the lead, Artie, so finally I said, 'I will play it.'"

According to Guare, one evening *Blue Leaves* and *Bedford Forrest* were performed at the same time. While *Bedford* was playing in the new Amphitheater, *Blue Leaves* was playing near the kitchen of the main house, its audience sitting on bleachers White had borrowed from the Little League. "The response to *Blue Leaves* intruded on the performance of *Bedford Forrest*," says Guare. "People came out of *Bedford* and wanted to know what was happening. They'd heard the response to *Blue Leaves*."

Bernhardt is less sure of this. *Bedford Forrest*, playing at night, was lit by equipment Michael Douglas helped set. Not so, Guare's play. "As I recall it, the sun hadn't gone down when we did *Blue Leaves*. We did it on the back porch, and there was no lighting over there."

Like *Blue Leaves*, another play presented that summer, *The Sudden and Accidental Re-Education of Horse Johnson* by Douglas Taylor, dealt with a man discontented with the ordinary existence fate had dealt him. Jack Klugman played Horse. (*Horse Johnson* would become the first play from the O'Neill to open on Broadway, on December 18, 1968, at the Belasco Theatre. It ran for five performances.)

Playwright John Guare and Peggy Pope perform in the first reading of *The House of Blue Leaves*, National Playwrights Conference, 1966.

Another reading that caused a stir was a one-act play by Horovitz called *The Indian Wants the Bronx*. *Indian* had been rehearsing in New York, and Horovitz brought it to Waterford with a cast that included John Cazale, Matthew Cowles, and a young actor new to most named Al Pacino. The story of an East Indian man (Cazale) lost in New York City who is viciously harassed on the street by a couple of young hoods (Cowles and Pacino) galvanized the audience with its air of menace.

Douglas also remembers that a group from the American Academy of Dramatic Arts presented Royall Tyler's 1787 American play *The Contrast*. One of the members of that cast was Danny DeVito. "We became best friends. After I graduated from school, we were roommates in New York." (When Douglas accepted the O'Neill's Monte Cristo Award in 2012, his remarks suggested that the initial bonding wasn't so much over art as a shared enthusiasm for cannabis.) They would later collaborate on

Al Pacino (center) with John Cazale (left) and Matthew Cowles in a scene from *The Indian Wants the Bronx*, by Israel Horovitz, National Playwrights Conference, 1966.

Danny DeVito (left) performing in the eighteenth-century play *The Contrast*, by Royall Tyler, National Playwrights Conference, 1966.

several films, including a film DeVito directed and in which Douglas starred, a hit black comedy called *The War of the Roses*.

In addition, the deaf students from Gallaudet College put up two performances of Euripedes' *Iphigenia in Aulis*, a precursor to the creation of the National Theatre of the Deaf at the O'Neill (see Chapter 4).

Guare believes that the response to the backyard readings was key to the adjustment that would come the next summer. His theory is that the comparison between the presentations of *Blue Leaves* and *Bedford Forrest* was the catalyst. "I think perhaps that was when the balance shifted, when the focus went from trying to put up full productions to doing staged readings."

Indeed, in the third summer, in 1967, the idea of producing full productions was abandoned. White decided that the National Playwrights Conference would be devoted to presenting staged readings.

One of those who would benefit from this decision was Ron Cowen, who at the time was 21 and getting his master's degree at the University of Pennsylvania. He wrote a play (eventually called *Summertree*) inspired by the shadow that the war in Vietnam was casting over society at the time. It was a shadow that had touched Cowen. "I had been called in for my [draft] physical. I was trying to fail everything, and I couldn't. I cheated on the hearing test, and I had a psychiatrist's letter." Neither the test nor the letter persuaded. "I remember the sergeant said, 'We don't care if you're gay, we don't care if you have no arms, you're all going.' And I thought, 'I passed everything, there's nothing I can do.' And at the very end, the last thing was the eye test. And they said, 'You can't see anything!' And I got out of it." Thousands of others were not so lucky and were drafted and sent to the war in Southeast Asia. Their stories were the inspiration for Cowen's script.

Before coming to the University of Pennsylvania, Cowen had attended the University of California, Los Angeles, where he had studied writing with Jerome Lawrence, the coauthor of *Inherit the Wind*. "He told all the students the usual bullshit. 'If any of you ever write a play, you should send it to me.'" Cowen did, and it turned out Lawrence wasn't bullshitting. "Jerry sent my play to the O'Neill. And they accepted me. I was at school. I freaked out."

Some weeks before the scheduled conference, he found himself in New York beginning rehearsals. He met his director, Lloyd Richards, and he met the young actor who would play the lead in his play, Michael Douglas. "Michael and I just laughed and bonded immediately because we looked like cousins. And then I met Phil Sterling, who played my father, and he looked just like my father."

Playwright Ron Cowen, National Playwrights Conference, 1972.

In an article for the September 3, 1972, *New York Times*, Cowen described the first reading. "We sat around a table with the actors and read *Summer Tree*. It was about 130 pages long, and I loved every precious luscious, golden word. Wow. Real actors, the first ones I'd ever seen off a stage, sitting right across from me like human beings and My Director and My Play. [W]e read the play through. Lloyd took notes. I took down his notes. He told me to take my own notes. I didn't know what to take. It all seems perfect to me. The next day we cut 40 pages. I learned to take notes. To cut. To scream. To cry. To beg. Oh, please don't cut it, I'll do anything, don't amputate! Lloyd was merciless, of course, and so were the actors. How about taking out this line? And that one there and that one. . . . And somehow it made it all better. . . . I couldn't figure it out. How come I didn't see when I was writing it that a ten-page monologue delivered from under a bed wouldn't hold the audience's attention? Then Lloyd suggested we make *Summer Tree, Summertree*. One word. Boy, he's really a smart man."

Looking back from the perspective of several decades, Cowen acknowledges, "I really didn't have a clue at that point what to do. The whole thing was a birth. I was an infant. And Lloyd was my father. I loved him so much. He didn't 'tell' you, he shared his thoughts with you, and you came to a decision together." Meanwhile, Cowen was learning. "I learned what blocking is. It's when the actors move around. They don't do that on their own, you know. They are directed to, by Lloyd."

Douglas (who roomed with Cowen at the O'Neill) remembers the play having personal resonances for him. "In those years—especially at the University of California, where I had been—we were actively involved in protests, in kicking ROTC off the campuses. A strong anti-Vietnam vibe." The play begins with the image of a young American soldier dying under a tree in Vietnam and then shifts to images and incidents from his life under the tree in his back yard at home in the States. "It was a lovely piece," Douglas recalls. "The play was focused on this young man, a principal character with a lot to carry. I had just recently decided to pursue acting. I was very undeveloped. I remember a lot of personal direction from Lloyd Richards, who was a great teacher. He was very articulate. And when something was funny, he had one of the greatest laughs—just from the bottom of his soul. Nothing made you happier than pleasing him."

Douglas was also directed by Richards the following summer in a play by a paralyzed playwright named Neil Yarema called *Rainless Sky*. "We were in wheelchairs in the play, and the actor I was playing with couldn't do it—he was sick or whatever—so Lloyd came in and played this role at the last second. It was just great realizing how good he was as an actor."

The first performance of *Summertree* in Waterford was in the Barn. Cowen remembers, "Everybody was crying. The same thing would happen [later, during the run] at Lincoln Center. The lights would go out at the end of the play, and everyone would just sit in the dark. Not applauding, not doing anything. Just sitting, just sitting in the dark. And then the lights would come up and everyone would applaud, wiping their eyes. And I said, wow, you know, you make people cry, you have this great sense of power. (But then you realize it's not so hard to make people cry.) But people were very moved in the Barn that night."

In addition to *Summertree*, 1967 saw the first stagings of Frank Gagliano's *Father Uxbridge Wants to Marry*, John Guare's *Muzeeka*, Oliver Hailey's *Who's Happy Now?*, and Horovitz's *It's Called the Sugar Plum*—all four directed by Melvin Bernhardt. Besides *Summertree*, Richards directed *Man Around the House* by Joe Julian and *Just Before Morning* by Tom Oliver Crehore.

New York City finally got a sense of what was cooking in Connecticut when some of the works from 1966 and 1967 were given full productions in the 1967–1968 season.

Father Uxbridge Wants to Marry was the first. Produced at Theater at St. Clement's Church by the nonprofit American Place Theatre, it opened on October 28, 1967, for a limited run of eleven performances with a cast led by Gene Roche as Morden, an elevator operator who comes to crisis when informed that his job is about to be made redundant by the switch to an automatic system. The various women in his life were played by Olympia Dukakis. Melvin Bernhardt returned as director for this production. *New York Times* critic Clive Barnes gave it a mixed notice, saying "its

Peggy Pope and Charles Kimbrough perform in John Guare's *Muzeeka*, National Playwrights Conference, 1967. Guare is behind the scenery.

Michael Douglas (seated) performs in Tom Oliver Crehore's *Just Before Morning*, in the Barn Theater, National Playwrights Conference, 1967.

Daniel Goldman and Linda Segal in *It's Called the Sugar Plum*, by Israel Horovitz, National Playwrights Conference, 1967. At this time, plays at the O'Neill hadn't yet begun using modular sets. Photo by William Auwood.

depiction of inescapable human misery proved effective," but expressing his opinion that it did not live up to its apparent inspiration, Georg Büchner's *Woyzeck*. He had words of praise for Bernhardt and the cast. Edith Oliver, the off-Broadway critic of the *New Yorker*, was dismissive. "The style is religious delirium. And the script is clogged with theological and personal symbols, the former as opaque to me as the latter. I must say I was not even tempted to try to crack the mysteries."

The second evening of work developed at the O'Neill to open in New York did so on January 17, when a double bill of one-act plays by Horovitz, *The Indian Wants the Bronx* and *It's Called the Sugar Plum*, began a run at the Astor Place Theater, across the street from the recently opened Public Theater of Joseph Papp. The bill was directed by James Hammerstein, who had directed *Sugar Plum* at the O'Neill. Cazale, Cowles, and Pacino were still in the cast. A promising young actress named Marsha Mason was featured in the companion piece. This time Oliver was more appreciative. "Mr. Horovitz is a natural dramatist with a keen ear for regional talk," she wrote. She found the depiction of "aimless cruelty" in both plays "frightening."

Summertree opened on March 3, 1968, in the downstairs space at the Lincoln Center Theater Company that would later be renamed the Mitzi E. Newhouse Theater. "Perhaps the most important point to be made about *Summertree* is that it is written by a writer, as you can tell three minutes into the show," said Oliver. In the *Times*, Barnes complimented it as "soft-centered but sensitive," and a reply to the "oft-heard question: 'What have those guys at Lincoln Center done for us lately?'"

However, the production did not feature two elements that had made *Summertree* go over so well in Waterford. According to Ron Cowen, Lloyd Richards had a scheduling conflict due to a project for the State Department and was not available

Director James Hammerstein (left) and playwright Israel Horovitz during rehearsal of *The Primary English Class*, National Playwrights Conference, 1975. Photo by Andrew B. Wile.

to direct the play at Lincoln Center. The reason Michael Douglas didn't play the part with which he had connected so strongly was more complicated.

Says Douglas, "Ron asked me to come back and audition for it. I auditioned a number of times, and finally Ron came back one day saying, 'You got it.' And then the stage manager called and said congratulations, and said, 'Tomorrow would you come in and read auditions?' And the next day I went in, and amongst the actresses was Blythe Danner, not really realizing that I was still auditioning. The next thing they told me was, 'You don't have the part.' I think they just wanted to get someone more established and more experienced. I think the decision came more from Jules Irving, rather than the director." (The director was David Pressman, the man who introduced George C. White to David Hays. In an interview shortly before his death in 2011, Pressman would call directing *Summertree* one of his proudest achievements.)

Poster from the Lincoln Center production of Ron Cowen's *Summertree*, 1968.

Cowen's vivid memory is of Lincoln Center artistic director Jules Irving approaching him, saying, "We're going to fire Michael. He's not strong enough to act against Blythe Danner." Cowen says, "I had a shit fit. I said, 'You can't do this.' Jules said that he wanted David Birney. I was furious, and Jules said, 'You have two choices. You can either have your play produced at Lincoln Center with David Birney, or we'll put it on the shelf and we own it for the next five years, and it won't be done.'"

David Birney was now a fact, and Douglas couldn't do anything about it. Douglas wasn't finished with *Summertree*, though. "My father—I guess out of spite or revenge or whatever else—acquired the screenplay rights."

Cowen began work on the script for producer Kirk Douglas. And then it was Cowen's turn to be pushed out. "*I got fired. I'm not surprised I got fired. I didn't know how to write a screenplay.*" The experience damaged his friendship with Michael Douglas. They lost touch until decades later, when schedules brought them both to Toronto and gave them the opportunity to have a long lunch and patch things up.

As for the movie, Cowen says, "You don't want to see the film of *Summertree*. It does not have a word of the play in it." Michael Douglas has fond memories of the project. The actress who played opposite him was Brenda Vacarro, and it was the beginning of an extended romance.

Of the 1967–1968 New York productions that had originated at the O'Neill, *Times* critic Clive Barnes was most enthusiastic about a double bill of plays, *Muzeeka/Red Cross*, that opened April 28, 1968, under the direction of Melvin Bernhardt at the Provincetown Playhouse (a small theater in Greenwich Village that was once home to early works by Eugene O'Neill). *Red Cross* was a short piece by the young Sam Shepard, who had fled the O'Neill in its first year. According to Barnes, Guare's *Muzeeka*, which featured Sandy Baron, Kevin Conway, and Marcia Jean Kurtz, was "a mind-opener, a play of realistic fantasy. . . . Mr. Guare wants us to laugh, but he does not want us to forget. He has a wit like a poisoned arrow (such as when he suggests that soldiers fighting in Vietnam are under contract to individual television companies) but he does seem to have a big understanding of what we are and what we are doing."

Though the record was not of unanimous huzzahs, most of these writers were remembered when honors season came around. Ron Cowen won the Vernon Rice and Drama Desk Awards for playwriting, and both John Guare and Israel Horovitz won Obie Awards for their plays.

Rehearsing *Dream on Monkey Mountain*, by Derek Walcott, in the Amphitheater, National Playwrights Conference, 1969. Walcott, a poet and playwright from St. Lucia, would win the Nobel Prize for Literature in 1992. Shown, left to right, are Albert Halder, Walcott, and Slade Hopkins. Photo by Howard E. Moss.

The season in New York had established the O'Neill as a major source of new work and new writers. This success carried with it new danger. The writers who had made a splash in the city returned to the country in the summer of 1968 with the strut of conquering heroes. Cowen says, "It all of the sudden became the star system. The second season was about getting producers up there, getting the most finished production you could get on, trying to get star names in your play, trying to get your play done on Saturday night, because that's when the producers could drive up and see. And all of the sudden it's pre-Broadway tryout. And all of the sudden it was not the O'Neill anymore."

With so much energy put into presentation, the exploration of text was given less attention. Cast in multiple roles, the actors ran from rehearsal to rehearsal, desperately trying to master lines, and a lot of time was devoured by dozens of sound and lighting cues. As White wrote, "The losers were the playwright and the texts. They were virtually run over in a scrabble to get the work on its feet. All these elements began to breed a sense of competition among actors, playwrights, designers, and directors."

Cowen was working again with Lloyd Richards. In his article for the September 3, 1972, *New York Times*, Cowen described how his piece, *Redemption Center*, which was supposed to be a modest two-hour musical, got so swamped by presentational concerns that the first performance ran three and a half hours. The length seemed all the longer because of the heat in the barn space where it played. "Lloyd and I sat on the steps at the back of the house, our heads between our hands, eyes blank, dried tongues hanging out, stunned. I think that's the best word I can think of other than hot. Stunned." They cut and rewrote furiously for the second performance, but Cowen deemed the result "an unsalvageable mess."

Nor were they the only team that had difficulties. "Disaster after disaster," Cowen remembered. "People were going crazy, screaming, leaving, coming back, leaving. Everybody was mean. I went away a lot."

The high visibility of the O'Neill had also attracted the attention of producers, scouts, and agents, who flocked to check out the properties and talents. Deals and schemes were being discussed all over the grounds. This only increased the competition among writers. White comments, "What had begun as an attempt at building a temple of creativity had now allowed the money changers to enter."

Despite the chaos, the 1968 session introduced works that would be heard from again—John Guare's *Cop-Out* and Lanford Wilson's autobiographic *Lemon Sky*, which later opened in New York starring a young Christopher Walken, was made into a film with Kevin Bacon and Kyra Sedgwick, and is frequently revived.

A month after the Conference, White invited some of its veterans to Waterford to identify the problems and discuss how they should be addressed. He remembers, "This representative group was unanimous in its call for an artistic director with a firm hand, who would put the house in order."

As White saw it, he had two strong candidates. "I knew it was between Mel Bernhardt and Lloyd Richards. Mel was brilliant and a wonderful director—flamboyant and inventive and very, very cutting edge. I knew he would be good in his own way, but Lloyd—Lloyd and I just got along. And I thought, Lloyd has a wisdom. So it was a tough decision, but I finally opted for Lloyd."

Bernhardt's memory is that White inquired about his interest, but that his career as a director in the city was taking off, and he didn't care to be considered. He didn't want to commit to spending the necessary time in Connecticut. "I had things happening back in NYC. I didn't want to tie up that much time when I could be doing plays in other places."

Playwright Lanford Wilson and a young actor watching a rehearsal of *Lemon Sky* outdoors in the Instant Theater, National Playwrights Conference, 1968. Photo by Phyllis Kaye.

Bernhardt also says that he and Richards "didn't see eye to eye. Lloyd was much more academic than I. I was more interested in communicating what a play could be to the audience that we had. I wanted to use anything we could find around the place to help the audience picture what a full production might hold. Lloyd was much more interested in working with the playwrights on textual matters."

With Richards named to the post, he and White set about the task of reordering priorities. The focus would now be on the text. Because the writer was supposed to feel free to change text until the last moment before a performance, the actors would have to remain on book. This also meant that chasing after production values was a thing of the past. Whereas Bernhardt would have used whatever tables or chairs or props were at hand, Richards wanted a consistent house style based in sparseness to direct all the attention to the writing.

White turned to designer Peter Larkin. "I said, 'Okay, you only get fifty bucks. I want something that will be scenery that can be used for everything.' That was about as specific as I could get. And then Peter came in one day to my office in New York and dumped these wire things on my desk; he said, 'I think I got it.' 'What are these?' 'Well here, you take this and combine it with this, and you've got a platform, you put it this way and you've got. . . .'" These aluminum rectangular shapes, designed to be assembled in different configurations, became the building blocks of such physical production as the O'Neill employed. A rendering of a set for each play by Fred

Ron Liebman and Linda Lavin in *Cop-Out*, by John Guare, National Playwrights Conference, 1968.

An example of the set modules ("mods") designed by Peter Larkin and used throughout the National Playwrights Conferences to suggest locations and furniture, a practice continuing to this day. Photo from 1973.

Voelpel or Neil Jampolis was posted near the entrance of the theater, so that the audience could bring in with them a mental picture of what a fuller physical production might look like.

But Richards wanted to offer the writers something in addition to the work on their scripts. "I gave them an opportunity to live with playwrights who were going through the same thing. This access is a rare opportunity for working playwrights. Here it is two o'clock in the morning, in the dorm that they stay in, and everybody is working. You have a community. The person whose play was coming up next, you and other playwrights brought him coffee, took care of him. You didn't come to the O'Neill just to get your play done. You came to the O'Neill and you made yourself available to other playwrights—as did directors, designers, actors—everybody was available to the people involved with their work. And that created this productive, wonderful community. You were the focus for a while, and later you focused on someone else."

One more thing Richards insisted on: though he couldn't keep producers and scouts and agents from seeing the shows, there was to be no more deal making on the grounds of the Center itself. The O'Neill was reconsecrated as a temple of creativity.

3. George C. White and Lloyd Richards

George C. White had a spy named Al Swatzberg.

"If the town had had a cracker barrel, it would have been in his insurance office. I would go in to check on the gossip, what was going on. I'd do that periodically, to find out where the torpedoes might be coming from. And he once said, 'What did you ever do to Frank Ferri?' And I say, 'Who?' And he says, 'Frank Ferri. He's the head of the bricklayers union. He's Italian. Boy, does he hate you and the O'Neill.' And I say, 'Get us together.' So finally he says, 'Frank has agreed to meet you at 7 a.m. at Howard Johnson's on Thursday.'

"So I traipse over to Howard Johnson's. Al says, 'George, I want you to meet Frank Ferri.' I put out my hand, and he [Ferri] goes like this—" White makes a dismissive noise. "And I know he's Italian, so I say to him, 'Perchè non stringe la mano?' 'How come you won't shake my hand?' And he looks at me and says, 'How come you know Italian?' And I say, 'I'm half Italian.' He says, 'White?' I say, 'Yeah, but my mother's name is Rovetti.' 'Rovetti? Rovetti! You any relation to Andy Rovetti, the plumber on Great Neck Road?' I say, 'He's my uncle.' He says, 'You're Andy's nephew?' I say, 'Yeah!' 'And Ding Rovetti—the filling station on Broad Street?' 'Yeah, they're my uncles!' He says, 'No shit. I thought you were some faggot from New York.' And he became our biggest advocate."

Lloyd Richards (left) and George C. White outside the Hammond Mansion, ca. 1975. Photo by Rob Rooy.

The importance of George C. White being a local boy cannot be overstated. The enduring partnership between White and Lloyd Richards was between a white Waterford native with a background combining New England and Italian roots and a black man who, as he commented, was lured to "a place I had never heard of" after a long journey beginning with a childhood in an industrial city during the Depression.

White was born in 1935 to a family that boasts three generations of painters, including White's father Nelson. Nelson's popularity as an artist helped his status in town; he was comfortable with what passed for aristocrats in the area—the

Harknesses and the Hammonds—but also, as White says, with "the 'hewers of wood and drawers of water.'"

A local girl named Aida spent some of her childhood in the early 1900s working in a New London sweatshop on Main Street. Across the street from the sweatshop, a man known as Doc Ganey ran an informal social establishment called the Second Story Club, where members drank, played cards, pored over books from Ganey's extensive library, and compared notes on visits to local brothels. A couple of brothers who were regulars noticed Aida on the street and would whistle at her. Aida's mother told her to have nothing to do with them. They were bad characters, those O'Neill boys, Jamie and Eugene.

Aida got a job substituting for the upstairs maid in the White home. "She never left," says White. In 1927 Aida married young Nelson; George was their son. Marrying a maid caused an uproar. "It split the family right in half," says White. Though Aida was born and raised in Connecticut, the Rovettis came from Italy. In summers, Aida would visit relatives in the old country, taking George with her, hence his ability to engage Frank Ferri in Italian.

The White family at their Waterford home, August 1968. Shown, left to right, are Nelson White, George White, Jr., Aida White, Juliet White, George C. White (standing), Caleb White, and Betsy White.

Roger Christiansen, who was raised in the area and now serves on the board of the O'Neill Center, observes that New London (to which Waterford is a rural adjunct) got much of its character from the institutions and businesses located there: "It was a blue collar, working-class area. Kind of a sailor town, with bars where they would get into fights." Christiansen remembers little awareness of Eugene O'Neill when he was young. "The locals could have cared less. I didn't even know that the O'Neill existed until I got hired to work there." Christiansen frequently drove by the Monte Cristo Cottage, where the playwright spent much of his boyhood and where both *Long Day's Journey into Night* and *Ah, Wilderness!* are set. "I had no idea what it was." It was in this less-than-welcoming soil White would try to plant a major cultural institution.

White's fluency in Italian was part of the reason he got his first job in the arts at age nineteen, managing the International Ballet Festival in Nervi, Italy. The production stage manager, Dale Wasserman, took the young man under his wing, later finding his former assistant a job with producer David Susskind in New York. Susskind hired him as a researcher on a landmark TV series, *East Side/West Side*, starring George C. Scott and Cicely Tyson, which confronted controversial issues of the day. Being connected with Susskind gave White access to people he could call for help, references, and advice as he put together the O'Neill. Among those he consulted was William Darrid, the producer-agent who suggested his stepson Michael Douglas spend those formative summers in Waterford.

To make the O'Neill fly, White needed support on two fronts—top-rank theater professionals from New York to give the conference substance and credibility, and the people in the Waterford–New London area, whose world these outsiders would inevitably invade and engage.

The TV/Cinema Panel at the first National Playwrights Conference, 1965. Shown, left to right, are Phillip Reisman, Dale Wasserman, and William Darrid.

Part of the justification of the Center being built there was the connection the area had to the early life of Eugene O'Neill. But this connection did not always impress those who lived there. As late as 1974, the proposal to change New London's Main Street (the location of the Second Story Club) to Eugene O'Neill Drive faced objections. Thomas Griffin, who had served three terms as mayor, spoke against the idea, saying, "O'Neill was a stew bum. What did he ever do besides write a few plays?" The proposal passed anyway.

What gave White an advantage was that his was a familiar face. "I played ball with half of the town officials when I was a kid. I got a thirty-year lease from the town, because they figured 'This kid went to Great Neck School. What the hell. Give him a lease on the property (not including the beach) and if something comes of it, fine. And if it doesn't, we haven't lost anything (and probably nothing will come of it anyway).' And also the townspeople figured, 'They're going to do summer stock. They're going to do *Three Men on a Horse*.'"

But the O'Neill opened in the sixties, and the plays chosen were far from summer stock fare. "The culture was changing," White comments. "Never trust anybody over thirty, Vietnam, and all that."

When a company of players faces an audience, they can either affirm that audience's values or challenge them. The theater of celebration does the former, based on the belief that society is structured so that most of the time it works pretty well. Characters get justice, often with a little mercy tossed in. Shakespeare's comedies exemplify this kind of work; at the ends of both *Much Ado About Nothing* and *Twelfth Night*, those we care about mostly get paired off in appropriate marriages, and the unsympathetic figures get punished by being exiled from the community. When the curtain comes down on *Three Men on a Horse*; *Oklahoma!*; *Guys and Dolls*; and the comedies of George S. Kaufman and Moss Hart, Jean Kerr, and Neil Simon, the audience leaves with a sense of well being, because everything has worked out satisfactorily and a sense of order has been reestablished. All is mostly right in the world.

But many of the most consequential achievements in drama are based on a different orientation, taking issue with assumptions the audience holds dear. In his book *The Theatre of Revolt*, critic Robert Brustein discusses how this tradition has been expressed on the modern stage by analyzing the work of Henrik Ibsen, August Strindberg, Anton Chekhov, George Bernard Shaw, Bertolt Brecht, Luigi Pirandello, Eugene O'Neill, and Jean Genet—all of whom found their cultures wanting in profound ways.

The bulk of the plays to which White lent his support in the first few years of the O'Neill Center were part of this tradition. Again and again, Center projects dealt with the alienation or destruction of the individual and the corrupt and often obliviously murderous nature of authority. *Muzeeka*, *The House of Blue Leaves*, and *Father Uxbridge Wants to Marry* offer critical assessments of organized religion, mass culture, and the military. Innocent, idealistic youth is slaughtered for no good purpose in *Summertree*. The image of the traditional father in the American family takes hits in *Who's Happy Now?* and *Lemon Sky*.

This was far from the summer stock operation many in the town pictured when White solicited support for a theater, as White acknowledges. "People would be passing by on their way to the beach with their little kids and there would be a play with people yelling 'You motherfucker!' And they were outraged that we were doing these dirty plays and there were all these awful people from New York. And then one guy—he was a Swedish critic who was visiting—changed on the beach. A nude guy on the beach! And, because he was from the O'Neill . . . well!

"As I say, I grew up here. I understood their outrage, but I wasn't about to change. That's why I said, 'Look, I'm perfectly willing to put up a sign that says this play contains bad language and don't come if you don't want to hear it, but I'm not going to have the playwright change it.' I had a local woman who was on the Park and Recreation Committee. She would read the plays and rate them, like movies.

"Today we are more than accepted by the community. The lease has just been renewed for a long time. The town owns this property, but we have the lease

The entrance sign to the Eugene O'Neill Theater Center (then named Foundation), 1969.

drawn so they can't break it. And the local newspaper, *The Day*, has always been on our side."

White created the O'Neill, but critic John Lahr believes that the O'Neill in turn created White. "I think George found his role in life. There was a way in which he was this lost guy, I felt, who found a purpose. Maybe we all were, but I certainly felt that he was. Because he created this place, he had a certain kind of cachet and he became sort of an impresario."

Frank Rich, the former first-string *New York Times* theater critic, got to know White socially through Alex Witchel, who had known White through her studies at Yale (Rich and Witchel later married). "He was what I remember as the spirit of the enterprise. He had a bon vivant quality but also just wild enthusiasm—loved everyone that worked there, loved every play, loved all the people. Was completely unpretentious, not the kind of person you tend to find in the theater world. He was, in my view, in the best sense of the word, a producer—a do-gooder, a theater-lover. It's kind of remarkable that this sort of WASPy guy from New England would play this huge important role."

For the first years, although he had assistance from a band of volunteers and supporters, White made the crucial decisions on his own. He chose which playwrights and panelists to invite and which projects to work on. (As noted in Chapter 1, he also secured the Hammond Estate; raised the funding; and supervised the travel, lodging, and feeding of the guests.) As he is the first to concede, he started with no master plan but adjusted course as he learned what did and didn't work. So the idea of a theater that might produce some plays transformed into a meeting among some handpicked writers, and that became a season of two produced plays augmented by some staged readings, and that became a season of staged readings, and that—in 1968—became a season of whatever the writers, directors, and actors could throw together, given the circumstances. And that, as Ron Cowen observed, almost sank the whole thing.

When White took the advice of some veterans of the 1968 conference to hire an artistic director of the National Playwrights Conference, it was an acknowledgment that the operation had grown too big for him to handle by himself. And also that he needed a partner who could bring to the O'Neill skills and experience that could only have been acquired from years of working in the professional theater. By choosing to create the post of artistic director of the Playwrights Conference and by choosing who would take on that role, White ensured that the O'Neill would find the stability it needed to move forward confidently.

White had had a chance to watch Lloyd Richards in action—first coordinating the ungainly project that was *Bedford Forrest* under improvisatory circumstances and then directing staged readings on the lawn. Sixteen years older than White, Richards radiated calm in the midst of chaos. Jean Passanante, who assisted Richards for two of the conferences, remarks, "I was completely enamored of him at first sight, because he was so principled and idealistic. He was true to his ideals about what the Playwrights Conference was meant to do and what it wasn't meant to do." Passanante's previous job had been at the Williamstown Theatre Festival, a well-regarded company in the Berkshires that often accommodated the imperatives of high-profile names. Richards emphasized to her that the O'Neill ran on other principles. "Lloyd said, 'Everybody makes the same money, everybody lives in the same dorms, and everybody's there for the same purpose, which is to serve the playwright.' That was music to my ears. And he practiced what he preached. He was a great patriarchal figure. Everybody wanted to please him. You wanted to be on Lloyd's good side. He wasn't really scary, but he was . . . he was sort of magisterial." Richards also decided that the post of artistic director made it inappropriate for him to direct any of the readings himself.

Born in 1919 in Toronto, Richards was raised in Detroit, one of five children. Reaching adulthood, Richards considered law and the ministry, but when he

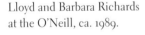
Lloyd and Barbara Richards at the O'Neill, ca. 1989.

attended Wayne State University, Detroit, his interest shifted to acting. It was not a shift that made a lot of practical sense. He could look to little evidence that there was much of a living for him to make in the theater. Few black actors did, and even stars like Canada Lee and Paul Robeson struggled mightily with the system. Richards still was intent on pursuing acting when he moved to New York in 1947.

Acting jobs were few and far between, but he was cast in a play by director Paul Mann. Mann invited Richards to join him as a teacher in his acting studio. One of Richards's students was Sidney Poitier. Richards spoke of the early days of their friendship. "He said to me one day, 'If I ever do a major Broadway show, I want you to direct it.'" Some years later, when Poitier had begun to make a name for himself in films, he redeemed that promise, recommending Richards direct a script headed for Broadway by a young black woman: A *Raisin in the Sun*. The 40-year-old acting teacher began working on rewrites with the 29-year-old playwright, Lorraine Hansberry.

Collaborating with Hansberry, Richards demonstrated the sure sense of how to be useful to a playwright that would serve him in good stead later at the National Playwrights Conference. "We met once a week and talked about it, and Lorraine would work on it. I would challenge her . . . and she would top me in what she wrote."

Raisin's opening on May 11, 1959, not only launched or boosted the careers of the extraordinary cast supporting Poitier (including Claudia McNeil, Ruby Dee, Diana Sands, Ivan Dixon, Lonne Elder III, Glynn Turman, and Douglas Turner Ward), it was also the first play by a black woman on Broadway. And Richards scored the distinction of being Broadway's first black director. The play, Poitier, McNeil, and Richards were nominated for 1960 Tony Awards.

The success of *Raisin* led to other directing opportunities on Broadway. Looking at the projects Richards undertook—including the musical *I Had a Ball* about a fortune-teller—critic Michael Feingold comments, "I think Lloyd's pre-O'Neill Broadway career is very indicative of his thinking, because what he did after the huge success of *Raisin* was immediately *not* do another black family play." In the meantime, Richards pursued additional employment in the academic world. The interplay between his professional and academic interests would grow more intense after Richards became artistic director of the National Playwrights Conference. White has a story about that:

"Bart Giamatti [A. Bartlett Giamatti], a friend of mine from undergraduate days, became president of Yale, to everybody's delight and surprise. I was teaching at

Lloyd Richards in his Yale School of Drama office, 1988. Note photos of his wife Barbara and O'Neill veterans Edith Oliver and August Wilson on his desk.

Yale then. Robert Brustein, who was the dean of the drama school, had hired me to teach theater administration. I get a call from Bart saying, 'It may come as no surprise to you that I am not renewing Brustein's contract.' And I say, 'No, that's not surprising.' So he says, 'I need a new dean. Do you want it?' I say, 'No, thank you, Bart. I've got my baby, and I'm not about to give that up. But I've got somebody for you that's a no-brainer.' He says, 'Who's that?' I say, 'Lloyd Richards. He's got everything. He's been head of the union [SDC, the Stage Directors and Choreographers Society, previously known as SSDC], he's a teacher, he's a director, he's an actor, he's got it.' But I add, 'If Lloyd accepts it, you've got to let him do the O'Neill as well.'"

Richards became head of the Yale Drama School in 1979, which also made him artistic director of Yale Rep. This put him in a position to practice vertical integration to a degree unmatched by anyone else in the theater. He was able to develop talent at the school, bring students and graduates to the O'Neill for seasoning, and then feature them at Yale Rep, often giving their careers lift-off. For example, Richards was familiar with Charles S. Dutton from his days as a Yale student. He cast him in the O'Neill presentation of August Wilson's *Ma Rainey's Black Bottom*. Richards subsequently directed Dutton in the production that played at Yale Rep and brought him to Broadway. Dutton was nominated for the Tony Award for best featured actor in a play in 1984. From there, he went on to a major career.

Directors who came to work at the National Playwrights Conference were advised by Richards that the director had different responsibilities there than in a conventional production. As director Barnet Kellman describes it: "It was your job to allow the problems to surface, not to cover them up with the tricks of our trade. You were not supposed to use sleight-of-hand, you were not supposed to use misdirection to take the audience's eye off of problems. But you were supposed to delve into the text and let performance come alive to let the problems reveal themselves. And then work with the writers to address those problems. On the one hand, it was self-effacing. On the other hand, it was tremendously aggressive, because you're on a very, very short clock. You would assure the writer, 'Look—that script you wrote? It exists. You can return to that anytime you want. Freed up by the fact that the script is safe in your desk drawer, let's play! Let's not be afraid. This is the time to try things.'"

William Partlan, who assisted Richards in the O'Neill Center's New York office, adds, "I liken it to the Hammond B3 Organ, because the people who know how to use that organ the best just show you glimpses of how powerful it can be. It sort of comes

George C. White (second from left) and Lloyd Richards (right) with O'Neill trustees Dina Merrill and Peter Van Slyck, ca. 1980.

at you and then goes back underground almost. Lloyd always had a kind of amazing intelligence behind his eyes, was inscrutable as well, but also—you knew not to mess with him, because under that was a great deal of power. . . . I think that's part of what George really wanted in an artistic director: someone with the inner kind of strength that Lloyd brought to it to tame all of those egos and establish a core set of values."

"They [White and Richards] laughed a lot," says G. W. (Skip) Mercier, resident designer for the National Playwright's Conference from 1983 to 2004 and a member for twenty years of the faculty of the National Theater Institute. "They were amused by each other. There were times George would say something that was just ridiculous, and Lloyd would just look at him and crack up. George was a firecracker. 'Let's go to Russia and have the Russians come!' And that happened because George had gone to Russia and had had a good time in Russia and all of a sudden we're surrounded by Russians! And Lloyd would look amused, as if to say, 'What does *this* mean? What ride are we all on now?'"

In his functions as critic, dramaturg, playwright, and a member of the selection committee, Feingold had the opportunity to watch Richards over decades. "I remember one occasion when a director and a playwright after the first performance of a play showed up the next morning, each with a different rearrangement of the second act that he proposed to put in that afternoon. Both of them yelling furiously at each other. I said, 'We must go to Lloyd.' I herded them off to his office, where Lloyd adjudicated, and we found a way into the second act that was rational, viable, and somehow managed to please everybody. That was the first time I thought his role model was Abraham Lincoln."

Dustin Hoffman (second from left) visits the National Playwrights Conference, 1969. Photo by Raymond Nash.

Richards reminds Feingold of Lincoln also in that he worked to broaden the franchise. "Gay came in, because that was always a part of the theater. But black, Asian, and Latino came in, because these were gifted writers and actors and they were part of the world and Lloyd wasn't going to exclude them."

Richards would sometimes encounter those who didn't understand the appeal of working as he did on new scripts. Partlan tells a story of the internationally renowned South African dramatist Athol Fugard, which illustrates a characteristic Richards response to such doubt. "Fugard did several of his new works with Lloyd at Yale. And at one point, apparently, he said to Lloyd, 'I don't understand how any playwright works in the way that you do at the O'Neill.' And Lloyd, being Lloyd, said, 'Then you're going to have to come and be a dramaturg.' So Athol came as a dramaturg to work with actually a Yale playwright, a young woman named Janeice Scarbrough, who had written a play called *Trinity Site* that I was assigned to direct. (Of course, Janeice was petrified when she found out that he was her dramaturg, but it turned out he was quite a good one.) I think he did come to understand how it could work for some playwrights, though not that it would work for him necessarily. But again, that was Lloyd's technique—if someone didn't think that the process would work for them, then he would find a way to make them at least see the process and understand it."

In 2005, six years after he retired from the National Playwrights Conference, Richards wrote a letter to Amy Sullivan, then the executive director of the Center. In the process of telling Sullivan that he regretted not being able to attend a celebration in honor of Eugene O'Neill, Richards wrote that if honors were to be given, it was about time that White got his due. "There is, in the harbor, a statue of the young Eugene O'Neill. . . . I look around and I question, where is the statue or significant acknowledgment to the 'patron' who welcomed arts and artistry with open arms[?] Where is the acknowledgment of the man who gathered his family around him to get it done and made it possible for me to front and develop his idea of a national playwrights conference to serve playwrights in honor of America's foremost playwright, Eugene O'Neill[?]" In the letter, Richards is particularly appreciative of White's personal support. "There are few around who are aware of what the local response may have been to the coming of a black man to the first O'Neill presentations and ultimately selecting that same black man to head up that idyllic playwrights place, never hearing any racial murmurs that may have existed. I know that without George White, President A. Bartlett Giamatti, and Edith Oliver[,] I never would have been invited to become the Dean of the Yale School of Drama, Artistic Director of Yale

Athol Fugard (left) and Lloyd Richards attend a rehearsal, National Playwrights Conference, 1992. Photo by A. Vincent Scarano.

Lloyd Richards, Betsy White, and George C. White (left to right) enjoy a laugh at the start of the 1988 National Playwrights Conference in the Instant (later renamed the Edith Oliver) Theater.

Rep, and [of] the O'Neill National Playwrights Conference, thus becoming the first black dean in the history of the Ivy Leagues and one of the few black artistic directors who was able to stand as a beacon to invite an August Wilson to submit a play." He went on to write, "I honor Eugene O'Neill, I honor August Wilson but I particularly honor George White without whom none [of] this would have happened. . . . I believe that the people of Waterford and the people of the theater should know and appreciate who they have in their midst."

Joel Oliansky isn't here to tell us what of Richards's work inspired his request for the latter to direct *Bedford Forrest*, but, by recommending Lloyd Richards, he introduced the director to White, and the axis of the American theater shifted.

4. National Theatre of the Deaf

 David Hays says that the impulse behind his founding of the National Theatre of the Deaf (NTD) was in part born out of irritation at the 1961 Tony Awards. Hays designed the Broadway play *All the Way Home*, Tad Mosel's adaptation of James Agee's A *Death in the Family*. The director was Arthur Penn. "Penn and I went to the Waldorf-Astoria to collect our Tony Awards. He didn't get his and he should have. I didn't get mine and I should have. What happened to me is that Oliver Smith won the Tony for [design for] a musical, but he was also nominated for play. So I said, 'Well, he's got his Tony and there's no one else nominated for play except me.' So I was halfway to my feet when they announced that he got that also. Nothing to do when you're halfway out of your seat except pretend you had a hemorrhoid.

"So we're coming out of the lobby and Arthur says, 'Listen, David, I'm saying what every loser says: this is shit. I've got a really wonderful project that's real. Not this Broadway crap.' So we go to some club which has zebra skins all over it. And I danced with Annie Bancroft, and she was the one who explained the concept of the Theatre of the Deaf."

David Hays teaching at the O'Neill, 1970s.

After Anne Bancroft had starred in Arthur Penn's 1959 production of William Gibson's *The Miracle Worker*, the story of how teacher Annie Sullivan brought language to the blind and deaf child Helen Keller, a psychologist named Edna Simon Levine approached Bancroft and Penn with an idea. As Stephen C. Baldwin commented in his book *Pictures in the Air*, Levine had "two passions, theater and the deaf community," and this "led her to the notion of a professional theater troupe for deaf actors." Levine had the impulse to approach Bancroft because of a feature of her performance in the Gibson play—she used sign language. Baldwin affirmed that, although earlier plays had featured deaf characters, *The Miracle Worker* was the first Broadway play in which sign language had been used "as an expressive medium."

Levine believed that a minority advances when members of the group achieve celebrity, giving human faces to people who would otherwise tend to be stereotyped and discounted. She reasoned that a theater featuring deaf actors could generate just such notable figures, individuals who would then create new professional pathways and inspire others. She thought that funding for such a company could likely come from the Vocational Rehabilitation Agency (VRA). Says Hays, "The government justification for the VRA was if you [came up with projects that] take people off the dole, you make taxpayers out of them." A theater of the deaf had the potential to do just that.

This is roughly what Bancroft told him during the dance. Hays expressed interest. Penn told him, "We want you to design it." Hays replied, "Of course." As conceived, the project was dependent on getting the VRA grant. Working with Levine, the three put a lot of time and effort into it. But the grant didn't come through.

Hays's interest in the possibilities of the form was reignited by a 1963 visit to Gallaudet College, a school for the deaf in Washington, D.C. (which changed its name to Gallaudet University in 1986). There he saw a student production of Thornton Wilder's *Our Town*. "I had just designed . . . for an off-Broadway production [of *Our Town*] with José Quintero, but this was more moving. I won't say it was more expert, because they were amateurs, but something about the sign language and the voice with it was very touching." Gallaudet was a leader in deaf theater by virtue of being the only school that offered training for deaf actors, a program that was initiated in 1961.

When George C. White approached Hays about getting involved with organizing the O'Neill, it occurred to Hays that the new center could offer the legal and organizational umbrella for the deaf theater. "George said, 'Great.' George helped me apply for the grant. He was more of a business man. So our relationship started." An initial grant of $16,500 was approved by the Rehabilitation Services Administration in 1966. They were on their way.

As a first step, Hays brought one of the Gallaudet productions, *Iphigenia in Aulis*, to Waterford. As mentioned previously, it was a special feature of the 1966 National Playwrights Conference, the first conference to feature readings of new scripts. It went over well, and some of the Gallaudet performers were invited to be founding members of NTD, which was formally launched in 1967.

The challenge of staging a deaf theater production is to appeal to both hearing and nonhearing audiences. Generally, deaf actors engage in the action onstage, signing their dialogue, while hearing actors stand to the side and speak the lines, functioning as human subtitles. In this format, language has particular force as words exist simultaneously as speech and gesture. Part of the fascination for the audience is in gleaning the correlation between the two modes of "saying."

The young company was given a shot of visibility when a Sunday afternoon television series called *NBC Experiment in Television* devoted an episode to it. Hays remembers, "They came up to the O'Neill Center and filmed things that we invented just for the program but which gave an indication of what was to come. Arthur Penn directed a scene, Joe Layton directed a scene, Gene Lasko directed a scene." The program included selections from *Hamlet, All the Way Home*, and three Broadway musicals.

The broadcast encouraged the loosening of purse strings. More grants came in, including a substantial one from the Rockefeller Foundation, which enabled Hays to move forward more confidently. "By this time more things were built in Waterford. And we had good enough rehearsal spaces. And the kitchen was good. And so on we went."

The following summer saw the first session of the Professional Training School established by NTD at the O'Neill, which developed the skills of the players. This

National Theatre of the Deaf, ca. 1972.

led to a first public performance by NTD at Wesleyan University in Middletown, Connecticut. An inaugural tour followed. Says Hays, "Luckily, a lot of the people I had come out of school with were reaching a certain maturity and had taken positions in various colleges. So three or four of those first gigs we got were from friends of mine who were now the senior design teacher or the artistic director or the field director of places like Brandeis.

"The summer school was one of the best things about the Theatre of the Deaf. Deaf people from all over the world came. And that helped start companies in other countries. And then people came to us from where other companies started—India, Japan, China. We would offer room and board to help them start, or we helped get them going as we toured."

International travel meant the necessity of international communication, which gives rise to a naive question—how international a language *is* sign language? Hays explains, "There are two parts to sign language. One is the signs like 'bore'/'you bore'/'this is boring' [Hays demonstrates], but you can spell it, letter by letter—B-O-R-I-N-G. And you can spell very fast. I can't spell that fast. But you see it just the way you see a word on the page. Zip, your eye goes right along. Signs are not the same in each language. Ours came mostly from the French. The British spelling is two-handed, which is a little more awkward on stage; you can't hold a drink and sign at the same time.

"Sign language is also different in all countries. But deaf people are so eager for the communication that they don't get stopped by words. You talk almost fluently with the signs a half hour after you meet. Not in any deep way, but, 'Where's the men's room?' 'How long is this going to last?' Stuff like that."

Hays not only worked at the O'Neill; in the early days he also called it home for much of the time. "I slept in my office. Me, my two kids, and my wife—we'd all pile into that room, summers when the kids were up there, many, many years. And now," he notes wryly, "there's a sign saying 'Edward Albee slept here.' I believe he was there one night."

If you want to make a splash in the general audience's consciousness of theater (assuming the general audience *is* conscious of theater), you have to play Broadway. NTD, which had grown to be a company of seventeen actors (including four hearing-speaking performers), got there within two years of its founding.

"There is a special intensity and force of communication among the deaf," wrote *New York Times* critic Clive Barnes of the company's first offering, which opened at the Longacre Theatre on February 24, 1969. "Hands gesticulate and flutter, eyes seek

The National Theatre of the Deaf cast outside the Long-acre Theatre on Broadway, after a performance in 1969 with Anne Bancroft.

out eyes, and to the outside what is being communicated takes on a visual existence of its own." Barnes appreciated aspects of the presentation. "The hand conversations sometimes have the airy grace of mudras in Kathakali dance, and the actors have become adept at blending them with ordinary hand gestures." For Barnes, though, the speaking actors carried most of the freight of meaning. "Time and again the mind flew to the voice, and the actors, however accomplished, became illustrations more than participants." His reservations aside, he particularly admired one of the pieces, *Gianni Schicchi.* Based on a short opera by Giacomo Puccini, it had a plot derived from the *commedia dell'arte* tradition, and Barnes thought it "brilliantly directed by Joe Layton," a famous director-choreographer of musicals of the day.

A second program, which opened a couple of weeks later on March 8, found Barnes more appreciative of the company's technique. "Where I think it exerts its strongest appeal to the non-deaf is in its uses of what I might call ideograms, graphic symbols indicating, often with great expressiveness, things such as a river or a snowstorm. But when it has to transmit ideas and emotions, which is done by the manual language, this is far less communicative, although in fairness the sheer deftness of the manual alphabet invented by the Abbé de l'Epée in the seventeenth century does have a visual fascination of its own." Barnes was particularly impressed by an adaptation of Sheridan's short comedy, *The Critic*, which again was directed by Joe Layton "with a very proper panache." Though Barnes still wasn't entirely sold on the mode of presentation, he thought the engagement "provided an excellent showcase for the company."

On January 12, 1970, at the American National Theatre and Academy, the company returned to Broadway with a limited run of *Sganarelle* (adapted from Molière) on a bill with *Songs from Milk Wood* (drawn from Dylan Thomas's *Under Milk Wood*) directed by J Ranelli. Generally, Mel Gussow, who reviewed this engagement for the *Times*, was more appreciative of the format than Barnes had been. "Narration blends with sign language, which blends with acting. Actors switch from one form of expression to another. Occasionally there is a chorus of signs. So fluid is the work that one cannot always tell who is talking, and who is gesturing, who is hearing and who is deaf. On this stage are only actors—good ones."

To date, NTD has not returned to Broadway, but in 1977 the company won a Special Tony Award.

Inevitably, the company found itself embroiled in some of the political issues facing the deaf community at the time. There had long been controversy about whether to employ sign language or lip reading. According to Hays, "There were people who didn't want you to learn signs. They said that would stop deaf people from speaking clearly. It would be a crutch. Well, this turned out to be bullshit. People like Spencer Tracy's son at the Tracy Clinic out in California, who is deaf, didn't grow up knowing sign language. But when he *did* learn sign language, he spoke better. This became obvious. The more goes in, however it goes in, the more comes out." By using sign language in their performances, NTD was seen as a high-profile advocate for signing.

David Hays (left), George C. White (second from left), and Phyllis Frelich with members of the Gallaudet University production of *Iphigenia in Aulis*, National Playwrights Conference, 1966.

Edna Simon Levine's belief that a company featuring deaf actors would produce celebrities who could make the community and its concerns more visible was prescient. The student who played the lead in the *Iphigenia in Aulis* that was performed at the O'Neill in 1966 was Phyllis Frelich, who became one of the founding members of NTD. Through her work there, she met a set designer named Robert Steinberg. They married. (Steinberg also had a hand in designing the outdoor space at the O'Neill called, first, the Instant Theater and then the Edith.) During a time as an artist-in-residence at the University of Rhode Island, Frelich met playwright Mark Medoff. The dynamic of the marriage of Frelich and Steinberg inspired Medoff to write a play about the relationship between a deaf woman and a hearing man. It was called *Children of a Lesser God*, and it eventually opened on Broadway starring Frelich. She won a Tony Award for her performance in 1980. (Medoff also won the Tony Award for Best Play.) This led to other work for Frelich in theater and television. In addition, as she reported in a February 25, 1996, interview with the *Los Angeles Times*, her success seemed to trigger a change in society. "After that, everywhere I'd go, there would be people who wanted to study sign language, if only just for the beauty of the language itself. Before that, there was nobody like that. People said, 'That's the language of the deaf. We don't need that.' If they were going to communicate with me, they wanted me to learn to speak. But with sign language onstage, it became more accessible, and those attitudes changed. So I'd love to think that theater has played a large role in that change."

Children of a Lesser God was the watershed for the deaf theater community in much the same way that *A Raisin in the Sun* was for African-American theater artists. Frelich's understudy, another NTD alum named Linda Bove, played the role on tour and later became famous as Linda the Librarian, a character on the children's television show *Sesame Street*. The play was made into a film that starred another deaf actress, Marlee Matlin, who won the Oscar as best actress in 1986. Matlin and Frelich co-starred in *Sweet Nothing in My Ear*, a TV movie on deaf issues, and Frelich was directed by Bove in a production of D. L. Coburn's *The Gin Game* presented by the Deaf West Theatre Company. A Los Angeles company that was partially modeled on NTD, Deaf West was founded by Ed Waterstreet, Bove's husband and another NTD alum. Deaf West brought deaf theater back to Broadway with a remarkable revival of Roger Miller and William Hauptmann's *Big River*, a musical adaptation of Mark Twain's *Huckleberry Finn*. At one point in that production, during the final number, the orchestra and the singers cut out and, in silence, the ensemble signed a chunk of the song in unison. The New York audience cheered.

The success of Frelich, Matlin, and Bove largely put a stop to hiring hearing actors to play deaf characters on the screen. With actors on the scene who had won

National Theatre of the Deaf actor Linda Bove (center, eyes closed) teaches introductory sign language at an O'Neill Center summer camp, 1980. Bove would later play a lead role on *Sesame Street*.

or been nominated for a variety of top acting awards, it became apparent that such roles could be cast from the deaf community without compromise.

In some respects, NTD's presence at the O'Neill was an anomaly. All the other programs based at the Center required that audiences interested in seeing their work go to Waterford. If, for example, you wanted to see what the Playwrights Conference was up to, you had to go to the Hammond Estate, a location far from conventional theater districts. In contrast, NTD used the O'Neill campus as its base and built its projects there, but it gave the bulk of its performances elsewhere, touring cities and venues around the country and ultimately around the world. As a result, the general public was much more likely to have direct experience with and exposure to NTD than any of the other programs hosted by the O'Neill. The other programs concentrate on development; NTD produced finished pieces. One can only speculate to what degree the

The 2012 National Theatre of the Deaf holiday show, *Christmas Past and Presents*, performed in New London, Connecticut. Shown, left to right, are Joey Caverly, Chrissy Cogswell, and Christina Stevens. Photo courtesy of Betty Beekman.

difference in focus and mission led to friction. But friction there was, and, after sixteen years, there was a divorce. The causes are still a matter of debate.

Statements in the press put a public face on the issues. In an article dated November 8, 1981, in the *New York Times*, the issue is described as one of space. "The umbrella doesn't quite cover us anymore," Hays was quoted as saying. "We have grown to almost the same size as the center, financially. . . . and although we don't anticipate severe budget cuts, we want the flexibility to face them as they come with our own board of trustees."

According to Hays, grant money that was earmarked for the NTD ended up being used for some of the O'Neill's general expenses. He also says that Lloyd Richards was inflexible in scheduling the use of facilities at the O'Neill, to NTD's detriment. "Every once in a while there'd be a conflict. And George always did whatever Lloyd wanted. That's all," says Hays. The result was a divorce between NTD and the O'Neill, and Hays, whose contributions to the early days of the O'Neill Center were many and substantial, hasn't spoken to White since.

At the end of a transition period, NTD moved its offices to Chester, Connecticut, in 1983, and it continued to produce and tour from that base. Between the Waterford and Chester days, the company built up a remarkable record. Hays rattles off a list of accomplishments: "It ran for 30 years, did 30 foreign tours, was the first company ever to play all 50 states, the first company invited to the new China after the ping-pong [referring to the so-called ping-pong diplomacy that was a prelude to the resumption of relations between China and the United States], the first company invited to South Africa when the ban was lifted, and it went to the Olympics. We went to all seven continents. No one else has ever toured all seven continents." Including Antarctica? "I was hired by a cruise line to do a lecture, and when we got inside the continental three-mile limit of Antarctica, I asked to do a workshop on board. The tourists came and heard my little lecture on the Theatre of the Deaf. And so that's our seventh continent. Now put an asterisk next to Antarctica if you will because that was a workshop, but we raised our flag there."

The biggest threat to NTD after leaving the O'Neill came from an unexpected quarter. In 1994, while Hays was still artistic director, an audit revealed that the then executive director, Charles M. Roper, had embezzled more than $100,000. Roper went to prison, but this did nothing to repair the company's situation. Between Roper's malfeasance and shrinking and disappearing grants, annual budgets were cut back from the low seven figures to the mid–six figures, the summer training academy had to be shut, and shows for adult audiences were eliminated. An article in the August 10, 2006, *New York Times* reported that the company had retrenched to focus on touring shows targeted to young audiences.

New management steered NTD through the crisis years, and the company, though smaller, is out of danger now. A rapprochement with the O'Neill led to the move of its office into the Monte Cristo Cottage in 2012. "We're not part of the O'Neill," says the current executive director, Betty Beekman, "but we're here *at* the O'Neill."

Beekman has deep ties with NTD, having first worked with the company in 1973. Over the years of on-again, off-again connection, she has worked "in just about every position" except accounting (but including acting). It is a deep satisfaction for her to schedule company rehearsals on the campus where the company got its start. "It's such a good space for us. We don't have our own theater. We've never had a building. We've always been a touring company." The loss of funding has forced a scaling back of the size of the operation from its heyday, "But the quality, no." The hearing daughter of deaf parents, she has been interpreting since the age of four. The motive that led Edna Simon Levine to push for the creation of the company is still alive for her. "To be able to create social change? Yes, I firmly believe that. Every time we perform, through our entertainment we also educate, and we enlighten [audiences] in terms of knowing about deaf people. 'Oh, wow! They're cool, they're funny! They make me cry, they make me laugh!'"

As for the possibility of a full return to the O'Neill, there have been conversations between her and the O'Neill's executive director Preston Whiteway, but Beekman jokes that the current sense is "Let's date before we get married."

Little Theatre of the Deaf's production of *Stories in My Pocket* while it was in development at the O'Neill in 2011. Shown, left to right, are Claudia Liolios, Ian Sanborn, Jari Majewski, and Sara Guarnieri. Photo courtesy of Betty Beekman.

5. Critics and What to Do with Them

After the confrontation between John Guare and Elliot Norton at the first National Playwrights Conference, George C. White might well have had second thoughts about inviting critics to the O'Neill Center.

He did. They weren't about blocking them from the Hammond Estate, but about reassessing the way in which they would participate. When the Conference shifted its focus to presenting staged readings of new plays, White proposed that playwrights and critics have post-performance conversations.

This plan hit a few bumps, one of which was *Women's Wear Daily* critic Martin Gottfried. Ron Cowen, still exuberant about the reception *Summertree* had received from the audience at the Conference, remembers, "They ushered me into this room with these four or five older men. Of course, when you're twenty-one, everyone's older than you are. So I sat down, and Martin said, 'I think you have absolutely no talent, but you're young and you still have time to go back to school and think of something else to do.'" The other older men in the room were also critics, one of whom was Ernest Schier of the *Philadelphia Bulletin*. "He exploded," says Cowen. "He turned to Martin and started yelling at him. 'You have no right to talk to him that way.' And the other critics, too—'You shouldn't say that.' It was like having four

Dan Sullivan (left) leads a session with the National Critics Institute fellows, ca. 1980. Formerly the lead theater critic for the *Los Angeles Times*, Sullivan led the Institute from 1999 to 2013. Photo by A. Vincent Scarano.

dads come to your defense because some bully was picking on you. I think the O'Neill [realized] that this is not the best thing to do, to throw the lambs to the wolves, the morning after."

Though Cowen has cause to remember Gottfried as an adversary, the breakthrough of a playwright into public consciousness is often the result of a critic taking up his or her cause. When John Osborne's *Look Back in Anger* opened in London in 1956, most of the press were dismissive, but Kenneth Tynan's review in the May 12 *Observer* famously included the line, "I could not love anyone who did not wish to see *Look Back in Anger*." Audiences flocked to find out why, and Osborne was made. Claudia Cassidy of the *Chicago Tribune* is often credited with launching Tennessee Williams's reputation in 1944 by raving about an out-of-town tryout of *The Glass Menagerie*. Later, a *Chicago Daily News* critic named Richard Christiansen defended a play Cassidy had called "very dull," writing on October 24, 1975, that "The play is a triumph for Chicago theater—and a treasure for Chicago audiences." The play was *American Buffalo*, and that review helped propel David Mamet to national attention.

So, yes, critics could indeed play a valuable role in support of new work and new writers. But the O'Neill had to figure out how they should function as part of the unique developmental process taking place in Waterford.

One young journalist had no idea at the time that his summer at the O'Neill would lead him to become a champion of new work. "I didn't even know I really wanted to be a critic," says John Lahr. "It was a way of getting tickets to go to the theater. I was writing for a giveaway paper on the East Side called *Manhattan East*." This led to an invitation to the playwrights conference the same summer as Cowen. "It was great for me, because I got a feel for contemporary American theater, for the theater makers. I had come out of Oxford, and the skill or technique of discussion and argument and deconstruction of material was something that was fun for me. When I got up to do it in front of these people, I could find ways into things that seemed surprising to them. Suddenly it occurred to me that this might be a legitimate avenue for self-expression that I had never entertained."

Lahr remembers that the shift in American playwriting in general at first caught the uptown world off balance. "They completely misjudged the scene. The *Times* initially didn't even send people down to review plays off-Broadway." Lahr soon was working as drama editor for Grove Press, known for being at the cutting edge of art and politics. While the *Times* was fumbling, he was busy tracking a rapidly evolving scene. "Suddenly I was going to 150 plays a year. I was writing about all this stuff, I was meeting all the new playwrights."

Playwright Lance Lee (left) and critic John Lahr in the Barn during a session after a performance of Lee's play *Rasputin*, National Playwrights Conference, 1969.

Left to right, Institute director Dan Sullivan and National Playwrights Conference playwrights Lauren Yee and Michael Yates Crowley listen to a critic fellow, National Critics Institute, 2013. Photo by A. Vincent Scarano.

One of Lahr's projects for Grove was editing and writing commentary for an anthology published in 1969 titled *Showcase 1: Plays from the Eugene O'Neill Foundation*. Looking at the titles in the book for the first time in years, Lahr remarks, "Wow, that's a damn good group." The scripts included are *Father Uxbridge Wants to Marry* by Frank Gagliano, *Muzeeka* by John Guare, *Who's Happy Now?* by Oliver Hailey, and *The Indian Wants the Bronx* by Israel Horovitz. The book achieved its purpose. It drew attention to a new generation of writers and encouraged their production by adventurous companies elsewhere. It also was another step in establishing the O'Neill Center at the heart of the new movement in theater.

Back in Waterford, George C. White was beginning to wonder whether, aside from what critics might offer to the O'Neill, the O'Neill might have something to offer to critics, particularly developing ones. Conversations between him and established figures like Norman Nadel, Judith Crist, and Ernest Schier led to the founding of the National Critics Institute (NCI) in 1968.

Though Lahr was not involved with the Institute—and in fact is skeptical about the value of a program to train critics—he articulates one of the reasons it was created. "The chronic problem with criticism is that the critics, even the ones who are considered the good ones, don't know about theater making. They don't generally know how to write a joke or a scene. They don't know that if they don't like the set, it's not necessarily the responsibility of the set designer. They don't know actually who is responsible for the apparent mistakes that they see. There's a way in which the theater critic is not seen as part of the equation of theater. Which is crap. It's just silly. But you have to earn that, you have to earn that place at the table."

Lahr elaborates, "If you don't create anything, if you've never made anything, the language that you use to criticize is—if it's really violent, like John Simon's—an indication of an absence of creativity. If you've made something and also write criticism, that tempers your idiom. I prefer the language of the makers to the language of the observers."

The Institute was scheduled to run concurrently with the Playwrights Conference, to help developing critics earn their places at the table by giving them access to the world behind the scenes of the art they presume to evaluate. However, from the start it was established that none of what the critic fellows wrote was to be shown to members of the Conference.

The founding director of NCI was the critic who had come to Cowen's defense, Ernest Schier, universally known as Ernie. In a conversation with Dan Sullivan for

Ernie Schier, director of the National Critics Institute from 1968 to 1999. Schier was the lead theater critic at the *Philadelphia Bulletin* and a dean among the nation's theater critics.

Judith Crist and Woody Allen speaking with the campus community under the Conference Tree, National Critics Institute, 1972.

the book *Under the Copper Beech,* Schier playfully said, "I think it can't be taught," even though, at the time of the interview, he had been teaching it for thirty years. Schier's own preparation as a critic had begun with an infatuation with the stage. A high school dropout, he had hoped to be an actor but drifted into a job as a copy boy at the *Washington Post.* He was shortly named assistant drama critic. The man he was assisting had a drinking problem, so Schier got frequent opportunities to write. With practice came assurance and a career that led to the post in Philadelphia, which established him as one of the most respected critics on the scene.

Michael Phillips, who has served stints as the theater critic for the *Los Angeles Times* and the *Chicago Tribune* and currently is the *Tribune's* film critic, arrived at NCI in 1984, lugging with him a manual typewriter. "I was 23 at the time, and it was a hell of a lucky summer to be there—August Wilson had *Joe Turner* [*Joe Turner's Come and Gone*], John Patrick Shanley had *Savage in Limbo.*" Phillips's impression was that he was one of the few young critics who had been backstage at a professional company. "Before I came to the O'Neill, I had been in some rehearsal rooms briefly for stories—including at the Guthrie in Minneapolis. But for those who came to NCI from smaller markets, that was a new experience. And some didn't know how to handle it. They were so bowled over by their proximity to good-looking actors that they lost their minds instantly. And they couldn't shut up about their opinions of how to fix the play they were observing—in *rehearsal!*

"Ernie Schier scared the living shit out of us. To be that irritable, that irascible, that mood-swinging in his amiable praise one minute and just bile the next. He was a tough customer in many ways. But he really loved and believed in that program."

Left to right, Institute director Dan Sullivan, O'Neill board chairman Tom Viertel, and Michael Phillips speak to the campus community, National Critics Institute, 2005. Photo by A. Vincent Scarano.

Left to right, director David Esbjornson, critic fellow Andrew Propst, and Edward Albee, National Playwrights Conference/National Critics Institute, 2001. Photo by A. Vincent Scarano.

Some of Schier's notes have stayed with Phillips. "His biggie was, 'You use the word *seems* a lot. What's the Hamlet line? I know not *seems*? Don't use that stupid word.'"

Phillips has returned frequently to teach at NCI. One of the aspects he concentrates on with students is how to begin a review. "People always feel they have to take on the world in the lede, sum it all up at the beginning. No. Start with one small thing that's on your mind. And then follow where that goes. And then you'll get what you feel you need to say about the production. Wherever I've worked, the sign above my keyboard reads, 'Be specific, be brave.'"

Chicago arts journalist Kevin Nance remembers an encounter with Edward Albee. "Albee was taking questions from the crowd, and we were all there — pretty much the entire O'Neill family." Toward the end of the session, the moderator opened the floor to questions, and Nance raised his hand. "The gist of it was: 'In your scripts, you do a lot of directing of performance. You give a lot of stage directions, and you give in particular notes on how the actors should pace a particular speech, or deliver it.' There's a speech in *A Delicate Balance* which he describes as an aria, and he gives quite specific instruction as to how it's to be performed. And then I said, 'But I notice that in your recent plays, for example in *Three Tall Women*, there's very little in the way of direction to do with staging or performance. I wonder, does that mean that you have changed your position on the playwright's role in determining how his plays should be performed these days?' And surprisingly, I thought, his answer was, 'No, my position has not changed.' He said basically it's the playwright's prerogative to write these things in the scripts, and he felt that the people who take on the plays should very seriously apply those directions. It was a pretty controversial statement. Actors and directors in particular felt like that was ridiculous. 'Albee's got his head up his ass and is being incredibly imperious and, you know, he needs to get over it.'

Joel Siegel (left, standing) and Frank Rich (second from right) address critic fellows, National Critics Institute, 1984. Siegel was the longtime critic on *Good Morning America*, and Rich was the first-string drama critic for the *New York Times*. Photo by A. Vincent Scarano.

That was the gist. I did not intend to put him in a position of being at odds with the crowd there, but that's what happened."

Ernie Schier retired in 1998 and died in 1999. Former *Los Angeles Times* critic Dan Sullivan, who served as Ernie's assistant for a number of years, succeeded him, with administrative support from Helene D. Goldfarb and Mark Charney. Under his leadership, the schedule of NCI was reduced from the four weeks that Phillips spent on the campus. Sullivan says of the decision to shorten the stay, "I began to fear for the mental health of some of the people at the end of the third week." Currently NCI meets for two weeks.

Sullivan sees a consistency in the problems he and his guest teachers address in the writing of the students. "Unclear writing, pretentious writing, glib writing, an ingrown sort of cynicism that wants to not like anything, or an ingrown fandom thing that makes them predisposed to love everything. And *meeting a deadline*. Here, you have to turn something out by—I think it's seven in the morning now—and it's not your best work. We always have people at first going, 'I don't want you to think this is my best writing.' I don't think this is your best writing. I *know* it isn't. But this is journalism, this is the best writing you could do in an hour and a half." (At the end of the 2013 session, Sullivan announced that he would step down as director of NCI but continue on the faculty.)

Linda Winer, theater critic for *Newsday*, who often teaches at the Institute, says, "What I love is watching these people who all came there and have been hanging out together for 24 hours a day—they all go to the same event, and they all write their reviews frantically in the night, and the next morning they find out that each

Linda Winer (*Newsday*) speaks with critic fellows, National Critics Institute, 2001. Photo by A. Vincent Scarano.

one has a radically different reaction. They find out that the person who looks pretty much like them sitting next to them is looking at something with an entirely different world view."

Part of the current challenge for critics in general, and for NCI in particular, is the shrinking number of writers actually being paid to write criticism for print publications. In May 2013, the *Village Voice* eliminated Michael Feingold's position. Since its founding in 1955, the *Voice* has been the chief outlet for discussion of off- and off-off-Broadway, and it has long sponsored the Obie Awards. Feingold's dismissal is a particular shock. If someone of his stature has no job security and a diminishing number of periodicals care to make room for theatrical criticism on their pages, one can't help wondering about the point of training people for a field in which there are ever skimpier professional opportunities.

Another concern is linked to the increased amount of arts-related journalism on the web. Some websites, such as Playbill.com and TDF.org, are under the sponsorship of respected organizations and pay their writers generally modest sums. But a plethora of blogs and sites are written by people of widely differing abilities—some (like David Spencer's *Aisle Say* and Martha Wade Steketee's *Urban Excavations*) feature writing that would do credit to any established publication, whereas others feature a profusion of adjectives and little craft.

"Blogs are a new ballgame," says Julius Novick, another frequent teacher at NCI. "I hope it doesn't entirely wipe out the idea that some people are better at theater criticism than others." Novick notices a shift in those he encounters at NCI. "We don't attract the mid-course professional critics as much as we used to. We see more academics for whom criticism is an important secondary occupation which

Left to right, Michael Feingold (*Village Voice*), J. Wynn Rousuck (*Baltimore Sun*), and Institute director Dan Sullivan, National Critics Institute, 2006. Photo by A. Vincent Scarano.

still employs their academic skills. They come to the Critics Institute to hone their journalistic chops. If it's possible to hone a chop." Novick believes that academic critics can profit by assimilating the skills required of journalistic critics. "Academic criticism of any art has become a highly specialized field in which some people are able to flourish even though they write very badly. These writers deal largely in matters that are of particular interest to specialists but that do not have a news peg or that are not related to a particular performance. Academic criticism, if read at all, is mostly read for the sake of its information, its analysis, its ideas. Journalistic criticism, when it's really good, is read for all of those things but also in order to make the acquaintance of distinctive personalities with particular views. Journalistic criticism places a higher value on writing well and being interesting. It takes off from a specific event, a specific production, seen on a specific night, and therefore the journalistic critic has an obligation to re-create the experience that academic critics don't [have]. Also, journalistic critics tend to know more about what goes into making theater." Novick sees as self-evident that academic critics would be of more value if they had the journalist's writing skills and greater familiarity with the practical considerations that go into putting on plays, both of which are addressed at NCI.

With NCI, the O'Neill realized White's goal of being of value to the critics. As for the critics being of value to the O'Neill, director Lloyd Richards had an idea for employing them differently than they had been so far.

In his interview with N. Graham Nesmith, Richards said, "We used to have major critics after each show [at the National Playwrights Conference]. Everybody would come back, and these critics would offer critiques, and then the audience would engage with the critics. . . . It was a brawl that the audience and critics had. And so I cut that out. But then I said to myself that there were some excellent theater minds. How do you take that excellent theater mind and put it into the theater process? So, I decided to use these critics, those who understood how working on drama could be helpful to playwrights."

Richards mentioned the idea to White. White responded, "Bertolt Brecht wrote of a thing called a dramaturg." Richards researched the concept and agreed that it fit what he intended. And so he began assigning each project a dramaturg as well as a director. Most dramaturgs came from the ranks of critics.

In the years since the O'Neill popularized the term, the word "dramaturg" (sometimes spelled "dramaturge") has become a common one in the American theater. From situation to situation, the job has covered a number of functions. In some companies the dramaturg is simply another name for a literary manager. In others, the dramaturg acts as a researcher for the director, perhaps elucidating the historical background of a Molière play or untangling how Freudian theory applies to *Henry IV, Part One*. In addition, the dramaturg may have a diplomatic mission, serving as liaison between a company's management and a writer.

A dramaturg's function differs depending on whether first loyalty is to an institution or to a playwright. At the O'Neill, a dramaturg could be called a critic who is on the side of the playwright. Dramaturgs with backgrounds as practicing critics can usually anticipate the problems they would have with new works were they to be assigned to review them, so they often can sound early warnings about what is problematic in a developing script. The more academically inclined dramaturgs may be sufficiently schooled in history and theory to make concrete suggestions or to engage in a Socratic dialogue that leads writers to solve problems on their own. And then there are dramaturgs who are themselves playwrights and who bring to the job the perspective of experience facing similar challenges and fighting similar battles.

Though he is also a scholar and a playwright and has served as a literary manager at Yale Rep, Michael Feingold is primarily known for his years as the critic for the *Village Voice*, in which position he had a unique perspective on the development of American playwriting in the years between 1971 and 2013. Participating as a dramaturg meant he had to make ethical decisions about which plays developed at the O'Neill he should cover as a critic. "The plays I fell in love with or grew to hate were the ones I wouldn't review afterward. The plays I was basically neutral about I [would] say, 'Hmm, let's look at this objectively. I'll be a different person now.'"

Dramaturg (and drama critic for the *New Yorker*) Edith Oliver and Lloyd Richards, National Playwrights Conference, 1987. Photo by A. Vincent Scarano.

From left (seated), dramaturg Edith Oliver, director Harold Scott, playwright OyamO, and Lloyd Richards during a critique session of OyamO's *The Breakout* in the Instant Theater, National Playwrights Conference, 1972. The Instant was later renamed in Edith Oliver's honor.

A measure of the esteem in which another O'Neill dramaturg was held can be gleaned in the living room of the Hammond Mansion. Three portraits hang there. Two of them are of George C. White and Lloyd Richards (both of them looking uncharacteristically glum). The third, which director Amy Saltz says its subject once described to her as "Portrait of an Old Lady in Need of a Bra," is of Edith Oliver.

Director William Partlan remembers Oliver being "curt, specific, and hugely supportive." Did she have any particular dramaturgical allergy? "If the characters kept saying each other's names all the time: 'People don't talk like that. No one uses somebody's name every time they talk to them. Get rid of it.' It was tart but it was out of love, and it was always in support of 'let's make this better.'"

Dramaturgs are generally eager to be useful, but one of Oliver's virtues was knowing that sometimes being useful means knowing when not to suggest "improvements." David Henry Hwang was twenty-one when he arrived at the O'Neill with his play *F.O.B.*, and she made an immediate impression on him. "The first time I met her, she said in that gravelly, kind of New York 'dame' voice: 'It's really great. Don't change a thing.' I ultimately learned that she was sort of correct. At the post-performance comments—I was onstage with Lloyd, my director Robert Allan Ackerman, and Edith—and everybody had ideas about how I should rewrite my play. I felt, 'This is my first play, and these people have a lot more experience and they're presumably well meaning.' I spent the next two or three weeks rewriting along those lines. And then, eventually, I threw all those rewrites out. Edith's advice turned out to be correct." Ultimately, through Ackerman, *F.O.B.* came to the attention of Joseph Papp at the Public Theater, where it was produced. Hwang won the Obie Award for it; one of the Obie judges that year was Edith Oliver.

Feingold has affectionate memories of his cranky colleague. "Edith used to write for the radio. She wrote for the *64 Dollar Question*. And she said she had also done some radio acting. I asked her what, and she said, 'Mostly gun molls.'"

A favorite Edith story is one that takes place in the room she regularly occupied at the Mansion. Susan Booth, now the artistic director of the Alliance Theatre in Atlanta, recalls, "I was back there for the first time since I'd been an NTI [National

Rehearsal in the Instant Theater for David Henry Hwang's *F.O.B.*, National Playwrights Conference, 1979. Photo by A. Vincent Scarano.

Theater Institute] student. The bedroom at the top of the steps on the top of the third floor of the Mansion had been the site of a major rite of passage for me. At NTI, I had met a lovely young man, and the rest was history. So I went running up the steps to that room, and I collided with this small, bespectacled woman standing in the doorway." Trying to explain the intrusion, Booth told her, "I'm so, so sorry. I lost my virginity in this room." Edith: "Well, you're not going to find it."

Playwright Jeff Wanshel remembers, "Once we were walking together, and she just brushed up against something, a large prop or something, and she began to topple. She was kind of hovering for a second on the way down. I reached out and steadied her. And she seemed to weigh nothing. I thought it was absolutely fantastic that somebody so tough with so much gravity, with that much personality, could be made of gossamer."

Another Susan Booth memory of Oliver dates from the death of director Dennis Scott. Some members of the community were in the living room of the Mansion, discussing Scott's desire to have his ashes spread in the sunken garden. "Edith said, 'When *I* die, I want my ashes spread in an ash tray.'" In fact, when she died in 1988, her ashes were spread under the Instant Theater, where she had attended plays for twenty summers. It was renamed the Edith.

The third dramaturg to cast a long shadow was Max Wilk, a screenwriter who had also worked as a story editor. Skip Mercier was particularly close to Wilk and had many opportunities to watch him at close range with the writers. "There was an Irish

Max Wilk and playwright Ursula Rani Sarma, National Playwrights Conference, 2008. Photo by A. Vincent Scarano.

Director Barnet Kellman rehearses John Patrick Shanley's *Italian American Reconciliation* in the Instant Theater, National Playwrights Conference, 1985. Shown are Edith Oliver (dramaturg), Kellman, and Shanley, with J. Smith Cameron in foreground. Photo by A. Vincent Scarano.

playwright who didn't think she needed a dramaturg. Good playwright. The first meeting, she just bristled. She had no idea why she had to waste her time talking to this man. And Max is cracking jokes. In the middle of him being very funny about silly stuff, he just turned and, looking right at her, he said, 'If you knew how to end your play, we wouldn't all be here.' Dead serious. And he leaned in and said, 'I can either help you or not. I'm pretty busy.' And he got up and walked away. She followed him down the path, and it was remarkable how she came to adore him. And they did find an ending.

"Max was always like a dog who knew where the bone was hidden. 'Yup, it's there. I know where it is. All you have to do is figure it out for yourself.' So you'd keep exploring stuff until you found the bone.

"But when a line was said onstage that he thought was a horrible line, he would literally groan. And some playwrights would get furious. Sometimes it would be, 'Oh, my God!' I'd go, 'Max, you've got to shut up.'"

The title of the book mentioned earlier, *Under the Copper Beech*, has particular meaning for critics who have spent time at the O'Neill. The copper beech in question is the same tree in the sunken garden near the Mansion that threw shade on many events of the first National Playwrights Conference. It was in this garden that, on August 3, 1974, Henry Hewes gathered a group of critics from around the country,

and they founded the American Theatre Critics Association, a national organization for those who write theater journalism. Best remembered as the critic for the *Saturday Review* and one of the past editors of the *Best Plays Annual,* Hewes was particularly interested in drawing attention to the work of regional companies. To this end, one of the functions of the Association is to recommend to the Tony Awards which nonprofit company outside New York City should be given an annual special award for regional theater. (As of 2014, nonprofit companies in New York that don't produce on Broadway will become eligible, a change that angers many in the Association.)

The original copper beech in question is no longer standing, having been hit by lightning and mauled by storms. New saplings from the old root system are sprouting on the site. The award that was conceived under it—the Regional Theatre Tony Award—was given to the O'Neill Center in 2010.

Executive director Preston Whiteway accepts the 2010 Regional Theatre Tony Award on behalf of the O'Neill, here in a simulcast of the broadcast in Times Square. In a perfect coincidence, the screen sits next to a billboard for *In the Heights,* a musical developed by the O'Neill in 2005. Photo by Tony Awards Productions; Thomas Robinson. © WireImage.

6. National Theater Institute

A flyer on the bulletin board of the Dartmouth drama department changed Barry Grove's life. It announced a program promising college students a semester of professional training in the theater. He applied. "I was nineteen, a sophomore at Dartmouth, and I came to the very first semester." The first semester of the National Theater Institute (NTI), fall, 1970.

As it was the first semester, much of the program was put together on the fly, but Grove was unaware of whatever organizational challenges the organizers faced behind the scenes. All he knew was that he was instantly immersed in training in a dazzling variety of theatrical disciplines. "One day, we were in kimonos with bamboo sticks banging on each other, and another, Margo and Rufus Rose appeared and we were playing with Howdy Doody and making puppets. Jess Adkins was teaching acting in a serious way, David Hays and Fred Voelpel were teaching design, J Ranelli and Melvin Bernhardt did some classes in directing. Our playwriting teachers were Frank Gagliano and Lee Kalcheim." Contemporaneous articles in *The Day* report that other teachers who shared their knowledge during that first semester included playwrights Robert Anderson and Paul Zindel, designer John Gleason, puppeteer Bill Baird, and directors Jules Irving and Stuart Vaughan. According to Grove, the

O'Neill's founder also pitched in. "George White taught us fencing." White also hosted a brunch for the kids at his Waterford house, during which he introduced Grove to his first taste of New York theatrical culinary culture. "My first Bloody Mary, and my first bagel and lox."

The semester culminated in putting together a show that the students toured to several colleges in the east. Grove's organizational skills must have attracted attention, because J Ranelli called him during Christmas break with an offer to assist director Melvin Bernhardt on the Broadway premiere of Paul Zindel's play, *And Miss Reardon Drinks a Little*. It meant taking a leave of absence from school. "One day I was home, back to just being a kid, and the next day I was having lunch with Julie Harris and Estelle Parsons at Sardi's." Harris, Parsons, and Nancy Marchand were among the stars of the production that he accompanied through out-of-town tryouts before opening on Broadway. This led to being invited to be a stage manager

Jim Henson giving a master class with Kermit the Frog, National Theater Institute, 1988. Photo by A. Vincent Scarano.

A movement class during the first semester of the National Theater Institute, 1970. Barry Grove is standing second from the left. Photo by Philip A. Biscuti.

at the 1971 Playwrights Conference. Grove then held a series of jobs at the O'Neill and met a young woman who assisted Lloyd Richards and Ernie Schier there. Her name was Rosemary Barnsdall Blackmon (known to her friends as Maggie), and they married soon after.

A few years later, George C. White found himself on the board of a new venture whose artistic director, Lynne Meadow, was a fellow alum of Yale. White gave Grove a glowing recommendation, the chemistry between Meadow and Grove clicked, and they built Manhattan Theatre Club into one of New York's key nonprofit institutions, now producing seasons both on and off-Broadway and regularly introducing major plays (including several Tony and Pulitzer Prize winners) to the canon.

The idea for NTI occurred to J Ranelli when he was a student at Wesleyan. "I was looking for a thesis project. I had brought a couple of people from the O'Neill

Morris Carnovsky, a member of the Group Theatre, teaching at the National Theater Institute, ca. 1985. Carnovsky originated roles in many of the Group Theatre's productions, including several by Clifford Odets. Photo by Frances L. Funk.

to Wesleyan to do workshops—[director] Gene Lasko and [writer] Frank Gagliano. The kids had loved it, we loved it. So I'm thinking, why can't this be part of the undergraduate experience? The liberal arts experience is different from the conservatory, but there could be a conservatory window. I was going to write a paper on subject curriculum, propose that Wesleyan, Trinity, and Central Connecticut—all close to Waterford—do this as a pilot. I'd get some O'Neill people, and we'd do a boot camp, three-week thing in the summer. I wrote the outline, but finally I decided that I didn't want to do that as a thesis project. I wanted to investigate directing. And so instead I did a paper on directing.

"Then David Hays and some others started talking about starting a school. I spoke to the president of Wesleyan, Victor L. Butterfield, and I said, 'I have this idea. Some schools offer a junior year abroad. I'd like to get the theater departments of a group of colleges together, create a little board, and administer what would be at the O'Neill.' Victor said, 'If you put eight chairmen of anything in a room, you'll never get anything done. Do it as an independent project, and tell them they can send their students there. You can invite them to advise, you can give them dinner, but don't give them any authority.' And so I brought that to George [C. White], and he went to his contact at the Rockefeller [Foundation]. I wrote the proposal—it would be one term, and we would look to bring the students in the second term of their sophomore or first term of their junior year. What they took from this could be applied to their choices in the remainder of their liberal arts studies. It really was in service of liberal education."

I was here one day when Morris Carnovsky was teaching at NTI [National Theater Institute]. The kids were nineteen or twenty, and they didn't know what the blacklist was. They didn't know that he had been blacklisted, and they didn't know that Elia Kazan had been a friendly witness in front of HUAC [the House Committee on Un-American Activities], and that he had named Morris as a communist to the Committee. After the class, Morris was standing, rapping with the kids. And one of the kids asked him, "What do you think of Elia Kazan?" And I thought, "Oh shit." I expected a mushroom cloud to rise over the barn. But he just paused for a moment and then looked at the kid and said, "Beware of Greeks wearing lifts."

—George C. White

J Ranelli (standing) teaches a group of Wesleyan students in the Barn Theater, 1967. This program was a precursor to the National Theater Institute. Photo by Kevin Donovan Films.

Barry Grove is just one of a number of distinguished theater managers who began their careers at NTI. Carol Ostrow, the producing director of the Flea Theater; Ted Chapin, head of the Rodgers and Hammerstein Organization; and Todd London, the artistic director of New Dramatists, also studied there. London was particularly impressed by the connection to the host organization's namesake. "For a kid coming from the Midwest who had never been by the Atlantic, the smells of the water, the sense of place and a playwright. . . . It wasn't like I had been steeped in knowledge of O'Neill, but suddenly you're in this place, and you hear this foghorn and smell these sea smells, and you live in this Mansion. . . ."

Ranelli served as the first director of NTI. "We had a faculty meeting. Lasted about ten minutes. It was the only one we ever had. David Hays, Fred Voelpel, and myself. Fred said, 'Well, all we gotta do is make the kind of school we wish we'd had.' And that's what we did.

"We figured that you could hire the best people in the theater and bring them to Connecticut in a limo, pay them a respectable fee, and you're still not talking about a tenth of the cost of one junior faculty member at a university for a year. And some of the big shot theater people came in their own limos and gave the check back. Said, 'Put this back in the kitty.'"

Fred Voelpel leads a class in the Sunken Garden, National Theater Institute, ca. 1980. Voelpel was the primary set designer in residence for the National Playwrights Conference and taught set, costume, and makeup design at NTI. He led NTI as its director throughout the 1970s. Photo by Roger S. Christiansen.

The range of approaches to the theater the students were exposed to ran the gamut from the high Broadway proficiency of director-choreographer Joe Layton to the cutting-edge explorations of Peter Brook. Ranelli has a particularly vivid memory of Jean-Louis Barrault demonstrating his famous mime from *Autour d'une Mère*, portraying both rider and a horse. "The bottom half is the horse and the top half is the guy trying to control the horse. He did that for us, and then he taught us how to do it. An amazing moment of history and craft."

Ranelli ran NTI for two years. Fred Voelpel took the helm in 1973. For the first three years, the program was supported by money from the Rockefeller Foundation and the National Endowment for the Arts. After that, it was supported by students' tuition. Indeed, at a certain point the tuition began to support much of the rest of the activities of the O'Neill Center. Executive director Preston Whiteway puts it plainly: "The O'Neill does not exist without NTI."

Jennifer Garner hadn't planned on being an actress. She enrolled in Denison University in Ohio with the idea of being a chemistry major. Her focus changed. "Once I got to college, my time and attention went to the drama program there. I think that I benefited from going to a small liberal arts school, where I could be on stage pretty much every night of the year. But what I really needed was a bit of conservatory education." She came to NTI in the fall semester of 1993 in search of an experience that would take her work to a different level. "It helped me know where the holes were in my theater education. By the time I left NTI, my goal was more to continue working in regional theaters. It was part of me taking my dramatic education more seriously. It took me from an undergraduate theater major, who figured

that I'd go on to law school or med school or do something else, to the idea [that] I really could keep studying this. Never once at NTI did I think, oh, I want to be in front of a camera. Never ever ever. I only wanted to do theater."

At NTI she got her first taste of a discipline for which she later had great use. "I ended up doing a job that required a lot of combat skills," she says, referring to her starring role as a CIA operative on the ABC TV series *Alias*. "I was so grateful to have had an introduction to stage combat at NTI. And even though what I had to do on camera was a lot scrappier, I felt like, 'OK, I understand what a miss is.'"

Henry Winkler leads a class shortly after completing his role as The Fonz on *Happy Days*, National Theater Institute, ca. 1981. Photo by Roger S. Christiansen.

Classmates Scott Lowell (left) and
Jeremy Piven in a scene from *The Odd
Couple*, National Theater Institute, 1985.
Lowell later starred on *Queer as Folk* on
Showtime, and Piven starred on HBO's
Entourage.

It also introduced Garner to aspects of the theater she had not previously
explored. "I had never done mask work before, and I could not believe how powerful
it was. How much you can bring something to life with intention. Your physicality is
all you really need to tell a story."

British director Richard Digby Day had first been involved with NTI as a guest
director. When the job of director opened up, he applied and in 1990 was hired to
share the position with critic Ernie Schier. Digby Day remained on campus, and
Schier would visit to consult and teach playwriting. After two years, Schier decided
to cut back on his responsibilities, and Digby Day became sole director, a position in
which he remained until 1998. "I suppose I was the first director who was ever there
on a sort of permanent basis. During the semester, unless I was away recruiting, I was
there the whole time. I lived in the Hammond Mansion."

Because of Digby Day's background, the program had a strong classical ground-
ing, and he began scheduling a visit to the United Kingdom at the beginning of the
semester. "We usually stayed in Stratford-upon-Avon for two weeks. They all saw the
same plays, they all went to the same art gallery, they all went to the same stately
home, they all went to the same concert." His purpose was to give students from various corners of America common experiences to help bind them together as a group.
(Later, he added the option of an alternate semester for students at the Moscow Art
Theatre School.)

When they returned to the States, he kept them relentlessly engaged. Digby
Day thinks one of his contributions was to move from the "catch as catch can" spirit
of scheduling to a more rigorous environment. "If you're going to keep people in the
middle of the country in not ideal living conditions (they were probably less good
than they are now), then you must keep them occupied all the time. Classes literally

Richard Digby Day, who
led the National Theater
Institute from 1991 to 1998.
The program's intensive and
demanding curriculum still
reflects his influence.

Ghost Stories

Fall of 1981. I was an NTI [National Theater Institute] student, I was 19. And George White was here a lot, and he was always telling us about the ghost. And he'd tell us when he'd first gotten the house. . . . No one was really even working yet. But they'd hear babies crying, and they could smell placenta. One of the people who was cleaning there or someone who was working there said, "What's that smell? I know that smell. That smell is the smell of birth."

We get a Ouija board and go up to the library and do séance stuff. Six or seven of us from NTI in a circle. It was late at night, and there was a party going on downstairs. So we were asking, "If you're in the room. . . ." All those things that you do. And the Ouija thing starts going around and around and around, and [at] one point, the library door opens and kind of closes and we were like, you know, so scared. And it just started spelling "H A M M O N D." And we went running downstairs. And we saw our playwriting teacher, David Berry. We said, "David! David! You're not going to believe this! It spelled out the name!" And he goes, "Hammond?" And we're like, "Shit, how'd you know that?" He says, "Well, 'cause this is the Hammond Mansion, this is the Hammond family," and he says that Mary, the ghost, haunts the house. Upstairs, we didn't know it was the Hammond house.

I was told this story that Mary had a baby, but with a guy who was a farmer around here, and the baby died or something, and so Mary haunted the house. Also Mrs. Hammond haunted the house. And if you had Mrs. Hammond, she was, "Get out of my space!" But Mary is much more friendly.

I remember being on my bed on the third floor one time, and the bed started to shake, and I was lying there, saying, "The bed is shaking. The bed is shaking." And I looked over and there was like this sort of depression in the bed, and I went, "I'm going to get out of the bed now and walk downstairs."

The second floor, you know, the back rooms—that always felt like the haunted area back there. One time I even fainted back there. I had been working out—I was a dancer back then—and I was taking a shower, and I got out of the shower, and I just fainted. And I just thought that that had to be either I was so tired or a ghost scared me or something. I found myself on the floor.

This was in the early eighties, [when] I think the ghosts were more active, because when I came back for the Playwrights Conference and there were so many people, nobody had ever encountered the ghosts.

—Annie Evans

began at 7:30 in the morning with a movement class, and then the classes, with proper lunch and tea breaks, went on through the evenings as well. The only time we didn't have a class, I think, was on a Saturday evening."

Digby Day felt that NTI could be a constructive presence in the community. "The O'Neill had been perceived by a lot of people as rather exclusive and private, and that it was a lot of New Yorkers and theater people coming up for the summer." Some of his projects involved performances open to the public. "We did *Murder in the Cathedral* in one of the churches of New London. And, with Connecticut College, we did a huge promenade play to celebrate the 350th anniversary of New London's founding. That was written by local authors. That brought the O'Neill onto the streets of the city." In collaboration with Sally Pavetti and Lois MacDonald, who supervised activities at the Monte Cristo Cottage, Digby Day also scheduled a series of events there to focus on the heritage of Eugene O'Neill.

"I think what one tried to do [was to instill] a sense that the theater demands—almost more than anything else—an extraordinary level of discipline. The theater's

Marya Ursin

Marya Ursin, the longest-serving member of the faculty in National Theater Institute (NTI) history, is a beloved guide, mentor, mother, and positive force for each successive class of students. Teaching yoga throughout the semester, she and her husband Dan Potter also lead the very first workshop that all NTI class members take as part of their first week of orientation—masks. By creating their own three-minute story and building a mask that reflects a part of their personality, the class members bond, and pretension is immediately stripped away. But most of all, Ursin acts as a mother figure to the class, attend-

Marya Ursin

ing nearly every presentation and scenework final throughout the semester. Beloved by students and successive NTI leadership alike, no NTI semester would be complete without her healing and loving presence.

David Jaffe, director of the National Theater Institute from 1998 to 2006, welcomes students during orientation, 2002. Photo by A. Vincent Scarano.

potentially the most disordered thing in the world, and there's a great pleasure in its practitioners discovering that the way you deal with it is by imposing order."

One of the things NTI students might discover was where they belonged in the theater. Rebecca Taichman arrived at NTI assuming she was going to pursue an acting career, and she was initially not very happy. "My memory—and maybe I'm making this up—was that you couldn't wear anything except blacks or sweats or something. You couldn't be expressing your own individuality. It was about being a canvas as an actor." As part of the program required experience in the different disciplines, she found herself assigned to direct scenes from Henrik Ibsen's *Peer Gynt.* "That week was a revelatory week. It's where I felt, 'Oh, this is where I can express ideas of my own.'" This led her to a career as one of the directors most in demand in New York's nonprofit scene.

Actor-writer John Krasinski cites David Jaffe (who succeeded Digby Day as director) as being a determining influence in his life. Krasinski came to NTI in the fall of 2001. His semester at NTI was designed to count as his last semester of college at Brown University, Providence. He had had a little experience with the college theater scene, mostly doing it for fun. Jaffe, then the director of NTI, gave a talk that prepared him for a different level of seriousness.

"I remember David saying, 'There's a voice inside every single one of you right now sitting in this room. And the only thing I'd encourage is that over the next fourteen weeks, you listen to that voice. Because that voice is the most honest voice you'll ever hear, and it's going to tell you if you have what it takes to do this professionally or not. The truth is you need to know it now. You will only be helping yourself have a very fulfilling life, either in the theater or not. But you have to listen, because I've seen so many people who disregard the voice and are very unhappy.'

John Krasinski in scenework, National Theater Institute, 2001. Photo by A. Vincent Scarano.

"We had meetings with David, and—God, I've never told this story, but—we had meetings with David. And he had a huge smile on his face when I walked in and he said, 'How are you liking it here?'

"And I said, 'Oh my God, I love it. It's the best. I'm having the best time ever.'

"And he said, 'That's great. Can I ask you one question? Because, you know, you seem like a great guy and I really like you, but I just want to ask you one question.'

"And I said, 'Yeah.'

"And he said, 'When are you gonna stop bullshitting people?'

"And I said, 'What?!'

"And he was like, 'When are you going to stop being a bullshitter? I'd just like to know when it's going to happen, just so I can keep an eye out on it.' For some reason the little alarm system in the back of my head didn't feel offended. And he said, 'What I'm noticing about your acting right away is that you rely more on people liking you than on doing a good job. I watch you do a monologue or a scene and you're going into some really interesting, really dangerous places, and you're doing stuff that's really, really interesting, as soon as you get nervous and you might have put yourself out there a little too much, you turn to the audience and make a joke or make a face and you bring the audience back in and everyone laughs at you. And it's almost like you clear the air and you get to start again. I'm telling you right now that

Colman Domingo (left) teaches a class for Theater-makers, the National Theater Institute's summer program, 2009. Photo by A. Vincent Scarano.

is extremely detrimental to your work. So I'm just asking *you* when are you going to step up and actually try acting.'

"I was floored. He was exactly right. Because I had never taken acting at Brown to be the beginnings of a career. I always did it just for fun. So there was this person who said, 'If you want to do it for more than fun you can. And I'm seeing right now that you're constantly pulling the ripcord and taking the parachute out rather than going in and actually doing some interesting work.'

"I'll never forget the next monologue I did after that was the monologue from *K2* [by Patrick Meyers], where the character is telling his friend to go on without him and basically leave him to die. And I got so emotional—not even that I was crying necessarily—but I definitely felt something very visceral and something that I had never felt before. And I could totally sense that the back of my brain was saying, 'Now would be a great time to make a joke. Or just tell people that you don't remember the line.' Or something like that, and I just overrode that for David, because he challenged me to. I don't think I've looked back since then. To this day, all my friends who were at NTI say it's one of their favorite things that I've ever done. I think it was probably one of the best, most honest, clear moments I've ever had acting. And it's because a man took the time to challenge me in a very honest way."

Krasinski was at NTI on September 11, 2001. "We weren't supposed to have radios or TVs in our room. But someone had heard the radio in the main office when they went to the bathroom or to make a call or something that a plane had hit the towers. And they came back and they told the group. And all of a sudden I was running. And I don't even remember getting up or leaving the room or whatever. A couple of us went off campus and went to this biker bar to watch the news footage. It was like a bad eighties movie where, you know, three or four young college kids were sitting in a bar with thirty or forty people central casting would put into a biker bar. And it was this connecting moment where every single person in there was there for each other. We were hugging each other, we were talking to each other, we were telling stories." The connection to the biker bar where they had found shelter on September 11 continued. "After that moment they took care of us and they treated us like we were their kids. And they came to our final project.

"The night of 9/11 we put on this show that we were rehearsing all day. It was a mask performance. And David Jaffe said, 'I just want to let you know that it would be hard for me to believe that there were any other people that got up and did theater tonight. And I just want to tell you that I've never been more proud of anybody in my career.'"

John Krasinski (standing) performs a scene with Danny Stessen, National Theater Institute, 2001. Photo by A. Vincent Scarano.

The group was scheduled to leave within the next few days to continue studies in Stratford-upon-Avon. "David had gotten tons of calls from a lot of parents saying 'Don't let my kids get on the plane.' When you're so close to college or you're in college or whenever it is that you come to NTI—you're not really an adult. And so this was a moment when we became adults before we ever thought we had to." Krasinski remembers, "David said, 'I will respect you for whatever decision you make. But to get on that plane and go to Stratford-upon-Avon has nothing to do with this school. It has nothing to do with theater. It has everything to do with the world. That if you get up and you get on that plane and you move forward and you weren't affected by it, we win.' And he said, 'And I'm not trying to make it dramatic, but truthfully, you have a family here. We can all do this together.' And then he told us that, believe it

National Theater Institute students after a performance at the Royal Shakespeare Company, Stratford-upon-Avon, United Kingdom, 2001.

or not, certain churches in NYC, had shut their doors after 9/11, but the theaters were open. And he said, 'I'm not going so far as to say theater needs to be your church, but I'm saying you have an opportunity to change the world in a big way right now by just saying you're not going to let this define you.'

"We were all just a mess, just crying. I mean it was a massive event for all of us. And sure enough, most of us chose to go forward and flew to Stratford.

"I credit NTI, truthfully, with everything as far as where my head is and what my goals are and dreams are. I would say it was probably one of the most influential moments of my life, being there."

Krasinski's visit to Stratford-upon-Avon was a continuation of the legacy of Digby Day to expose students to aspects of international theater.

Another NTI alum had an especially strong reaction to her foreign trip. Rachel Jett had first visited the campus during a summer with her grandparents, who lived not far away in Groton, Connecticut. At the age of twelve she asked to be driven up the driveway to the Mansion, where she picked up a brochure for the program. She returned as a nineteen-year-old student in 1994. At the time she was enrolled at Northeastern State University in Tahlequah, Oklahoma. After going to Waterford, she didn't return to Northeastern. Digby Day, who was then the director of NTI, apparently saw something in her from the start. "He took me under his wing and tailor-made a curriculum for me."

Through an NTI program, Jett was chosen to be one of three students who spent a semester at the Moscow Art Theatre School in 1996 (a program that continues to this day, now sending more than thirty students each fall). She looks back with wonder on the experience. Among her teachers there were Anatoly Smeliansky, the dean of the school (now its president), and Andrei Droznin, whose eponymous system of training forms the foundation of Russian stage movement and is a cornerstone of NTI's movement curriculum. "We saw seven or eight teachers every single day, and we took nine hours of classes. It was like being privately tutored in the back of the Moscow Art Theatre." The classroom they used was filled with history. Aside from the stage, there was a big *chayka* (the stylized drawing of a seagull that is the symbol of the company, referring to the Chekhov play that the Moscow Art Theatre famously staged, establishing the play's reputation in 1898), a chair where Constantin Stanislavski used to sit as well as the chair of the school's founder, Vladimir Nemirovich-Danchenko. To hear Jett tell it, she had found her paradise, and she slips into the present tense describing it:

"We have [the] run of the place. We can drop into any rehearsals, because there's only three of us. Anatoly can take us to every premiere, just sneak us in the back door. He takes us to the productions they make for only the other artists. At each little reception, he's saying, 'That's the best playwright in Russia. This is the best ballerina.'"

Her devotion to Droznin's system of movement led her to return to Moscow several times to apprentice with him. Finally, he gave her permission to teach his methods, which led to a job teaching at NTI in 1998, which in turn eventually led to her becoming artistic director in 2011.

From Jett's description of the program as she runs it today, NTI is still true to what J Ranelli initially outlined, later shaped by directors Digby Day, David Jaffe,

National Theater Institute director Lynn Britt (left) with a student, ca. 1988. Photo by A. Vincent Scarano.

Rachel Jett leads a Russian Movement class, National Theater Institute, 1999. Jett now leads NTI as artistic director.

Michael Cadman, and Jeff Janisheski. She acknowledges that it is designed to discourage the people who shouldn't apply. "If you tell most people that you're going to be in class ten hours a day, seven days a week for fourteen weeks with three days off in the middle—getting up at 7:30 in the morning and working until midnight every night—it doesn't appeal to everyone. When this sounds attractive to a student, we know they're probably our kind of student. It's always been an ensemble-based program that takes a small group of individuals. They come here thinking they know what they are and know what they want to do, and we give them the opportunity to find out that they can do other things. They may come to us as actors and find out that they are actually good playwrights or designers or directors. It's a practicum. It's their laboratory."

Mary Martin (seated far right) leads a master class in the Screening Room, National Theater Institute, 1988. Photo by A. Vincent Scarano.

The program now boasts semesters in advanced playwriting and advanced directing, and a summer term—the Theatermakers program—in addition to the Moscow and Waterford bootcamp-like semesters. New for 2014, NTI offers an undergraduate semester in comprehensive musical theater training.

Jett believes that one of the consequences of the NTI training is the degree to which it encourages self-starters. Many alumni have founded their own companies. "I think that comes from a sensibility of the way we work here. We say all the time they shouldn't wait for someone to give them a job, that they have to go out and make their own work. We give them some of those tools—they learn how to write, direct, design, they learn how to work in an ensemble without a big authority telling them what to do. A lot of the work is student driven. Their final project is largely

Class members rehearse for their final in Droznin/Russian Movement, National Theater Institute, 2010. Photo by A. Vincent Scarano.

student driven. So they leave here and they kind of know what it takes, at least to get their work done."

Those who have gone through the program feel a kinship for one another. An alumni organization called the Risk Fail Risk Again Theater Collective facilitates continuing contact and collaboration. ("Risk. Fail. Risk Again" is the motto of NTI.) Jett explains: "These folks make things together, they go and see each other's work, they do retreats. They have a web site where they chat and they post events. They're always close to their own class, but once they leave, they become a part of a large pool."

Also, just by virtue of training at NTI, they are welcomed into the larger community that hosts it. At the orientation it is said explicitly: "You are now part of the O'Neill family."

7. National Playwrights Conference — The Richards Years

A summer night in 1994. A portly black man with graying hair and a trimmed beard addresses an audience assembled on the bleachers of what was then called the Instant Theater:

"Ladies and gentlemen, welcome to another project in the thirtieth annual National Playwrights Conference. For those of you who are here for the first time, I am Lloyd Richards, artistic director of the Conference, and it is my privilege and my responsibility . . . [to] share with you what's happening here, what we're doing, what it's all about. Thirty years is a long time. Thirty years of what? Of following a vision."

He tells how George C. White founded the O'Neill Center and created the National Playwrights Conference. He describes the process of selecting the plays for the Conference, the nature of the work done on the scripts, and the conversations that go on before and after the performances. He draws to a close by talking about the audience's part in the Conference.

"We appreciate your being here. We appreciate all those who made this possible. We appreciate George for envisioning. We appreciate the town of Waterford for their . . . enormous continuing contribution. We appreciate the work of all of the

Lloyd Richards introduces a play at sunset in the Edith Oliver Theater (formerly the Instant Theater), National Playwrights Conference, 1994. Photo by A. Vincent Scarano.

parties who were involved, and particularly this evening, we thank Stuart Warmflash for permitting us to work with him on his play, *Owning the Knuckleball.* Thank you."

For the most part, Richards chose to be a quiet presence, doing his work in behind-the-scenes conversations and meetings. This was the big exception—introducing hundreds of performances, reminding all of the mission of the Conference.

The publicly accessible aspect of the Conference was the summer performances, but there was a community preparing for the Conference during much of the rest of the year. One of the helpers of this process in the late seventies would go on to win the Pulitzer Prize and the Tony Award in 1989. In 1976, Wendy Wasserstein was exhilarated to be running around town, delivering scripts to the readers who were helping to winnow the hundreds of submissions down to a manageable number.

Under White, recommended playwrights had been invited to bring up whatever they were working on. Under Richards, with a few special exceptions, writers were invited on the basis of submissions, opening opportunity to unknowns around the country. These scripts were initially screened by a panel who wrote detailed evaluations. The ones that made the cut went to the next level of readers. And these were reduced to a list of semi-finalists numbering in the dozens. From this, Richards and his advisors chose eleven or twelve works. Richards had the final say about which were chosen, but he sometimes allocated a slot to a work that had not particularly spoken to him but had excited the passionate advocacy of a panel member.

The plays chosen were not necessarily the best plays submitted, but rather what the committee felt would be best served by the process. William Partlan remembers a script of self-evident excellence. "Paula Vogel's *Baltimore Waltz* was one of the candidates. It was a truly extraordinary play, beautifully written. Ultimately, we as a committee knew this one was going to get produced. 'This one doesn't need what the O'Neill can bring to it.' And so we said no."

Richards then had to decide who would direct what. Certain directors inevitably developed reputations for proficiency with certain styles of plays, but for every piece

Judith Light (left) and Wendy Wasserstein (playwright), *Uncommon Women and Others*, National Playwrights Conference, 1977. Photo by Roger S. Christiansen.

Phyllis Kaye

Phyllis Kaye

Every National Playwrights Conference participant during Lloyd Richards's era remembers Phyllis Kaye. Local to Waterford, Kaye was introduced to George C. White as he was organizing the O'Neill Center in 1964. Kaye was named as one of the founders of the O'Neill, and she volunteered to help organize the first National Playwrights Conference, acting as a sort of company manager for the first decade—a role that was just coming into use in American theater. She arranged for artists' living quarters, transportation, and general well-being, though she remains best known for her calligraphy (to say nothing of her punch served at the welcome party). She hand-wrote each name tag worn by O'Neill artists from 1966 to 1999, many of which are shown throughout these pages.

Kaye also organized the first National Playwrights Directory, publishing it in hardcopy and distributing it nationally in 1989. Containing the contact information, biographical details, and listing of extant plays, the book's aim was to facilitate further productions for writers after development in the era before the internet.

Kaye continues as a fixture at the O'Neill, attending nearly every work offered throughout the year and often being among the first to welcome new staff members.

—PW

he would assign to a director's "sweet spot," he would assign something else outside his or her comfort zone.

Next came casting. From the actor's perspective, an invitation to Waterford had special meaning. "You were anointed," Caroline Aaron states flatly. "It was such a vote of confidence. If you were invited to go to the O'Neill in the summer, it meant that you belonged to the elite part of the acting community."

Cynthia Nixon and Justin McCarthy rehearse *I Have Often Dreamed of Arriving Alone in a Strange Country,* by Patrica Cobey, National Playwrights Conference, 1992. Photo by A. Vincent Scarano.

Richards's appointment to the Yale Drama School gave him a chance to offer encouragement to some of the promising young actors in the program. Courtney B. Vance remembers, "To be asked to the O'Neill was a very big honor. Miraculous. I didn't care whose play I was in. I just was so amazed and glad to be a part." Vance was invited in 1985 and that summer worked in two projects with another Yale student named Angela Bassett. A dozen years later, in 1997, they married.

Though there was never a formal O'Neill repertory company, from season to season, there were actors who could be confident that they would spend four weeks in Waterford, including Robert Christian, Bryan Clark, Jill Eikenberry, Kevin Geer, Brent Jennings, Peggy Pope, John Seitz, and Helen Stenborg. Actor Reed Birney remembers Edith Oliver telling him that some parts would never be played as well as they were at the O'Neill, because some of the most gifted actors on the scene would frequently play smaller parts that, in full production, wouldn't be played by actors of similar stature.

The first time the writers, directors, and dramaturgs met one another was at a weekend meeting held a month before the Conference. During this weekend, the playwrights would read their plays to the community. Partlan says, "It was important to Lloyd that we in the room got to know each other as artists first. After three days of the hell of listening to each other read the plays, the playwrights felt, 'We know who we are now.' The playwrights began to bond with each other."

Doug Wright, the Pulitzer Prize–winning writer of *I Am My Own Wife*, learned that the pre-Conference could trigger something other than bonding. Says Wright of his 1988 experience, "I had written this play that was pretty outrageous, *Interrogating the Nude*. I'd been fascinated by the artist Marcel Duchamp, and I wanted to write a play that was about his life but was written in an anarchic spirit that was true to that life. So I came up with this conceit—it was set in and around the Armory Show of 1918, where Duchamp's 'Nude Descending a Staircase' was introduced. He was the first cubist to depict a nude in motion going down a series of steps. So I concocted this potboiler plot in which an artist's model had been dismembered, fragments of her body had been found, and the only clue was this wet painting at the bottom of the stair. There was a big interrogation and Duchamp was a suspect. It was a metaphysical, cheeky little play about aesthetic crime versus literal crime. I wanted to find a way to make the painting as shocking to a contemporary audience as it had been in its cultural moment.

"You learned over the course of the play that the murder victim was a woman named Rose Selavy. If you know Duchamp's story, he created a female alter ego based on the phrase 'eros, c'est la vie.' She was his invisible female doppelganger that he had sort of murdered to create this painting. In fact, there had never been a crime. He was out to publicize the painting, and it was all sort of a ruse."

Initially, Wright's pre-Conference experience was a pleasure. "I was newly out of graduate school, and I'm a pretty affable guy, and everybody seemed to like me and was amused by my youth. Ann Commire, Thomas Babe, Neal Bell, Keith Huff,

Robert Christian

Robert Christian, the African-American actor Lloyd Richards had once cast as an old Jewish man, started having chronic health problems. Word came one morning at the National Playwrights Conference that he wouldn't be able to make rehearsal. He came down with pneumonia, and it wouldn't go away. Then he seemed to bounce back, but he subsequently fell ill again. It was a pattern that soon became all too familiar. At the time, it had no name. "That was the first memorial I went to," says Marsue Cumming. Gregory Hines did a tap dance in his memory. Christian was the first of the O'Neill community to succumb to AIDS, on January 27, 1983.

(*left*) Director William Partlan with Ebony Jo-Ann during rehearsal for *Pork Pie*, by Michael Genet, National Playwrights Conference, 1999. Photo by A. Vincent Scarano. (*right*) Left to right, Doug Wright (playwright), Ernie Schier (dramaturg), and Gitta Honegger (director) during rehearsal for *Interrogating the Nude* in the Amphitheater, National Playwrights Conference, 1988.

Michael Kassin, Mark St. Germain. Interesting group of writers and my first time being in their company. So I was feeling quite on top of the world.

"Then I read my play to the other attendees. And several of the female playwrights were deeply offended. It sort of luxuriated in the telling of this very violent crime against this purportedly female character, this Rose Selavy, and they were really unhinged by the play's graphic description of the crime. They were women of conscience, and I'd really upset them. A group of them went to Lloyd Richards and said, 'We don't want to be in festival with this play, and we don't feel safe with this writer in our midst.' I'm 23 years old and I'm thinking, 'I want to be a provocateur!' and then I find out what it *feels* like to be a provocateur. While I have at times an incendiary imagination, I flatter myself that I'm a pretty nice guy. I was young, I was unmediated, I hadn't had the twelve years of psychoanalysis I've had now, and at times I was too eager to push buttons. And at times I *was* dealing with provocative material in an irresponsible way.

"But I became an absolute pariah, and no one wanted anything to do with me. I would go to breakfast and sit by myself. I felt lost and alone." There was one writer who broke ranks with the others. "Jeff Wanshel. He took me under his wing and said, 'Don't freak out. You're young. There will be a learning curve here.'

"Lloyd Richards asked me, 'How are you feeling about all this?' And I said, 'The play may need work, it may be too untempered, it may be sort of issuing forth

Playwright Jeff Wanshel, who developed five plays with the National Playwrights Conference. Photo by A. Vincent Scarano.

out of my id without enough craft, but I'm happy to be here, and I want the play to work, and I don't want to be everyone's enemy.' And Lloyd was completely empathetic. I think he saw my youth.

"Then I remember [director] Gitta [Honegger] bravely came up to my table and said, 'I have a dramaturgical idea. It doesn't involve a rewrite, but it's a casting notion. You have an actor playing the role of Duchamp, and you have an actress playing Rose Selavy. Since she's his metaphorical twin sister and ultimately a creation and doesn't exist in the real world, let's just cast a man. We'll have two men, and sometimes Actor A will play Duchamp and sometimes Rose, and sometimes Actor B will play Duchamp and sometimes Rose. And the two of them will continually trade off the two roles, because they are dimensions of the same psyche.'

"So I went home and I did a modest rewrite, keeping this casting idea in mind. When I returned for the conference, there were more people there instead of just the playwrights, so I had a chance to make new friends and not be the pariah any more, even though some of the playwrights regarded me with a jaundiced eye. And we worked and worked and worked on the piece."

The changes Wright had made during the break paid off. "People appreciated that we'd reconceptualized it to a degree. They now recognized that it was inherently

Dramaturg Edith Oliver, 1994. Oliver was a drama critic for the *New Yorker* and an O'Neill institution in her own right, spending each summer from 1975 to 1995 at the National Playwrights Conference. Photo by A. Vincent Scarano.

Lloyd Richards (left) and John Patrick Shanley, National Playwrights Conference, 1983, during the first of Shanley's four residencies, with *Danny and the Deep Blue Sea*. Photo by A. Vincent Scarano.

a black comedy, less Anthony Shaffer and more Joe Orton in tone. Very much to their credit, the women who were particularly incensed by the play now saw it was a rumination on art, not an attack on its sole female character. Through this casting coup, the play thematically fulfilled itself in a richer way. So the feedback session was actually very, very warm. It ended up being very positive, and in being positive, it pieced me back together after the very soul-shattering experience I'd had there.

"And it was, dare I say it, the hit of the festival. Lloyd adored it, it went on to be produced at the Yale Rep and was optioned for Broadway for years and got a number of resident theater productions and got a very nice review in *Variety*.

"But that summer taught me what it means to take full moral and personal responsibility for your work and what you put out in the world. And even now, after admittedly provocative plays like *Quills*, I still look back on that summer as when I had to face down my two selves—the aesthetical provocateur and the nice Texas boy who just wants to be loved. That's probably been the biggest war in my life— between those two disparate aspects of my nature. It taught me more about both defending your work but also articulating your work in the clearest possible way, because I learned that you are absolutely held accountable for it. I think of that as the summer that forced me to grow up."

The O'Neill's entrance
sign, ca. 1979.

Lee Blessing first came to the National Playwrights Conference in 1983 with *Independence*, and he attended his ninth conference in 2005 with *Great Falls*. One aspect in particular stays with him from his early years. "I loved the renderings. It felt very old Broadway to me, how somebody would sit down and imagine your world for you, and then actually draw it, paint it." The renderings were posted next to the entrances to the theaters, so that the audience could carry in an image of the world in which the action they were about to see was intended to take place. "The O'Neill gave you a lot of the sense of what it would be like if you were actually having your play done in a major production. Things like the rendering made you feel you were being taken seriously."

Left to right, director Barnet Kellman, play-wright Lee Blessing, and Mary McDonnell rehearse Blessing's *Independence*, National Playwrights Conference, 1983. Photo by A. Vincent Scarano.

One particular O'Neill experience stands out for Blessing, working on what became his most famous play, the story of the relationship between an American and a Soviet diplomat. "The reading of *A Walk in the Woods* was done in the Instant Theater on July 4th. We literally spent that week watching nuclear submarines rolling out from Groton [a naval submarine base across the river] and sailing into the Sound, standing next to guys that we knew were KGB. Some of George's Russian invitees, you know. He invited Russian writers and directors and actors. But they came with companions."

Not every playwright invited to the Conference came away from the experience in a mood to be complimentary. In the same issue of the *New York Times* in which Ron Cowen wrote enthusiastically about his experience—September 3, 1972— another Conference playwright from that summer, Kenneth H. Brown, had his say in an article called "The Average Was Lousy." Brown's piece begins (the punctuation is his): "Once upon a time and a very good time it was there was a mansion on a road by the sea owned by a very rich town in which there lived a very rich man named George C. White who, after trying very hard to get involved in the theater for a very long time, finally succeeded in doing so by making the mansion a summer camp/Johnny Carson show for theater people called The Eugene O'Neill Theater Center." Brown found little of value in the conversations with visitors Woody Allen,

Playwright Lee Blessing, 1983. Photo by A. Vincent Scarano.

Rendering for Lee Blessing's *A Walk in the Woods*, National Playwrights Conference, 1986. Rendering by G. W. Mercier.

Paddy Chayefsky, Robert Downey, Arthur Penn, and Kurt Vonnegut (the Johnny Carson reference). He goes on to offer synopses and criticisms of the majority of the work done by his fellow playwrights.

One of those playwrights, Sandra Scoppettone, articulated the general sentiment in a September 24 letter to the *Times* in which she called his piece "a complete betrayal of everything the O'Neill stands for." She continued: "[A]ll the writers were in a workshop environment with plays in progress. To have those plays reviewed, good or bad, even in capsule form in the *New York Times*, violates those conditions."

Contacted during the writing of this book to see whether he had had any thoughts on the matter since he wrote the article, Brown demurred.

Though the *Times* generally was supportive of the O'Neill, this was not the first piece it ran that was critical of the Conference. Rose Leiman Goldemberg reflected on her time there in a September 20, 1970, story called "Woman Writer, Man's World." "For the first time, because of the Waterford experience, I'm forced to confront what it means to be a woman playwright, judged in the same scale as Dr. Samuel Johnson's dog." She couldn't help but notice that she was the only female in the group of twelve writers selected.

Her submission, *Gandhiji*, was a portrait of the private life of Gandhi, dealing with his failures as a husband and a father. "In my play," says Goldemberg, "a group of actors make him improvise his life, to make him understand what he did, and how he treated the people who loved him. Everything in the play is true and comes out of his autobiography."

Left to right, Judith Crist, Kurt Vonnegut, George Roy Hill, and Lloyd Richards during a panel session, National Playwrights Conference, 1970.

Charles S. Dutton performs in *Seven Guitars*, by August Wilson, National Playwrights Conference, 1994. Photo by A. Vincent Scarano.

Part of her problem was a matter of bad luck. She thought the director originally assigned to her, Glenn Jordan, was "terrific," but illness forced him to withdraw. She was assigned another director, Mel Shapiro. She remembers, "He didn't get my play at all; he seemed resentful that they'd given him another job. I couldn't talk to him. When something didn't work the first time, he'd give up and say the play didn't work. There's a scene where Gandhi tells his wife that he'll never sleep with her again, that he's taken a vow because his passion for her is destroying him, and asks her does she mind. And she says, 'You've taken the vow. No, I don't mind.' Well, Mel couldn't stage the scene. He couldn't figure out how they could confront each other. Finally, I think it was Margaret Linn, who was playing Gandhi's wife Kasturbai, who said 'What if we turn our backs to each other?' And boy, did that work!"

In her *Times* piece, Goldemberg described the morning-after discussion of her play. "To dramatize the kind of putdown a woman playwright encounters: the Conference 'rap session' after the staging of my play *Gandhiji* was a particularly rough one. My chief critic, who didn't like women and who didn't like me, attacked me personally, faulted my integrity, told me I'd written the *wrong play* about Gandhi (I'd chosen to explore the controversial private man projected against the image of the public saint), patronized my craft by extolling it as 'razzle dazzle,' kept begging me 'not to hate' him but to admire his 'frankness' and would not stick to the play. I made the best answer I could, tried to keep my cool, and let the personal stuff lie and sour in its own juice." In a conversation for this book, Goldemberg added, "I got questions like, 'What does your husband think of it?' 'What do your kids think?' I wanted questions like, 'Why did Gandhi do that? Why did you want to tell it in that way?' I felt it was wrong, that my work wasn't taken seriously."

Forty plus years later, Goldemberg comments, "I don't know if the O'Neill liked the *Times* article, but it was indeed what I'd felt, and there was a big response to it—letters from women, gay playwrights, black playwrights, Indian playwrights, saying, 'We just want to be *playwrights*, period.'

"The O'Neill was hard, but it did a lot for me. I went there wanting to be a playwright. I came away saying, 'I am a playwright.'" *Gandhiji* went on to full production and helped establish her reputation as a dramatist (she went on to write a number of other plays and won a Writers Guild Award for her teleplay *The Burning Bed*).

She continues to feel it was wrong to condition a reading on the writer's acceptance of sitting still for the public discussion. "Playwrights had to buy a performance or a tryout by sitting for the audience to tell them what they thought or what to do. It was like telling an actress, 'You can have this part, but first you have to take your clothes off and walk naked in Macy's window.'"

Though Yale rejected White's early offer to link the O'Neill Center to its drama school, many writers, actors, and directors can claim both institutions on their résumés . Yale's graduate playwriting program has long been a magnet for aspiring dramatists. The competition for the small number of available openings each year is intense, and Yale has a history of choosing its students wisely. The Conference selection committees and artistic directors have often chosen with similar wisdom.

Albert Innaurato first went to Waterford when his play *The Transfiguration of Benno Blimpie* was accepted for the Conference in 1973. This was some compensation for the hostility he describes at the hands of the dean of Yale's Drama School at the time. When he complained to Robert Brustein that students assigned to rehearse *Benno* were failing to show up, Innaurato says that Brustein replied, "Albert, we're trying to prepare you for the real world. We don't like your work and they won't either." Time has not mellowed Innaurato's opinion. "I hated his guts. I still hate his guts." A few years after its performance at the Conference, *Benno Blimpie* made its way to New York and won Innaurato an Obie Award in 1977.

One of Innaurato's classmates at Yale was Christopher Durang, with whom he collaborated on a play called *The Idiots Karamazov*, a mash-up of all things literary and Russian in which, in a student production, a young Meryl Streep played the 80-year-old

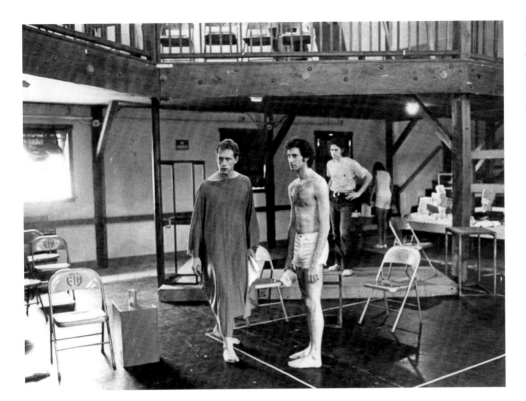

Michael Sacks (left) and Lenny Baker rehearse *The Transfiguration of Benno Blimpie*, by Albert Innaurato, National Playwrights Conference, 1973.

translator Constance Garnett, roaming the stage in a wheelchair, abusing morphine and ultimately morphing into Mary Tyrone from O'Neill's *Long Day's Journey into Night*. Durang found a soulmate in another student, Sigourney Weaver, beginning an ongoing collaboration on a series of projects, including the Broadway run of his *Vanya and Sonia and Masha and Spike*, in which she starred and for which he won a Tony Award for best play in 2013. He also met and bonded with an aspiring young playwright some years before she began delivering scripts around Manhattan.

Durang got his MFA from Yale in 1974 and his invitation to the O'Neill in 1976. "I tell this to students in the hope that it will encourage them to keep trying: I applied four times before I got in, and it was for *A History of the American Film*. In retrospect, I'm kind of glad I got in on that one, because my previous ones all had been one-acts."

As described on Durang's website, *A History of the American Film* establishes five archetypal characters—"Loretta the good girl, Jimmy the tough guy, Bette the tough gal, Hank the good guy, and Eve the wisecracking friend"—and runs them through decades of plot conventions, styles, and genres familiar from revival cinemas and TV. The scenes play like a series of skits, albeit with a pungent aftertaste. Durang has a deeper purpose than making the audience laugh, charting how the changing values of American society are reflected in popular entertainment. So it is that the same actress who has a "We're the people" speech invoking Ma Joad from the film *The Grapes of Wrath* in the forties finds herself strapped to an electric chair for being a communist, a reflection of the Red Scare melodramas produced in the fifties.

The Conference also employed Durang's talents as an actor in Amlin Gray's *Pirates*, which featured Dianne Wiest, masquerading as a man. "We would hold our scripts, doing swordfights. Dianne was very unhappy with this, and I also didn't want to be hurt, so I went up to her and said, 'When this happens, why don't you and I fight together? I'm going to be really gentle, so don't worry.' That was the beginning of our friendship."

In those days, rewritten pages were copied onto different colored paper. "The original copy was white, and then there would be pink and yellow and blue. Arthur [Kopit] paid me the compliment of saying that he was impressed, because he thought whenever we got to colored pages they were very good."

Durang has some thoughts about why *American Film* proved to be his break-out play. His earlier works were more absurdist and darker, mixing strong tragic and sexual elements that general audiences of the time found off-putting. In contrast, *American Film*—though it has streaks of black comedy—was more accessible. As Durang observes, "the audience of the time was my parents' age, and they knew all those movies and had lived through World War II."

American Film did indeed get to Broadway in 1978, where it had a modest run, though Durang was nominated for a Tony for best book for a musical. At one point, the character of Mickey reveals to his girlfriend that he has lost his hands in the war, and (referencing the part Harold Russell played in *The Best Years of Our Lives*) he shows her his hooks. At the O'Neill, these were suggested by coat hangers, the hooks of which protruded from between the actor's knuckles, the rest of the hangers completely visible. At the Taper, the actor wore real prosthetics. The coat hangers, being metaphoric, were funny. The prosthetics were not.

Though Durang appreciated the imaginative responses his play unleashed in the designers of the full productions at Hartford, the Mark Taper, and the Arena, there was something about the atmosphere of the Conference—reminiscent of skits performed by the fire at Camp Whateveryoucallit—that was "really charming. The O'Neill was obviously not a costumed production." The biggest production value came during a parody of a Busby Berkeley number called "We're in a Salad," during which "the girls did carry celery stalks."

Wendy Wasserstein, who graduated from Yale in 1976, followed Durang to the Conference the following summer (1977) with a play she had begun writing while

(*above*) Dianne Wiest rehearses for *Pirates*, by Amlin Gray, National Playwrights Conference, 1976. Christopher Durang, there as a playwright for his *A History of the American Film*, also acted in *Pirates*. Other Conference playwrights to act and write in the same season are John Guare (1965), John Patrick Shanley (1984), and Neal Bell (1989). Photo by Roger S. Christiansen. (*right*) Rehearsal in the Amphitheater of *A History of the American Film*, by Christopher Durang, National Playwrights Conference, 1976. The play would be Durang's first on Broadway. His fifth, *Vanya and Sonia and Masha and Spike*, won the 2013 Best Play Tony Award. Photo by Roger S. Christiansen.

a student. *Uncommon Women and Others* started as a one-act play based on Wasserstein's classmates when she was a student at Mount Holyoke College, a group portrait of young women dealing with the insecurities of approaching adulthood as they note with both excitement and trepidation the changes in society the women's movement is bringing about. Durang remembers, "Some of the male students were not that crazy about the play, so she had insecurities about it." Innaurato says much of the Drama School establishment disdained to call the play by its name: "They called it 'that play.' They were very nasty about her."

After leaving Yale, Wasserstein got connected with a new off-off-Broadway theater called Playwrights Horizons, which was founded in 1971 by Robert Moss and was struggling to attain lift-off. A young former actor named André Bishop soon joined Moss, and one of their early projects was a musical cowritten by Wasserstein called *Montpelier Pizzaz*. Bishop remembers, "Then she brought us *Uncommon Women and*

Others, which we did a staged reading of. I felt strongly that it should be made into a full-length play." By the time Wasserstein got to the Conference, the play had grown, including a scene in which the classmates reunite six years after their graduation.

Bishop visited Waterford under an assumption. "Playwrights Horizons was always going to produce it the following season. It was in the days when you could go into production very quickly, and it wasn't elaborate and all.

"I spent a week there with her. I was very nervous the whole time about it. You know, all these plays being put up and then these talk-backs. Everyone eating together and sleeping in the dorms and all that. And if you're sort of basically an outsider. . . . But I met a number of writers that summer who we then went on to produce besides Wendy: Neal Bell, Ted Tally, Peter Parnell."

Bishop saw *Uncommon Women* both nights. Word apparently got out, because Bishop remembers seeing producers at the second performance. "T. Edward Hamilton was there from the Phoenix [Theatre], and I thought, 'Uh-oh.' And of course he fell promptly asleep. But that in no way prevented them from making an offer to do the play."

At the time, the Phoenix was a higher-profile company than Playwrights Horizons, and "Wendy was embarrassed. She didn't owe anything to us. But we developed it, and my boss had done her plays before I even got to Playwrights Horizons. We

Cast of Wendy Wasserstein's *Uncommon Women and Others*, National Playwrights Conference, 1977, including Swoosie Kurtz (far left), Judith Light (second from left), and Kathryn Grody (middle). Photo by Roger S. Christiansen.

went out for breakfast, and she said that she had decided to go with the Phoenix. I was devastated at first. Then I thought, OK, Playwrights Horizons has got to start focusing on refining its productions. We have got to, frankly, spend more money, get better actors, have longer runs, and have better designers so that we can—I don't want to say compete—but so we don't lose plays like this again. And that's what we did."

The Phoenix production of *Uncommon Women* (directed by Steven Robman, who also directed it at the O'Neill) featured an extraordinary lineup of up-and-coming actresses—Swoosie Kurtz and Anna Levine from the Conference were joined by Glenn Close, Alma Cuervo, Jill Eikenberry, Cynthia Herman, Ann McDonough, Josephine Nichols, and Ellen Parker. (A TV version for PBS featured Meryl Streep in the role played by Close.) The review by Richard Eder in the November 22, 1977, *New York Times* announced the arrival of an important talent: "Wendy Wasserstein has satirical instincts and an eye and ear for the absurd, but she shows signs of harnessing these talents to a harder discipline. . . . [She] uses her very large gift for being funny and acute with a young virtuosity that is often self-indulgent. But there is more. Unexpectedly, just when her hilarity threatens to become gag-writing, she blunts it with compassion. She blunts her cleverness with what, if it is not yet remarkable wisdom, is a remarkable setting-out to look for it." Not a bad welcome to have from the *Times*.

The relationship between Wasserstein and Playwrights Horizons was repaired, and Bishop (who took over the artistic directorship of the company when Moss decided to step down) went on to produce *Isn't It Romantic?* (1981) and *The Heidi Chronicles* (which won Wasserstein the Pulitzer and the Tony in 1989). When Bishop took over the artistic directorship of the Theater at Lincoln Center, he continued to produce her work (including the hit *The Sisters Rosensweig*, 1991) until her death at age fifty-five in 2006.

James Earl Jones (left) and Lloyd Richards on the O'Neill Center lawn, ca. 1984. Photo by Roger S. Christiansen.

From left (front), Lloyd
Richards, Marilyn Stasio
(dramaturg), Wendy Wasser-
stein, and Martin Esselin at a
critique the morning after a
performance of Wasserstein's
*Uncommon Women and
Others*, National Playwrights
Conference, 1977. Photo by
A. Vincent Scarano.

Part of Wasserstein's importance, aside from the quality of her work, is as a pioneer, one of the first female playwrights of her generation to achieve prominent success. The commercial theater at that time still offered few works written by women.
As for women directors, only a few had managed to acquire important New York
directing credits. Margaret Webster and Eva Le Gallienne were well-regarded hands
at the classics, and Agnes de Mille expanded her celebrity as a choreographer to take
on full responsibility for a few musicals. Regionally, others like Zelda Fichandler,
Margo Jones, Alvina Krause, Viola Spolin, and Nina Vance also attracted notice,
often establishing theaters to have places to work.

As someone who was frequently cited as the first African-American to do this or
that, Richards was probably aware of the significance of the first woman to be asked to
direct at the O'Neill. In 1975, the gender barrier for directors was broken. Fresh from
a critical triumph in New York staging David Rudkin's *Ashes* at Manhattan Theatre
Club (where she has served since 1972 as artistic director), Lynne Meadow got the call.

She remembers, "I definitely felt as the first woman directing there that I wanted
to do a great job. So I was nervous. Young. And so I walked around looking very serious
all the time. I think I probably was wearing, you know, a suit or something. And Lloyd
came over to me and he said, 'Lynne, um, why don't you go put on a pair of shorts?
And relax.' That was Lloyd. I put on my shorts and proceeded to have a great time."

The first project she worked on was *Hollinrake's Gambit* by Lance Lee, which featured the husband-and-wife acting couple, Michael Tucker and Jill Eikenberry. "I had scheduled an hour and a half or something to work on one scene, and I was going over. Everyone was lying around on the grass. And I said, 'I'm running behind and I'm sorry that you all have to wait for a little bit.' Jill said to me, 'Lynne, we're not in New York. We don't have other appointments to go to. We're just lying around in this beautiful place. Don't worry about it.' That was a great piece of advice."

The season Meadow made her debut, she directed a play written for a family audience by Jonathan Levy called *Marco Polo*. Meadow relates the story of casting Meryl Streep: "I said, 'I would like her to play the princess in *Marco Polo*. The other people in the cast were Chris Lloyd and Ben Masters. And I also cast an actor, Joe Grifasi, who was a friend of Meryl's from New Haven, to play Harlequin. It was children's theater, really sort of family theater. I had never really done that but I agreed to

Neal Bell (playwright) and Lynne Meadow (director), *Two Small Bodies*, National Playwrights Conference, 1977. Meadow founded Manhattan Theatre Club in 1970 and continues as its artistic director. Bell has developed four plays at the Conference and now teaches playwriting at Duke University. Photo by Roger S. Christiansen.

do this, because I thought the piece was charming. And so the moment comes when the bad guy, who was being played by Chris Lloyd, says to the Princess Meryl, 'Give me your ring.' We're rehearsing it, and Meryl started to take the ring off. But then she was having a hard time, so she was yanking on her finger. Finally she put her finger between her knees, trying to yank the ring off, and then she rolled on the floor, still trying to get the ring off. It was hysterical.

"Jonathan Levy, the playwright, said, 'But Lynne, she's the *Princess*. What's she doing?' And I said, 'What she's doing is just marvelous.' He said, 'I don't think a princess would act this way.' So I stopped the rehearsal. And Meryl and Jonathan

(*below*) Meryl Streep rehearses, National Playwrights Conference, 1975. Photo by Andrew B. Wile. (*right*) Joel Brooks and Meryl Streep rehearse in the Barn Theater, National Playwrights Conference, 1975. Photo by Andrew B. Wile.

Director Sheryl Kaller (center) rehearses Molly Smith Metzler's *Close Up Space*, with Michael Chernus and Jessica DiGiovanni, National Playwrights Conference, 2010. The play premiered in 2011 at Manhattan Theatre Club. Photo by A. Vincent Scarano.

and I walked to the side to talk about it. Jonathan said, 'I'm not sure a princess would behave in quite such a way.' And Meryl said, 'I did a lot of work with kids when I was in New Haven. It seems to me that kids really like to see their heroes have flaws. They prefer when their heroes are real people and have problems.' She used those words — 'have flaws.' So I will never forget that moment of dealing with her, and Jonathan Levy then saying, 'Yes, I think you're right.' So we left it in and it was very funny."

The O'Neill also introduced Meadow to new playwrights. "Right from the beginning of my career I was very interested in doing work by exciting writers, and I wanted very much to produce work by African-American writers. I wanted the profile of Manhattan Theatre Club to be as encompassing as my own taste. And I thought Richard Wesley and OyamO were those writers."

For three years, 1975–1977, Meadow spent her summer vacation working at the O'Neill. "I think that's a fine thing when you're in your twenties. But as the Manhattan Theatre Club became increasingly more demanding, I found that I needed to have a vacation in the summer." Though she hasn't visited the O'Neill in years, work developed there continues to make its way to her company's stages.

Amy Saltz was determined to follow Meadow's lead to Waterford. When Joseph Papp opened the Public Theater arm of the New York Shakespeare Festival on Astor Place in 1967, she got a job assisting Gerald Freedman on the initial off-Broadway version of *Hair*. In 1970, a small-scale musical she directed called *Touch* was a surprise hit off-Broadway. Nevertheless, her phone didn't ring. "I didn't get offered one show, and couldn't figure out why." Saltz found more opportunities regionally, including notable success with new work in Chicago. A job with John Houseman's Acting Company (a troupe made up of graduates of the Juilliard Theater Program) gave her experience with the classics, and she put together new projects for them. She kept hoping to get invited to the O'Neill. "I wrote Lloyd a lot of letters, and then I finally gave up. And then he actually came to see a play that I did at the American Place Theatre. I got a call."

She arrived in 1982, the first of seventeen seasons she spent at the O'Neill. That first year she brought in an actor she knew from the Acting Company named Kevin Kline to do "a terrible Russian play," Edvard Radzinsky's *Theatre in the Time of Nero and Seneca.* Kline played the emperor, and Michael Tucker played the philosopher he killed. It was Kline's only season at the O'Neill.

Saltz's first project was Carol Williams's *AWOL.* "It was about a man who was ostracized by his friends. I learned a really serious lesson working on that play. There were all of these stage directions, and I dismissed them, because I didn't understand them. And at some point in rehearsal the playwright very cautiously came up to me and she said, 'Would you mind just doing those stage directions?' And there was a whole subtext of the play that was in the stage directions, and I had just totally missed it. It's what the play was really about."

Saltz also had difficulty with Neal Bell's *Raw Youth,* which was presented at the 1984 conference. She says, "It was very dark, very sexual. When I read it, I was

The 1982 directors for the National Playwrights Conference on the Hammond Mansion Seaporch. (Top, left to right) Dennis Scott, John Pasquin, Amy Saltz, Barnet Kellman, and William Partlan; (middle) Tony Giordano; (bottom, from left) Bill Ludel and Lloyd Richards. Photo by A. Vincent Scarano.

Kevin Kline (left) and Michael Tucker rehearse *Theatre in the Time of Nero and Seneca*, by Edvard Radzinsky, National Playwrights Conference, 1982. This play was one of the first developed at the O'Neill by a Soviet playwright. The O'Neill became (and continues to be) a leader in cultural exchange between Russia and the United States. Photo by A. Vincent Scarano.

disgusted by it. And it's Neal, so the language is difficult language. I didn't understand it, I was offended by it, and I asked Lloyd to take me off of it. I said 'I don't know what to do with this play.' And he said 'You'll find something.'"

Says Bell, "The play was loosely suggested by the Abscam scandal. The FBI used a con man to set up a sting to trap congressmen who were accepting bribes from Middle Eastern countries. The play began to revolve around the idea of the con man using his son as the bait in a trap. And that's when it shifted over into dealing with gay issues."

Michael Feingold, who served as dramaturg, describes it: "It's a tight little play about a young, troubled ex-cop who has been kicked off the force for doing some kind of shady business which seems to have been coming out of his realization that he might be gay. His father has been let out of the federal pen because the FBI wants him to set up a male hustler ring as an entrapment scheme for gay politicians. He recruits his son to be a working boy, OK? We're already in deep shit. It's a play in three scenes. The young man and his father. The scene with the first client. And then another scene with the father at the end. In the last scene, the son, who has discovered who he is, persuades the father to destroy the videotape, tell the Feds he can't go through with it, and to go back into the pen."

Bell remembers having difficulty reading it aloud at a pre-Conference weekend. "I'm naturally shy anyway, but since this is the first time I had written a play that was openly about gay issues, I was a little . . . tender about it? Afterwards, Amy comes up to me—I had never met her before—and she says, 'I don't think I'm the right person to direct this play.'"

Saltz's version of that first conversation: "I asked him, 'What are you trying to do?' because it was very murky. It turned out that there was definitely a play in there, but it was obscured by too much other stuff. He hadn't found it yet, but he was really trying to do something. I was nonplussed. I had thought it was just someone writing nasty stuff to get his rocks off, you know? So I said, 'We are going to go through this play line-by-line practically, and I'm going to tell you every time I want to throw this play in the ocean.' I mean I think I was hysterical. Neal—you know he's a very gentle man, and he was very patient with me. We started going through the play, and I found out that I just totally, *totally* misunderstood the tone of the play. And we started working. . . . We did it in the Amphitheater, and it was one of those magical nights when everything comes together."

Bell says, "She did an ideal job with it."

As was the case with every play presented during the Richards years, the morning after the second performance of *Raw Youth* came the critique supervised by Richards. Usually, he had a sure control of these sessions. Barnet Kellman describes the Richards manner: "He had a look, a quiet look that he would give that you knew you had just done the wrong thing." If you got that look, you had to stop and take stock. "You would think about why that was somehow out of bounds. But at those critiques, if somebody went off, Lloyd would kind of stare for a second, take a ridiculously long pause, and then move on to somebody else."

Well, *usually* that was sufficient. Which brings us back to the morning of the critique of *Raw Youth*.

Feingold remembers, "Neal was very nervous. The director and the dramaturg spoke, as was the custom, at the beginning of the critique. And I said that

John Turturro and Mary McDonnell in *Danny and the Deep Blue Sea*, by John Patrick Shanley, National Playwrights Conference, 1983. Shanley developed four plays at the O'Neill, including *Savage in Limbo* in 1984, *The Dreamer Examines His Pillow* in 1985, and *Italian American Reconciliation* in 1986. Photo by A. Vincent Scarano.

George C. White, Lloyd Richards, and Ernie Schier (National Critics Institute director) lead a post-show critique, National Playwrights Conference, 1983. Photo by A. Vincent Scarano.

the difficulty of the play was that it had what I called a 'buy or die' premise. Once you accept the premise, the rest is a matter of watching it unreel. And then a few people made a few comments that were polite, friendly—nice, cautious, tentative. Then Martin Esslin rose to speak." Esslin was a critic famous for coining the phrase "theater of the absurd" and writing a book on the dramatists he considered to be working in that vein.

"Martin began to rant," Feingold says. "I can't remember which word he used repeatedly—it was either 'swill' or 'kitsch.' He started out talking calmly but accelerated. The play had disturbed him very much emotionally, and he was furious about it. By the end, he was literally screaming. He was a man with a florid complexion, and his face had gotten purple like a beet. Lloyd said, 'Martin,' several times, trying to stop him. 'Martin, Martin.' And finally he shouted, 'Martin, I don't think this is helping the playwright!' And Martin stopped in mid-word, as if he suddenly realized where he was and all the color went out of his face and he sat down. Then Lloyd poured some mollifying oil on the troubled water, there were one or two other polite comments, and the critique was adjourned. I think Amy [Saltz] and I had to carry Neal out of the room."

Asked about his reaction to Esslin, Bell in turn asks about what others recall. When details are supplied, Bell says, "Oh my God, I'm starting to remember that." A pause, then: "Thanks for bringing that back."

Ernie Schier and Amy Saltz, National Playwrights Conference, 1994. Saltz directed August Wilson's *Seven Guitars* that year. Photo by A. Vincent Scarano.

Martin Esslin's opinion did not discourage André Bishop. He picked the play up for production at Playwrights Horizons. Saltz directed it, the only time she directed the New York premiere of a play she had worked on at the conference.

The value of the critiques continues to be debated today, when they are no longer regularly scheduled. Few of the writers interviewed say that the public discussions proved useful to them. One common refrain, though, is that these sessions often created such frustration in those witnessing the comments that some would sometimes approach the writers in private with more useful observations. Playwright Matt Witten observes, "I got the most out of going out with the director and actors for drinks afterwards, or at the O'Neill just talking to August Wilson about the play over coffee. For me personally, having the two nights of performance in a row was freaking awesome, and being able to talk to these incredible people that night or the next day in a noncritique situation was the most valuable."

Jeff Wanshel remembers Meryl Streep in his play, *Isadora Duncan Sleeps with the Russian Navy*. "She was sensational in it. She was cast to do the full production at the American Place Theatre for Wynn Handman. But just before rehearsals started, she got her first movie: four lines in *Julia* in a black wig. And they had the right to keep her until they scheduled her scene. So Wynn, who was extraordinarily flexible, postponed for two weeks. But finally he said to me, 'We can't wait.' So we cast Marian Seldes, who won an Obie in the role. She was a good sport, but she was aware that she was a last-minute replacement. If we ever disagreed she'd say, 'I'll try to do it as Meryl Streep would have.'"

When Kevin Geer first arrived at the O'Neill in 1982, the process was new to him. "I had never done a reading of a play. I didn't know how to do it. 'You mean we are going to hold the scripts?' It was a different technique. We always said 'four days of rehearsal at the O'Neill are like four weeks of rehearsal,' because each day was like a full week. Now readings are everywhere. I do readings all the time now."

Jill Eikenberry says that the particular kind of work that the Conference demanded of her redefined her as an actor. "I felt I was on the flying trapeze all the time. Forging these relationships so quickly, because you had to. In Albert Innaurato's play *Earthworms*, I remember just latching on to John Harkins, because that stuff was so raw and emotional. And then having Albert rework it after the first night so there was new stuff to play the next day. There was never any resting, never any 'Oh, we've got that section.' I got a lot of confidence in my first instincts. I was a much better actor after that.

"I did *Primary English Class* [by Israel Horovitz], which was a huge hit at the O'Neill [in 1975]. And then Diane Keaton was cast in it in New York. I knew that kind of stuff happened, but it was rough, because I felt like I *owned* that part. Israel called and asked me if I would come to rehearsals and sit in the back and watch [what] she was doing and tell him what she should do. Staggering. Then I was cast as her replacement, but it only lasted a month after that. But that was a little discouraging about the O'Neill. You couldn't own anything."

Nancy Mette speaks of working on Keith Reddin's *Life and Limb:* "I was in rehearsal and I was saying this line and I would think, 'I guess eventually I'm going

Meryl Streep, director Hal Scott, Joel Brooks, Ben Masters, Edith Oliver, and cast during the first read-through of *The Spelling Bee*, by Marsha Sheiness, in the Amphitheater, National Playwrights Conference, 1975.

Jill Eikenberry, National Playwrights Conference, 1975. Eikenberry and her husband Michael Tucker (Conference, 1982 and 1983) later starred in *L.A. Law* on NBC (1986–1994).

to figure out what that means.' And then, I was onstage and realizing right then what it meant. And I said the line and got a huge laugh. Part of the charm of the process at the O'Neill was that it had to happen right then. That was the way it worked. You could take a crazy chance, because that was the only time you were ever going to get to take that chance. And everybody else was taking the same chance."

The shortness of the rehearsal schedule was matched by Richards's injunction to keep production elements in the readings to a minimum. William Partlan, who served a term as production manager before becoming a regular director at the conference, recalls, "Every single prop listed by a stage manager was considered and either approved or disapproved at a morning meeting every single morning. Because the tendency was, naturally, to keep adding props. And so it became a bit of a system essentially controlled by a production manager but always with Lloyd's eye [on it]." This meant drawing case-by-case distinctions: "What's most important—to not confuse the audience, to have the prop there, so that they knew what it was supposed to be rather than miming it? When I became a director later, I would of course be a victim of it as well."

Christine Estabrook remembers working in 1976 on Kevin O'Morrison's *Lady-house Blues*. "Tony Girodano directed it. It was all about the kitchen and preparing a whole meal that's then served at the end of the night. When Lloyd saw it, Tony came back and he said, 'He doesn't like all the props.' And I said, 'I can't mime. I don't know what to do. I have the script in one hand, and if I have to mime that I'm like mixing stuff and cracking eggs. . . .' I was lost."

With the same eye that was on guard for unnecessary props, Richards kept looking for new people to invite to the Conference. Oz Scott came to his attention through a feat of theatrical legerdemain—taking a sheaf of poems by Ntozake Shange and organizing their presentation into what became a hit Broadway attraction (via Woodie King, Jr.'s New Federal Theater and Joe Papp's Public Theater), *For Colored Girls Who Have Considered Suicide/When the Rainbow Is Enuf.* Scott came to realize that, for him to serve the writer in the O'Neill process, he would have to restrain his facility. "I know how to pull tricks. And that is one thing that I tried not to do at the O'Neill is pull tricks. I said to myself, 'I'm gonna keep it clean.' One writer came with a script that had four scenes in the first act with complete changes and four in the second act with complete changes. We did those changes, just to show the writer, 'This is what you've got.'"

Another major African-American talent got a key opportunity at the O'Neill in 1980 when Barnet Kellman was assigned to direct a TV project called *A Thousand Miles to Freedom.* Says Kellman, "It was about a black girl who decided that she had

Angela Bassett, National
Playwrights Conference, 1985.
Photo by A. Vincent Scarano.

had enough with slavery and that she was going to get on a train and go north by passing herself off as a white girl." Kellman observes that he was facing this casting problem "at a time when I think white people were much less sophisticated about the shades of colors within black families that all black people were aware of. I thought, 'OK, thank you very much. You can't cast a white person and say they're black. So how do we cast a black person and believe that they're white?" Richards suggested Anna Deavere Smith, whom he knew from work in the New York office (like Wendy Wasserstein, she delivered scripts). "Anna had done almost nothing at that point. But, besides being a beautiful light-skinned African-American, she is an incredible mimic and a great shapeshifter." That ability to shapeshift was part of what made *A Thousand Miles to Freedom* persuasive, and it was at the heart of the solo shows that made her reputation later, in which she was convincing playing every race, gender, and age.

A Thousand Miles to Freedom was part of a program called the New Drama for Television Project that ran concurrently with the Playwrights Conference for

> *We were probably drinking on the porch, and it was getting really dark. It's probably the last week there, and we decide to go skinny dipping. So Roc [Charles S.] Dutton and Deborah Hedwall and I go down to the beach. You can't see anything. So we take off our clothes. We all get in the water. I'm freezing. And Roc is there. Of course, you can't see him at all. And these kids, these townies, come by and start messing with our clothes. Well, Roc gets up— starts coming toward them from out of the water. "What the fuck are you guys doing?" He's a big guy. And they look at him and go "Ohhhhhh!" and run. We found our clothes. They were kinda scattered a little, but we found 'em. I was laughing so hard. But that's so unlike me. I don't, you know, I don't . . . mess . . . when I have to work. I don't mess around. I don't have a lot of fun. I'm very serious.*
>
> —Christine Estabrook

a number of years. The program, sponsored by the ABC television network, was designed to encourage quality writing for the small screen. It was hoped that each year one of the scripts developed there would make the leap to broadcast as a television special. In some years, though, ABC preferred to adapt one of the scripts that had been written for the stage, such as Kathleen Betsko's autobiographic *Johnny Bull*, the story of a British woman who marries an American, assuming that she is coming to the America she knows from the cinema, only to discover she has married

Oz Scott (left) and August Wilson,
National Playwrights Conference, 1994.
Photo by A. Vincent Scarano.

The O'Neill Process

THE DIRECTOR: *After the morning read-through in the Instant [Theater], the director is setting up the stage to begin the afternoon blocking rehearsal. The playwright objects to the floor plan, but the director prevails. Blocking begins, and as the first actors enter the stage, the playwright again objects to where they are standing. The director decides to "take five" and disappears into the [Hammond] Mansion. (When Lloyd's office was there.) When he returns, he tells the playwright that Lloyd [Richards] wants to see him, and the blocking rehearsal continues. Sometime later, the playwright returns, takes a seat in the bleachers, and remains silent for the remaining days of rehearsal. (director: James Hammerstein, playwright: Israel Horovitz)*

The best way to find out how well your boat floats is to turn it over to a seasoned captain.

THE DRAMATURG: *When questioned about that morning's first read-through, the dramaturg replied: "Once we scrape most of the 'shits' and 'fucks' off, I think we're going to find a rather good piece there." (Edith Oliver)*

Playwriting is an honorable profession. It's good to have a doyenne around to teach the children some manners.

THE SCENIC DESIGNER: *While explaining to an actor why he probably was not going to get a chair with arms on it, the designer praised the use of the simple aluminum box that could become either a throne or a sled or a small hill. He pointed out that once an actor treats the box in a specific way, the audience is invited to participate by using their imagination, and once they are invested in the performance, they are more actively engaged on the evening's journey. (Fred Voelpel)*

Every "thing" here is to support the playwright.

THE AUDIENCE: *In the Amphitheater, the character is telling a rather long and very involved story that ends with a very bad pun. Most of the audience groans, with a few light-hearted "boos" and several extended "Noooooos." The actor goes to a desk, picks up a pencil, and scratches out the offending paragraph. General applause.*

When an audience hears the play, the playwright can hear the play.

THE ACTORS: *Almost all of the returnees think they've died and gone to actor heaven.*

There is nothing—repeat, nothing—the playwright can ask that those actors wouldn't try.

THE PLAYWRIGHT: *"It wasn't until my fourth week here that I realized—nobody has a second act!"*

Sometimes siblings are what a playwright needs most.

—Bryan Clark

Filming a scene for the New Drama for Television program, National Playwrights Conference, ca. 1982. With a grant from ABC, the O'Neill developed television and film screenplays in the 1980s. Photo by A. Vincent Scarano.

into a coal mining family struggling for existence in Pennsylvania. (Jason Robards and Colleen Dewhurst played the miner's parents in the TV version.)

One of the projects selected for the New Drama for Television Project brought members of its cast into open conflict with Richards. Tom Wright: "It was called *Three Against Possum Bend*. It was by two white people, and it was probably the most racist piece of literature I've ever read. It was supposed to be a satire, but it completely missed the mark. Roc [Charles S.] Dutton's character was a chicken-stealing guy, somebody else's character was a preacher who was out taking money and sleeping with women on the side . . . it was this really, really big broad thing. Very, very insulting." In addition to Wright and Dutton, the cast included such African-American luminaries as Mary Alice, Angela Bassett, Rosanna Carter, and Howard E. Rollins, Jr.

"Well," Wright continues, "we all did it. Everybody bit their lip. Because Lloyd. . . ." Wright hesitates, and then plunges ahead. "This is one of the other things I think: for African-Americans that worked at the O'Neill—Lloyd also put you under the African-American ultraviolet ray, and he wanted to see what came back fluorescent. Lloyd would sort of scan you with these eyes saying, 'Don't fuck up while you're up here.' Anyone who's African-American, they know what that means. And so you were on your best behavior for a number of reasons. But it's an old school way of dealing with people. That's as much as I'm going to get into that."

Ron Lagomarsino was assigned to direct it. It was his first year at the O'Neill, and all he could think as he—a white director—approached the material was, "What the fuck am I going to do with this? I was given it because I was a TV director and I had done some soap opera in New York at that time. And here I was working with the crème de la crème of African-American actors in New York and it was *offensive*. But everybody came to work, and we all gave it our best shot."

Tom Wright picks up the story after the video had been shot and edited and was going to be shown at the Conference. "Everybody knew this was a volatile piece of work. So everybody in the Conference showed up. And I mean it was packed. And we watched the video, and after it was over, there was this really polite applause. And you could feel everyone in the room turning around looking at one another going, 'Who's going to address this?' Well, they started off the critique and one person raised their hand and said, 'I didn't understand when the characters really weren't able . . .' blah blah blah. And the second person raised their hand and said, 'Well, in the context of this particular story . . .' blah blah blah.

"And I couldn't take it. So I raised my hand. I stood up and I spoke and went right to the heart of the matter—that we as human beings should hope to elevate, hope to raise the human condition, not drag certain themes and certain images over the fire. And I got standing applause from the entire O'Neill. As I sat down I looked up and Lloyd was sitting there with his legs crossed burning a hole through my skull. He did not want me to address that issue. But I thought, 'Fuck it, there are some things that are more important than whether Tommy Wright gets to come back to the fucking O'Neill next year.'

"Then someone asked the question: how did this play get here? And that was the volatile question. For whatever reason, one play slipped by Lloyd. My personal opinion is that he did not oversee this play whatsoever. As you can imagine, it put a serious dent in my relationship with Lloyd." (Nonetheless, Wright was invited back for another two seasons.)

Lagomarsino sees the incident as a window into Richards's thinking. "It felt to me like Lloyd was out on his own on the whole race thing. We were just coming out of a period when, if the subject was a black subject, you had to have a black director, right? You didn't mix this up, right? African-Americans had to tell their own stories. But Lloyd would say, 'Barnet, you're doing *A Thousand Miles to Freedom.*' He opened up my life. He gave me an opportunity to work with people I would never get to work with otherwise. I got sent to the Caribbean to work as sort of a State Department bring-the-O'Neill-to-the-Caribbean project, because Lloyd felt anybody can do anything. Oz Scott doesn't have to direct black plays, and Barnet does not have to do white plays."

One aspect of the Conference that many veteran O'Neill actors and directors prized is something that Wright began to question. "There was this cadre of people

Helen Hayes and Lloyd Richards, ca. 1991. Hayes was nicknamed "the First Lady of American Theater" and is one of eleven people to have won an Emmy, Grammy, Oscar, and Tony Award (EGOT). Hayes often joined the National Playwrights Conference as a mentor. A Broadway theater is named in her honor. Photo by A. Vincent Scarano.

Playwrights John Patrick Shanley (left) and Lee Blessing settle a friendly argument on the Hammond Mansion Seaporch after lunch, National Playwrights Conference, 1984. Photo by A. Vincent Scarano.

who came back every year. The same directors, the same actors." It got to a point where, as he saw it, the only new people there were some of the playwrights. "And so the question was: who was actually serving whom?" He wonders whether the plays got to be more or less the fuel for a community that began to exist for its own sake rather than for the writers. Concerns such as this may have been a factor in the changes James Houghton put into place when he became the Conference's artistic director.

Director Steven Robman believes that Richards's tendency to invite the same people back from year to year was based on practicality. He knew that veterans wouldn't have to be brought up to speed on the reasons the Conference was organized as it was. "There developed almost an O'Neill technique. I think one of the reasons Lloyd asked people back was that some people were better at that than other people, or they weren't scared of it."

At summer's end, Richards assigned himself one final task. Says Marsue Cumming, who assisted Richards several seasons, "Lloyd would dictate a thank-you note to everyone. It was an amazing experience sitting with him. I'm here to tell you, they were all personal. He knew everybody."

8. August Wilson in Waterford

Few would deny that August Wilson belongs in the front rank with such figures as Eugene O'Neill, Thornton Wilder, Arthur Miller, Tennessee Williams, and Edward Albee. The plays that make up his Century Cycle—all but one of which take place in Pittsburgh's Hill District—offer a sweeping account of the journey of African-Americans over ten decades, with one play set in each decade. Wilson consistently credited the National Playwrights Conference with giving him the opportunity to find his place. The O'Neill also introduced him to the person he needed to develop his gifts to their fullest. Critic John Lahr speaks for many when he says, "I think Lloyd [Richards]'s collaboration with August is, along with [Elia] Kazan's with Tennessee [Williams], the great collaboration of the twentieth century."

While giving Wilson his due, one should not forget how much other black writers accomplished in Waterford before and after his arrival in 1982. Derek Walcott's *Dream on Monkey Mountain* was a guest production in 1969; it went on to be produced by the Negro Ensemble Company in 1971 and won an Obie Award. Between 1969 and 1976, three plays by Edgar White were presented at the O'Neill, focusing on stories drawn from his background in the West Indies; five of his plays were produced by Joseph Papp at the Public Theater. OyamO (sometimes referred to as Charles F. Gordon) made the first of his five visits in 1972 with a play called *The Breakout,*

August Wilson in front of the
Rose Barn at the O'Neill,
National Playwrights Confer-
ence, 1994. Photo by A.
Vincent Scarano.

and another of these plays, *The Resurrection of Lady Lester*, was presented on CBS
Cable in a television production directed by Richards. Charles Fuller worked on
The Brownsville Raid in the Amphitheater in 1975, seven years before winning
the Pulitzer for *A Soldier's Play*. Phillip Hayes Dean, whose *Paul Robeson* (starring James Earl Jones) played Broadway in 1977 under the direction of Richards,
worked at the Conference twice, as the author of *The Last American Dixie Band*
(1977) and *King Crab* (1979). J. E. Franklin, best known for her play *Black Girl*,
worked on a play in 1981 called *Christchild*. Franklin's dramaturg was the prominent African-American playwright-screenwriter Richard Wesley, who worked at
the O'Neill on projects in 1973, 1974, and 1985; one of these included a play called
The Mighty Gents, which ran on Broadway in 1978 with a cast that featured Morgan Freeman, Dorian Harewood, and Howard E. Rollins, Jr. John Henry Red-
wood's *The Old Settler* was developed at the Conference in 1995 and had multiple
productions regionally before being produced as a TV special for PBS in 2001.
Other significant voices have included those of Leslie Lee (*Willie*, 1980), S. M.

Shephard-Massat (*Deeds*, 2003), Kia Corthron (*Breath Boom*, 2000), and Regina Taylor (*Magnolia*, 2008).

Wilson's submission for 1982 was just one of several hundred that arrived in envelopes without recommendations. Jean Passanante remembers when *Ma Rainey's Black Bottom* began to separate itself from the rest of the pack. "Every play would get one reading by a freelance reader, and then if it got a certain rating, it would go on to a second reader, and then, if the second reader liked it, it would be brought to Lloyd's attention, and he would determine that it would be sent to the selection committee. Probably about thirty or forty went to that selection committee. There was some debate about the play. It wasn't a shoo-in. My sense was that it was possible that it hadn't been read completely by some of the people because it looked like a telephone book—it was huge, and the typeface was very small."

Set in Chicago in the 1920s, the play presents Ma Rainey, a real-life blues singer, and (invented) members of a band assembled for a recording session. The session is disrupted by Ma Rainey's extravagant behavior and tensions among the musicians. Much of the script is made up of the musicians trading stories of their backgrounds, describing the roads that brought them to the studio, and articulating their hopes. At the play's end, a young trumpet player named Levee explodes in rage and stabs a fellow player to death.

Scene from Derek Walcott's *Dream on Monkey Mountain*, National Playwrights Conference, 1969.

Charles S. Dutton performs in the first reading of *Ma Rainey's Black Bottom*, by August Wilson, National Playwrights Conference, 1982.

At any rate, this is a summary of the finished play. The manuscript the selection committee evaluated was huge and somewhat shapeless. Michael Feingold recalls the discussion about it. "Lloyd was a little cautious at first. August's plays, with very few exceptions, aren't linear. And Lloyd came from a traditional mode of drama where you started at the beginning and went to the end."

"Lloyd reserved a discretionary slot," says Passanante. "If there was something that was controversial, he gave himself the privilege of putting it through. But that was not the case with *Ma Rainey*; it was definitely voted in by the majority. But I don't remember any particular buzz about it at the very beginning."

In a 1991 interview published on the website of the Academy of Achievement, Richards looked back on the selection of *Ma Rainey*. "[Wilson was] a poet who was in the process of teaching himself to become a playwright at the suggestion of some friends. He was rejected by us five times. . . . He even tells the story that once he didn't believe that we had really read his play, so he submitted the same play the next year, and it was also rejected. He thought, maybe these people have a point. . . . [T]he important part of that is the fact that August Wilson did not arrive full blown. He was a person who did not, in getting rejected, turn around and say, 'Aw, there is something wrong with you,' the rejector. He ultimately accepted the fact that he was in process, and there may have been something wrong with what he was doing, and he had to learn more and he had to do more. He did, and he finally got to that point where his work was accepted for work. Finally, that was when he came to the Playwrights Conference and our relationship began."

Passanante had the job of contacting Wilson to arrange for his first visit to Waterford. "August was living in Minneapolis. All the playwrights got a telegram telling them they'd been selected and to report to the pre-Conference weekend, and then I would call them and say, 'Fly in. We'll pick you up at the airport, you can give us your receipt and we will reimburse you.' My first phone call with August—he said, 'I can't afford to buy the ticket.' So I had to figure out a way to send him a ticket."

Constanza Romero, Wilson's widow, shares a story she was told of the first time Wilson and Richards met. "Lloyd had, of course, read *Ma Rainey's Black Bottom*. He looked at the group of writers and wondered, 'Which one is August Wilson?' Looking for the face that matched the play. You know, August was a very light-skinned black man. But then he heard August's voice and he said, 'Ah, *that's* the man who wrote that.'"

Passanante says, "There were a lot of sort of eyeball-rolling jokes among the directors and me about how much time this was going to take. The guy didn't open his mouth. He seemed very, very nervous. He smoked a lot of cigarettes and he held back a little. And the play seemed like it was going to be eight hours long. We were all worried that we were settling in for a long nap."

"No one fell asleep," says William Partlan.

"He read with his head down," designer Skip Mercier remembers. "He never made eye contact with anybody." Amy Saltz elaborates, "There was a podium with a desk. Most people would sit behind it and read. August couldn't sit still. He would be walking around, and this language would just sweep over the room."

Passanante says, "He almost was in a trance when he was reading it, kind of

From left (top row), playwrights John Patrick Shanley, Lee Blessing, and August Wilson listen during a critique session, National Playwrights Conference, 1986. Photo by A. Vincent Scarano.

rocking back and forth on his feet, being all the characters. For everybody in the room it was utter captivation. People were rapt. 'Oh my God, that play is brilliant.' And everybody knew it. Whatever playwright was supposed to read next said, 'Oh great, now I get to read *my* play.' But I think from that moment on everybody knew we were dealing with something really profound."

Saltz remarks, "At the end of the pre-Conference weekend, the playwrights got O'Neill jackets. This particularly affected him. Getting his—he felt like he was recognized, that he had arrived . . . that he was a *playwright.*"

When he returned for the full Conference, Wilson quickly came to appreciate what the O'Neill had to offer him. "August had started his own theater and he had had some theatrical experience, but I think he felt that this was a whole new ballgame," says Partlan, referring to Black Horizons on the Hill, a small company Wilson had helped found in Pittsburgh. The "whole new ballgame" was a different standard of professionalism. The value of the O'Neill was not just that it helped him find his play, but also that he began to learn how to be a playwright with claims to craftsmanship. Joan Herrington, who interviewed Wilson for her valuable book, *I Ain't Sorry for Nothin' I Done*: *August Wilson's Process of Playwriting*, quotes him as saying, "At the beginning, I got confused. I was still relatively new to play writing, and a lot of the stuff people were saying, I simply didn't understand. One playwright, he said all this stuff and I didn't know what the hell he was saying. But I knew it was right. I could tell that this is entirely what this play needs. But it wasn't in a language that I could understand. . . . I got better in the sense that I can understand more of what people were saying. My own response became that I understood more and I

Angela Bassett performs in August Wilson's *Joe Turner's Come and Gone*, National Playwrights Conference, 1984. Photo by A. Vincent Scarano.

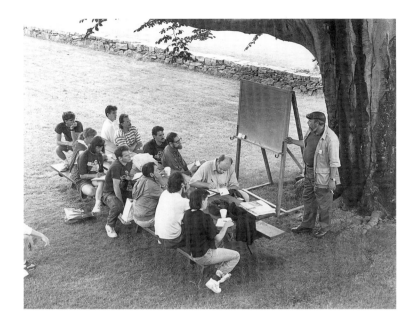

August Wilson teaches critic fellows in the
Sunken Garden, National Critics Institute,
1990. Photo by A. Vincent Scarano.

think that consequently I was able to do better work. And if I could understand the
criticisms that the people were making, I could change the work."

Richards assigned Partlan as a director and Feingold as a dramaturg of *Ma
Rainey*, and they went to work on the doorstop of a manuscript. Partlan says,
"Michael and I sat down together and compared notes, and we figured there were
numerous cuts that probably needed to happen in this play. As the band waited in
the band room, we heard story after story. The stories were evocative and wonderful,
but the storytelling didn't keep the dramatic action building. So we tried to figure out
where stories could be cut whole that would allow action to take over earlier. The
first day the whole cast got together and we did the read-through. It was over four
hours long. We identified where we felt probably cuts were needed. August looked
at us, and he said, 'I think you're probably right. But I need to hear it with an audience to know.' And the wonderful thing about the Playwrights Conference is that,
as director, I could look August in the eye and say, 'Then that's what we're going to
do.' The only thing that I said to August about this was, 'You have to promise me that
you won't pace in the back of the theater or anything else. Please promise that you
will sit in the middle of the audience, and notice when they lean forward and notice
when they sit back and let it wash over them.' And I then proceeded to stage — in four
days — the four hours and fifteen minutes of *Ma Rainey's Black Bottom* in the Barn."

Wilson later took pains to praise Partlan and Feingold for their help in making
Ma Rainey stage-worthy, and Romero says that Wilson was particularly appreciative

of the knowledge and advice Feingold offered. When asked what he thinks he did that was of specific help, Feingold says, "I think I talked to him more about clarity of structure and holding the character in the moment. August learned how to incorporate what was a storyteller's art into a dramatic form. By the end [of his career], he was going gangbuster with the skill he had acquired. But he had not had an academic training in playwriting or theater. For August, everything in the theater was a new beginning and an unparalleled miracle. I was fairly good with an anecdote about somebody who had a problem like such-and-such. The thought that there were parallels was simultaneously a surprise and a source of strength."

After the uncut *Ma Rainey* of the first night, Partlan recalls, "August comes to Michael and me next day with huge cuts. Having sat with an audience, he now trusted that he needed to make them. We got an hour and a half out of the play."

The second night, the first string critic of the *New York Times*, Frank Rich, was in the audience. Rich says it was pure luck. He just happened to be visiting then. "I had never heard of August Wilson. I don't know if many people had." Partlan describes the situation: "He was there not officially as a critic for the *New York Times*, because he couldn't be. But he could come and see the work. And so he watched that second performance, and I have to tell you, that second performance was extraordinary." Says Rich, "It was incredibly long, it was incredibly hot. Some people left. But it was such a striking theatrical experience, and his voice was so fresh and exciting, I felt, what the hell, I'm going to bend the rules slightly and write about it. And I did."

The Rich piece in question, "Where Writers Mold the Future of Theater," was published August 1, 1982. Rich wrote: "Like most of the audience in the Barn Theater in Waterford, I was electrified by the sound of this author's voice. And surely I wasn't the only one who left *Ma Rainey's Black Bottom* with goosebumps brought on by the play's unexpected esthetic resonance. Mr. Wilson is the kind of writer who fulfills the Conference's goal to replenish our theater's future—yet, eerily enough, he works in the same poetic tradition as the man who inspired the O'Neill Center's mission and who gave American theater its past."

Richards offered to produce the play at Yale Rep.

Partlan, having directed a few plays at Yale's Winter Art Festival, held out a hope. "I naively wrote Lloyd a letter and said, 'Lloyd, I sure would love to do this for you at Yale. I so enjoyed working with August.' And Lloyd, bless his heart, sent me a letter saying, 'Bill, I totally understand that, but you have to understand that I don't get to work on the plays that we do with the O'Neill. I can't. But this is one I've had my eye on and I have to do this work with August.' So he let me down gently." (In

Rehearsal for August Wilson's *Ma Rainey's Black Bottom*, in the Rose Barn, National Playwrights Conference, 1982. Photo by A. Vincent Scarano.

1988, Partlan finally directed a full production of the play at Trinity Repertory in Providence, which *Boston Globe* critic Kevin Kelly called "searing, powerful.")

The text still needed revision, and, as he had with Lorraine Hansberry, Richards asked detailed questions about the characters, what drove them, and how they acted on those drives. He didn't so much propose changes as cause Wilson to see for himself what changes were necessary.

Mercier observed and worked with both men at close range for years and has his opinion about the chemistry of the relationship: "August was a kind of offbeat poet who wrote character studies that went all over the map. Lloyd basically taught August what a playwright *is*. The difference between a poet and a playwright. It was the idea of understanding the motivation of a person through a world as a whole, and how to move that person through that world. And how every aspect of that world can either support or block the journey of that person. Suddenly August—rather than seeing a story from the inside—saw it from the outside."

A refined *Ma Rainey* opened on Broadway on October 11, 1984. It earned Tony nominations for the play and for actors Charles S. Dutton and Theresa Merritt.

Partlan worked again with Wilson at the O'Neill on *Fences* in the summer of 1983. This time the dramaturg was Edith Oliver. An early meeting with Mercier offered a crucial step in its development. Mercier says, "The first draft of *Fences* was all over the house. There were scenes in the kitchen, on the front porch, up in the bedroom. I asked him what he saw. He talked about Pittsburgh and the Hill District and the yard

Set rendering for August Wilson's *Fences*, National Playwrights Conference, 1983. Each Conference play receives a rendering of what it might look like in full production, a result of a Dream Design conversation between the playwright and the set designer on the morning before the first rehearsal. Dream Designs are a unique feature of the Conference to this day. Rendering by Fred Voelpel.

and that tree. Just what he saw in his mind. So I asked him, 'What do you see in the kitchen?' He didn't see anything. 'What do you see in the bedroom?' He didn't see anything. So I said, 'Why are we going there?' And the next morning, he grabbed me and he said, 'Do you think this can all happen in the back yard?' I said, 'That's your play. It's a boxing ring between a father and a son around that tree that you see.'"

The play centered on Troy Maxson, a former player in the black baseball league whose rage at an unjust world threatened his relationship with his wife, son, and half-brother, Gabriel. It was filled with great speeches and enormous promise, but in its early stages, it was also just plain enormous. In a performance in the O'Neill's Amphitheater, intermission came at about the two-hour mark. At that point, an elderly woman rose from her seat, turned to actress Tandy Cronyn (a veteran of the

Dramaturg Edith Oliver and August Wilson during a rehearsal of his *Fences*, National Playwrights Conference, 1983. Photo by A. Vincent Scarano.

Conference) and with a nod said, "I think I've had enough theater for one night." And so Helen Hayes left.

Partlan figures she saw the first night. "Like the first year with Michael, Edith and I pre-talked and tried to figure out where cuts could be made. But essentially August said the same thing to us that he'd said the year before. 'I need to hear it with an audience.'"

That evening made a vivid impression on a young writer-actor named Keith Reddin who was spending his first summer at the O'Neill. "I remember it started in the Amphitheater about 8:30. At the end of the play, it was something like 12:20, and we had been sitting on that concrete for four hours. And then the character of Gabriel started walking up a ramp and blew that horn as the fog rolled in and the

Howard E. Rollins, Jr., playing Gabriel in the final scene from August Wilson's *Fences*, National Playwrights Conference, 1983. Photo by A. Vincent Scarano.

I was going to graduate school at Yale, and I did not have a good time. For whatever reasons, they often said periodically "Why are you here?" And "You should leave." "Find another line of work." I graduated, and for two or three years after that, I didn't write anything. I was just so discouraged. And then I wrote a play, and I sent it into the O'Neill. I said, "Well, if I don't get accepted at the O'Neill, I guess it just means that I shouldn't write anymore." And it got accepted.

It was called Life and Limb. *It was my first play. I had a great cast, and for whatever reasons, people responded to it.*

Richard Christiansen, who used to write for the Chicago Tribune, *was there that summer. This was in the eighties, and Chicago was home to young companies like Steppenwolf, Victory Gardens, the Organic, Remains, Wisdom Bridge—some of them are still there, some of them have grown, some are gone. But it was a very exciting time. Richard saw the presentation of* Life and Limb *at the O'Neill, and he said to me, "I like this play very much. Do you know anybody in Chicago?" And I said, "I once briefly met Robert Falls, because I had friends who went to college with him." So he said, "You should get in touch with him." I said, "I don't know him. I can't send him a play. I met him once." So the story is—supposedly—he had lunch with Robert Falls, who [at the time] was running Wisdom Bridge, and he said, "I saw this play at the O'Neill when I was there for the Critics Institute." Bob went, "I don't know anything about it." Richard says, "Well, you know, if somebody did this play in a theater in Chicago, I bet they would get a very good review in the* Chicago Tribune." *And Bob said, "Really." And Richard said, "A very good review." And that afternoon Bob Falls gets in touch with me.*

And he did the play, and it got a very good review. As my family used to say, you couldn't have written a better review yourself. And so I would call Bob, and I would say, "How's the show going?" And he'd say, "Oh, people hate the production, hate the play, they left. I lost subscribers." I'd call the next week and say, "How is the show going?" And he'd go, "A lot of people are upset, they didn't like the play, they're walking out, they're leaving." Finally, the last week I called, I said, "Bob, I know the show's closing. I hope you got some good responses." He says, "I got a nice letter. Actually it's the only letter that was positive for the whole run of the show." And he read me this letter. It's like: "Dear Mr. Falls, Thank you for doing this play. It was really wonderful. I thought it was a great production. How great of you to do this." I said, "That's a fantastic letter!" He said, "It's from your mother."

But after that it got easier. And I've been lucky enough to go to the O'Neill fourteen summers.

—Keith Reddin

foghorns in the Sound started to blow. And at that moment I felt, 'This is why I go to the theater, why I want to be in the theater, why I want to write theater.'"

The performance was a profound experience that everyone, including Wilson, knew was again too long. Saltz remembers, "The next night it was 45 minutes shorter."

Again, *Fences* received its premiere at Yale Rep under Richards's direction. For the Yale production, Richards decided to cast Yale student Courtney B. Vance in the role of Troy's son, Cory. (At the Conference, Cory had been played by Richard Brooks, who would later have a regular role on *Law and Order*.) As mentioned previously, Richards had had a chance to see Vance's work outside of Yale when Vance had participated in the National Playwrights Conference of 1985.

By his own description, at the beginning of the rehearsals for *Fences*, Vance still had a lot to learn. "I was a young green kid at the time. We sat around the table for seven days just reading the play, stopping, starting, anecdotes. And by the second or third day I was going: 'Why can't we just get on our feet? This is boring.' The second week, we got up on our feet and I said, 'Oh, I have messed up.'" Vance realized that the rest of the company had been using that time to come together. "Sitting around the table, they were starting to know the play emotionally. So now everybody knew the emotional journey of the play, and they were matching up their physical to the emotional. And because I was behind, I had to do both at the same time. I realized from that point on the time around the table is probably the most valuable time."

Fences was the first time Vance worked directly with Richards. The process was not always a comfortable one. "Lloyd never spoke to me. I'm sure Lloyd told all the other people, 'Don't talk to Courtney.' And if I ever brought something up, they would just look at me like I was crazy. And I felt exactly like the little boy." And then, one day Vance realized that Richards was giving him an experience in the rehearsal that mirrored his character's experience in the play. Cory, too, was treated by the adults around him in the play as if he were still a child.

Fences played its run at Yale Rep, and then Robert Falls, artistic director of Chicago's Goodman Theatre, offered Wilson and Richards a slot so they could continue the work. Richards decided to bring Vance to Chicago. This decision was controversial. Vance was in his third year at Yale, and there were rules. "Students weren't supposed to do professional work. He took the heat. The whole faculty and the students were in an uproar because I was allowed to go."

As a result of the Goodman run, producer Carole Shorenstein Hays took a commercial option on the show and brought it to San Francisco. Then she made

The cast of August Wilson's *The Piano Lesson* at the O'Neill, National Playwrights Conference, 1986. Courtney B. Vance is standing. Photo by A. Vincent Scarano.

plans to bring it to Broadway. But Hays had one firm opinion about how the play should end, and Wilson and Richards had another. Vance remembers, "She thought the play should end with Cory singing the song to his father. And Lloyd and August knew the play had to end with Gabe [Gabriel, Troy's brother] blowing his horn and getting his brother into heaven. You've got to get him into heaven. So in San Francisco, every other show, we would do alternate endings. And it got so acrimonious that two days before we were to open [on Broadway], Lloyd announced at the theater that he was stepping down as the director because August and Carole Shorenstein Hays were at an impasse about the play. He supported his playwright. He said, 'I will not go against my playwright.' And then a day later, August came in, and said he and Carole had worked out a compromise and Lloyd would stage it." In the acting edition, Gabe does indeed get Troy into heaven.

Another pre-opening controversy finally generated a deeper connection between Vance and Richards. Vance says, "I had gotten wind that the little girl playing Raynell—playing my sister, had been playing her since we were in New Haven, for two years—was going to be fired. Before we opened on Broadway. I was so furious. Granted I was a little boy and nobody talked to me. So I was just fuming on stage. And Lloyd saw it. And he came up to me and said, 'Courtney, what's wrong?' And I said, 'Nothing, Lloyd.' And he said, 'Courtney, what's wrong?' And he asked me a third time. And I said. 'Lloyd, is she being fired?' He said, 'Courtney, in forty years I've never seen anything like this.' Evidently, because August and Lloyd sided together, and James and Carole Shorenstein Hays sided together. . . . It was a classic power struggle between the creative end—the playwright and the director—and producing. Classic. James Earl wanted the understudy, who was a small, fair-skinned young girl, to do the role when we opened, because if there was a fair-skinned young girl in the role, that let everybody know what the mama looked like. [The woman] he messed with. (You don't meet her—she died in childbirth. You meet the little girl seven years later.) So he wanted a fair-skinned girl so that you would know what the mama looked like. It was storytelling.

"But you juxtapose that wish against. . . . She was this girl who had been with us since New Haven and yes, she is getting too big, but—*let her* open on Broadway!" Telling the story, Vance is still upset. "It was a bitter, bitter fight. And I got wind of it." In that moment, a bond between Richards and Vance was forged. "That was the first time he shared. The relationship turned from professional to personal. I went deeply into him."

Fences was an even bigger hit than *Ma Rainey*. It won both the Tony and the Pulitzer, and Richards won a Tony Award for his direction. Vance was nominated for the Tony the first time. (He won on his third try in 2013, taking home the award for supporting actor in Nora Ephron's *Lucky Guy*.)

Wilson continued to bring plays to the National Playwrights Conference for first exploration through the staged readings. Though he eventually made public statements that he wanted only African-American directors to direct his work, in fact, at the O'Neill, he continued to collaborate with white directors, including Amy Saltz. Michael Feingold remembers, "I asked August, as part of an interview that I ended up not using, if he had found any difficulties in working with Amy. And he said, 'Oh,

Early table reading rehearsal of *Joe Turner's Come and Gone*, by August Wilson, National Playwrights Conference, 1984. Wilson is sitting at the back. Photo by A. Vincent Scarano.

August Wilson and director Amy Saltz during rehearsal in the Amphitheater for Wilson's *Seven Guitars*, National Playwrights Conference, 1994. Photo by A. Vincent Scarano.

you mean because she's white?' I said, 'No, because she's a woman.' And it had never occurred to him that there were other issues apart from the black-white one."

Saltz says that in fact she had mixed feelings about working on *Joe Turner* at the O'Neill. "I didn't think I should be directing it. I was very intimidated by the mysticism of the play. I didn't know what of that was because I was white. I didn't know what was cultural in it and what was August in it. As if there's a difference—but there is, and so I was intimidated by it."

Director Barnet Kellman believes that Richards had a purpose in not assigning black directors to work with Wilson at the O'Neill. "I think his view was: we are artists, we're craftspeople, we have a discipline to bring to the matter. And don't forget— he was not encouraging directors to tell their personal story on the writer's material. So the fact that they were black and might have a more personal connection to the specifics of the material, that wasn't the point of being at the O'Neill."

Wilson used the O'Neill not only to work on the script he brought, but also on the ones he was planning. Saltz describes long nights sitting in Blue Gene's, the on-site pub at the O'Neill. "Those *long* stories that are in all those plays, he practiced those stories. Each year, he was telling me stories that ended up in the next play. I remember him talking about a man who stayed up all night wrestling with the devil and that ended up being Troy in *Fences*. Another year, he talked about an image of a little girl standing by a piano and the piano was all carved with her ancestral story. *The Piano Lesson*. The next play was always in the works."

The man who struck many as being shy during his first visit to Waterford evolved into an outgoing and sociable presence. Says Saltz, "I remember, August's second year, he and John Patrick Shanley getting super-drunk together at the end of the pre-Conference. Shanley was there with *Danny and the Deep Blue Sea*, and August was there with *Fences*, and Shanley was like, 'You son-of-a-bitch, you wrote that stage direction at the end of that play'—the stage direction where Gabriel blows the trumpet and blows open those pearly gates so Troy can get into heaven—and Shanley was like, 'You son-of-a-bitch, nobody can touch that.'"

Wilson reveled in the camaraderie with the other writers. Says Douglas Post, "When I was there the summer of '94, August was working on *Seven Guitars*." That summer the playwrights shared living quarters. "There was kind of a kitchen area, where you could pick up a little coffee, and there was a refrigerator. That refrigerator was always stocked with beer. That was August going out and buying beer for the building. He would never take credit for it. It just showed up. Also that summer, it didn't look like there was going to be enough money for all the new playwrights to get their O'Neill jackets. Suddenly those jackets showed up. And we all knew who had made that happen.

"One night, we'd all been sitting out on the sea wall and drinking. We knew that August was still up in his room working on his play, so we all stood outside the window and we serenaded him. 'You Are My Sunshine / My Only Sunshine.' And the next day he was telling Lloyd and everybody how honored he felt that the other playwrights had come by in the middle of the night to sing to him."

Seven Guitars was one of an extraordinary run of plays Wilson brought to the O'Neill after *Ma Rainey* and *Fences*—along with *Joe Turner's Come and Gone*, *The Piano Lesson*, and *Two Trains Running*. In the wake of their O'Neill presentations, Richards would take over as director and present them at Yale. To avoid confrontations such as the ones they had had with producer Hays, Wilson, Richards, and

> One night, we'd all been drinking. It was after all the plays were over. And I was with John Patrick Shanley. He was always fascinated by the blue moon. And it was July 31st, and it was supposed to be a full moon that night, which would have made it a blue moon. But the sky was overcast and was really dark. It was late. Well, Shanley wanted to see the full moon. So he got us all out there in the field in front of the Mansion, and we all started screaming at the top of our lungs out there. And the clouds parted and the full moon came out. And he was so happy.
>
> —Roger S. Christiansen

Charles S. Dutton (left) and Rocky Carroll in August Wilson's *Seven Guitars*, National Playwrights Conference, 1994. Photo by A. Vincent Scarano.

Yale Rep managing director Ben Mordecai became the key producers of these plays. Wilson and Richards would continue to shape them through engagements at various regional theaters before arriving in New York. At every step along the way, the plays lost ten or fifteen minutes, until they were in fighting trim for Broadway.

The partnership between the two men evolved. Partlan comments, "I did see them grow closer and sort of more equal, and that was hard to do with Lloyd. Lloyd had a kind of quality to him that made you sort of feel like he was the principal. As August brought more plays to the O'Neill, his relationship with Lloyd evened out in some ways. Lloyd respected August a lot and recognized that August was a major force and a writer to be reckoned with. But I think, even within that, Lloyd needed to be the person that he had started out as for August, which was a mentor and someone who needed to be looked up to by August. My sense is that it's almost like the good student who rises and rises and now is kind of on an equal par and then gets recognized by the world as seminal. That was probably hard for Lloyd, because—I'm putting words into his mouth, I don't know this—but my instinct is that he wanted August to keep looking to him for ways in which he could continue to develop the work."

Wilson acknowledged a psychological aspect to his relationship with Richards. In an interview published in *Vanity Fair* in 1989, he was quoted as saying, "I'm a great

I was there one of the summers that the whole NEA [National Endowment for the Arts] argument came up. It was looking like [North Carolina senator] Jesse Helms was going to win, that he was gonna convince Congress to cut the funding. Lloyd [Richards] invited Frank Rich to come up that summer. Everybody got in a big tent out by the house, and Frank started on about the NEA and funding, and . . . was basically telling us everything we already knew. I'm standing in the back, and you know when you're a kid, you've got this irrepressible thing in you. And at the end Lloyd said, "Does anybody have any questions?" And I said, "Frank, you sound like you really care about this. If you care so much about this, why don't you write about it in your column instead of writing reviews?" And everybody gave me a look like, "You're never gonna work in this town again." And thank God for Lloyd, because he said, "I think that's a great idea." And Rich did.

That afternoon August Wilson and I were sitting in Blue Gene's. He's like, "Sit down, Rob." I sat down, and all of a sudden, just out of his mouth he said, "You know, I gotta tell you, I really respect Jesse Helms." And I said, "You respect that racist? That man has caused so much pain for so many people and now is causing a lot of pain with the NEA! You respect that man?" And he said, "Yeah, because I know exactly where he stands." For the first time ever, I understood how people on either side of the aisle could respect each other, could actually go and have a drink with each other. Even though they hated what that person stood for, at least they knew they stood for something.

—Rob Knepper

boxing fan, and boxing is like writing. I look at Lloyd like he's my trainer. Now, Lloyd is old enough to be my father. Having grown up without a father, that has a lot to do with my relationship with him. I always view him in a fatherly way. You know, you want to please Pop. You want Pop to be proud of you. I want to score a knockout."

It is in the nature of a father-son relationship that at some point the son usually stakes his claim to being an autonomous adult. Success wrought changes in Wilson's manner. Sought after and lionized, the man who had struck people as retiring and shy during his first visit to the O'Neill now carried himself with greater confidence. John Lahr believes that the inevitable happened when they were in preproduction on what would be the only filmed version of a Wilson play, the CBS *Hallmark Hall of Fame* television production of *The Piano Lesson*, directed by Richards. "August threw an amazing scene, because the designer had not designed the sculpture on the piano in a way that made a proper statement. It insulted his sense of African-American sensibility. Lloyd took great offense to the kind of fury that came out of August at that point."

Saltz has more information. "In 1995, Lloyd was going to do *Seven Guitars* in Chicago, which was the first production of it after the O'Neill, but he got sick and he couldn't do it. Walter Dallas did it. I think August found out that someone else could do it, someone else could direct the play." Richards came back to *Seven Guitars* for the Boston production, but, according to Saltz, "They never really made it up."

Scott Richards adds, "Let's put this into the mix: My father had to have an operation. There was blockage in his carotid artery. This would have been before going into rehearsal on *Seven Guitars*. It's considered a somewhat dangerous operation. So, we're sitting in the waiting room at Mt. Sinai [Hospital, New York], and August shows up, and he is sweating and he's scared to death. He is more freaked out and frightened than any of us in the family. I think he realized how vulnerable he was and how dependent. I think there was something about my father becoming less powerful or less healthy that scared him." Scott Richards believes that it was then Wilson began to think of working with others; Wilson didn't want to be at risk of feeling that vulnerable again.

The situation deteriorated further at the Huntington Theatre Company in Boston, where South African actor-playwright Zakes Mokae, an old friend of the director and known for his collaborations with Athol Fugard, joined the cast as Hedley. When the play opened, Mokae didn't have his lines down and read his part from a script. "August made Lloyd fire him," says Saltz. "Lloyd was furious and I think humiliated by having to do that." Saltz was present at the opening night on Broadway. "I was walking with August from the theater to the party, and I guess we went through the Edison Hotel, through the lobby, and we passed Lloyd—or Lloyd passed August—and there was nothing. It was awful. Really, really awful."

Constanza Romero's comment on the break: "More than anything I want to emphasize that every person who starts under the auspices of somebody, when you gain your wings, you have to try out how you're going to be going on your own. August felt he needed to experience the work more on his own." Wilson teamed with Ben Mordecai to create a production company called Stageworks, and they continued to use tours through regional companies to revise the work before coming

Charles S. Dutton performs in *Joe Turner's Come and Gone*, by August Wilson, National Playwrights Conference, 1984. Photo by A. Vincent Scarano.

Lloyd Richards (right) and August Wilson, 1984, when Wilson was developing *Joe Turner's Come and Gone*. Photo by A. Vincent Scarano.

to Broadway. Romero believes that Wilson called Richards to tell him about the decision to team with Mordecai.

When N. Graham Nesmith asked him about the break, Richards replied, "What happened is simply a play came that he did not invite me to direct. That's all. We didn't have a fistfight or draw guns or anything."

Says Saltz, "I think that his plays suffered by not going through the O'Neill process. I mean, when I got *Seven Guitars*, there was no play there. There was the bookend of the wake after the funeral and there were characters and there were stories and big speeches, and August knew that Hedley would kill Floyd, but there was no play. What we did at the conference was find out who Floyd was and why he went to heaven and what the story was. I also kept asking him for more for Vera. And one day he came in shaking, and he gave me a speech and he said, 'Here, what do you think?' It was that 'Floyd touched me here, Floyd touched me there'—that *incredible* speech of hers. And *I* was shaking by the time I finished it. He found the play during that process at the O'Neill. There was something about the focus and the intensity and the pressure of those four days that helped him enormously in the writing." The final three plays he wrote—*King Hedley II*, *Gem of the Ocean*, and *Radio Golf*—did not go through the O'Neill process (though *Gem* was partly written as a writer-in-residence at the O'Neill during James Houghton's tenure as artistic director). Though generally well received, all three had disappointing runs on Broadway.

As with many splits, collaborators and associates took sides. Vance's impression is that most people chose to give Wilson their primary loyalty. "When Lloyd and August split, everybody went with August, and nobody went to talk to Lloyd anymore. And I said, 'You know what? The man has given me so much and done so much for me. This man will have my allegiance until he goes to the next world. That's the way I was raised. He took care of me. I gotta take care of him. Every free moment I have I'm going to spend with Lloyd Richards.'" Vance was based in New York shooting the TV series *Law and Order: Criminal Intent*, which put him in the same town with Richards, and Vance remembers a series of meals over which they had "the best conversations."

Inevitably they talked of the way Richards had worked with Wilson. "Lloyd told me, 'Courtney, I set up this whole regional theater network so that all I needed was a playwright. I'd been waiting for a playwright so we could go around to all the regional theaters, work the play, and come on into New York.' He set the whole thing up, and he put Ben Mordecai in place as managing director. Then the two of them, August and Ben, took over and cut Lloyd out. Lloyd said, 'Every playwright that I've worked with eventually wants to direct, they want to act, they want to write, they want to do the lights, they want to do the sound, they want to do everything. Basically August Wilson wanted to be me. And he cannot be me.'"

Lahr believes, "The debt that August owed Lloyd was beyond repayment. When you think of the odds of August succeeding as a writer, let alone a playwright, it's mind blowing. I mean you can't even imagine it. Because he left school at 15, and how he found his way toward his vision. It was just an amazing story. Unique. And I think, at least six of those plays are great pieces of theater. No writer ever had a chance to sustain the growth of a piece in a systematic way more than August. That never existed. He is sui generis."

Vance insists that "August Wilson would not exist if it weren't for Lloyd Richards. Lloyd Richards plucked him out of nowhere. And he guided him and taught him. What Lloyd had set up was so amazing and wonderful, and everybody benefited. Everybody. August got Pulitzers and Tonys and accolades. And all he had to do

Mary Alice (left) and Ebony Jo-Ann rehearse *Joe Turner's Come and Gone*, by August Wilson, National Playwrights Conference, 1984. Photo by A. Vincent Scarano.

August Wilson revises *Seven Guitars*, National Playwrights Conference, 1994. Photo by A. Vincent Scarano.

was just let it happen. And you know that August did not win a single award after they split. No more Tonys. No more Pulitzers. Lloyd taught him dramatic structure. And without Lloyd, there was nobody [to teach him]. Everybody else told him, 'Yes, yes, yes, it's wonderful, wonderful, wonderful.' Even with *Gem of the Ocean* being three hours long." Vance says that both he and Wilson owed their artistic lives to Richards. "I was his son, and August was his son. It's one of the great tragedies in theatrical history that August decided he needed to go his own way. It's oedipal."

The chill between Wilson and Richards lasted until a final conversation shortly before Wilson's death. In August 2005, Wilson announced that he was suffering from liver cancer that doctors expected would take his life in a matter of months. In fact, he died on October 2, 2005. (Before he died, he learned that Broadway's Virginia Theater would be renamed in his honor. The ceremony occurred on October 17.) Wilson's passing occurred only a few days before Nesmith interviewed the director. Richards said, "I was not shocked by the news. August had called me and I talked with him a couple of days before that. He sounded very weak. He called because he said he was feeling good that day, but good did not mean up to his normal strength." With his customary reticence, Richards did not describe the phone call in detail, so the extent of the reconciliation is unknown. But Richards did say, "I thought that we might have had another conversation, but it did not happen and it will not happen. Whatever we had, that was it. We completed our relationship at this place, and in this time."

9. Cabaret and Performance Conference

It was exactly what Laila Robins needed.

The award-winning leading lady (and O'Neill veteran) had just finished an extended run in the off-Broadway Signature Theatre's 2012 revival of Edward Albee's *The Lady from Dubuque*. The project had been fulfilling. In 1980, the play's premiere had been roasted by the press. This production brought the general conclusion that the original critics had been, well, wrong. (One of those original critics even apologized for his earlier review.) All in all, an exciting undertaking.

The downside was that Robins was playing a woman dying a painful death from cancer. And the part was getting to her. "I thought at one point it was going to kill me. I thought that if I did it much longer, I could really get sick."

Rescue came in the form of an invitation to the 2012 Cabaret and Performance Conference from its then artistic director. "Michael Bush invited me. He knew that I'd sung at benefits and sort of pulled it off. He said, 'I think you should come up.'" So Robins arrived as a cabaret fellow. "There were about eight of us. Our fellows were quite an eclectic bunch. All different ages. An older distinguished lady from Texas, a boy straight out of high school practically, and people like me trying something new. . . . We became a tight bunch."

Table setting for the Cabaret and Performance Conference in the Dina Merrill Theater at the O'Neill, 2013. Photo by A. Vincent Scarano.

Laila Robins performs, Cabaret and Performance Conference, 2012. Photo by A. Vincent Scarano.

No sooner had they unpacked than they were in the middle of it. "The first night, with no warning, we had to get up and perform in front of the entire conference. 'You gotta get up and sing tonight.' 'What??!?' So I sang 'Woodstock.' It was baptism by fire."

This began two weeks of intense study with master teachers Penny Fuller and Barry Kleinbort. "Every single day we were working on songs. It was scary. It was you being yourself. That's what we talked about a lot in class. You were sort of exposing yourself. Marilyn Maye is a master of that. She came up and did an act. She would say things like, 'These three guys in the band are the closest guys in my life.' Or she would mention ex-husbands. . . . She wouldn't get maudlin about it, but you got a picture of the whole woman and why she had the right to sing certain songs. She let you into her life, but she finessed [it] in such a way that she didn't make you feel uncomfortable with too much information. She had a mastery of the form."

Each fellow had a concrete goal—a mini-set of three songs. Assembling their presentations, the students had to learn the art of sequencing numbers—when to use an up-tempo number, when you earned the right to sing a ballad, how to connect the selections with patter.

Asked to describe her act, Robins says, "I began by saying what a wonderful time I'd had up there and how much I'd learned. [Actress] Veanne Cox was up there working on a musical, and I made a little joke about Veanne and how some people

Marilyn Maye (left) performs with her band, Cabaret and Performance Conference, 2012. Photo by A. Vincent Scarano.

are crazier than others, which led into 'Twisted,' a song that Joni Mitchell used to sing about seeing an analyst. Then I talked about how one's neurosis can create an obstacle to sustaining a relationship, and I went into 'I Can't Make You Love Me'—a Bonnie Raitt song. And then I talked about how sometimes people just miss each other, bad timing. And that went into 'Send in the Clowns.'" Robins later made her New York cabaret debut with a revised version of her act at Feinstein's, shortly before that high-profile venue shuttered.

"The Conference was just two weeks of music, and it was a blast. In my usual gigs, I do so much, you know, crying and screaming and more crying. But this was a really healing experience. Like a balm. It was such a gift, at this point in my career, to have a chance to play outside my comfort zone. I feel I came out a different person."

In Elaine May's 1971 movie, *A New Leaf*, George Rose, playing a butler, compliments spoiled playboy Walter Matthau on managing "to keep alive traditions that were dead before you were born." This could be said about cabaret. For the most part, the nightclubs of the sort featured in black-and-white movies—the elegantly dressed singer leaning against a piano with a combo's backing—are gone, as are the sophisticated intimate revues, such as those produced by Julius Monk and Ben Bagley. At any given time, only a few artists can support themselves substantially through their work in the form. Most often, intimate evenings of performers singing an assemblage of songs are adjuncts to other aspects of their careers. A large percentage of the stars who grace 54 Below, the popular room opened in 2012 by O'Neill board chairman Tom Viertel, are figures familiar from careers on Broadway—for example, Patti LuPone, Tonya Pinkins, Norbert Leo Butz, and Tom Wopat.

Director, choreographer, and performer Tommy Tune tacks his program to the wall at Blue Gene's Pub, the on-campus watering hole at the O'Neill, after his cabaret show in August 2013. The pub's walls and rafters are hung with signed program inserts from authors and performers from nearly all O'Neill conferences. Photo by A. Vincent Scarano.

But as financially impractical as cabaret is, aspects of it nourish performers as no other form does. For some, like Robins, it provides a needed change of pace from a part. For others, it's a chance to exercise different muscles. For yet others, it's a particularly personal form of self-expression.

Ellie Ellsworth describes the germination of what was initially called the Cabaret Symposium in 1989. A log cabin built as a children's playhouse on a nearby property (belonging to a cousin of the Hammond family) had been lugged onto the Waterford campus and opened as a pub called (in honor of Eugene O'Neill) Blue Gene's. Betsy White remembers she and her husband George showing the space to Ellsworth, and Ellsworth's reaction: "'This is the perfect-sized space for a cabaret. As a matter of fact, there's a club in New York that's just closed, and I bet we could get all the lighting equipment from them cheap.' George, who's always up for a new challenge, said, 'Gee, that's a great idea!' So, Ellie got started." As it happens, Ellsworth is related to both the Whites. Yes, nepotism. But, aside from her credits as an actor and a teacher, she was a veteran performer on the scene, notably alternating with Ellie Stone in the long-running off-Broadway revue, *Jacques Brel is Alive and Well and Living in Paris*. Ellsworth signed on as artistic director, and Betsy (who had years of experience working in producer Ken Marsolais's office) took the title of producer.

There was an attempt to rush into activity with three weekend shows. It was so late in the season that most of the people on Ellsworth's A-list were already booked and unavailable. She remembers that one person she booked (no name given) was "embarrassing. Someone who was so false, who just by his performance described the very thing that I can't stand about cabaret."

Her reaction was so intense that it galvanized her determination to do it right. "I wanted to combine people who came to learn with people who knew how to do it. To have teachers who had various aspects of knowledge in this field, whether they were songwriters or performers themselves, artists of note, arrangers, music directors—even Fred Voelpel, who was a designer, because the solo performer has to know how to put themselves on the stage and not distract you from what they're trying to do. What we learned was that the program was more expensive than most students could afford." In search of income to support it, Ellsworth arrived at the idea of presenting performances that were open to the public. "An extraordinary list of wonderful people—Julie Wilson, Karen Akers, Sharon McKnight, Tovah Feldshuh, Kay Starr, and Andrea Marcovicci—all of them came at one time or another.

"I knew I had to have a name to help me get all the rest of the people I wanted to teach for me. One night, I was in a cabaret where Margaret Whiting was in the audience. I went up to her and I said, 'Miss Whiting, I admire you greatly. Would you be interested in teaching for me? I've been given the go-ahead to start a program for cabaret at the Eugene O'Neill Theater Center.' She said, 'Yes, absolutely.' Just

(*below left*) Co-founders of the Cabaret Symposium at the O'Neill, Betsy White (left) and Ellie Ellsworth, ca. 1992. Photo by A. Vincent Scarano. (*below*) Cabaret and Broadway star Julie Wilson performs in the Rose Barn, Cabaret Symposium, ca. 1995. Photo by A. Vincent Scarano.

Kay Starr (left) and Margaret Whiting perform, Cabaret Symposium, ca. 1997. Photo by A. Vincent Scarano.

boom, like that. Well, of course, that meant her musical director, Tex Arnold, would also come. I was off and running."

Whiting's commitment came to the attention of Enid Nemy, a writer for the *New York Times*, who made mention of it in a column. This attracted the first students.

Whiting was also one of the celebrities whose performances at the end of the week helped raise money for the program. According to Betsy White, the program almost paid for itself. The gap of about $20,000 was filled by private support, and securing that support became part of Betsy White's mission. Cabaret may have been fading in the public consciousness, but some people with affection for the form were still inclined to write supportive checks.

The work with the students started at the beginning of that week. Says Ellsworth, "The formula involved thirty-six cabaret fellows and twenty teachers. Everybody stayed at the O'Neill. We started at nine o'clock in the morning, and we went until after midnight every day. Evenings were usually cabarets in Blue Gene's. The fellows would perform, three or four or six a night. They'd each get a mini-act to do, three songs each. All week long they had their chance to perform. And then the final night there was a finale that involved only the fellows. We figured out how to do it so it wouldn't be just a list of people getting up to sing. We put together six teams—six pods—and each pod got to develop an act. The rest of us wouldn't know what they were going to do. They would have a theme or a throughline.

"We didn't really give them much time to plan it either. Purposely. I remember Lloyd Richards saying that why the readings worked so well at the O'Neill was that he learned from acting in radio that if you just give out a script to the cast and they

Conference fellows rehearse in the Rose Theater Barn, Cabaret Symposium, ca. 1993. Photo by A. Vincent Scarano.

plunge in, the instincts of the actors will take over. If you go past four days of practice, they lose all the instinct, and they're now at a loss again. They start second-guessing themselves, and none of the spontaneity is left. They need another two weeks to get it back. If you don't have any time to figure it out, you're going to throw yourself into it for survival, and you're going to come out with something fun and exciting and funny and spontaneous."

The program closed on Howard Sherman's watch, but Ellsworth believes he didn't want it closed. "Three funding sources dried up on me, and I was not very good at going around and saying, 'Give me ten thousand dollars.'"

A version of what Ellsworth had done was attempted at Yale by a former associate at Waterford, something she chooses not to discuss. She moved on to other projects and continued to consult privately.

Michael Bush, who had long been associate artistic director of Manhattan Theatre Club, was approached by Viertel and Amy Sullivan to take a shot at reviving the cabaret program. "I was more interested in making it project based. I was interested in doing what I call cabaret theater. (I never liked the term 'cabaret.') I decided if I was going to run the conference, I would change it to 'Cabaret and Performance Conference.' I wanted another word in there. Cabaret, to me, is any kind of an entertainment in an intimate space that breaks the fourth wall."

Bush started by cutting the number of fellows admitted. No longer were there groups as large as forty people. "I knocked it down to eight or nine."

Bush speaks with warmth about the two teachers who so inspired Laila Robins—Barry Kleinbort and Penny Fuller. "They were the core of the program. I made Joel

Michael Bush (artistic director of the Conference, 2005–2012) introduces a show at the renamed Cabaret and Performance Conference, 2008. Photo by A. Vincent Scarano.

Silberman the associate artistic director of the program. As a Steinway Artist, he was able to get a Steinway concert grand donated to us every year."

Robins was brought in as one of the fellows. Bush says, "The fellows arrived on Wednesday morning. They had their first class Wednesday afternoon. . . . I started the Open Mike, so that if you were coming up there—whether you were on a scholarship or you were paying full tuition—you could sing every night if you wanted to. If you had been working on a number in class, you could go in front of the audience during the Open Mike session that night. It followed whatever show happened, where anyone who was a part of the conference could sing.

"It was more about acting than singing. I think songs are stories, and they need to be approached that way. I used to say you have to not let the song sing you, you have to sing the song. It has to have some personal truth to it. Because you're singing to someone who is sometimes five feet away from you, you can't be phony. You have to sing it personally. I'll give you an example: One woman sang, 'I Have Dreamed.' She had had a child who was born with birth defects and was challenged. By the time she sang it in the final show, she was singing it about that child."

Under Bush's definition, small musicals that broke the fourth wall were also eligible for the Conference, which is how he came to develop two projects that later went to Broadway—[title of show] and The Story of My Life. "They were unlike the readings that are done in the musical theater program. I produced them as entertainment—they had production values." He also presented evenings organized around themes. He speaks with particular satisfaction of an evening called Ac-cent-tchu-ate the Positive: The Songs of Johnny Mercer that he presented with support from the Johnny Mercer Foundation.

The evenings Bush scheduled with the high-profile artists (Marilyn Maye, Leslie Uggams, and Lillias White, among others) brought in an enthusiastic crowd. "I had a core audience. They would line up a half hour before my shows. What's great about the audiences at the O'Neill—they've been trained to see something that's not finished. They're a very generous audience that will forgive you everything, but that core group would say to me they would wait all summer long to come to my conference because they were knocked out by it.

"I had guest artists who came up to participate in the projects. I would usually put them in as many as two, sometimes three, to keep them there over the two-week period." The projects were often organized around the work of a songwriter, such as evenings devoted to the songs of Ed Kleban and Charles Strouse. "Then on the last night I would produce this huge gala that always sold out. It was called the Grand Finale. The box office was paying for my conference. I did two evenings where I had a nine-piece orchestra in there. I knocked the place out with a Jule Styne kind of sound. I really was pushing the envelope. Maybe I pushed it over the edge."

The current artistic director of the Cabaret and Performance Conference is someone Tom Viertel met through 54 Below. John McDaniel has a long résumé

(*above left*) Barry Kleinbort (associate artistic director, 2005–2012), Cabaret and Performance Conference, 2006. Photo by A. Vincent Scarano. (*above*) Penny Fuller (associate artistic director, 2005–2012) performs, Cabaret and Performance Conference, 2006. Photo by A. Vincent Scarano.

Tony Award winner Lillias White performs, Cabaret and Performance Conference, 2011. Photo by A. Vincent Scarano.

in musical direction, including six years leading the band for *The Rosie O'Donnell Show.* He appeared at Viertel's nightclub one evening accompanying Dee Hoty and Donna McKechnie as well as another evening on which he sang some of his own songs. McDaniel came into the program with a template he largely inherited from Bush (the two haven't had direct communication, though Bush thinks highly of McDaniel). Guest artists would give performances that helped raise money for the program and also acted as examples for the fellows of what successful cabaret performances look like.

But then the priorities shifted. Reflecting on his conversations with executive director Preston Whiteway and Viertel, McDaniel says, "What they wanted to get away from a little bit was so much creation of new shows. It [the program] had been inching toward the creation of musicals. I imagine this was blurring the lines with Music Theater [see Chapter 10]. They wanted to simplify a bit." This shift was in line with McDaniel's focus. "Developing the artist is more interesting to me than developing product." That said, he was very pleased with an evening he put together with guest artists saluting songwriters Sammy Cahn and Jimmy van Heusen called *Come Fly with Me*, for which he saw a future.

The 2013 Cabaret and Performance Conference featured eight fellows—four women and four men. Most paid full tuition, partial scholarships were offered to some, and one was on full scholarship. "We had a strong pool of applicants," says McDaniel. The digital age has arrived in this field; there were no live auditions. Everybody applied with video clips. "Sometimes clips of their shows with audiences hooting and howling. Sometimes them singing into a bathroom mirror."

One of the people McDaniel encouraged to participate is a performer familiar to him from Broadway, Kerry O'Malley. "I first met her when she was standby for Bernadette Peters on *Annie Get Your Gun*, for which I did arrangements and music supervision. Now she's in L.A. We're Facebook friends, and she wrote and said, 'This Conference sounds cool,' and I thought, 'Oh my God, she's perfect to come and be with us.' She said, 'Save the scholarship for someone who needs it. I can afford to pay.' So she's here and doing beautiful work."

Artistic director John McDaniel introduces the kickoff performance, Cabaret and Performance Conference, 2013. Photo by A. Vincent Scarano.

Kerry O'Malley performs
with Mark Hartman at the
piano, Cabaret and Performance Conference, 2013.
Photo by A. Vincent Scarano.

Indeed, the evening when the eight fellows presented their mini-sets, O'Malley closed the show. Lounging vampily in a snug dress on top of a grand piano, with red hair and flashing eyes, she sang Cole Porter's "So In Love" (from *Kiss Me, Kate*) to a bemused accompanist.

For those with a taste for historical connections, two of the cabaret fellows in the program performed songs from Stephen Sondheim's score for the musical *Company* under the appreciative eye of one of their master teachers, Donna McKechnie. McKechnie had been one of the stars of that classic's original 1971 production.

When asked what concerns her when she coaches young performers, McKechnie says, "Popular culture today—the emphasis is put too much on the highest note." In much of contemporary Broadway choreography, she also sees the desire to impress overwhelm the impulse to express. "Too much today is about the result. I want to go back to 'what is it about?'"

One thing McKechnie has learned from coaching is that some songs are more elastic than others, more open to different legitimate interpretations. For instance, when Barbra Streisand sings "Happy Days Are Here Again" at a crawl, that choice reveals profound new aspects of the composition. "'They Can't Take That Away from Me,' though, you can't distort that too much or it loses all meaning. Singers will tell me, 'I have all these songs,' and I'll say, 'You picked this song for a reason. So find out—what are you saying?'"

(*left*) Brad Simmons performs, Cabaret and Performance Conference, 2013. Simmons, a Broadway music director, leads the Junior Fellows program at the Conference, drawing local middle and high school students into cabaret. Photo by A. Vincent Scarano. (*below*) Tony Award winner Donna McKechnie (*A Chorus Line*) puts on her new show, Cabaret and Performance Conference, 2013. Photo by A. Vincent Scarano.

The idea that cabaret and performance skills are in the service of an antique form was contradicted by a show given in the summer of 2013 by the Junior Fellows, a program offered by the Cabaret and Performance Conference gratis as a public service to the community. Under a pair of splendid trees in the open-air Edith Oliver Theater, a group of young people presented an hour-long revue devoted to the songs of Stevie Wonder. Singing; dancing; and wielding instruments as varied as a tuba, a French horn, a ukulele, and a battery of kazoos, they brought a gathering of friends, neighbors, and (it must be said) more than a few longtime veterans to their feet. Cabaret performance may no longer be a way to celebrity and fortune, but it can connect artists to an audience with a directness and intimacy that is exhilarating.

Lyricist Sheldon Harnick recalls working within the traditional Broadway system on the out-of-town tryout of *Fiddler on the Roof*. "We had a good first act and a very troubled second act. We didn't open too well in Detroit. I remember Austin Pendleton [who originated the role of Motel] asking [director-choreographer] Jerome Robbins, 'What do we do?' And Jerry said, 'Every day we're going to fix four things.' And he did. Because he was organized and he was smart, and because we'd had that six months of discussions before we went on the road. We had the luxury of three stops, and Robbins did exactly what he said he was going to do: three or four things every day. And by the time we got to New York, we had a terrific show."

Harnick had the fortune to get started when it was indeed still possible to fix a show on the road. Michael Kanter, in his film *Broadway: The American Musical*, identified the golden age of the commercially produced musical as occurring from 1943 to 1959. One might quibble with those specific years, but in general the classic shows of the repertory were created as commercial ventures—often as vehicles for stars like Ethel Merman, Mary Martin, John Raitt, and Robert Preston—and refined in the Broadway tryout system described in Chapter 1. As time retired many of the leading figures of that era and the commercial system declined, the survival of the musical required creating new strategies involving the nonprofit world.

Composer-lyricist Sheldon Harnick rehearses at the O'Neill, National Music Theater Conference, 1983. Harnick developed two pieces at this Conference and acted as a mentor at several others. He is best known as the lyricist for *Fiddler on the Roof*. Photo by A. Vincent Scarano.

In 1961, Allan Becker, the head of the musical theater division of the performing rights organization Broadcast Music Inc., collaborated with Broadway conductor-theorist Lehman Engel to create the BMI Musical Theatre Workshop (now called the BMI Lehman Engel Musical Theatre Workshop) in which Engel articulated his theory of the form and gave composers and lyricists assignments based on scenes in existing scripts to help them develop their skills. Two participants of the workshop—Edward Kleban and Maury Yeston—were involved in projects that led to the creation of new ways to build shows.

In 1974, Kleban was selected by director-choreographer Michael Bennett to partner with composer Marvin Hamlisch on songs for a project being developed under the sponsorship of Joseph Papp's Public Theater. The result was *A Chorus Line*, which went from its engagement downtown at the home of the Public to a record-breaking run at the Shubert Theatre, winning the Tony Award and the Pulitzer Prize. The show was built using the then-unusual process for musicals of workshopping—writing with a cast and staff present to instantly test material and facilitate changes. The workshop process presented an alternative to the increasingly expensive method of testing and changing material in a series of tryout engagements before opening in New York.

As the workshop idea was already in place for nonmusicals at the National Playwrights Conference, it was logical for the O'Neill to address developing musicals in a similar way. To head the National Music Theater Conference, George C. White recruited Paulette Haupt. Like Engel, Haupt had a history as a music director and conductor, from which vantage she had had the opportunity to study music drama intimately. "I thought it would be a wonderful thing to do for a couple summers," said Haupt, making this comment as she approached her thirty-sixth season as the artistic director of the National Music Theater Conference.

For the inaugural summer in 1978, Haupt chose a project that brought the O'Neill Center back to its namesake—an opera based on Eugene O'Neill's *Desire Under the Elms* with a score by Ed Thomas and a script by Joseph Masteroff, who was well known in musical theater circles for his work on the Broadway classics *She Loves Me* (written with Harnick and composer Jerry Bock) and *Cabaret* (score by John Kander and Fred Ebb).

In that kickoff year, the Conference was held at Connecticut College in New London, and members were housed in dorms. Masteroff laughs at the memory of his initial encounter with the dorms. "For the first time I saw how actors actually lived. It was so awful that everybody, as soon as they saw their rooms, had to get into a car and

Full Conference photo, National Music Theater Conference, 1986. George C. White and Paulette Haupt are behind the piano, Ed Thomas and Joe Masteroff are in the first row to the left of the piano, and Ray Bradbury (*Fahrenheit 451*) is immediately to the right of the piano. Photo by A. Vincent Scarano.

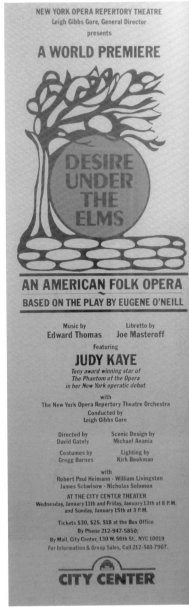

NEW YORK OPERA REPERTORY THEATRE
Leigh Gibbs Gore, General Director
presents

A WORLD PREMIERE

DESIRE UNDER THE ELMS

AN AMERICAN FOLK OPERA
BASED ON THE PLAY BY EUGENE O'NEILL

Music by   Libretto by
Edward Thomas   **Joe Masteroff**

Featuring
JUDY KAYE
Tony award winning star of
The Phantom of the Opera
in her New York operatic debut

with
The New York Opera Repertory Theatre Orchestra
Conducted by
Leigh Gibbs Gore

Directed by   Scenic Design by
David Gately   Michael Anania

Costumes by   Lighting by
Gregg Barnes   Kirk Bookman

with
Robert Paul Heimann · William Livingston
James Schwisow · Nicholas Solomon

AT THE CITY CENTER THEATER
Wednesday, January 11th and Friday, January 13th at 8 P.M.
and Sunday, January 15th at 3 P.M.

Tickets $30, $25, $18 at the Box Office
By Phone 212-947-5850;
By Mail, City Center, 130 W. 56th St., NYC 10019
For Information & Group Sales, Call 212-581-7907.

CITY CENTER

Poster from the 1989 City Center production of the musical *Desire Under the Elms*, which was developed in the first National Music Theater Conference, 1979. Photo by City Center.

rush to the Stop & Shop to get the most basic things for life. Like an electric bulb. I thought, 'Aren't actors wonderful to put up with this? This is really pretty shitty.'" Masteroff and Thomas, having the resources to do so, opted to move to a local hotel.

Accommodations aside, Masteroff's memories are happy ones. "To me it was always a vacation. There was an ocean, and you got your meals free. I loved it. And most everybody did."

Similar to the approach used for *Bedford Forrest* and *The Bird, the Bear and the Actress* (see Chapter 2), the presentation of *Desire Under the Elms* involved substantial scenery. Haupt says, "Our whole concentration for I think ten days and two performances was on building the house, lighting the house, staging, going up and down from the first to the second floor. We learned very quickly that that was not the way to work." Following the model laid down by Lloyd Richards for the National Playwrights Conference, Haupt decided from then on to focus on testing and revising material and writing new pieces with a minimum of technical support.

(*left*) Maury Yeston presents a scene from *Nine* (then titled 8.5) in the Barn Theater, National Music Theater Conference, 1979. Photo by A. Vincent Scarano. (*right*) Jerry Mitchell (director) and Christiane Noll discuss *Take Flight*, by Marsha Norman, Richard Maltby, Jr., and David Shire, outside the Barn Theater, National Music Theater Conference, 2001. Mitchell later directed and choreographed *Legally Blonde* and *Kinky Boots* for Broadway. Photo by A. Vincent Scarano.

This is where Maury Yeston enters the story. While in the BMI Workshop, Yeston started work on a wildly impractical project, an adaptation of Federico Fellini's classic film, 8½, called *Nine*. Yeston remembers, "I was in love with 8½ the film and I just started writing it. I didn't even have a book writer." Kleban introduced Yeston to Italian playwright Mario Fratti, who joined him on the project. Failing to draw interest from producers, after some time, the two put it aside. And then, Yeston recalls, Fratti called with news. "'We've won.' I said, 'We won what?' He said, 'We won being able to do a reading at the O'Neill Music Theater Conference. I applied.' So we joined forces again to go up to the O'Neill and to read what it was that we had.

"Thus we came to the O'Neill and Paulette Haupt, who is a brilliant woman, a natural born teacher, unbelievably versed in opera, operetta, and musical theater. It was her then-husband who played Guido there—Timothy Nolen." Yeston believes that to a large extent, two weeks at the O'Neill is a substitute for the out-of-town tryout system. "The writing team, the producing team, and the cast become a family. If not for three weeks in Chicago, then it's for two weeks in Connecticut. The whole idea is to throw open the windows, allow ideas to come in, and allow the piece to breathe. And give the director and the cast enough time to develop ideas, to make contributions, and at the same time give the writers enough time to write new things, and then to present them simply and see how they work with an audience.

"And so we presented the show. And it was very well received. Katharine Hepburn, who lived reasonably nearby, came to see it. I found out later, Hepburn wrote a letter to Fellini about it. 'I've just seen this remarkable thing, a musical on your wonderful movie, and I'm very taken with it. There's a very talented young man who's written the music.' Fellini told me this."

Yeston credits the O'Neill and the BMI Workshop as being crucial to the success of his show and his growth as a writer. "What you're going to learn at BMI is basically writing theater songs—how to interact with an audience, what works and what doesn't work. And also how to find premises of musical storytelling. What you will *not* find is interactions with actors. What you will not find is full scenes. What you will not find is the structure needed. And that is the kind of thing that you will find at the O'Neill. So the two—the O'Neill and BMI—absolutely complement each other."

The show Yeston and Fratti developed went through other stages. When Tommy Tune joined the project as director, there were other discoveries and shifts. Fratti left as primary writer of the book (the final credits say that the show is "adapted from the Italian by Mario Fratti"), and Arthur Kopit joined the project and has sole credit as the book writer. The resulting show won Tony Awards in 1982 for best musical and for Yeston's score, among other honors.

Yeston sought to repay his debt to the BMI Workshop by teaching there after Engel's death, and in this position, two decades later, he got an early peek at another

Cheyenne Jackson rehearses *Red Eye of Love*, by Arnold Weinstein, John Wulp, and Jan Warner, National Music Theater Conference, 2007. Jackson frequently stars on Broadway (*Xanadu, Finian's Rainbow*) and TV (*30 Rock, Glee*). Photo by A. Vincent Scarano.

project that went to Waterford. A couple of young students brought in work based on an intriguing premise. Robert Lopez and Jeff Marx didn't have a story in mind when they started introducing the songs, just a concept: that the characters from the children's TV show *Sesame Street* are now a decade or so older and face the challenges that come with young adulthood. *Sesame Street* addresses the issues of childhood through songs and sketches. Lopez and Marx had the idea that the less innocent issues of people in their twenties could be explored satirically through song forms drawn from the show most of the audience had probably been exposed to when they were kids.

Producer Kevin McCollum took an option on the material when Lopez and Marx thought that what they were developing was a TV show. McCollum and his associates saw potential for a book musical. Jeff Whitty says, "There were very funny, smart, fresh songs, but no particular story. A sort of grab bag of characters. I drop in, having never written a musical before. I was not the kid that listened to the *Gypsy* cast album, you know what I mean?" Notwithstanding his lack of experience with the form, the producers had a hunch about Whitty and asked him to join the team to coauthor the book.

McCollum says, "And then we needed a place to create the alchemy of what these ingredients were." McCollum was familiar with the Conference from having

Creators of *Avenue Q*, working in the Barn, National Music Theater Conference, 2002. Shown from left are Stephen Oremus (music director), Robert Lopez (music and lyrics), Jeff Whitty (at back; book), Jason Moore (director), and Jeff Marx (music and lyrics). Photo by A. Vincent Scarano.

done a site visit for the National Endowment for the Arts. "[Co-producers] Robyn Goodman and Jeffrey Seller and I felt the O'Neill was the place, so we sent in the application and were accepted." Another addition to the team was director Jason Moore. "It was a place for Jason to work out what the relationship was between the puppets and the people. And we built some more puppets to explore what [more] the show would need. [Without] the O'Neill, I'm sure it would have taken at least another year."

Lopez remembers, "This was really for us the crucible of—would this thing go on? Would it make the transition from something with a lot of funny songs to a working full-length story with two acts? That was the challenge that the producers and Paulette [Haupt] presented us before we came up. We had to give it a beginning, a middle, and an ending. We had some of it in place, and we kind of were hopeful that we had solved a lot of it."

Whitty says, "At that point Jeff [Marx] and Bobby [Lopez] were cowriters of the book. And this is what the O'Neill did for us: it very clearly established what our boundaries were. I was working with Jeff and Bobby who were, shall we say,

Avenue Q in its first reading at the O'Neill, National Music Theater Conference, 2002. Shown (left to right) are Jordan Gelber, Stephanie d'Abruzzo (back of head to camera) with Lucy the Slut, John Tartaglia with Princeton, Kate Monster, Trekkie Monster with Rick Lyon, and Amanda Green. Photo by A. Vincent Scarano.

Jordan Gelber and Stephanie D'Abruzzo performing with Kate Monster in *Avenue Q*, National Music Theater Conference, 2002. Photo by A. Vincent Scarano.

brimming with confidence about their abilities based on this huge success that they'd had at the BMI Musical Theatre Workshop. They had no experience with storytelling and could just toss out any idea. Meanwhile, I'm trying to channel it into something that is the story, so there was a lot of conflict going on between us. And no new music. So we were working with these fragments of songs, a lot of which weren't finished. And what the O'Neill did—it prompted Bobby and Jeff to write new music, because we needed it."

Julia Murney and Paul Kandel in Andrew Lippa's *The Wild Party*, National Music Theater Conference, 1997. Photo by A. Vincent Scarano.

McCollum says that the Conference provided not just a place for the collaborators to work, but also a way to test the work. "The O'Neill has a very, very sophisticated audience that are fans of the theater. They're not cynics. They're smart—they're not going to love everything—but when they love it, you know you've got it."

Lopez remembers the first performance in front of an audience was an eye opener. "It kind of didn't work. We had a scene instead of an opening number that started off the whole story. And we knew that there was going to be an opening number, but even with the scene that we knew was wrong, the whole thing just felt flat." They were used to delighted responses from performing the songs out of context or as part of other presentations, so it was a shock that material that they knew usually landed did not land as part of the show in performance. The point was to learn from the audience, and they had learned that a bold change had to be made. Lopez and Marx asked Whitty and director Moore if they could try their version of a new opening, and they received a go-ahead. "It was the first 25 pages that really didn't set the audience up for what the show was. It didn't tell the audience what the theme of the story was. It just had someone coming to Avenue Q and being welcomed into the neighborhood, and then they sang the Avenue Q theme song. It didn't tell the audience that this show is about that feeling after you graduate from college that you're not special anymore, that you're not a kid anymore. So Kristen

Rick Lyon and Trekkie Monster in *Avenue Q*, National Music Theater Conference, 2002. Photo by A. Vincent Scarano.

[Lopez's wife], Jeff Marx, and I took the script and combed through it and reordered a bunch of things and wrote something that introduced that theme of 'special' in the first part. It wasn't a song, it was just another little scene." As "clunkily written" as Bobby thinks that scene was, it served its purpose at the next performance. Clued into what the show was about, the audience began to find the humor of the songs, and the story started to cohere.

As for Whitty, the experience of seeing how and where the audience reacted gave him a new appreciation of what was required of a book. "Even though I wasn't able to reach the full vision of the show in those two weeks, something inside me clicked—this is how the show should move. Bobby and Jeff eased up on the book writing, and then at the end of the two weeks said, 'We want to take our names off the book,' which made just the hugest difference. So I thank the O'Neill so much, because there really would be no *Avenue Q* without it. That creative team was headed for the rocks."

Whitty remembers a moment when he knew everything was going to be OK. "It was 4:30 in the morning. I was trying to figure out how to get Rod, the gay character, out of the closet in a way that was funny. We were so tired. We'd all been working so hard, and I was sitting in the living room of our little house where we were staying, and I just started howling with laughter. Jason Moore, the director, came in and said, 'What is it?' And I had just written this exchange where Nicky, thinking Rod is

Jason Moore (director, left) and Jason Sellards (aka Jake Shears; music and lyrics), *Tales of the City*, National Music Theater Conference, 2009. The musical is based on Armistead Maupin's *Tales of the City* novels, set in San Francisco. Photo by A. Vincent Scarano.

not listening, says, 'Yes, I think my buddy Rod is a closeted homosexual.' Rod says, 'Nicky, what?' And Nicky [realizing he's been overheard] says, 'All I said was, 'I think my buddy Rod has an undescended testicle.' And I just—we were so tired, we had to laugh for like an hour. And the joke works fine. It's not as funny in the show. But I kept it in because of the memory of that moment with Jason, because we were all so punchy at that point."

It's almost axiomatic that the opening number of a musical is the last one written. Whitty confirms this was the case with *Avenue Q*. "It's tough, because you have to write [a provisional one] first to get started, but then you also have to go back and rewrite it. So you have to go back and sort of see the journey you've taken while writing it and then set that journey up." Understanding what the "clunkily written scene" had achieved, the team had a better sense of what the musical opening that would replace it had to accomplish. Says Whitty, "Out of all the numbers in the show, that was the number that was the most collaborative, like, beat by beat. 'OK now this character is going to come in and say this. We'll work through this. And yeah, I mean, the first half of that song.' . . . Everyone thought that this was going to be the sort of temporary song. 'This will do until we find the right opening number.' But then by the time it was done, it was like, 'Okay, this is it. This is how the show's going to start.' "

Paulette Haupt, artistic director and co-founder of the National Music Theater Conference, conducts a rehearsal, 1981. Photo by A. Vincent Scarano.

Avenue Q was that rare thing, an original musical. And so was the next big hit to emerge from the National Music Theater Conference, *In the Heights.* Like *Avenue Q*, it's about the life of young adults in an urban neighborhood.

Lin-Manuel Miranda says this is not a coincidence. "I'll tell you a story that overlaps the DNA of *Avenue Q* and *Heights.* At the beginning, I was doing book, music, and lyrics by myself. It was becoming an operetta, because I'm really much better at attacking dramatic problems musically. If I write dialogue, it's pages and pages, and no one wants to hear it. That's how my brain works. Working with [director] Tommy [Kail] for a year, we'd created the best two-act version of what *In the Heights* was. Kevin McCollum came to one of our readings and said, 'I like this musical world, but I would like to give you a pair of tickets to this show we have in previews. It's called *Avenue Q.*'

"One of the main plots of *In the Heights* in its original incarnation was that Nina had a brother named Lincoln who (because I [started writing it] in college, and this is a big twist when you're in college) was in love with his best friend, who was a guy, and he comes out and that's the big revelation of the show." Miranda went to the *Avenue Q* preview and discovered that elements were more than a little similar. "This guy who's in love with his best friend and in the closet and can't tell him. I turn to Tommy and go, 'That's our plot! They got there first.' And it's better and it's

Tommy Kail (director, left) and Lin-Manuel Miranda (music and lyrics) during the first rehearsal for *In the Heights*, National Music Theater Conference, 2005. Miranda did not play the role of Usnavi at the O'Neill, at the recommendation of Paulette Haupt and Kail. Miranda instead focused on improving the story and structure of the musical while it was in development at the Conference. He later played the part on Broadway, picking up one of two Tony Awards for his performance. Photo by A. Vincent Scarano.

funnier and more irreverent than the very earnest way we were telling it. And that was the beginning of the way [the character] Lincoln Rosario left the show.

"The year *Heights* opened on Broadway, there was a show called *Glory Days* about a guy who was in love with his best friend and that was the big twist. I was like, 'Oh, this is what we *all* write first!' That's just a thing we grapple with when we're young."

Again, similarly to *Avenue Q*, producer McCollum brought in a book writer to provide a context for songs that had already established a milieu. Quiara Alegría Hudes, one of several accomplished playwrights who had the benefit of being taught by Pulitzer Prize–winning playwright Paula Vogel, remembers: "I had a reading at Manhattan Theatre Club of a play that was set in a similar neighborhood in West Philly. Someone came up to me after and said, 'A friend of mine is working on a similar project, but it takes place in Washington Heights and they're looking for a playwright. Could I get your number and pass it on?' That's how that connection was made. They handed me a 110-page script. Lin and I sat down to meet, and it was very clear that we had a similar story that we wanted to tell. We worked on it for about a year before the O'Neill."

Her memory of the time spent at the O'Neill? "I think I slept four hours a night. We kept throwing out song after song. At first, we were still working within the confines of the story that Lin had created initially, which was about the father-son relationship and about two love triangles. At the O'Neill we saw that those little fixes weren't going to change the larger problems. That's when I had the idea that it really needed to be about the community." She and Miranda found a model of what they hoped to accomplish in *Fiddler on the Roof*. "That was the piece that we felt most closely aligned with. Obviously, the ending was different. [In *Fiddler*], they're leaving their home and ours is about staying home. The draft at the end of the O'Neill was kind of a mess, but it was crystal clear what was wrong and what needed fixing."

Miranda says that, given the structure of the program, the focus was on the script and songs to the exclusion of other elements that are part of a successful musical. "A big piano and a percussionist. That's all that we had for all of our presentations at the O'Neill, and you learn that way." Nothing was staged at the O'Neill. "It was music stands. You stood up, and it didn't get more complicated than that."

When a project accepted for the National Music Theater Conference has connections with producers, the producers sometimes offer enhancement money. *In the Heights* had been accepted into the program on its own considerable merits, but McCollum, recognizing that the cast of twenty-two and a three-piece band would strain the O'Neill's resources, offered additional funds. "We're talking ten, fifteen,

Left to right, Paulette Haupt, Quiara Alegría Hudes (book), and Lin-Manuel Miranda (music and lyrics) speaking with students in the Barn after a performance of *In the Heights*, National Music Theater Conference, 2005. Photo by A. Vincent Scarano.

Betsy Wolfe and Steve Kazee rehearse *Tales of the City*, National Music Theater Conference, 2009. Kazee won the 2012 Tony Award for Best Actor in a Musical for *Once.* Photo by A. Vincent Scarano.

twenty thousand dollars." This is considerably less than the hundreds of thousands a workshop in New York might cost.

McCollum says that apart from the financial aspect, there are other advantages to working at the Conference rather than workshopping in New York. "When you do a reading in NY, everyone is in their real lives, and it's hard to turn off their brains. I think our artists are wildly distracted. Through no fault of their own, but just because they're part of our culture today. To have a place where you can get out of your everyday routine to concentrate on being an artist . . ." McCollum thinks that the distractions of the contemporary wired life keep musicals from being written as they used to be—getting everybody in a room to work intensely, knocking out a draft powered by enthusiasm in a short time. The relative isolation of Waterford screens out much of the inessential. "I think that kind of old school way of working is rare and is why the O'Neill is so important in the ecosystem of the musical theater.

"The thing about the O'Neill is, it's one of those oases of development where everyone's there for the right reason. The creative process wins because the author is king. I don't think people realize commercial producers like myself feel this: the author is king. And my job is to support their inspiration. So that's what the O'Neill provides me—a home to do that for two weeks, and I don't have to find NY hotel rooms. We're all going up to the O'Neill. We're getting in the van, we're gonna have a cocktail at the bar, and we're gonna get to work."

Kristen Anderson-Lopez, who cowrote the book and score of *In Transit*, a piece developed in the 2008 National Music Theater Conference, came to Waterford with the advantage of having experienced the Conference with her husband Robert during the work on *Avenue Q*. "I used what I had observed. A few weeks before, I took our group and said, 'OK, any beefs we have, we need to bring out now, so that it doesn't happen on day three of the O'Neill.' We had our own little cleanse and purge before we got there." Kristen saw a distinction between her team and the one Robert was part of. "They were new to each other, in the intense experience as collaborators who had been put together. I was with people who had been best friends for ten years. We all knew our issues before going in."

Among the issues Kristen and collaborators James-Allen Ford, Russell M. Kaplan, and Sara Wordsworth faced was the unusual nature of the project. *In Transit* is an a cappella musical. When they arrived, it had never been performed. "We were concerned with how on earth six actors, five of whom had never done this material before, were going to learn 300 pages of music without any piano help in a four-day rehearsal process. I think they showed up Sunday night, they started on Monday, and I believe we had a presentation Thursday night. We had Friday to rewrite and then Saturday was another presentation. And we were meeting our new director for the first time at the O'Neill. Joe Calarco had been assigned to

Continuing a tradition at the O'Neill, the authors of *In Transit* sign and pin their program to the rafters of Blue Gene's Pub, 2008. Shown, from left, are Kristen Anderson-Lopez, Sara Wordsworth, and James-Allen Ford. Russell Kaplan is out of the frame. Photo by A. Vincent Scarano.

us. So we met with him when we got there Sunday night, and he said what you want your director to say, which is, 'This piece really, really speaks to me.' Then he proposed—ready for a surprise?—writing a new opening number. And restructuring the rest of the show. And so we said, 'OK, let's do it.' Our original seven-minute opening number was in the trash that night. We went out to CVS and bought a peg board and put every little moment in the show on index cards and started swapping them around. And by the next morning, we had a brand new order of the show. And we were writing lyrics to the new opening number while the cast was learning everything else that they could.

"It would not have happened anywhere else, because you've got four days for six strangers to come in and become the tightest-knit a cappella group you could possibly imagine. It could only happen if you took them all out of their own lives, stuck them in bunk beds someplace in Connecticut in the woods. I mean, the other thing about the O'Neill is that, as opposed to when you do a workshop in NY, you end the day but the work never ends. The cast was leaving, having dinner, and then they would all go back to the common room where they were at Connecticut College, and they would all rehearse on their own all night together, too. It never ever could have happened in that amount of time if we didn't have the incredible cast that we had, but also just everybody working with full burners 24/7."

Shown left to right, Farah Alvin, Wesley Taylor, Theresa McCarthy, and Tommy McDowell rehearse *Broadcast*, by Nathan Christiansen and Scott Murphy, in the Rufus & Margo Rose Theater Barn, National Music Theater Conference, 2013. Photo by A. Vincent Scarano.

Tom Kitt, a composer who did not work at the Music Theater Conference as a writer, nevertheless counts his experiences in Waterford as key to his development. "I spent two summers at the O'Neill as a musical director, and I would love to develop a piece as a writer there. It's what you live for as a writer—the real opportunity to take risks with your piece, and then make some big changes. When you're in full production, you have to keep all the technical elements in mind, you have to allow everybody else to do their work. As you get closer to a production, your window starts to close in terms of the kinds of changes you can make. But the O'Neill is really about the material. You're up there with phenomenal performers, and you're given lots of rehearsal, and you're given multiple presentations. And you're encouraged to really look at each presentation separately and determine some exciting things you might want to try. The writers who took that to heart and did daring work—it was thrilling to be a part of and see." Much of what Kitt absorbed during his time at the O'Neill was applied to a show he wrote with Brian Yorkey, *Next to Normal*, which went on to win him the Pulitzer Prize and the Tony.

Visits to the National Music Theater Conference teach writers not only about their works but also about themselves. Composer Jeanine Tesori says, "It's the first place that I realized that I don't write unless I have a reason to write. Which is the deadline. Which is aptly named." Tesori (another veteran of the BMI Workshop) was working with librettist Brian Crawley on an adaptation of Doris Betts's *The Ugliest Pilgrim*. A few years earlier, she was supporting herself as a conductor and arranger. What she wanted to do was write. "So I left the city for a year to try to re-jigger my life and reboot." In fact, she retreated so far as living for ten months in a lighthouse in Westport in upstate New York, where she worked on her project. She and Crawley completed six songs and sent them to Haupt. "And that was really the beginning of everything." Having had a reading for the first act in New York at Playwrights Horizons in the winter, Tesori and Crawley arrived in the summer of 1994 at Waterford to solve problems.

"What was most important was we could rewrite and feed in rewrites immediately, and not waste time wondering if they were going to work. It's almost like a couture fitting. You're making something and then you're putting it on the models right away, as opposed to getting very far down the line before all the seams are tight and you have to rip them back up. I've used that model ever since I was there." Ultimately, she and Crawley had a musical called *Violet*, which opened at Playwrights Horizons in 1997, won the Drama Critics Circle Award for best musical, and launched Tesori on a high-profile career as a theater composer.

Jeanine Tesori (music) watches rehearsal for *Violet*, a musical she wrote with Brian Crawley, National Music Theater Conference, 1994. After a revival run at New York's City Center in 2013, *Violet* was scheduled for a full Broadway production in spring 2014. Photo by A. Vincent Scarano.

Sheldon Harnick had the opportunity to contrast his experiences on the road with the Conference approach in 1983, when Haupt selected a musical for which he wrote book, music, and lyrics. "Paulette knew that I was working on a musical based on a play by a Soviet writer named Yevgeny Schwartz called *The Dragon*." On the surface, the story is about a town plagued by a three-headed dragon. A knight arrives to destroy the dragon, and the monster's place is taken by the mayor, who becomes ruler of the town. "What he was really writing about was, 'We've all lived through the horrific siege of Leningrad, and our reward is that we get to live under a tyrant, Stalin.'" Schwartz wrote it as a fairy tale to get it past the Soviet censors. But when it was performed, it was evident what the real meat of the piece was, and the piece was immediately withdrawn until after Stalin's death.

"The first opportunity I had to see what the audience response was to what I was writing, was at the O'Neill." Harnick believes that writers who come out of the BMI Workshop benefit from a different kind of evaluation at the O'Neill. He's listened to tapes of presentations of material out of BMI (and also out of a program run by another American performing arts organization, ASCAP). "They have an audience which is so enthusiastic that no matter what they're presenting, it's as though they've written a show-stopper. Whereas at the O'Neill, people want to be helpful, but I think they're a little more judgmental, a little cooler, and that's more helpful."

Kristen Chenoweth and Andrew Lippa on a break during a performance of Lippa's *The Wild Party*, National Music Theater Conference, 1997. Photo by A. Vincent Scarano.

Paulette Haupt introduces a reading, National Music Theater Conference, 2013. Photo by A. Vincent Scarano.

In 1989 Douglas Post had the unique experience of working on a musical in the Music Theater Conference a couple of weeks after working on a play called *Earth and Sky* in the Playwrights Conference. The musical, *The Real Life Story of Johnny De Facto*, was warmly received. Immediately after the performance, Haupt introduced Post to Michael Price, artistic director of the Goodspeed Opera House in East Haddam, Connecticut. "Michael shakes my hand and says, 'I like your musical very much, and I would like to do it next season at my theater.'" Mindful of Lloyd Richards's injunctions against business talk on the campus, Post was apprehensive. "I'm thinking, 'This is wonderful, but I can't be talking to you.'" He brought up his concern to Haupt, and she informed him that "her rules at the Music Theater Conference were different than Lloyd's rules at the Playwrights Conference." Price went on to produce Post's musical that fall.

Sometimes the simple presentation of the O'Neill is missed when a project moves to full production. Jeff Whitty returned to the O'Neill in 2009 to work on a musical version of Armistead Maupin's *Tales of the City* novels, which featured a score by Jake Shears and John "JJ" Garden. Whitty remarks, "I think our big lesson so far was the most satisfying version was the O'Neill version. We went on and did a production in San Francisco [in 2011, at American Conservatory Theater]—hundreds of costumes, big lavish set, things moving up and down. The show was engaging

Shown left to right, Jason Moore (director), Jeff Whitty (book), and John Garden (co-composer) watch a rehearsal of *Tales of the City*, National Music Theater Conference, 2009. Photo by A. Vincent Scarano.

enough in San Francisco. It was entertaining, but it missed a certain heart. It missed a certain inclusion of the audience that comes with trusting them to imagine what is there, which they would much rather do than see it depicted in front of them." Whitty and his collaborators now agree that less would be better. "The soul of the show is about letting the audience imagine this place that feels like home instead of trying to *show* them this place that looks like home. The next version will be pared down to 10 percent of what the production was."

The necessarily spartan circumstances of a Music Theater Conference presentation motivated the creation of a device that ended up becoming a part of the final version of Douglas J. Cohen's musical version of writer-director Frank D. Gilroy's film, *The Gig*. The show is about a group of hobbyist musicians who put aside their daily jobs to get together for an opportunity to perform together under professional circumstances for the first time. Cohen says, "It starts with all the guys in their respective nine-to-five worlds. I had written a prologue which encompasses musically each of their worlds. They come together on a song called, 'Farewell, Mere Existence, Hello Jazz.'" The performers hired did not, in fact, play instruments. Cohen took the suggestion that the actors *sing* their instruments. "I went ahead, on the spot. Started giving one a bass line, and then someone doing a piano riff, and another would be miming a horn." What had started as a solution to a problem of how to present the show at the O'Neill became the signature device of the piece. "It transformed the whole show. In fact, in the Samuel French acting edition, I urge people not to use real instruments but to keep the singing device."

A benefit party in Waterford in 1988 helped launch another hit show. Stuart Ross, who several times came to the National Music Theater Conference as a director or dramaturg, was working on a project about a quartet of male singers in the fifties mode, à la the Four Freshmen. Ross had put up bits and pieces of this work in the cabaret in the basement of the West Bank Café on 42nd Street. "I had about forty minutes of it then. Paulette [Haupt] came to see what I was doing, and she said, 'Can we do this for a special event up at the O'Neill?' I did some work on it, and we did it as an entertainment for the party for the tenth anniversary of the Music Theater Conference." The enthusiastic response to this chunk encouraged Ross to keep working on it until it became a little something called *Forever Plaid*. It opened off-Broadway in 1990 and is probably playing somewhere as you read this. Though the piece wasn't developed at the Conference, Ross says that the method he used to develop it was based on the methods employed there, where he has often directed.

Though the Music Theater Conference runs concurrent with the Playwrights Conference today, the processes necessarily are different. It is possible to put the staged reading of a play on its feet in four days. Musicals require the performers to learn scores that are frequently complicated, involving significantly more time. Haupt explains, "The first rehearsal day, the cold reading, is Tuesday morning, and

Composer Stephen Schwartz speaks during a lunch, National Music Theater Conference, 1997. Schwartz, the composer-lyricist of *Pippin*, *Godspell*, and later *Wicked*, was attending as a mentor. Photo by A. Vincent Scarano.

Cast of *The Noteworthy Life of Howard Barnes,* by Michael Kooman and Chris Dimond, National Music Theater Conference, 2013. Hunter Foster is sitting at the center. Photo by A. Vincent Scarano.

then they start learning to sing. We rehearse the first week Tuesday through Saturday, and we do our first reading Saturday night. Second reading Sunday afternoon." There are two subsequent performances the following Wednesday and Friday, which gives the writers time to make cuts, add a bit of new material, and do some revisions. "So they're there almost a full two weeks. Usually we have two going at the same time. In rep in a way. We start with project A, and then we add B to it the second week. Then A goes away, and we add C. Each piece has its own separate cast, director, music director. Sometimes musicians." In a typical summer, the National Music Theater Conference works on three pieces, though sometimes they find a way to do four.

"The first reading is always pretty rough, because the actors don't know the material yet." Haupt recalls the reaction of one team of writers after one such initial read-through. "They were sitting in the bar crying. It'd been a pretty rough reading, and I went over to console them. Before I could say anything they said, 'Paulette, thank you, it will never sound this good again.' They were crying from joy. They'd never heard it. After all these years, it's still hard for me to imagine what it's like to have something in your head for so long and to suddenly have it come to life in front of you."

The changes between the first performance and the fourth can be striking. Haupt says the big differences tend to come between the Sunday afternoon run and the one on Wednesday night. "They have all day Monday to write. They have all day Tuesday to rehearse. And they have half a day Wednesday." But surprises can come later in the process, too. "When we did *Picnic at Hanging Rock* [2009], Daniel Zaitchik [book, lyrics, and music] got to the Wednesday evening reading and said, 'That's it. I can't do anymore. I don't know what to do.' So we had no rehearsal on Thursday. He came in on Friday morning with forty pages, I think—a different structure and he had cut one character. We did an entirely different reading on Friday night. Just incredible."

As at the Playwrights Conference, Haupt is committed to open submissions, though she will sometimes approach projects she hears about that are in process. In a typical year, there will be something north of 150 applications. "We initially ask for thirty pages. The first thirty pages and a CD of six or more selections. They all go out to readers. I listen to every CD. Just to kind of get a sense of the strengths and weaknesses of what, if only based on the music, I would not choose. Then they all go out to readers, and the reports start flooding in in December, basically. If a piece is recommended, we usually ask for the full scripts. Those go out to readers. Sometimes a full script will be read by two people before it comes to me. Then they start coming in boxes to me."

Cast of *Goddess*, by Michael Thurber and Mkhululi Mabija, National Music Theater Conference, 2013. Photo by A. Vincent Scarano.

Cast of *In the Heights*, by Lin-Manuel Miranda and Quiara Alegría Hudes, National Music Theater Conference, 2005. Photo by A. Vincent Scarano.

As confident as Haupt is that the Music Theater Conference is now structured correctly, it still requires good faith on the part of the participants. One project written by a team of famous and talented people she counts as among "the worst two weeks I think I've spent. The whole attitude from everybody, except [the composer] was, 'We're here to put on a backers' audition.' It wasn't, 'We're here to work on the piece.' It was, 'We are here to get this in front of the right people.' That is not what the O'Neill is about."

11. National Puppetry Conference

"Puppeteers tend to be solitary—or work in very small companies of two or three people," says Pam Arciero, artistic director of the National Puppetry Conference. "When you find a big group of people who understand what you are doing—it is such a gift. That is what the Conference grew out of—the need for us to do that."

Puppetry was in the bones of the Center from the early days. Rufus and Margo Rose, the married couple who were creators of TV's *Howdy Doody Show*, lived in Waterford and were longtime friends of George C. White. To be friendly with White meant to be recruited to his cause, and Rufus found himself drafted to be what his son, Jim, describes as a construction superintendent, bringing the buildings of the Hammond Estate to a point where it was safe for the Center's programs to function indoors. "I know for a fact that my mother was one of the persons who emptied the cow stalls [in the barn] of the years of, uh, cow occupancy. She was never one to let somebody else take the shovel." The Roses lent a hand on various aspects of the O'Neill facility, including the roof of a space extended at a right angle from the Barn now called the Dina Merrill Theater (previously called the Barn El, because from above the structure looked like a giant L), which Rufus designed and for which he and Margo executed the mechanical drawings. As Barry Grove recalls, the Roses also taught at the National Theater Institute from its beginning.

Marionette performance,
National Puppetry Confer-
ence, 2001. Photo by Richard
Termine.

Jim and Jane Henson arrived in the New York area in 1963. Having already experimented in Washington, D.C., with techniques to make puppetry address the specific challenges of television, Jim sought out Rufus as a mentor. The Hensons were frequent visitors at the Rose house, where, according to their daughter Heather, the friendship extended to tournaments of "killer croquet." In 1969, the Hensons and their growing crew of puppeteers found a berth on the PBS children's TV show, *Sesame Street*. The popularity of their appearances on that program led to other projects highlighting the Muppets—a repertory of well-loved characters headed by Kermit the Frog and Miss Piggy, who would go on to star on TV and in several movies.

Rufus Rose died in 1975. His son, Jim, remembers, "George White called me and asked if it would be acceptable to our family to name the theater barn after my father. And I said, 'On condition that my mother is given equal billing.'" And so it came to be called the Rufus & Margo Rose Theater Barn.

In 1976, Connecticut College cosponsored a festival with the O'Neill Center in observance of the thirtieth anniversary of a National Festival of the Puppeteers of America that the Roses had hosted shortly after World War II. Part of the objective was to bring together from across the country many of those often-solitary artists. In pre-internet days, puppeteers were less aware of others working in the same field, so this was an opportunity for many of the artists to see what others were tackling.

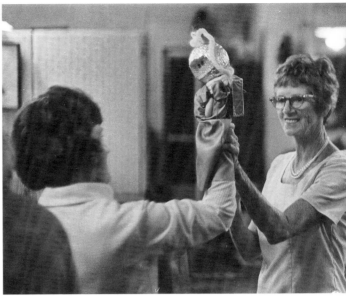

(*left*) Rufus Rose with Howdy Doody, ca. 1965. Rose and his wife Margo lived locally in Waterford and were among the founding trustees of the Eugene O'Neill Theater Center. The Roses often hosted Jim and Jane Henson at their home, and they introduced the Hensons to the O'Neill. (*above*) Margo Rose (right) teaches a student, National Theater Institute, early 1970s.

Bart P. Roccoberton, Jr., who is the director of the Puppet Arts Program and is associate professor of dramatic arts in puppetry at the University of Connecticut, Storrs, recalls festival performances held both at Connecticut College and on the O'Neill grounds. Master puppeteer Allelu Kurten has a vivid memory of the legendary Burr Tillstrom setting up a small stage by the stone wall near the Mansion and performing with his iconic characters, Kukla and Ollie. Ollie was a dragon who ordinarily had one large tooth, but when he opened his mouth that day he had a set of choppers instantly recognizable as being modeled after those of Democratic presidential candidate Jimmy Carter. Kurten reports, "It brought down the house."

Puppetry continued to be a part of the O'Neill in the person of Jim Henson, who would occasionally find room between his work on film and TV projects to teach at the National Theater Institute.

At the time only a handful of schools offered majors—including the University of Connecticut and the University of Hawaii. In the early eighties, the puppetry

Gonzo visiting the O'Neill and a bit of puppetry history—the Rufus & Margo Rose Theater Barn, August 2012. Photo by Jean Marie Keevins.

community was alarmed by the rumor that the Connecticut program was in danger of being cut for budgetary reasons. Margo Rose kept pressing for assurances that the program would continue, but the school was not quick to offer her any. So she took action.

Roccoberton says, "One day, Margo called me. It was right after the Theatre of the Deaf had left the O'Neill grounds. She said, 'We need to create a safety net for the UConn program, because the university is not responding, and we must have puppetry training in this country.' So I worked with her for probably a little over a

A puppet mask performance, National Puppetry Conference, 2008. Photo by Richard Termine.

Jim Henson (center) visits
the O'Neill with George
C. White (left) and Bart
Roccoberton, Jr., 1988.
Photo by A. Vincent
Scarano.

month, and we walk in with all our papers and our folders and our notebooks and Margo says to George, 'George, you must be pretty lonely around here now that the Theatre of the Deaf has left.' We tell him what we have in mind. And in the next second, George says, 'I agree. What's the budget?' Margo and I say, 'B-b-b-b-budget?'" Roccoberton laughs. "Of course we never did figure out what the budget was."

A meeting of interested parties gathered together to discuss the structure of the program. Roccoberton continues, "I thought that my role was to make sure everything was going OK, make sure everyone's coffee cups were filled. And then: 'So who's gonna direct this thing?' And Margo pointed at me and said 'Bart will.' And so that's how we got it under way.

"As I said, there was no real budget. George looked at my résumé and said, 'Oh, you're tech theater-trained. We need a technical director here at the Center. So why don't we start you off as technical director of the Playwrights Conference, and then you can work, and we'll build the program from there!' So, my first year was as technical director. I didn't realize the technical director also had to take care of the plumbing and the roofs and stair units, so I spent the year crawling. I know every space at the Center. It was actually a great time because, as I crawled down through the boiler room and under the dining room, my head was at work. I put together a full plan for IPPA [Institute of Professional Puppetry Arts] in those six to eight months that wouldn't have happened if I was sitting at a desk. And so it actually turned out quite good."

A poster dating from 1985 reads, in part: "The Eugene O'Neill Theater Center . . . is proud to announce THE INSTITUTE OF PROFESSIONAL PUPPETRY ARTS. . . . As part of its goal to increase the perception, growth and quality of the puppet theatre, the Institute of Professional Puppetry Arts offers programs for the professional, the student and the general public." Two programs were designed for students—one a single semester described as introductory, and the other a two-year program. The single-semester program promised instruction in "Acting, Directing, Movement, Voice, Playwrighting [sic], Costume and Scene Design, Figure Design, Construction and Manipulation, Masks, Hand Puppetry, Rod Puppetry, Shadow Puppetry and Marionettes." Accreditation was offered by Connecticut College. At the time the poster was published, accreditation was still pending for the more exhaustive two-year program "intended for the career-oriented student," but eventually an MFA was offered. Jim Henson's participation was promised along with that of Margo Rose, Roccoberton, and White, as well as Vincent Anthony, Bil Baird, Frank Ballard, Lynn Britt, Paul Vincent Davis, Peter Lobdell, Rudy Shelley, Richard Termine, Fred Voelpel, and Brad Williams. As per Margo Rose's insistence, Roccoberton is indeed listed as the Institute's director. The first students arrived in 1986.

Roccoberton recalls, "All of our teachers were professional artists who were commuting from either New York or from Europe. The students were on call seven days a week. We did three three-and-a-half-hour classes each day, and we also designed clear time. The way that we ran, they used to say it was 'Roccoberton Standard Time.' If Roman Paska was coming up out of New York on Friday and he missed his train, I would go to the students and say, 'The session we have clear tomorrow morning is now filled. You have this evening to do your laundry.'"

The main difference between what a student would get at IPPA and the University of Connecticut was that the university program expressed the vision of one person, Frank Ballard, and IPPA offered a constant turnover of professionals from a variety of backgrounds, much in the way NTI operates at the O'Neill.

IPPA ran for four and a half years. Roccoberton says the difficulty in perpetuating the progam lay in trying to start a new arts program during the Reagan era. He says of Reagan, "One year, he cuts funding for the arts, saying, 'Business will take up the slack with contributions,' and the next year he cuts the tax credits for businesses to give money."

Jim Henson died in 1990. Richard Termine, who had worked with the Henson organization for several years as a builder and designer for *Sesame Street* (one of the characters he created was Meryl Sheep), says, "I think a lot of us were really

Jane Henson (right) teaches during the first National Puppetry Conference, 1991. She would later serve on the Board of Trustees of the O'Neill. An enormous supporter of new puppetry talent, she passed away in the spring of 2013. Photo by Richard Termine.

impacted by Jim's passing, just as we had been by Rufus's. This was another milestone that we needed to process and deal with, and that really, I think, motivated us to be involved."

The form of that involvement was proposed by Jane Henson, Jim's widow. She called on Termine, some IPPA veterans, and other interested parties to organize an annual puppetry conference. Jane Henson honored the family that had been so welcoming to her and Jim by dubbing its sponsoring organization the Rose Endowment for Puppetry. The National Puppetry Conference website states it is "dedicated to the legacies of such visionary puppet artists as Bil Baird, Jim Henson, Rufus and Margo Rose, Don Sahlin, Martin Stevens, Burr Tillstrom and Brad Williams and to the spirit with which they shared their creativity and themselves." George Latshaw (whose puppets sang with Leslie Caron in the movie *Lili*) was initially named artistic director and Termine associate artistic director, but after the first conference, they switched roles.

Termine, who was artistic director for eleven years, says that being based at the O'Neill had an influence on how the National Puppetry Conference was conceived. "We wanted to take up the model of the O'Neill and see if we could make that work for puppetry—workshopping, developing new work for our art form."

Margo Rose (top, with Howdy
Doody) and Jane Henson, 1991.
Photo by Richard Termine.

The O'Neill has exerted another influence. Heather Henson, Jim and Jane's daughter, who also serves on the O'Neill's Board of Trustees, has been experimenting with soaring kites and large translucent figures that glide through the air, and she cites the Hammond Estate grounds and beach as a catalyst. "I've been inspired by the landscape of it, of being on the water, being in that beautiful area."

To draw attention to the new enterprise, the inaugural conference in 1991 focused on the Muppets. The guest performing artists working with the approximately twenty participants were Pam Arciero, Cathy Mullen, and Martin P. Robinson, all of whom had history with the Hensons. In addition to Termine, the puppet builders present included Peter MacKennan and Jan Rosenthal, also Henson veterans. But Heather Henson says that her parents were always determined that, whether via IPPA or the Conference, efforts at the O'Neill not be seen as devoted to Muppetry. "Jane was adamant that the Muppets were not going to be the legacy of the work. My father also. So many people were doing Muppet-style work, and he really wanted to encourage people to use their creativity for their own work."

In the years that followed 1991, the Conference—first under Termine and then, beginning in 2002, under Arciero—has put effort into giving support to and showcasing the broad range of approaches to puppetry, including styles and techniques far from Kermit and Miss Piggy. "It is very hard to find any other program that is going to give that amount of intensive education to you in all forms of puppetry. On our campus you can find any form of puppetry happening at any time," says Arciero.

She observes that a significant number of the people who find their way into puppetry do so on their own. "Very often they are self-taught. We have people who have been working in their garage, as well as people who have masters of fine arts in puppetry." Arciero notes that one of the inhibiting factors in university training is its expense, with college credits often costing $3,000 or $4,000 a pop. You might well be asked to pay $8,000 or $10,000 to take a puppetry class at a university. The O'Neill's conference—which combines workshops to develop new skills with professional development—currently offers eight days of training, room, and board for

Founders of the National Puppetry Conference, 1991. (Back) Bobbi Nidzgorski, Bart Roccoberton, Jr. (with Telly Monster to his left), Margo Rose (sitting with Howdy Doody), Martin P. Robinson, Jane Henson, George Latshaw, and Peter MacKinnon; (front) Richard Termine, Kathy Mullen (with Mokey Fraggle), and Pam Arciero (with Graziella the Grouch).

Behind the scenes of a shadow puppetry piece, National Puppetry Conference, 2001. Photo by Richard Termine.

something in the neighborhood of $1,000. "You can't even stay in a motel for $1,000 for the week on a beach in Connecticut," says Arciero. "I have tried to maintain that lower cost. To do that I do solicit funds outside. That is something Jane Henson and her family have always been great about, helping us keep the price to an amount that allows starving artists to come in and learn."

Arciero sees part of the National Puppetry Conference's job as preserving the heritage. "We are passing on what we learned from our elders to the next generation."

An example of Bunraku puppetry, National Puppetry Conference, 2001. Bunraku typically needs three puppeteers for each puppet: one to operate the legs, one for the body and head, and one for the arms. Photo by Richard Termine.

Kevin Clash (with Elmo) and a guest, National Puppetry Conference, 2002. Photo by Richard Termine.

She compares some puppeteers of the past to the old-time magicians—neither group used to be inclined to share its techniques. The masters who come to the Conference these days have put this proprietary attitude behind them. "We make each other better by sharing this information."

The idea isn't merely to pass on traditions, but also to support the transmission of craft in the service of continuing development. Says Arciero, "We usually invite two or three guest artists, and our participants sign up to be with them all day long, so that they can understand the artists' technique—their style of design, how they think about a show, where a show comes from, how their shows are written. You have a group of people to help you with techniques you don't know. Maybe you are starting with a different style of puppets, or you just don't have the people who have the skill sets to help you in the outside world. Say you want to do a shadow puppet show—you can have a shadow expert help you block your show and make it look right. Most puppeteers begin on their own, reinventing the wheel. They don't know that there is a common language." Arciero emphasizes the personal transmission of craft. "You can buy books on it, but it is not the same as working with the artists who know this [craft]. One of the advantages of our conference is that you really work with people who are excellent in the art form. I try to get the best people to come teach."

Two participants practice their marionette skills in a puppetry workshop in the Dina Merrill Theater basement, National Puppetry Conference, 2009. Photo by Richard Termine.

Associate artistic director Jean Marie Keevins describes the perspective of the first-time participants arriving in Waterford. "They're daunted. They want to know what they're going to leave with. You tell them they're going to leave with a new family. At the end, you have to push them off the campus. They come, they learn, they grow, they find this family, and it's all over the world."

"Part of the orientation is an instant puppet theater exercise," says Termine. "We divide up into small groups, and they have ten or fifteen minutes to create a puppet performance with found objects—anything from a music stand to someone's bag, a ladder, anything. Collaborating in their group, they animate them, they create characters, they bring the objects to life, they interact, and there's a story— beginning, middle, and end. We present them to each other."

"One year," says Keevins, "in my backpack I had a bag of plastic razors, and everybody in the group took a razor to make a flock of birds. There was some scene that took place with a tree. It was far from outstanding, but it was a moment where we all told a story with things we had just found as a group." Keevins sees the tradition of beginning this way as "a great equalizer, because it starts out with participants and staff together."

Another tradition is the circle pitch, during which participants propose new short pieces to be created at the Conference. Keevins explains, "The circle pitch is absolutely everybody there in a big circle. Once everybody pitches, basically the answer is yes! You can do that idea. Whatever idea that is, yes! And then they talk with

Bart [Roccoberton], and they figure out how they're going to do it technically, and they work with the musicians and figure out the soundscape, if they even need it."

One project that started with a pitch stays with Keevins. "It came from this guy who said, 'I kind of have this idea. I don't really know what it is, but it kind of goes like this. What do you think?' He literally made no sense, but within the next day we were all, like, 'Yep, I want to be involved in that project. It's amazing.' It went on to be the show-stopper of the evening."

Connor Hopkins's *Dustbowl* begins with a brief audio introduction—a snatch of a Woody Guthrie song—and a quick sighting of a small plane flying in the sky. Then the lights come up to reveal a house and a clothesline standing in a bleak landscape described by sheets of brown paper. The stick figure of a boy emerges from the house and makes his way past the clothesline to a fence, where he sits. A wind blows headlines across the stage, spelling out the disaster of the Depression and the news that dust storms are striking the Great Plains. The boy's mother emerges from the house as a storm threatens. She goes to the fence and embraces her boy. The dust now covers the house and the fence. The mother tries to protect her son as the small figure of a plane (fashioned from a Coca-Cola can) appears in the sky above, fighting the storm. Now a larger version of the plane lands, and a dapper figure wearing pilot's gear emerges, carrying a map that he consults. He sees the boy and his mother and distractedly pats the boy on the head as he continues to peruse his map. The mother drops to her knees and beseeches the pilot for help. He rebuffs her and returns to his plane. He takes off, leaving the boy and his mother alone. She coughs and falls

Connor Hopkins (far back) rehearses for his *Dustbowl*, using Bunraku-style puppets, National Puppetry Conference, 2009. Photo by Richard Termine.

to the ground. A layer of dust—represented by a small sheet of brown paper—covers her. The boy is alone. He hears the sound of an engine, looks up, and sees the plane disappear. The lights go down as a taste of Woody Guthrie returns to the soundtrack. The entire piece has played without words.

Roccoberton comments: "The boy sees that the man had no concern for other human beings. By the end of the piece, you realize that the interloper was Charles Lindbergh." Keevins remembers members of the audience weeping by the end.

Much of the activity of the week is devoted to participants supporting guest artists working on projects in progress. While assisting the artists, participants pick up practical experience of various aspects of production, which they will then be able to apply to their own work.

Around Thursday of the Conference week, Roccoberton puts on his producer's hat. The shows are a mix of pieces by the guest artists as well as a sample of work created by the participants based on ideas from the circle pitch. "Our goal is to put these things in front of an audience. Puppetry does not work without an audience. So the audience is a very important element for us. Of course we want them to look good, but we have to work very simply—make sure things are illuminated and that we work out the flow of the evening, so that we're not there for five or six hours. There are two performances, Friday and Saturday nights. They're generally in the Dina Merrill Theater, but we've used the grounds as well—Heather [Henson] has performed outside. Saturday afternoon we try to have a session, so that revisions can be made on the projects for Saturday night."

Short pieces by members of the Conference are sometimes featured in late-night sessions in the on-campus pub, Blue Gene's. In a blog entry on *Playbill*'s website, Sophia Saifi described some of what was shown in the 2013 session: "Puppeteer Estee Taylor's saucy Jessica Lange-esque marionette sang Etta James while a snarky Black Eyed Susan turned down her puppeteer Madison Cripps's romantic advances."

The proliferation of short pieces has given rise to a variant on poetry slams—puppet slams, many of which are supported by the Puppet Slam Network, a program of IBEX Puppetry, an organization founded by Heather Henson: "We give little grants—$2,000—to theater organizations that want to present evenings of short puppet works, like those pieces by participants that come out of the circle pitch. There are about fifty venues that do it now. Most of the people who run puppet slams across the country are like that one person from Austin who does puppetry, comes to the Conference, and gets so jazzed that they'll then start a slam in their own city."

Leslie Carrara-Rudolf performs as a character transformed by a gypsy skirt, National Puppetry Conference, 2009. Carrara-Rudolf is a frequent instructor at the Conference and plays Abby Cadabby on *Sesame Street*. Photo by Richard Termine.

Arciero has built on the program that she inherited from Latshaw and Termine. "About a year after I took over, I started what we call our intensive puppetry conference—a three-day intensive where people will come and study one specific technique. For example, we had HuaHua Zhang, who teaches a specific form of Chinese rod puppetry. You spend three days, twelve hours a day, working on the technique, so you learn only that. Or we have Jim Kroupa, who comes in and does the mechanics workshop. He will take one mechanical element—say a blinking eye, a nodding head, a turning head—and you will learn how to do that in about thirty hours of work. Basically that's all you do. You eat in between, go to bed, and then wake up and do the same thing for three days."

Arciero gets particular satisfaction when the participants evolve into guest artists themselves. "We have had a couple of people who started out as participants, and [we] ended up inviting them back to do master projects. You know they just keep developing their stuff on and on."

One such project was developed by Michael Bush (not the same Michael Bush as the former head of the cabaret program, discussed in Chapter 9) and Stefano Brancato, two puppeteers Roccoberton knew as students in his program at the University of Connecticut, who first came to the Conference as participants. "They brought in a piece called *Icarus*. It showed promise, and we worked on it more back at UConn over the following year. They were accepted into the emerging artist slot at the next Conference, and the performance here was a major success."

O'Neill executive director Preston Whiteway and Kermit the Frog at the O'Neill's 2010 Summer Gala, which honored Jane Henson and the founders of the National Puppetry Conference. Kermit made a surprise appearance. Photo by A. Vincent Scarano.

Arciero gives details of the emerging artists program into which Bush and Brancato were accepted. "Emerging artists are people who have come a couple of times and want to develop longer pieces. They are given a ten-minute segment to do. A staff helps them develop the writing, and we give them people to direct—however many puppeteers they need. They get to show the project at the end of the week, along with everyone else.

"*Icarus* involves a Greek chorus made up of both humans and puppets and brings to the stage the Minotaur and its father Poseidon in a huge form. I would refer to it as a great piece of theater that involves puppetry, not a 'puppet show.'" It also goes against the assumption by many that anything that involves puppets is designed for children. Roccoberton adds, "Stefano [Brancato] described it as OK for young people from thirteen and up, but it's actually an adult piece." He adds that some have suggested that the audience appropriateness might expand if they "could get rid of the bull sex in it."

Not all puppetry is designed for live audiences. The Hensons, the Roses, Shari Lewis, and Burr Tillstrom all achieved their fame via screens, some on TV and some additionally on film. The National Puppetry Conference also supports artists working in these media. Martin P. Robinson (perhaps best known for playing Mr. Snuffleupagus and Telly Monster on *Sesame Street* and designing Audrey II for both the off-Broadway and Broadway productions of the musical *Little Shop of Horrors*) has run workshops in which participants, instead of presenting live pieces at the end of a Conference, have been represented by video segments. This requires learning about framing, lighting, and editing.

Different concerns apply, depending on whether one is building something for live or video presentation. Live offerings often account for the presence of the puppeteer. As Arciero comments, "The person standing behind the puppet either is acknowledged as somehow being part of the play or is intended to be invisible." The Tony Award–winning *War Horse*, a co-production of England's National Theatre and South Africa's Handspring Puppet Company, makes a bargain with the audience not to see the puppeteers, even though they are plainly there. The team of three who manipulate the leading horse wear black, and the audience chooses to concentrate on the puppet of the horse, tricking themselves into removing the team from their consciousness. In other situations, as in *Avenue Q*, the presence and participation of the puppeteers, often having dialogue with the puppets, is a highlighted feature and, indeed, is the basis of some of the humor of the show.

In contrast, video puppetry mostly works to keep the puppeteers masked or out of frame (sometime removing them digitally). We don't see Frank Oz playing Miss Piggy in the Muppet films and TV episodes.

Martin P. Robinson's *The Halloween Project* uses giant puppets, National Puppetry Conference, 2013. Photo by Richard Termine.

This speaks to essential differences between stage and screen. The stage is metaphoric. The audience knows what it is seeing is not literally true. (Even in the most conventional naturalistic plays, the audience makes allowances for the fact that the actors live in rooms with three sides and somehow always face in the direction where a fourth wall would be.) However, the screen usually tries to counterfeit the literal, putting effort into rendering fantasy momentarily credible by giving it detail and body.

Robinson, a regular at the Conference, continues to put together new projects in whatever medium he deems appropriate. In 2013, he returned with a live work in progress called *The Halloween Project*. Loosely based on the story of Hansel and Gretel, the excerpt presented in the Rose Theater Barn featured a girl being terrorized by three huge figures manipulated by strings and rods—a pumpkin-headed creature whose head blinked as he spoke, a menacing clown, and a ghostlike figure who sailed and swooped over the audience. Initially terrified (and who wouldn't be terrified of being raised in the branch-like arms of a giant pumpkin creature?), the girl managed to touch the points of compassion in her would-be tormentors and win them over. Robinson's video side was expressed in a 2008 project that employed his collection of handmade Italian bottle stoppers featuring character heads on their tops. For that, Robinson led a contingent of Conference participants to downtown New London to shoot material that established the action in a bar.

A piece by another participant in 2013 also used video—a brief comic riff on the adventure movie *Jurassic Park*, in which the voracious dinosaurs were not the Spielbergian computer-generated wonders but figures sketched in pen on pieces of paper. The effect was hilarious.

The rest of the pieces by participants in the 2013 Conference were live. A notable one featured three women slamming the wooden deck of the Amphitheater with sodden mops and then suddenly being moved to transform the mops into the three Weird Sisters from *Macbeth*, playing passages of the witches' scenes, the strands of gray mop fabric suggesting frazzled hair. Another piece featured a young woman so disappointed by the book she has just finished reading that she fashions from its pages paper puppets that enact a story she prefers. Another suggested that the three little pigs were bullies picking on a young wolf in a schoolroom.

A piece developed and shot at the 2004 Conference married puppetry and social action. Created for No Strings, an organization that teaches disaster coping and preparedness to children in various cultures through the medium of puppet

Kathy Mullen (center) and Lindsay Briggs (right) film an early version of *No Strings*, National Puppetry Conference, 2004. *No Strings* is an educational program that was later used in Afghanistan in a program about the dangers of land mines. Photo by James Stidfole.

videos, the piece in question taught children how to protect themselves from land mines. Something that originated in the peaceful countryside of Connecticut ended up being shown to the young audiences in Afghanistan on monitors in the back of a truck.

Arciero mentions that, because of the increasing sophistication of computer imaging, new territory in film is opening. "It is a new field that I am very interested in, which is a crossover between puppetry and CG [computer-generated] animation." She cites the character of Yoda in *Star Wars*. "The first time around, he was a puppet performed by Frank Oz magnificently. In the second set of *Star Wars* pictures, they did Yoda all as CG animation. There was something really appealing and human about the first one, but I didn't really care about the computer-generated Yoda. But I am really interested in the crossover fields and how that works. I think that with computer-generated stuff, we will be able to do things like have a puppet's hands really pick something up or write a letter. If we combine those techniques, it's gonna be spectacular. That is the way of the future, and I do want to keep working in those arenas."

Arciero continues to be concerned about the scripting side of her art. "There are a lot of great puppet builders out there, tremendously beautiful puppet builders, and there are people who can move puppets very well out there. What there aren't are a lot of good writers for puppetry. It is like you have to be able to write

Tim Lagasse (left), Pam Arciero (artistic director), and Martin P. Robinson at the opening of the 2009 National Puppetry Conference. Both Arciero and Robinson are regulars on *Sesame Street*. Photo by Richard Termine.

a ballet and a Shakespearean show, and then combine them. The movement is as important as the words, very often. Finding playwrights who understand that is difficult. Puppets are very freeing. There are things that puppets are free to do by not being human—puppets can fly without any problem." Arciero is pushing to involve more writers who are not themselves puppeteers, and to that end has begun a strand of the Conference that is strictly about writing. Getting puppeteers themselves interested in the discipline of composing scripts has been a struggle. "It has been hard to get that going with puppeteers; we have been kinda ADD, you know."

Robert Smythe, who has taught writing at the Conference, has theories about how the very nature of puppets creates obstacles to effective narrative. "Puppetry seems to bring out a design response on the part of artists. 'If I build it, I can figure out what to do with it.' When I started teaching writing here at the Conference and started to speak about the concept of character, people would very often say, 'But I *have* a character!' and they'd hold up a completed puppet. And I'd be, 'Let's talk about what a character might mean. That there's a being that has wants, faces obstacles.' General playwriting concepts. And they sometimes go, 'Well, why would I want to do that?' I've been trying to impress them with the idea of story. It's not thematic: 'We need to save the oceans.' No, we need an individual who comes into it. We need a way in." Smythe has come to understand that writing for puppets does not involve a one-to-one substitution of puppet for actor. Puppets (like comic strips) represent an edited version of reality. "Human beings onstage are not edited. The human being is always living and breathing and is always 100 percent. Even the most lifelike puppet is an edited representation. When we start to realize that, it gives us an opportunity. We can basically break the laws of physics, play with space and time in the way that two-dimensional film representations can. We can do this with puppets in a way that is absolutely impossible with human beings."

Arciero would like to see the community expanded. "Puppetry is really a white event. It just is, for whatever reason. It is very hard to find that many different ethnic groups working in it. For a lot of reasons. I mean, we are playing with dolls. It is not a real macho thing to do for most people. More macho cultures are not necessarily going to tolerate a guy going into it. So I push really hard to get those ethnic and minority scholarships in. I want the field to be as diverse as humanity is.

"And there are some people who send [endow] scholarships specifically for one form or another, say marionettes or shadow puppets. Sometimes scholarships have

Heather Henson (left) and Lisa Willoughby perform *Panther and Crane* at the Detroit Institute of Arts in 2012, after developing the piece during the 2011 National Puppetry Conference. Henson is also a trustee of the O'Neill. Photo by Stephen Henderson.

been given in memoriam. There is a Nikki Tilroe scholarship. She was a beautiful movement person, so that scholarship is being put out to those who are specifically interested in movement and puppetry. Then there is a Jerry Nelson scholarship. Jerry played the Count on *Sesame Street*. That scholarship is for someone who is extremely good at character voices and developing characters. So there are specific support systems for that."

Aside from the knowledge participants pick up at the Conference, not a few find that the O'Neill is a first step into the professional world. Preston Whiteway observes, "So many of the young artists who first start as participants even now are working on *Sesame Street* and the other major opportunities for puppetry professionally in this country."

Heather Henson says that because specific works in the field aren't well known, the Conference risks looking like a sideshow in comparison to other O'Neill projects. "We don't have quite as many shows on Broadway as other conferences, but the impact on the community is immense, it's national. Our program is known internationally throughout the puppet community. All puppeteers in America and abroad know about the O'Neill program."

Termine adds, "The puppeteers come here to find their voice as artists. They don't have to go home and rely on fairy tales. They can create work with their own vision. Within the course of that week, they can find the impulse to form and the sense of creativity to go on and do more work like that." Arciero echoes this sentiment when she says, "I don't want puppetry to be relegated strictly to children, as it has been—not that there is anything wrong with that—but people hold different standards for children than they do for 'legitimate theatre.'

"There are probably at most three or four thousand puppeteers in the whole country. So it is a very small community. For us to find each other and then to work on keeping that standard as high as we possibly can—that is a really rare thing. That is what I love doing—getting the community together."

During the Conference, the basement of the Dina Merrill Theater is turned into a space completely filled with puppets and people working. The last night of the Conference, after the second performance, Arciero says, "We put the campus back to exactly the way it was before we moved in, back into perfect condition. That is

Jane Henson speaks at the National Puppetry Conference, 2009. Photo by Richard Termine.

one of my rules. Then we go down to the beach. That is when everybody gets a little crazy, a little loose. We do a roast. Everyone acts out funny things from the week. There's a bonfire, and any puppets that you don't like, any script that you don't like, you burn them in the fire, or put them in little boats and send them flaming out to sea. A Viking puppet funeral."

Jane Henson died on April 2, 2013. At the memorial service on April 9 at Manhattan's Church of St. Vincent Ferrer, attendees—including many veterans of the National Puppetry Conference—were given angel puppets to wave, and Heather Henson's aerial creations whooshed overheard.

12. The Changing of the Guard

Lloyd Richards announced that he would retire as head of the National Playwrights Conference in 1999. A search committee recommended James Houghton. Houghton had come to prominence by building from scratch the off-Broadway Signature Theatre Company in New York. Founded in 1991, the Signature devoted each season to a single playwright. Some of the writers who had been celebrated by the Signature had also attended the Playwrights Conference in one function or another—Edward Albee, Lee Blessing, John Guare, and Sam Shepard. (More would have their seasons later—Athol Fugard, David Henry Hwang, August Wilson, and Lanford Wilson.) In the July 18, 2000, *New York Times*, George C. White affirmed that Houghton's lack of experience at the O'Neill was part of what made him an attractive candidate. "I wanted somebody to come in and see it fresh," White was quoted as saying by reporter Mel Gussow. "He brought no baggage, none of this, 'It's always been done this way.'"

The change in the leadership of its best-known program came against the background of other changes and challenges at the O'Neill Center. In the previous year, White, in reaction to the appearance of a six-figure deficit, eliminated the role of development director, took over most of those responsibilities himself, cut some programs, and reduced the budgets of others. Frank Rizzo, longtime theater reporter of the *Hartford Courant*, quoted White as saying, "I could probably last five or ten

Director James Houghton (left) and playwright-performer Bill Irwin in *Mr. Fox: A Rumination*, National Playwrights Conference, 2003. Photo by A. Vincent Scarano.

years, but I don't want to do it. I was at a point where I could just be the founder and chairman and designated hitter in fundraising. But I'm working my ass off now." Having steered the Center back into the black, he thought about who might take on a leadership role in the future. He was to find a candidate through an associate of his wife Betsy. Betsy was friendly with a woman named Pat Daily, and she suggested that Daily and her longtime companion Tom Viertel might enjoy visiting the O'Neill.

Some years before, Viertel's energies had been primarily devoted to real estate. Then he had happened on a show in Los Angeles featuring Penn and Teller, the duo who perform magic mixed with a dose of satire and a healthy contempt for the trappings and conventions of traditional magicians. Despite having had no experience in producing, Viertel and one of his business partners, Steve Baruch, decided to collaborate with producer Richard Frankel to bring the two for a run in New York. That

George C. White (right) introduces James Houghton in the Edith Oliver Theater at the opening of the National Playwrights Conference, 2000. Photo by A. Vincent Scarano.

O'Neill chair Tom Viertel (center right) attends a reading, National Playwrights Conference, 2010. On his right are Sandy Block and Liz Furze, respectively of Serino Coyne and AKA, both Broadway advertising agencies. Photo by A. Vincent Scarano.

proved successful, and they had followed this by bringing improvisational legend Paul Sills and a company of his players to New York in an offering called *Sills and Company.* Hooked, Viertel continued to put together new projects, off-Broadway and on.

Though he had begun producing, he had little understanding of how theater was built. "I'd been a theatergoer all my life, but I didn't know my way around the theater community to any great extent. I had no serious background, no educational background, nothing." Viertel and Daily took the Whites up on visiting the 1991 Playwrights Conference. Though he enjoyed himself, Viertel doesn't remember thinking much of the plays he saw. "I wasn't used to plays that weren't finished, so I didn't really have perhaps the breadth of thinking about it that I might have."

Viertel returned to the O'Neill in 1993 while involved in the development of a musical based on the Jack Finney novel, *Time and Again,* which featured a book by Viertel's brother Jack and a score by Skip Kennon. He approached Paulette Haupt about bringing it to the Music Theater Conference. Viertel recalls, "I stayed for the whole two weeks while it was being workshopped. *Time and Again* had tricky issues, many of which we were never able to solve. [Critic] Frank Rich came up to see it, because he and my brother were friends. In the pub afterwards, he said to me, 'You know, you don't have an active hero.' I didn't know what he was talking about. I had never thought of musical theater in those kinds of structural terms, but I realized he was right. From that moment on, we knew we had a problem, and we were never able to solve it."

In the process of working there, Viertel "fell in love" with the O'Neill. The following year, 1994, when White asked him to join the board, he immediately agreed. "From that time onward, I was at the O'Neill a good deal of my summer. George and Betsy [White] were kind enough to let us use the little boathouse on their property, which is a wonderful little stone building that looks straight out on the water. (It also looks straight out at the nuclear power plant, but nonetheless, it's a beautiful little spot.) So Pat [Daily] and I used to come up, and we would stay at the boathouse, and it became part of our life." Viertel became chairman of the board in 2000.

In the meantime, Howard Sherman had succeeded White as executive director. Sherman didn't respond to a request to discuss his time at the Center for this book, so the controversies that arose during his stewardship won't be discussed at length here. More than a decade later, though, White still feels that Sherman paid insufficient attention to the community that gives the O'Neill its home. In contrast, Houghton gives Sherman great credit for introducing a new level of discipline to the management of the place.

Houghton arrived in 2000, shortly before Viertel took on the chairmanship. In fact, he spent the summer of 1999 at the Playwrights Conference, Richards's last. Houghton recalls, "Lloyd gave me all sorts of great, sage, wonderful advice in terms of trying to deal with priorities and the nature of the beast itself, nurturing and supporting the writers and the broader community. I had never been to the O'Neill prior to that as a participant or observer."

As per White's hope that he would "see it fresh," Houghton made structural changes. Chief among what he wanted to address was an issue some in the Richards

Howard Sherman (executive director, 2001–2003; left) and 2002 Margo Jones Medal recipient Mel Gussow, 2002. Photo by A. Vincent Scarano.

Playwrights with James Houghton (bottom left), National Playwrights Conference, 2001. (Back row, from left) Victor Lodato, Judy GeBaur, Michael Feingold, Susan Johnston, and Lee Blessing; (third row, from left) Patricia Smith, Adam Rapp, Jeffrey Hatcher, and Karen Hartman; (second row, from left) David Cale, Kirsten Greenridge, Allison Moore, Gina Gionfriddo, and Cusi Cram; (first row, from left) James Houghton, Brooke Berman, Keith Reddin, Dan O'Brien, and Regina Taylor. Photo by A. Vincent Scarano.

era had discussed—the actors and directors regularly invited back were the stable community of the O'Neill. "Not out of anything but goodwill and good intentions, the only outsiders to it were the writers. That had manifested itself to the point where the only people housed on the campus itself were the directors, the administrative staff, and some of the long-term people. And so I flipped that and brought the writers onto campus."

It was a change appreciated by at least one writer. Lee Blessing laughs as he talks about a summer when he and his colleagues were lodged in Seaside Sanatorium, which had a history of being first a tuberculosis clinic and then a mental institution. "It was a building that clearly had been built I think in the nineteenth century. Brick, three or four stories high. Metal gates blocked some of the stairwells. It felt like Shutter Island. Creepy. We were all on the first floor. If you went down to the basement, I'm told you could see equipment that had been used to, uh, help people with mental and emotional problems over the years." Aside from the macabre nature of the lodging, Blessing points out, "We were some miles from the O'Neill itself."

Douglas Post believes that he was there when the facility housed playwrights on the first floor and patients on other floors. The first day the playwrights were there, Kate Robin ventured out to jog. "She got lost, and she flagged down a car, and she said, 'Can you help me? I'm trying to get back to Seaside.' And the people in the car were like, 'Oh sweetheart, just get in the car. We'll get you back to Seaside.' She didn't realize until she was returned that they thought that she was a patient."

Blessing talks about the practical value of moving the writers to home base. "Suddenly, if you had a problem in rehearsal, you could go back to your room, work on it, and come back without wasting a great deal of time. I think people felt that that was really helpful in a practical sense, but even on a subtler plane . . . you know, you felt as though, if this is a *playwrights* conference—" he says, laughing, "—we need to be where it *is*, you know?"

Houghton also changed the approach to inviting directors and actors. "I thought it was important to open the doors to a broader community, because more people should have the experience. That was not to shut people out who had been there before—in fact, while I was there I brought a lot of people back—but to open the doors up more. Finding that equilibrium between having enough people who are seasoned there who can give you a strong foundation, but not so many that they're defining what the experience will be beforehand."

Says Blessing, "Jim [Houghton] had looked around New York for some of the better known and/or hotter young directors. I think he was looking to hook up these

Rehearsal of *Klonsky and Schwartz* in the Barn Theater with (left to right) Mark Blum, Chris Noth, Harris Yulin, and Romulus Linney (playwright), National Playwrights Conference, 2002. Photo by A. Vincent Scarano.

Director Pam MacKinnon (right) works on *Father Joy*, by Sheri Wilner, National Playwrights Conference, 2003. Photo by A. Vincent Scarano.

young playwrights with people who could do the most for them in the long run. I think Lloyd didn't feel that that was as important as running an O'Neill where the problems would be minimized. I benefited, obviously, from my five years in Lloyd's system. There were people I saw there in 1983 that I also saw there in 1999. Jim wanted to open it up. In 2000, we had something like a dozen plays, and we had about a dozen directors, and each play [was] cast [independently]. Somebody would be up for maybe a week rather than a whole month."

Director Pam MacKinnon was invited to Waterford in 2001 because of a play-wright. Gina Gionfriddo was accepted to the Playwrights Conference with *Guine-vere*. She and MacKinnon had enjoyed working together on a project in one of New York's downtown theaters. Richards would probably have assigned Gionfriddo a director of his own choice, but Houghton's view was different. Says MacKinnon, "Jim's response was, 'I believe in supporting good marriages.' He wanted to honor what the playwright requested." Whereas directors under Richards usually came up for the entire Conference, under Houghton, the directors came up only when they were working on their assigned projects. The playwrights, though, continued to be in residence for the whole Conference. MacKinnon also remembers that, on the first day of rehearsal, the playwrights were expected to read their plays to the company. Her writers "were a little bit mortified," but MacKinnon found she valued hearing plays interpreted by their authors, and she has sometimes employed this in her non-O'Neill projects. "Subsequent to that—never in front of actors—I have read plays aloud with writers like Adam Bock. And actually when I was working with Edward

Albee on *The Zoo Story* as act two of what is now called *At Home at the Zoo*. From memory, sitting next to me on a sofa, he talked through Jerry's dog story. You do hear rhythms and at times intent that is sort of ineffable. And with Edward in particular, you can see when there's a twinkle in his eye, and that informs the tone."

MacKinnon's association with Albee began because of someone she met in Waterford. "Michelle Volansky, who was then the literary manager at Philadelphia Theatre Company, was there as a dramaturg. One afternoon we went down to the beach, and she in a very offhand way said that Philadelphia Theatre Company had just gotten the regional premiere rights of *The Play about the Baby*. Would I be interested? And I said, 'Absolutely.'" MacKinnon got the job and soon found herself having her first meeting with Albee over a lunch. "It was the perfect way for a director and a writer to get to know each other." That they had a specific play to talk about made it easier. "In retrospect, it was probably a job interview, but I didn't really think about that until years later." The meeting must have gone well, because Albee kept approving her as director for various productions of his work. One of them, a production of *Who's Afraid of Virginia Woolf?* for Chicago's Steppenwolf Theatre, was so well received that it was brought to Broadway for a run, which led to her winning the 2013 Tony Award for best director. "And that definitely comes from, you know, sitting on that sliver of beach at the O'Neill."

Houghton decided to modify the invitation policy to combine the Richards and White approaches. The bulk of the writers were offered spots on the basis of submitted scripts, but, echoing White's first experiments, Houghton decided to also invite writers he thought would benefit from residencies. "They didn't necessarily have to be there doing a project. I thought they would add to the conversation of the community. The minute I got there, I wrote August a note saying, 'August, you're welcome back at any time.' I think I sent it out snail mail back then. He must have gotten the letter a few days later, and he called me right away. I put a room aside for him, and he came." This was after Wilson and Richards had parted company (see Chapter 8). Wilson worked on *Gem of the Ocean* while in residence, though he didn't have a reading of it there.

Houghton continues, "We also had community meetings after a couple of lunches each week. I would bring anyone from a sculptor to someone of a political persuasion or fellow writers. It was meant to be provocative. It was meant to take this community of really smart, wonderful artists who were all giving so much of themselves and to fuel conversation to spur more context for what we do. You know, in any theater experience, the walls can come closing in on us. Everything that

Kevin Geer and Rebecca Nelson in Victor Lodato's *The Bread of Winter*, National Playwrights Conference, 2001. Geer has acted at the Conference for more than twenty-five years. Photo by A. Vincent Scarano.

happened in those community meetings, no matter what subject matter, was always about theater, but theater is about the things going on in our world. So it was a way to broaden our perspective, to bring other influences in." MacKinnon adds, "It was sort of like a town meeting. It gave us another time, besides mealtime, when we all came together. I thought that was really great."

One might guess that the man who shaped the Conference for decades might have had some issues with the changes, but Houghton insists otherwise. "Lloyd felt like I respected the tradition, that I was carrying it forward [consistent with] the foundation on which the O'Neill stood. He was very complimentary and very generous. And George seemed to be as well. And the board was very supportive." He hesitates, then adds, "As you know, it didn't particularly end well."

The first controversy arose over the submission process. Houghton explains the roots: "There were only, at most, a handful of readers. And in some cases, readers were reading 200 to 400 scripts for the O'Neill. How can someone who's reading over 200 to 400 possibly give a script a full shot with a single read? As disciplined and as good as those readers were, nobody can live up to that." He was also determined to broaden the backgrounds of those involved in reading. Most readers had been drawn from the East Coast; he recruited more people from around the country and cut the number of scripts each was responsible for reading to 25. Each play was read twice, and reports commented on the plot and the themes engaged. The readers also gave the scripts grades, which helped flag works that were potentially controversial. "If there was real disparity between reactions [to] a play, I sent it out for a third read. I wanted to make sure every script was getting a good equal read, and that there were multiple perspectives on it. Not only in terms of, obviously, different readers, but

Rob Morrow (left) and Alvin Epstein rehearse *Tuesdays with Morrie*, adapted by Jeffrey Hatcher, National Playwrights Conference, 2001. Hatcher developed four other plays at the Conference under the tutelage of Lloyd Richards. Photo by A. Vincent Scarano.

different regions of the country that certain issues may be more relevant to—the Southwest versus the Deep South, or the Northwest, or the center of the country, or whatever. [The idea] was to bring the rest of the country to the O'Neill, even if they never stepped foot on the campus. I think at one point I printed a thank-you to everyone who had participated at the O'Neill during my time there. I listed everyone who either was at the Conference or read for the Conference. There were well over 800 to 1,000 names of people, and every region of the country was represented. We were reaching out, and the country was reaching back."

The country was reaching back with more and more candidate works to go through a more expensive open submission process. "At the same time," Houghton says, "George [White], as president of the board, was struggling with the financial aspects of the O'Neill. There was a lot of pressure to address budgetary issues. Then Howard [Sherman] came in [as executive director]. I think what Howard was trying to do was what I was trying to do—which was take this great thing and create an infrastructure that could support it. And the board was working feverishly to do that as well, but were coming up a little short. I needed more resources to continue the reading process the way I had it. And basically what I proposed was taking a year or two-year hiatus on the complete open submission, so that we could kind of right the ship for a few years, get the financial house in order, and then reestablish the open submission."

Taking this step meant justifying it, and Houghton felt that this involved risks to the O'Neill's reputation. "There were things that I felt were confidential. Financial matters. I did not want to upset the entire community or put the infrastructure of the

O'Neill in jeopardy. And so I did one interview for the *New York Times*. That's the only one I would do." In an article dated September 26, 2003, reporter Jason Zinoman quoted him as saying, "I had to make a very tough decision. . . . But the bottom line is that between the bad economy, increased demand and limited resources, we can't sustain open submissions." Instead he proposed a system in which scripts would be nominated by professionals from around the country.

Houghton stresses that he had run the idea by the board, but "they then basically backpedaled once it got controversial and the community had gotten upset about it. There was a big pile-on." For some, to curtail open submissions was to damage part of what made the Playwrights Conference unique.

Most producing organizations—commercial or not—decline a script that is not by a writer known to them or referred by an agent or someone trusted professionally. It was to open up opportunity to new people that Richards established that the Conference was willing to take a look at anything submitted. The irony Houghton faced was that the cost of maintaining open submissions was endangering the financial health of the Conference, and without the Conference the new writers would have less of a chance to move up.

The "big pile on" to which Houghton refers included a *New York Times* article published September 26, 2003, quoting several writers alarmed by the change in policy. Conference veteran Adam Rapp was quoted as saying, "If I wasn't able to submit *Ghosts in the Cottonwoods* in 1996, I never would have become a playwright." Houghton felt that the opposition didn't take into account the urgency of the O'Neill's financial vulnerability, but felt hamstrung by his determination not to offer specifics he thought would be damaging:

James Houghton (left) and August Wilson outside the Hammond Mansion, National Playwrights Conference, 2002. Photo by A. Vincent Scarano.

"I did meet with playwrights privately. Writers who had been at the O'Neill during Lloyd's time talked to me about their concerns. And I went to New Dramatists. August was with me when I went to New Dramatists. He saw that there was a real issue at hand, that I was trying to deal with it in a reasoned way. I didn't allow any press in that New Dramatists meeting. This was to talk to anyone who wanted to come—writer or otherwise—and hear what some of these more confidential aspects were that had no place in the press. It would have hurt the institution, and I had no interest in doing that."

The break came in October 2003. Houghton learned that, during a board meeting, some decisions had been made without his knowledge or input that he felt directly affected his ability to lead the Playwrights Conference as he felt it should be led. "That was unacceptable to me. There are things I would do differently, and I'm hopeful that there's some things the O'Neill would have done differently. I still would have left, because I felt that things were mishandled. I had lost trust in the O'Neill and how they were working with me."

Houghton is at pains to affirm his continuing regard for the O'Neill and his determination, even in leaving, to serve the Conference. Remembering that his early days of orientation were haphazard—picking up information, customs, and practices in a catch-as-catch-can manner—he was determined that those who succeeded him would have a guide to which they could refer. "If all of us got hit by a bus, I wanted there to be a document [so a successor] could walk in and at least go, 'OK, this is how it functioned.' Like for instance, I worked for, I think, two years to figure out how to do the schedule to have multiple readings all at once that dealt with the [scheduling

National Playwrights Conference technical team on break outside Blue Gene's Pub, 2002. Shown (from left) are Travis Walker, Melissa Mizell, Mike Salvas, Jane Cox, Devin Lindow(front right), and Justin McClintock. Photo by A. Vincent Scarano.

of the] air conditioners. When I left, I wanted to be sure—no matter when I left, or how I left—that there was a bible in place."

Houghton has continued to helm the Signature Theatre. Under his leadership, in 2012 the company opened a new complex on the southeast corner of 42nd Street and Tenth Avenue in New York. Like the O'Neill, the complex features multiple stages in varying configurations (three public ones and a fourth for private workshops). The O'Neill has its pub, Blue Gene's, where artists and guests socialize. The Signature has a café and bookstore that offers free WiFi and aims to be a public place where members of the theater community can converse or set up their computers and write. Houghton has also served as the Richard Rodgers Director of the Drama Division of the Juilliard School in Manhattan since 2006, calling to mind Richards's simultaneous positions at the O'Neill and the Yale School of Drama.

The leadership of the Playwrights Conference continued to be problematic. O'Neill veteran J Ranelli was asked to both run the Conference and serve as producing artistic director, supervising all artistic programs. His associate, Richard Kuranda, remembers thinking this was ill advised. "Holy smokes, so many years had passed since he had been involved as a start-up guy with the institution. These programs had evolved into their own unique production and operational models. We didn't have enough space, there wasn't enough money, there wasn't much transparency about the budget. It was a stressful period." Abruptly, Ranelli resigned on the eve of the 2004 Conference. The official explanation was "exhaustion," a characterization Ranelli disputed, telling the *New York Times* the reasons were "entirely professional."

At this point, one of the ideas explored was asking Wendy Wasserstein to step in to run the Playwrights Conference. Critic Frank Rich remembers, "She talked to me about it. If memory serves, her attitude was—even if it was somewhat ceremonial— she did not want to be an administrator of an institution when she had her own work to do." Wasserstein was to make her last visit to the O'Neill campus on October 16, 2004, during which she gave a funny and passionate speech about what the O'Neill meant to her and to the playwriting community. She died on January 30, 2006.

Kuranda was now named interim artistic director for the National Playwrights Conference. In the fall, he was given the title of producing director. "I did not necessarily have a great time there, but I am proud of the work." Theatermakers, the summer program affiliated with the National Theater Institute, began in the summer of 2005, and an attempt was made to begin a Conference for Film and Television Writing with Oz Scott (which didn't make it to a second year). "I was happy we were able to bring J. T. Rogers up off-season to work on *Madagascar*. And I was really happy

Excerpts from Speech at the O'Neill, October 16, 2004

Wendy Wasserstein

The O'Neill to me is certainly one of the most important places in my theatrical history, and I also think in the last half of the twentieth century in American theatrical history.

I'll tell you my personal experiences with the O'Neill. When I got out of the Yale Drama School in 1976, as you know, there are no ads in the NY Times that say "Playwright Wanted"—$80,000 a year plus benefits. I didn't know what to do with my life, and my friend Pat Quinn—who was in my year at the Yale School of Drama—told me her sister Nancy was Lloyd Richards's assistant at the O'Neill Center [winter offices] in New York. And in fact she was the managing director at the O'Neill Center in New York. And [Pat] said, "Why don't I call Nancy, and maybe we can get you a job." So there I was with a Mount Holyoke degree and a degree from Yale School of Drama, and basically I got a job as the messenger girl at the Eugene O'Neill [Theater Center].

And what I did was I delivered all the scripts to the readers for the O'Neill competition, and I took dictation for Lloyd Richards. And I always thought that if Lloyd thinks I know how to take dictation, he deserves the letters I'm sending out. Lloyd would say things, and I would pretend I was Thelma Ritter in a "B" movie and say, "Hey Lloyd, I don't know what you're saying to me, but I'm sure I'll write a lovely note."

I saw in the most intimate way how the O'Neill works, because I was taking the plays to the readers, and I would pick up the plays from the readers and bring them back to the O'Neill. So what I saw was all of these playwrights from across the country were submitting plays, and they were taken seriously. That is an amazing thing. Being a playwright is a very lonely and serious profession. You're alone in your room, you're writing plays. It's not like your parents and the world are saying, "Yes, yes! Be a playwright!"

The O'Neill used to send out form rejections to the playwrights. Well, I felt the need to write personal notes to all the playwrights. "Keep writing." "You're so talented." And then I would sign it "Lloyd Richards." And about four months into these rejections, Lloyd Richards was getting like all of these letters from these playwrights saying, "You're so wonderful, you're so kind." And finally he caught onto me and he said, "What's going on here?!" I said, "Look, you know they're all aspiring playwrights, they need, you know, I'm not saying they were all accepted, but I feel they needed a little boost."

So, that stopped.

But it was a really uplifting experience, because it was not-for-profit, but it was a high regard for . . . the individual voice. I loved working with Lloyd, and I loved working with George White. And I thought their vision was a really excellent one. Because they were setting high standards, and it was all so inclusive. And also Lloyd Richards's commitment to the diversity of voices was one of the strongest in this country, and the one that initiated a lot of change in the theater.

Uncommon Women [and Others] when I was at Yale was just my thesis; it wasn't a big deal. When it was done at the Yale School of Drama, afterwards, there was an after-play discussion, and someone got up and said, "I can't get into this. It's about girls." And I looked at them and said, "I spent my life getting into Robin Hood and Lawrence of Arabia, so why don't you try it?" I submitted it to the O'Neill and I thought, "Well, let's see what happens." And happily, they decided to do it here over the summer. I remember it all so clearly, because Edith Oliver was a dramaturg then, and Edith Oliver came up to me and said, "I went to Smith College. I know what this is." I felt like I had a home and I had a community.

And there was Lloyd Richards, and I have to say Lloyd gave me the best advice about playwriting I ever had. Lloyd said to me, "The actors can feel ambiguous, but you can't feel ambiguous. You have to know where this play is going." And I thought, "That is absolutely right." And I think because

(continued)

> *they took us so seriously, we took our work seriously. So I remember rewriting* Uncommon Women *again and again upstairs in the main house. I would sit there and rewrite. We were all rewriting all the time and taking our work and the work of others very seriously, and interestingly, not competitively. I think you often hear about writers talking about one another or whatever. That didn't happen here. There was actually a real interest in each other's work. From that summer at the O'Neill, I submitted my play to the Phoenix Theatre in New York, and that's why that play was done in New York.*
>
> Uncommon Women *moved on to become one of the most produced plays in American colleges, and certainly a play that, I think, opened up other women playwrights' eyes to the possibility of becoming a playwright. And I think it's all because that play was nurtured here.*
>
> —Wendy Wasserstein

we were able to get back to empowering the artistic directors again." Other new faces appeared on campus, including director Michael Bush to head the regenerated Cabaret and Performance Conference and Wendy Goldberg as new artistic director of the National Playwrights Conference. Then, on August 19, 2005, Kuranda was told that the O'Neill would be undergoing another reorganization, and that his job was being eliminated. Citing a three-year contract that said they were obligated to him through August 21, 2007, Kuranda sued. A settlement was negotiated.

Howard Sherman, too, had left in 2003. Tom Viertel says, "He didn't want any more of it. He couldn't afford adequate staff, so he would literally go out and fix the gardens himself." Sherman moved to a job as executive director of the American Theatre Wing, New York, with Viertel's support.

Viertel picks up the story. "Amy Sullivan had gone to Yale Drama School and had a real passion for the theater. She had been at the O'Neill as a development officer as a young woman and was at the time the development director of the Lyme Art Academy [in Connecticut]. As news of Howard's imminent departure started circulating, Amy came to me unbidden and said, 'I want this job. I love the O'Neill, I grew up at the O'Neill. This is hugely important to me, I want to do this.' And I thought, 'Well, yes, but we should really do a national search and go through this in an ordinary way.' We started to do it [the search], and I realized that it was going to cost us several tens of thousands

Amy Sullivan (executive director, 2003–2006; left) and Zoe Caldwell, recipient of the 2003 Monte Cristo Award, outside the Barn Theater before the award ceremony. Photo by A. Vincent Scarano.

of dollars that we didn't have. I knew Amy was sincere, and I also knew that her fundamental orientation was fundraising, something I desperately needed some lessons in. So I went to the board and said, 'I think we should just pick Amy.'" The board took his recommendation, and she was named executive director in September 2003.

"Amy taught me a lot about fundraising. She had a certain number of people who just funded whatever she did. They funded the Lyme Art Academy because she was there. Once she came to the O'Neill, they funded us. I don't think they had a particular affinity for either that or this, they just believed in Amy. There were four or five of them, and she had made a relationship with them that they were going to support her. I had never heard of such a thing. We ramped up our fundraising really substantially under her in an organized and systematic way.

"Very early into her tenure, she needed a general manager, someone to kind of run the place while she was doing the fundraising. [Producer] Manny Azenberg, who teaches at Duke [University], periodically came to her and said, 'There's this kid who is only twenty-two years old but he's amazing. He produced stuff down here like he was a professional. You've got to look at him if you're willing to take the chance on someone.'

Amy Sullivan

Amy Sullivan was the daughter of a crooner from New Jersey, and O'Neill Center DNA flowed through her veins. Named executive director in September 2003, Amy had previously acted in the National Playwrights Conference for a summer in the mid-1980s, served as director of development from 1992 to 1995, and returned to lead the O'Neill during a financially challenging time for the organization.

Amy Sullivan

Sullivan immediately began a reorganization after her appointment as executive director and sought to maximize collaborative opportunities among the O'Neill programs. Trained at the Lee Strasberg Institute in New York, she brought an artistic understanding to the Center, and reengaged and rebuilt trust among artist alumni. Several lasting legacies of her time include the decision to make the O'Neill's Monte Cristo Award a benefit dinner and move it to New York, rather than keeping it a simple reception in Waterford; lay the groundwork for a summer term of the National Theater Institute, called Theatermakers; and overlap the National Playwrights and National Music Theater Conferences, so that they operated simultaneously—providing vibrancy and new collaborative opportunities for the authors, directors, interns, and audiences.

Early in her tenure, Sullivan hired Preston Whiteway, a young graduate of Duke University, to be the O'Neill's general manager. Like founder George C. White, she believed the O'Neill thrived on youth. Late in 2006, Amy pulled back professionally to fight her breast cancer, and she recommended to the Board that Whiteway be named full-time executive director; he was confirmed in January 2007. Sullivan passed away in June of that year.

—PW

The Hendel Family

Rita and Myron Hendel

Other than the Whites, no family has contributed more to the O'Neill Center's success over generations than the Hendels. Longtime fixtures of the Waterford community, Rita and Myron Hendel first got involved about ten years after the founding of the organization, and Rita quickly joined the board. Through their leadership in philanthropic support, generous terms for fuel oil delivery (one part of the Hendel family business— and important for the O'Neill, given the many antique buildings on campus), and role as ambassadors to local circles, the Hendels helped secure the O'Neill's future on both practical and strategic levels. Rita's passion for the organization was kindled by the National Theater Institute (NTI), and she formed a deep professional friendship with Richard Digby Day, NTI director from 1991 to 1998. The two of them raised the local profile of the O'Neill, which was often better known nationally than it was locally, through public showings, lectures, and concerts.

The family tradition continues, with Rita and Myron's son Stephen and his wife Ruth now serving as the O'Neill's treasurer and vice chair, respectively. Their first date as a couple was at the O'Neill, and they've continued as enthusiastic and expert trustees, helping to expand NTI's and the O'Neill's reach and response to changing landscapes. Their love of theater has led to frequent producing credits in New York, including as originating producers on FELA! (2010 Best Musical Tony Award nominee), as well as to serving on many high-profile boards (Yale School of Drama, Theatre Communications Group, and the Bill T. Jones/Arnie Zane Dance Company). Their artistic home has always been in Waterford, however, and the O'Neill—and the American theater—is the stronger for it.

Steve and Ruth Hendel

—PW

Trustee Rita Hendel and Preston Whiteway in the Sunken Garden, summer 2007.
Whiteway, initially hired in 2004 as general
manager, was named executive director of
the O'Neill in January 2007, at the age of
twenty-five, following Amy Sullivan's resigna-
tion for health reasons. Photo by A. Vincent
Scarano.

And of course we were, because we didn't have much money to spend and this is an isolated world up here. You can't promise people the big lights of Broadway. So we did it. We hired Preston Whiteway, who came in and did a magnificent job as general manager. He looked like he was sixteen, and we just had a marvelous time, the three of us.

"Amy was with us for about three years, and then she got very ill and she had to back off. She had cancer, and she needed periodic treatments for it. The treatments would lay her low . . . anywhere from six weeks to three months, and during those periods of time when there was kind of no way to manage the situation, Preston would just step into the job. So he kind of got used to being the number one guy from time to time. Finally Amy couldn't continue anymore, and she left and passed away about six months later.

"I went to the board this time with much more certainty, and said 'We should simply let Preston do this. I've watched him do it during the time that Amy hasn't been with us, and I think he can do this.' By that time he was twenty-four or twenty-five, so he'd actually grown up a little bit. And so he stepped into the job. He has taken this organization to what I think of as new heights. And that's where we are today in terms of leadership, and it's terrific."

13. National Playwrights Conference — The Goldberg Years

In the 2013 staged reading of Samuel D. Hunter's *A Great Wilderness*, Brian Murray and Christine Estabrook handled a liquor bottle filled with something that could pass for cognac. There was a tomato (standing in for three tomatoes). And there was a jacket, smeared with something suggesting blood. In Lloyd Richards's day, these would not have passed muster with the prop police. But we are in the middle of Wendy Goldberg's days, and she doesn't mind the judicious use of props. (She can also lay claim to having started Samuel D. Hunter's career.)

Wendy Goldberg was a 31-year-old artistic associate at Arena Stage, the landmark regional theater of Washington, D.C., when she was recruited to take on the National Playwrights Conference. At the Arena, she had directed a number of productions and had run its program for the development of new scripts. She had also staged new works at other institutions, including New Dramatists and several non-profit companies.

"I came in in 2005," she says. "Tom [Viertel] called and said, 'I'm going to give you the weekend, but we would like you to do this.'" She came with the opinion that the O'Neill "was a club that I had not received a membership to." She believed that the Conference favored those who had gone to Yale or had endorsing credits

Wendy Goldberg, July 2013. Goldberg has served as artistic director of the National Playwrights Conference since 2005. Photo by A. Vincent Scarano.

in New York, neither of which could be said of her. "I was coming from working in Washington [D.C.]. I hadn't even lived in New York yet when I got this job. So I wanted to open it up. I didn't want it to feel like a secret society. Also, I'm the first artistic director [of the Conference] who doesn't run another theater. It became pretty clear that this place needed full attention. I continue to direct and do other projects, but this is home. I don't think the person who runs the Conference could also run a producing theater [any more]. Producing theaters need so much more [attention] than they ever did, and they also run during the summer."

One way Goldberg went around "opening it up" was to look specifically for voices from elsewhere in the country. That started as soon as she accepted the position. "I think I got the job at the end of March, and then I received the scripts that made it into the finals. I had a month to create a season." She found something of what she was looking for in a script that had already been rejected, called *Norman Rockwell Killed My Father*, written by Hunter when he was a student at the University of Iowa. "Sam was writing about Idaho. I had never quite seen anybody writing about that region in that way, and so I called him and said, 'I know you've been told no, but I'm new and this is what I'd like to do. Would you be interested in coming?'"

This call was particularly welcome, given how discouraging much of Hunter's experience had been. "I had never done anything professional as a playwright. There was a part of me that had listened to all of my playwriting teachers who had this constant mantra of 'You're not going to make it' and 'There is no life in it' and 'You won't find a career' and 'Find a different job.' I feel like every playwriting teacher I had in college told me that."

Hunter wasn't entirely through with discouraging words when he got to the O'Neill. The dramaturg Goldberg assigned to him was Max Wilk. Hunter's first couple of weeks in Waterford were idyllic, going to the beach and seeing a lot of his colleagues' plays. "And then," Hunter recalls, "a few days before my rehearsal

Samuel D. Hunter (playwright; right) and Braden Abraham (director) listen to a rehearsal of *A Great Wilderness*, National Playwrights Conference, 2013. Photo by A. Vincent Scarano.

Roberto Aguirre-Sacasa (playwright; right), Peter DuBois (director; center), and Edward Sobel (dramaturg; left) laugh during *Good Boys and True*, National Playwrights Conference, 2007. DuBois is the artistic director of the Huntington Theatre Company in Boston. Photo by A. Vincent Scarano.

week, Max and I had our first meeting, and I remember he told me that my second act wasn't worth two cents. He said, 'I don't understand what the characters are doing.' So that night, I rewrote the entire second act. I left it at Max's door. The next morning, I'm waking up and all of the sudden Max appears in my doorway. 'You rewrote the entire . . .? You actually did something and it got better.' And for that week and a half, Max and I just tore the play apart. I had never torn apart a play before. I had never rewritten a play. In that young way, I just wrote a lot of plays. And they were all flawed, and they were student plays." Hunter doesn't claim that at the end of his work at the O'Neill *Norman Rockwell* was a successful piece. "It's not like this turned into a great American play. It was still a very young, very flawed play, but I learned more than I think I learned in any of the two grad school programs that I attended. I learned more from that week of just tearing apart a play with Max Wilk."

Norman Rockwell Killed My Father may not have been the play that would establish Hunter's reputation, but it started him on the path. His *A Bright New Boise* won an Obie Award in 2011, and the Playwrights Horizons production of *The Whale* was one of the critical successes of the New York 2012–2013 season and was subsequently produced successfully around the country.

Hunter is one of the flood of playwrights who have trained in graduate programs, but Goldberg isn't married to the idea that writers must come through the academic track. Hilary Bettis never went to college and claims that finishing high school was a chore. She fell in love with theater as a child growing up in Michigan and discovered there was nothing she preferred to sitting in a room and writing.

Anne Morgan, now the literary manager at the O'Neill, is one of the reasons Bettis was invited. Goldberg asks fellow members of the selection committee, "If there's one [play] you would fight for, really fight for, what is it?" Morgan fought for *Alligator* for the 2012 season, and Goldberg assigned her to be Bettis's dramaturg.

Bettis wrote *Alligator* after completing two relatively simple plays. "I get really bored easily. So I decided to write a play that broke all the rules of playwriting. I didn't care if it never got produced." Bettis was spending much of her time in "dirty rock clubs," aware that, though her friends would happily attend live music performances, few of them came to readings of her plays or went to the theater in general. "They didn't have that sort of visceral reaction to theater like they did with live rock. So I started looking up plays that were structured with music. I sort of fell in love with Greek plays and the structure of the choral lyric and operas as well, the different

Elizabeth Moreau (production stage manager; left), Wendy Goldberg (director; center), and Wendy MacLeod (playwright; back) rehearse *Thrash*, in Goldberg's first season as artistic director, National Playwrights Conference, 2005. Goldberg is the first artistic director of the Conference to direct a play each season. Photo by A. Vincent Scarano.

Alan Ruck (well known from the film *Ferris Bueller's Day Off*) during an early rehearsal of *The Language Archive*, by Julia Cho, National Playwrights Conference, 2009. Roundabout Theatre Company later produced the play. Photo by A. Vincent Scarano.

movements, and so this play became like prose with this band, but it's set up like a choral lyric, and there's a talking alligator."

Though Bettis and Hunter come from substantially different backgrounds, Goldberg notes something *Alligator* has in common with Hunter's work. "I felt as I did when I read Sam's play about Idaho—that no one had really dug in there yet."

Director Davis McCallum feels that his job is not only to serve the play but also to serve the playwright, particularly new and uncertain ones, such as some of the writers Goldberg invites, who have never been in a professional situation before. "I did have a playwright who had just graduated from Juilliard—or maybe she was still at Juilliard. It was her first time working with professional actors, and so I felt protective of her, making sure that she doesn't take in too much opinion about her play all at once, so she could maintain confidence in what she had written." As it happened, the first day her play was read, a group of playwrights from other MFA programs were visiting. "So there was this really young playwright and then there were like fifty other young playwrights watching her play. I sat right next to her, trying to bolster her through." Happily, the reading went well. "All of those playwrights were there to congratulate her at the pub afterwards as she was pinning her program up." (An O'Neill tradition now involves the pinning up of programs in Blue Gene's after the first performance of a project.)

More of the underexplored territory Goldberg looks for came courtesy of Julia Cho. "She was interested in exploring the first- and second-generation Korean-American experience in the desert [in the area of] Phoenix, Arizona, writing about three separate families and how they were connected. She called [the plays] *The Desert Trilogy. Durango* [the last work in the trilogy] is a play that everyone had passed on. She had already put it out there, and nobody was biting. Here she has [the opportunity] to rewrite and restructure and rethink . . . the play. Gordon Edelstein [of Long Wharf Theatre, New Haven] came up and saw it and fell in love with it." Ultimately, Long Wharf and the Public Theater collaborated on producing the play. "Both institutions had said no to the piece [in its earlier form]. Obviously she was able to do what she had to do to move it to the next level. Then Julia came back through the open submissions with *The Language Archive*, which was her first play that wasn't about Korean-Americans. It ended up winning the Susan Smith Blackburn Prize and getting produced at Roundabout [Theatre Company, New York]."

Goldberg talks about finding what she feels is the right mix for a season. In so doing, she considers "where people are in their careers, their age, their ethnicity, where they come from. I don't ever want it to feel like we have one singular aesthetic.

I think there are a lot of stories. I think about it [representing] a national conversation about what I think we should be talking about."

The National Playwrights Conference was born during the contentious sixties, and the issues of the time spilled onto the Waterford stages. Plays produced at the O'Neill still tend to belong mostly to the "theater of revolt" class, challenging the values and assumptions of the audience, but Goldberg notes that she perceives a lag between when political issues arise in the public conversation and when they make their way to the scripts she sees. "I do think that in terms of overtly political writing, it seems to take a little longer for us to respond to events. I remember thinking when we went to war with Iraq, 'Where are those plays?' It took us a little while."

She reaffirms her commitment to the open submissions process. Of the eight plays that typically are chosen for Conferences these days, "at least six—if not seven—come from the process. The open submissions tell you what stories need to be told right now." In memory of O'Neill alum Wendy Wasserstein (the two Wendies were friends and colleagues), and with the benefit of a generous donation from Meryl Streep, executive director Amy Sullivan established the Wendy Wasserstein Fund in 2006, "an endowment," Goldberg stated in a speech, "that will ensure the open submissions program in perpetuity." "It's an incredibly expensive process to maintain," she says. "When you get a thousand scripts, it's difficult to make sure that nothing slips through the cracks." Alumni of the Conference who submit to it have one advantage:

First presentation of David West Read's *The Dream of the Burning Boy*, in the Edith Oliver Theater, National Playwrights Conference, 2010. *Burning Boy* would be premiered the following season in New York by the Roundabout Theatre Company. Photo by A. Vincent Scarano.

they skip the first round of readers and get what is called a "priority read." "I want to continue to discover new people, but at the same time maintain it [the Conference] as an artistic home for people who have come through there. It's a big balancing act."

Anybody new in an administrative post is going to look at the assumptions and practices of predecessors, embrace some, and react against others. Goldberg decided not to revert to the Richards days and mandate post-show public conversations about the plays. "I'd heard all kinds of things about these sessions during Lloyd [Richards's time]. Certainly a lot of the audience was really engaged and loved them. But I don't think we need to engage the audience in that way. Unlike at a producing theater, where you have to get people excited about a new play, we're more artist focused. I do ask the writers if they'd like to have [a critique]. And if they want to have one, I will facilitate the dialogue. My first year, I think we had a couple of them, and later one more. And that was it. The writers feel they are getting what they need."

Among the challenges that Richards didn't have to deal with is the explosion of social media. "Everybody's on Facebook, everyone's on Twitter. If you want to say, 'Come see this reading' on Facebook and Twitter, that's one thing." But comments on the work? "We have a no-Facebook, no-Twitter policy. We have to have that. These plays are at the very beginning of their lives. The idea is for the writers to live in an environment of safety."

Where Facebook, Twitter, and the rest have started appearing on campus is in the plays by some of the younger writers. They have grown up in geography never

Lisa Peterson (director) and Jennifer Haley (with pencil) during the first read-through of Haley's *The Nether*, National Playwrights Conference, 2011. *The Nether* won the 2012 Susan Smith Blackburn Prize for best play in the English language written by a woman. It was produced by the Center Theatre Group in Los Angeles in 2013. Photo by A. Vincent Scarano.

Rehearsal for *Leveling Up*, by Deborah Zoe Laufer, in the Rose Barn, National Playwrights Conference, 2011. Photo by A. Vincent Scarano.

imagined by such wanderers as Eugene O'Neill, Tennessee Williams, and Lanford Wilson—the world of the internet and cyberspace. Goldberg observes that these younger writers have "been looking at technology and virtual communication, and how that has both helped and harmed us as a culture. We're spending so much of our time in an alternate universe, the virtual world has now co-opted reality. I would say that has been a huge concern of writers right now."

The Nether by Jennifer Haley (presented at the 2011 Conference) starts deceptively with what looks like a standard interrogation from a cop show. Soon we are into a tale in which a webmaster runs a site in which murderous and pedophilic fantasies are indulged. Is a crime possible if it takes place not in the real world but in an increasingly persuasive constructed one? This disturbing view of a plausible near future was warmly received in its premiere in Los Angeles in 2013 and won Haley the Susan Smith Blackburn Award.

Another play Goldberg cites as engaging this subject matter is *Leveling Up* by Deborah Zoe Laufer. Goldberg describes the play: "Four gamers live in a house in Nevada, in Las Vegas, where they just graduated from college. They don't have jobs. They're trying to make ends meet, but they're addicted to video games. One of them is really good. He ends up being recruited by the NSA to do drone warfare. And it's about how he thinks it's just a game. 'I can do it, it's fine.' And then you see what happens to him recognizing that it is real and his not being equipped to deal with it."

The pretend violence of the video game has led to his complicity in the shedding of real blood.

Goldberg directed *Leveling Up*, and that she staged a play at the Conference marks another contrast with the Richards model. Whereas Richards thought that he needed to maintain objectivity by not directing at Waterford, Goldberg says, "I felt like I needed to put myself as an artist inside the process. As a director who works on a lot of new plays and develops new plays all over the country and who created a model for new play development at a producing organization, I wanted to figure out—What worked? What didn't work? Was it enough time? Was it not enough time? Who else do we need in the room? And thinking about what's the best way to handle rewrites. What works for us, and what takes up too much time?" She thinks that being inside the process has been key to administering the process. "Although I obviously have a great interest in arts management, I've always been a director. I try to do both equally in terms of putting myself in the artist's seat in the process but then spend the rest of my time really curating and helping to develop everyone else's work."

As carefully as Goldberg plans, sometimes the unplanned inevitably requires some scrambling. Adam Bock remembers, "I was a last-minute replacement for a playwright who wasn't able to attend." The play that was pulled had included Jayne Houdyshell in its cast. Bock's play, *The Receptionist,* is a dark comedy about unsettling doings in the office of a business involved in unsavory matters. The title character seemingly wields power in her small domain, but during the course of the play . . . well, that would spoil the secret of the play. But Bock needed a receptionist, and Goldberg wondered if Houdyshell would be suitable. "I said, 'Yes, please!'" Bock recalls. "The receptionist is a character who is tied to a location. She couldn't leave her desk, so I needed to know whether I could have someone so bound to a spot and still have a play, because really, she couldn't be farther than the phone." He found that the conceit did work, not the least because of Houdyshell's virtuosity even in physically limited circumstances. Of the experience, Bock says, "It was quick and dirty and really fast; it was a little shocking actually. It was good." Houdyshell stayed with the play when it was produced at Manhattan Theatre Club in 2007, and the performance was among the most praised of the season.

Though Goldberg likes to keep business talk off the grounds for the bulk of the Playwrights Conference, one of her innovations comes at the end of the session, when she addresses the possible futures of the works that have been seen that summer. "The very last two days of the Conference, I have a slew of meetings, and we talk about where the plays can go. I work with the agents very closely and try to pick

up the phone, figure out what theater company might be interested in this work. We try to do a lot of that beforehand. I try to figure out who's going to be the best director and dramaturg and who [will] take the play forward. I'll think about the region of the country that the story might make more sense for the first time out. And then I work all through the season to try to help put these plays into production."

Goldberg also endorses more flexibility in presentation than the previous tendency toward a "house style." "In the past, you basically were staging the play in four days. If a play is ready for that and wants to do that, we have that ability. But if it's never been read aloud in front of an audience, maybe we should not really think about the physicality of it. Maybe for that play we should just hear the words. Every play comes to us at a different place. Every play needs different things."

Invitations to individuals, as reported in previous chapters, began when George C. White started the Playwrights Conference and James Houghton extended an invitation each season during his tenure. Goldberg continues the tradition by offering a room on campus to those she thinks could benefit from the visit. One of these individuals was Lynn Nottage, who, when asked for a comment on her experience, wrote, "I was working on *Ruined* when I was in residence at the O'Neill. It was extremely hot which helped create the tropical atmosphere." *Ruined* went on to be produced around the country and won the Pulitzer Prize for Drama in 2009. Another Goldberg "pick" was Quiara Alegría Hudes, who won the Pulitzer Prize in 2012 for *Water by the Spoonful,* part of a trilogy she is writing. Goldberg invited Hudes to the O'Neill in 2011 to work on another play in the trilogy, called *The Happiest Song Plays Last.* (Hudes, of course, had some prior experience with the O'Neill from her work

(*above left*) O'Neill general manager Jill Anderson (left) and National Playwrights Conference lighting designer Raquel Davis in Blue Gene's Pub, 2009. Photo by A. Vincent Scarano. (*above right*) Marin Ireland performs in *Bird in the Hand*, by Jorge Ignacio Cortiñas, National Playwrights Conference, 2006. Photo by A. Vincent Scarano.

on *In the Heights* in the Music Theater Conference—see Chapter 10.) *Happiest Song* was done as part of another of Goldberg's initiatives: occasionally collaborating with a nonprofit company on a play in which that company has a particular interest. *Happiest Song* was one of several associations with the Goodman Theatre of Chicago during Goldberg's administration.

The Goodman's artistic director, Robert Falls, had known Goldberg as a freelance director with whom he had never quite gotten around to working. When she became artistic director of the Conference, she told him of her idea to collaborate with producing organizations and asked whether he had an appropriate piece to propose. Says Falls, "We happened to have a play at that time that we were very serious about by a writer named Ifa Bayeza. *The Ballad of Emmett Till.* It clearly needed a lot more sort of dramaturgical work, and at that point we were not in a position, for a couple of reasons, to do a workshop or to assemble a cast [at the Goodman]. [Wendy] read the play and responded very strongly, and that led to kind of a first collaboration." *Emmett Till* was included in the Conference of 2007. Says Falls, "The Goodman did provide some financial support, so there was a sort of a collaboration on that level. [Director] Kate Whoriskey worked on it at the O'Neill. Tanya Palmer was the

Reading of Ifa Bayeza's *The Ballad of Emmett Till* in the Dina Merrill Theater, National Playwrights Conference, 2007. Daniel Breaker stands at the center, and Colman Domingo walks on the right. Both would later star in *Passing Strange* on Broadway. Photo by A. Vincent Scarano.

dramaturg. They did great work on it, and it was subsequently produced in 2008 in a production directed by Oz Scott." This play turned out to be the first in a series that the Goodman worked on in association with the Conference.

One can't help but wonder what the O'Neill could provide that the Goodman, one of the larger and most successful nonprofit companies in the country (and one based in a town with a reputation for dynamic theater), felt it couldn't. Falls responds, "I think *Emmett Till* might have had a month of residency at the O'Neill, which was considerably longer than most workshops that we've done. Clearly we do commissions and, of course, we do readings in house. I think the Goodman has a pretty good record: when we commission and workshop, those projects tend to get on stage. We don't do like a lot of theaters that put money into workshops and then can sort of say on grant proposals that they are developing all these new plays, but [don't mention they're] not actually producing them. We have ended up producing most of the plays that we've either invested in through workshops or through commissions. The relationship with the O'Neill is a way to continue to work on them. To give playwrights the opportunity to just spend even more time under different circumstances." Three of the plays the Goodman and the O'Neill have worked together on have ended up scheduled for full production in Chicago: *Emmet Till*, Regina Taylor's *Magnolia*, and Hudes's *The Happiest Song Plays Last*.

The presentation of *Magnolia* was unusual in that Regina Taylor directed her own script. Taylor seems surprised when told that she is the only person in the history of the Conference who has been given the opportunity to direct her own play. As an associate artist at the Goodman (she is also well known as an actor), she has a history of staging her own writing and, at the time of our conversation, was preparing to direct her play *stop. reset.* for James Houghton's Signature Theatre. "I write for actors, and I feel I have a common language with actors." Whatever changes there have been in the Conference, as she describes her experience in Waterford, her words could be those of most other writers who have worked there over the years. "The O'Neill gives you time for contemplation. I love traversing the grounds—the main house, the Barn, the beach. You have the opportunity to be alone or to have great conversations with other wonderful artists. An essential part in creating new pieces is to be able to disconnect if you need to and really deeply think about the piece that you're working on. To carve out that time away from your usual life, in which you can fabricate a lot of interruptions."

One reason for the lack of interruptions at the O'Neill is its notoriously lousy cell phone reception. Through trial and error, some have found a few places on the

Carey Perloff (director; standing), Martin Kettling (dramaturg), and Lucy Caldwell (playwright) rehearse *Guardians,* National Playwrights Conference, 2007. Perloff is artistic director of the American Conservatory Theater in San Francisco and has also attended the Conference as a playwright. Caldwell was part of the O'Neill's Irish playwright program. Photo by A. Vincent Scarano.

campus where, if you don't move too much from side to side, you can occasionally grab a signal. Though writers at the Conference may be writing about the internet, for various technical reasons, WiFi service is also less than robust. On breaks during meals and between rehearsals, the attempts by scores of people to try to connect through their computers and devices frequently overwhelm the system. Though participants at the O'Neill hardly languish in a cone of silence, the lack of instant, easy access to the world outside the campus helps the artists there maintain focus. The recent introduction of WiFi to the campus, however, spelled the death of a beloved tradition. Well, a tradition, anyway.

Raquel Davis recalls the days when, every morning during the Conference, everyone gathered before breakfast for a meeting to talk about the day's agenda. An incentive to be on time involved the skunk cap. "It was this baseball cap that had a skunk tail attached to the back of it. And every morning it was given out to a person who had to be on skunk patrol." If a skunk were found in a room, it was that person's job to encourage the skunk to leave. "This is how people were encouraged to be prompt—the last person in the door got the cap." With the introduction of more or less functional WiFi, an e-mail report could be sent out each evening at about 11 p.m., obviating the need for the morning meetings. No morning meetings, no investiture of the skunk cap.

Davis has a more elevated responsibility than the keeper of skunk lore. She is the resident lighting designer. The relaxing of the prop police betokens a general relaxation of the strictures under which readings were done in the Richards days. "Actually, all areas of design have a little more leeway now. All of us were more interested in what we needed to flesh out for the playwright and for the director. Still keeping it in the world of rehearsal, making sure everyone understood that we're not anywhere near production, but the scenery and the props do not need to be battleship gray and do not need to be cubes that represent something else. If the scene takes place on a couch and we've got a couch on campus that they like, we haul it into the theater." Davis doesn't recall any reports of White weeping for the loss

Rosie Cruz (production manager) hangs lights in the Amphitheater, National Playwrights Conference, 2009. Photo by A. Vincent Scarano.

Raquel Davis (lighting designer) at a Dream Design meeting on the Farmhouse porch, National Playwrights Conference, 2006. Photo by Brian Hashimoto.

of the concept of cubes, and in fact, the concept hasn't been retired entirely. "We use the mods to suggest walls sometimes, or if they need something that can easily transform from being a bed to a table to a phone booth, then we might bring a large mod out and then in the scene changes stand it up, lie it down, stand it on its side. But we haven't had that many of those kinds of plays in the last few years that want that kind of rapid-fire changing of location across the entire stage. Instead we seem to have pockets. Like this area of the stage represents this place, and this area on stage represents somewhere else. We tend to not do as much shifting around anymore." Davis's lighting is particularly useful for defining different playing areas when there is a paucity of conventional set pieces available.

As Goldberg was finishing her ninth season (and anticipated having her tenth land on the fiftieth anniversary of the O'Neill Center), she paused to review. "I had the luxury of having a legacy that I inherited of the way in which one develops a play. But at the same time, all around the country, every theater has some form of new play development program, and I wanted to figure out how we could continue to be relevant. We had to be relevant."

Goldberg believes that one thing that makes the O'Neill process distinct from those of other theaters is the continuing commitment to Skip Mercier's concept of the "dream design" process. Set designer Rachel Hauck finds herself in the situation of maintaining a tradition she knew of only by report. "The job was described to me as this conversation of speaking directly to the playwright about what the world of their play could look like, and how the play would move. This is the dream design conversation. That is the most important thing I do all summer—those eight conversations.

(*above*) Jeremy Cohen directs Jayne Houdyshell in Adam Bock's *The Receptionist*, National Playwrights Conference, 2006. The play would be produced by Manhattan Theatre Club in 2007, starring Houdyshell. Both Cohen and Bock are National Theater Institute alumni as well. Photo by A. Vincent Scarano. (*left*) Rachel Hauck (set designer) leads a Dream Design discussion on the Farmhouse porch, National Playwrights Conference, 2006. Photo by Brian Hashimoto.

"Normally, in production, you would have this conversation with the director about how you're going to take the ideas and the locations and the realities in the play and put them on stage. You don't want writers to worry about that too much. The writer's perspective is always welcome and invited and encouraged, but when it comes to the actual production decisions, those often happen between the director and the designer. And then you re-invite the writer into the conversation.

"The difference with the dream design conference is that, though the director and the dramaturg are there, we ask them not to speak but just to listen to the conversation as it happens between the writers and the designers. The writers are so used to imagining this world but not actually needing to answer the specific details of it, that they often will say, 'I don't know what it looks like.' And I'll say, 'Well, when I imagine your world, this is what I imagine.' And I'll turn to my peers, the other designers, and say, 'Do you guys agree, disagree?' Maybe I'll say, 'I think it's blue.' And the writer says, 'Oh it's definitely not blue, it's red.' 'OK, tell me why, because this is why I thought it was blue.'

"The writer is so used to looking at the play from the intense focus of character, motive, moment to moment. Designers look at a script from the back and the side, largely in terms of texture and color and mood and emotion. So it's a very intimate, but different, look at the play than they've seen." The conversations may trigger changes or clarifications in the text. "Sometimes as soon as the first reading the next morning. Usually, in small things, clarifications. And sometimes the results of that conversation are longer term.

"The plays are in process, so much of what we're doing is speaking to the writers about what the world of their play could look like. If I were actually going to design the play after having had that conversation, the first step for me would be to do

Keith Reddin (playwright) and Rachel Hauck (set designer) discuss the design for *Acquainted with the Night*, at Reddin's Dream Design, National Playwrights Conference, 2011. Photo by A. Vincent Scarano.

Participants in Theatermakers, the summer course in the undergraduate National Theater Institute (NTI), rehearse in the Amphitheater, 2010. Bringing the NTI into the summer professional season allows the students to meet with and be mentored by hundreds of working theater professionals; it also allows the professionals to see the students' work. Photo by A. Vincent Scarano.

that research. I feel like it's so valuable to hand the writers that research—just the imagery that would further inform the design. I'm not trying to answer the design of the production, but rather . . . [offer an] initial impulse." Whereas in the days of Fred Voelpel the audience would be offered a rendering to suggest what a set would look like, Hauck and her team like to post a selection of what their research has uncovered. "Just an idea of what the set *could* look like, to help them imagine it.

"When I first took the job, I couldn't believe it when I heard that Skip had done it for seventeen years. And now I totally understand, because it's the thrill of a lifetime to have those conversations with playwrights when they're at that point."

Goldberg's arrival also triggered a shift in the relationship between the Playwrights Conference and the other programs at the O'Neill. She swiftly came to the conclusion that "all the programs needed to be talking to each other in a deep way, in a way that I'm fairly certain did not happen before my time here. In order to survive we had to economize and put everybody together, and it ends up that that model was incredibly valuable for us artistically. We could all learn from each other, we could all actually speak to each other. It didn't feel like there were separate things happening." Goldberg speaks of the added benefit of having students present during the summer, seeing it as an extension of the Center's mission. "We are only a professional organization for a few months of the year; the rest of the time we are training theater artists.

"Amy Sullivan and I realized that the Playwrights Conference had to commit to the National Theater Institute in the summer, and I had to be a constant presence in the teaching throughout the year. Certainly Lloyd [Richards] taught in the National Theater Institute, but there was never a summer program." The result was the creation

Dina Merrill

Stage and screen icon Dina Merrill has served on the board of trustees since 1980. The daughter of Wall Street baron E. F. Hutton and cereal heiress Marjorie Merriweather Post, Merrill enjoyed a film career alongside Elizabeth Taylor, Cary Grant, Katherine Hepburn, and others, including films such as Butterfield 8, Desk Set, *and* Operation Petticoat. *In 1991, with husband Ted Hartley, she acquired RKO Pictures, and together they have successfully remade several films (*Mighty Joe Young*) and transitioned others to the stage (*Top Hat*).*

Dina Merrill

At the O'Neill, Merrill has been a high-profile advocate and philanthropist for the O'Neill's mission of discovering and nurturing new talent for the stage. In 1998, the Barn El, the largest indoor performance space at the Center, was renamed in her honor. Her generosity, creative spirit, and board leadership will benefit the O'Neill for years to come.

—PW

of the Theatermakers program mentioned in Chapter 6. "What I love is that we have this broad range of young people here who are from all walks of life. We've also deepened our commitment to . . . the Kennedy Center's American College Theater Festival program. The fellows who are working in the various departments—lighting fellows, sound fellows—come from schools all over the country, and the Kennedy Center's helping by giving them scholarships to be here and work for us."

Goldberg summarizes the challenge as "trying to honor the enormous legacy but also move forward. I think that there's been a renewed sense of excitement about what's happening here for funders. I know they're excited that work continues to get better and better and has the capacity to move into world premiere productions after being here."

From the perspective of the playwrights, the Conference continues to provide an environment conducive to doing the work. Ken Weitzman wrote in an e-mail of

Night life in Blue Gene's Pub after a performance, summer 2011. Photo by A. Vincent Scarano.

his experience in 2012 working on his play, *Reclamation*. "We get two readings, as does every play. Between reading one and two I make a very major change that reverberates through the entire script. Saturday morning after the Friday night read, I (and the crack literary staff) bring in a large stack of new pages. Upon seeing this enormous stack of new pages that needed to be incorporated and rehearsed in just the two hours of rehearsal we got that day, my director Lisa Peterson and dramaturg Martin Kettling stare at the pages, then up at me, then break into applause. As do my very generous, brave actors. Lisa and Martin, as O'Neill veterans, venture to claim that I set the unofficial record for the greatest number of pages written/revised in-between the two readings."

Oh yes, Weitzman also participated in his first live karaoke, singing "Twist and Shout," which, he adds, "I now feel was a huge cop out of a song. I continue to imagine myself singing songs that I was not brave enough to attempt at the time."

Executive director Preston Whiteway observes that the works chosen for the Playwrights Conference by Goldberg have tended to fare well in their post-Conference lives. "Seven of the eight plays from the 2011 season have been put up for full productions around the country. That's an extraordinary record, comparable to the 'classic' days of the seventies and eighties."

The "classic" days and the man who was their chief architect were remembered in a memorial celebration on the Hammond Estate campus. Richards died

Lloyd Richards Memorial

Executive director Preston Whiteway remembers, "We did it on Sunday, July 29, 2007, in conjunction with the barbecue that Tom Viertel hosts every summer, so that it would be a happy day. Many of the artists who came were people who hadn't been to the O'Neill for ten years, so we wanted to welcome them back with laughter and song and good food.

"As it was my first summer as executive director and my fourth summer at the O'Neill, I didn't yet know every individual who should be invited, so I asked five or six people to help me plan the event—Bill Partlan, Amy Saltz, Scott Richards, Marsue Cumming, Mary McCabe (who had been an assistant to Lloyd), and Jeffrey Hatcher.

"I opened the remarks. I played a voice greeting from Michael Douglas talking about how much Lloyd had meant to him and the start of his career. Then, I introduced Wendy Goldberg. This happened during her third summer with us, and it was the first time she was meeting some of the people who had worked with Lloyd for years, so I wanted to underscore the continuity of the program.

"Jeffrey Hatcher wrote a ten-minute spoof of the critique sessions, with different alumni playing the different kinds of iconic people who would show up for those sessions. One was 'The Old Lady with a Hat Whom Nobody Knows' played by Tandy Cronyn. Somebody else played 'The Firebrand.' And through it all, there was an empty chair onstage with sunglasses like Lloyd's. As you might expect from Jeffrey Hatcher, it was equal parts poignant and hilarious."

Some of the tributes at the memorial were culled from ones given at events honoring Richards during his lifetime. One of them was a piece by August Wilson. There was some behind-the-scenes debate as to whether, given the subsequent estrangement of the director and playwright, it was appropriate to read the Wilson comments, but to speak of Richards without highlighting his most memorable artistic partnership would have left a palpable vacuum. (Indeed, in 2013, when WNYC, the New York public radio station, produced audio versions of the August Wilson Century Cycle, it scheduled ancillary panels, and the first was called "The Lloyd Richards Effect.")

August Wilson's comments began, "In the old days, in ancient Greece, in Africa and China, and all over the world, when you wanted to learn something, you left your village, your town, your hamlet, and went to sit at the feet of the master of what you wanted to learn. In 1982, I left my home in St. Paul, and came to . . . sit at the feet of Lloyd Richards. It was crowded. But I made a little space for myself and sat down. I came to learn about theater and in the process learned so much more."

Following some more introductory remarks by Wilson, a playlet by Wilson was performed. It took place at "6 p.m., Thursday, October 20, 1988," in "Reaves Barbershop, New Haven, Connecticut." The scene featured Reaves and two friends, L.D. and Thompson. L.D. mentions that he's going to miss a big ball game, because he has something else to do. "They having a big banquet for this Richards fellow up at Yale. I'm gonna go see what they doing up there." Thompson at first doesn't know to whom L.D. is referring.

L.D. says, "Richards. Lloyd Richards. . . . He a big man. I shook his hand once. . . . They having some big to-do up there for him. They having a banquet and all kinds of people coming from all over to take off their hats to him. I'm going up there to take off mine. The man done made all kinds of accomplishments with the theater and television and whatnot. They got him running part of the school up there. Colored fellow. Running part of Yale University. See now, most time they don't let us do nothing like that. But this Richards fellow, he come on through. He didn't start at the top. He come on through . . . did a little bit of this, a little bit of that. I hear tell he was a waiter at one time. . . . He was living in New York, waiting tables, hanging out with Sidney Poitier. That's before Sidney Poitier got to be a star. It was Lloyd Richards helped to make him one. Of course now, he had some talent . . . you can't get blood from a turnip . . . but they was up there together. Living at the YMCA . . . splitting hot dogs. He take one half and Sidney take the other."

L.D. continues to talk about "this Richards fellow" (a phrase that was also the title of the playlet). L.D. says of him, "[He can] go out to meet life knowing he feel right with himself. He can go anywhere and sit with his back to the door. He ain't like Wild Bill Hickock. He can sit with his back to the door and be relaxed. He can sit down and be real comfortable, 'cause he know he ain't done nobody wrong. Now ain't many men can say that. Ain't many men can sit with their back to the door. The kind of man Lloyd Richards is come along every once in awhile. You got to wait till God get up out of bed on his good side and catch the devil sleeping. That's when you come up with somebody like this Richards fellow."

Left to right, Najla Said, Armando Riesco, and Demosthenes Chrysan in *The Happiest Song Plays Last*, by Quiara Alegría Hudes, National Playwrights Conference, 2011. The play was premiered at the Goodman Theatre in Chicago in 2013 and mounted by Second Stage in New York in 2014. Hudes won the Pulitzer Prize for Drama in 2012 for another play in her trilogy. Photo by A. Vincent Scarano.

on his eighty-seventh birthday on June 29, 2006, and the following summer, friends, colleagues, and collaborators filled the Dina Merrill Theater to celebrate his life and accomplishments. Having honored the memory of its founding artistic director with this ceremony, the next day Wendy Goldberg and the Conference honored his memory by continuing his work.

14. Beyond Waterford

The 1960 TV production of *The Iceman Cometh*, with Jason Robards re-creating his stage performance as Hickey, offered the young Robert Redford one of his earliest major roles as the guilt-ridden Don Parritt. This and the desire to better understand his Irish background led him to want to learn more about Eugene O'Neill. Reading about Doc Ganey's Second Story Club in New London, and knowing that his grandfather, Charles Redford, had been a violinist in the local theaters and was likely a member, he asked the old man the logical question. Redford recalls, "He was reluctant to get into it." Redford showed him a picture of O'Neill. "I said, 'Now look at this guy. You were there at the same time.'" Charles finally conceded that he indeed had known Eugene, and that he also had run into Eugene's brother, Jamie. But he still wasn't forthcoming with details beyond a comment that Jamie was "a bum."

Robert Redford returned to New London in the early eighties. He was there to consult with the son of the Italian-American girl who once worked on the other side of Main Street from where his grandfather had bent elbows with the O'Neill brothers. Redford had an idea to start an organization that could do for filmmakers what George C. White's organization had done for dramatists.

Robert Redford with George C. White, 1980. Photo by A. Vincent Scarano.

"George had put together a process and a structure with the O'Neill that I thought could be applied to film. We started to talk. There was little to no support for the idea of starting this idea with independent film. There was no money in the till. George came in as one of the first board members. That's my big connection to George. He was instrumental in translating the O'Neill project into the Sundance Film Lab Project."

Though there were various sightings of Redford at the Waterford campus (director Robert Falls remembers that, when visiting the O'Neill as a young man, he once heedlessly barreled down the stairs of the Hammond Mansion and literally knocked Redford to the floor), he didn't clock many hours there. "I was not that much of an observer in the actual process. I didn't have time; I was working as a filmmaker. I was basically taking that structure and converting it with George's help. It started with George and the O'Neill. [Sundance is] just sort of an offshoot of this. [The O'Neill] was there first, and it was the original concept that we keyed off of."

The similarities go beyond shared process. As discussed in the first chapter, when White began the O'Neill, many communities had scant representation in mainstream theater. Redford noticed a similar lack of diversity in Hollywood films.

"What attracted me to the O'Neill concept was just that. Way back in my life, I realized that I was going to be committed to doing whatever I could with whatever success I had to create a new opportunity for voices who would not normally have a chance to be heard. [Sundance] was designed to create opportunities for blacks, Asians, gays, women—all those people who were not going to get a chance. We could have a development program to get them started. Then we would do whatever we could to enhance that opportunity. The O'Neill was the first to do that. I think more people need to know the role that the O'Neill [played]. I can't say enough about George White."

That important plays and playwrights emerged from the National Playwrights Conference in so swift a time did not go unnoticed. Other organizations with similar objectives began to spring up, many with the participation of people who had worked in Waterford. The Playwrights' Center of Minneapolis was founded in 1971, its current producing artistic director is National Theater Institute (NTI) alum Jeremy Cohen, and its advisory board and alumni include such veterans of the O'Neill as Edward Albee, Lee Blessing, and James Houghton. In 1979, a playwriting class taught by an O'Neill veteran at the Victory Gardens Theater refused to disband when the course was over; instead, they founded Chicago Dramatists, which, under the leadership of Russ Tutterow, has seen many of its writers become important figures in the Chicago theater scene and work from its lab reach Broadway. In New York, in addition to the venerable New Dramatists (currently headed by NTI alum Todd London), there are a variety of play-development organizations, notably the Lark Play Development Center, which was co-founded in 1994 by current artistic director and NTI alum John Clinton Eisner and has included

George C. White (right) and Robert Redford (second from right) at a Sundance Institute planning meeting in the O'Neill Center's library, 1980. Photo by A. Vincent Scarano.

the involvement of such O'Neill veterans as John Guare, David Henry Hwang, Arthur Kopit, Lynn Nottage, and Theresa Rebeck. In 2001, an O'Neill playwriting alum named Jeni Mahoney founded the Seven Devils Playwrights Conference in McCall, Idaho, drawing on those who had worked at the O'Neill during the Richards years, including Blessing and Amy Saltz. Mahoney was particularly moved that the bell that used to be rung before each performance at the O'Neill was sent to be rung again at Seven Devils and that she regularly heard from Richards wanting to know how she was faring. All these organizations employ staged readings, and usually the writers can field feedback, often from the audience or an invited panel. (In addition to inspiring these groups, the O'Neill birthed the National New Play Network with White's early support. It immediately established itself as an independent organization, much as the American Theatre Critics Association had been hatched in the sunken garden.)

Falls, the artistic director of Chicago's Goodman Theatre (and the man who collided with Robert Redford), remembers the days when foundation money flowed freely to programs hosted by various nonprofit companies around the country. "There was money in the early seventies into the mid-seventies that was being directed towards playwright development and the development of new plays through resident theaters. But I fear that a lot of theaters were receiving money, and they were indeed developing plays, but they weren't putting those plays on. A lot of money went to theaters who were able to [state] on grant [applications] that they were doing public readings of plays, but [they were] producing very few of them. That [practice] has faded a bit as the money has faded. The roots of that could go back to the O'Neill in terms of being a model. But God knows lots of models get picked up and diluted."

The O'Neill has had an impact on international theater as well, being instrumental in inviting foreign artists to the United States and in getting Americans to consider the world beyond their borders. Part of this was rooted in White's reaction to the insularity of much of the American plays he was seeing. "I once saw graffiti over the urinal in the old Ginger Man Restaurant; someone had written, 'My mother made me a homosexual.' Under which, somebody else had written, 'If I get her the wool, will she make me one too?' God, that was so emblematic of the times. In the early days the theme for all the playwrights seemed to be, 'How I've been screwed over by my parents.'

"I got a call in 1968, from a guy named Jerry Freund, the director of the Rockefeller Foundation. 'Do you know about a playwright by the name of Derek

Soviet directors and writers at a session under the Conference Tree, National Playwrights Conference, 1984. Oleg Efremov (seated, second from right) was the artistic director of the Moscow Art Theatre. Lloyd Richards is second from left. Photo by A. Vincent Scarano.

Walcott? He has a theater workshop in Trinidad. Would you like to go down and see it?' And I went down and saw *Dream on Monkey Mountain* and just flipped. With the help of the Foundation, *Monkey Mountain* came to the O'Neill." Lloyd Richards brought it to Yale Rep. After that, it moved to success in New York (see Chapter 8).

This episode marked the beginning of White bringing foreign artists to Waterford. He saw that work from elsewhere had an effect on the American writers. "They could see other cultures doing other themes in different ways. Something besides navel gazing. American theater is very parochial."

The longest ongoing relationship between the O'Neill and theater in another country has been with Russia. It began in 1980, shortly after the Carter administration ordered sanctions against the Soviet Union because of the latter's invasion of Afghanistan. At one point, the only cultural ties between the United States and the Soviet Union were via the O'Neill Center, which began inviting over Soviet playwrights and sponsoring visits by American playwrights to the Soviet Union. Six Soviet plays were presented at the National Playwrights Conferences in the eighties. (The Soviet playwrights were accompanied by other Soviet citizens, including some strongly suspected to be members of the KGB. Groton Naval Base is not far from Waterford.) In 1987, White and a group of Soviet theatermakers organized the American-Soviet Theater Initiative to facilitate cultural exchange.

The Russian ties survived the fall of the Iron Curtain in 1989. As noted in Chapter 6, for more than twenty years, the O'Neill's educational program has maintained a vital connection with the Moscow Art Theatre School. The president of the school, Anatoly

Larissa Borisnova, former prima ballerina of the Bolshoi, leads O'Neill students in the National Theater Institute's Moscow semester at the Moscow Art Theatre, 2010. Photo by Kelly Van Dilla.

Smeliansky, is articulate about the importance of the connection. "Hillary Clinton visited the school and called it a model Russian-American relationship." Because of its years under a communist regime, Russia's theater was isolated from the rest of the world, so the exchange is very much two way. Americans are directly exposed to the traditions of Anton Chekhov and Constantin Stanislavski, and the Russians visiting Waterford catch up on what has been going on in other theatrical cultures. Smeliansky remarks, "Theater is not just for one country, or for another country. Theater unites us. For seventy-five years—*more* than seventy-five years—we had a very strong ideology, and a very wrong ideology, and many people grew up in that. So to erase that ideology means first of all to open the horizons. To open for the Russian teachers and for the Russian students new horizons in the cultural relationship. To open the world."

The relationship with the O'Neill, says Smeliansky, established a precedent that led to associations with other American theaters and schools. "It was the first. It was before the Carnegie-Mellon program at the Moscow Arts School. It was before the Harvard and the ART [American Repertory Theater] program. It was before many American colleges and universities started coming to Moscow. The O'Neill was the pioneer of that."

As for what visiting Americans learn, Smeliansky affirms that Russian theater is not only Chekhov and Stanislavski. "Moscow is like New York. It's the Mecca point, with hundreds of companies working every day." The big difference he sees between Russian and American theater is the emphasis in Russia on ensembles. "In Moscow, you have real companies—companies from twenty-five people to ninety people at the Moscow Art Theatre. Of course, we have now, like America has, production houses, giving space to different shows. But the idea of Russian theater is a company, which we consider like a good family." The world of Russian theater has proved attractive to some Americans. One student who studied in the NTI Moscow program, Caz Liske,

Anatoly Smeliansky (left), dean of the Moscow Art Theatre School, and David Jaffe, National Theater Institute director (1998–2006), speak at the O'Neill, 2002. Photo by A. Vincent Scarano.

is now teaching at the Moscow Art Theatre School—a first. Another, Odin Biron, has become one of Russian television's biggest stars on a comedic medical serial called *Interns*. Both first attended the Moscow school via the O'Neill's program and have since established careers for themselves in Russia.

In 1995, playwright Douglas Post and director Tina Ball were invited to the Shelykova Playwrights Conference in Shelykova, Russia, to restage, in Russian, a play they had worked on at the O'Neill the previous summer. Post's *Drowning Sorrows* told the story of a woman confronting a bartender in an obscure bar on an island with the claim that he is a former fiancé who abandoned her decades ago. (One can easily see how this theme would appeal to a Russian audience, given the history of personal and political betrayals from the days of Stalin's purge trials.)

Ball says of White, "He is the great adventurer. If you understand that about George, then you understand what it was like to go someplace like Russia with him, which was not a country that was very open in 1995. You could move around freely, sort of. But it was the first trip I ever took where I didn't know exactly what hotel I was staying at, in which city." Ball had a sense that arrangements were made on the fly, some of them, she remembers, involving cash deals negotiated in a Mexican restaurant in Moscow owned by someone with undefined but substantial influence. "In Moscow, we stayed in the Rossiya, this enormous 3,300-room hotel in Red Square, which was at one time the place where all the dignitaries stayed. Because all the Russian dignitaries stayed there, it also apparently became a very popular place for prostitutes."

An overnight train, a ferry across the Volga River, and a bus took Post, Ball, White, and the others in the party to Shelykova, whose playwrights conference was

Cross-cultural diplomacy at work: American barbecue champion Mike Mills (second from left) meets Senator Chris Dodd (Connecticut) and Russian Minister of Culture Mikhail Svidkoi (right) at the O'Neill's summer barbecue, 1994. George C. White is at left. Photo by A. Vincent Scarano.

modeled on the one at the O'Neill. It was held on the estate of nineteenth-century Russian playwright Alexander Nikolayevich Ostrovsky, which, as Post describes it, was "out in the middle of nowhere. You are really in the wilderness." They came prepared for the visit; Ball recalls White and a burly O'Neill-affiliated actor named John Seitz lugging a couple of cases of vodka onto the train.

The Russian hosts had cast *Drowning Sorrows* for them, and the play was presented in a Russian translation, directed by Ball with the assistance of a translator. The oddest problem they faced was translating the title. To Post's amusement, given the Russians' reputation for vodka consumption, the phrase "drowning sorrows" didn't make sense to the cast. "I kept saying, my gosh, you know—you're sad, you drink. Why do I need to explain this to *Russians?* And what they came back with was, in Russia, sadness comes, it stays with you for a time, and then it goes away of its own accord. There's really nothing that you can do to alleviate [it]. I said, 'In the United States, we go to the gym, we take pills, we see a therapist.' They said, 'Well, none of that would work for a Russian.'" The conversation spoke to a profound cultural divide between Russian and American assumptions. "Do we have control over our sorrow? In the States we kind of think we do. And I think the Russians would say we're fooling ourselves." The title that finally emerged from these discussions was *When the Sorrows Go Away.* Says Post, "This is why I came to Russia."

The trip to Russia also gave Post a chance to talk with Russian playwrights about the dilemma of what playwriting would become. "Playwrights in Moscow said one of the big difficulties they were facing was trying to figure out what to write about. For so long, the impetus for their work was essentially either covertly or overtly

Director Göran Graffman (Sweden; left) and Harry Carlson work on a script, National Playwrights Conference, 1983. Photo by A. Vincent Scarano.

to rebel against the government. And now that there was much less to rebel against, they were wondering what the topic of their plays should actually be."

Russia was not the only formerly closed country to open its doors to the O'Neill. White received an invitation to China, too. He was originally invited to direct a production of an O'Neill play there, a production that would have made him the first American to direct a play in China. This invitation was modified when Arthur Miller let it be known he was interested in directing a production of his *Death of a Salesman* there, which he did in 1984. (Miller wrote a book about his experience, *"Salesman" in Beijing*.) Shortly after, White directed *Annie Christie*, followed by *The Music Man* in Beijing in Chinese, giving him the distinction of being the first American to direct an American musical in China.

In 1991, a Swedish delegation brought a play of particular relevance to the National Playwrights Conference. *And Give Us the Shadows* by Lars Noren depicts Eugene O'Neill at age sixty and an encounter with his two sons. "Too long, and it was kind of turgid," says White, "but it was a fascinating idea that the boys confront their old man [just] as O'Neill had confronted his old man in *Long Day's Journey into Night*."

One African-American playwright contacted White because he was particularly eager to meet a guest of the O'Neill Center, Nobel Prize–winning Nigerian playwright Wole Soyinka. Author of *Dutchman*, a particularly vivid play about an encounter in a subway between a predatory white woman and a young black man, Amiri Baraka (formerly known as LeRoi Jones) met White and Soyinka in Greenwich Village. White remembers, "We met down on MacDougal Street, and they were like people from two different planets. They had nothing in common. When the governor of the Biafran province was going to get on the radio to cancel habeas

Poster advertising the O'Neill's undergraduate National Theater Institute at the Moscow Art Theatre. Photo by Kelly Van Dilla.

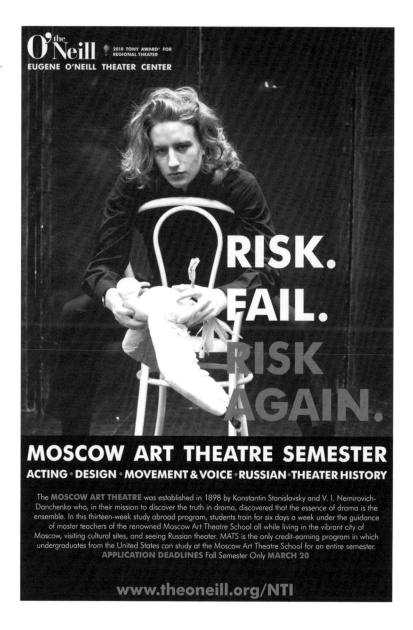

corpus, he walked into the radio station, and there was Wole with a pistol saying, 'Get on the radio and say you're not.' He was not screwing around. After he met Baraka, Wole asked me, 'Who was that? What was this all about?' And I said, 'Well, he wanted to meet you.' I mean Wole was the real thing. At one point, he was in this country because the Nigerians were trying to kill him, and only Lloyd knew where he was."

Perhaps the moment when the O'Neill's foreign involvement reached critical mass was 1984, when a variety of nationalities visited the National Playwrights

Chinese delegation arrives at the National Playwrights Conference, 1984. Photo by A. Vincent Scarano.

Conference. White remembers, "We had the Russians, of course, but we also had people from Australia, China, Argentina, Sweden, and probably someone from the Caribbean. And Danes.

"I was sitting in my office and the second or third day [of the Conference], my door flies open and the leader of the Danish delegation came in and he's all upset. He says, 'It has come to my attention that the Australian delegation has challenged the Russians to a drinking bout at Chuck's Steak House tomorrow night, and we

John Beryle, U.S. ambassador to the Russian Federation (left foreground), celebrates the twentieth anniversary of the O'Neill–Moscow Art Theatre student program at the U.S. embassy in Moscow, December 2011. The program is the longest continuing cultural exchange between the two nations. Also pictured are (to Beryle's left and behind him) Mikhail Svidkoi, special cultural envoy from the president, and (holding certificate, foreground) Anatoly Smeliansky, dean of the Moscow Art Theatre School. O'Neill executive director Preston Whiteway is at the center. Photo by Anastasia Korotich.

Danes are not invited.' I told him that I thought I could arrange things but also that we have in this country an expression called 'the big leagues.' I told him, 'I've been to Denmark, and I know you Danes are great at it, but I warn you . . .' Two days later, he staggers into my office, looking like he's been hit by a truck. And he says, 'George, I want to apologize. I have never, ever seen drinking like that. They drank Chuck's dry. We left at two in the morning, and they were still going at it.'"

15. Eugene O'Neill and the O'Neill

Director Robert Falls has a relationship with the Monte Cristo Cottage that goes back decades. "I went the first time when I was a kid, when I was working on a production of *Ah, Wilderness!* at the University of Illinois. I won't say it was life altering, but it was certainly a very inspirational moment. Over the years I visited it on other occasions."

The most vivid visit was on March 31, 2003, when Falls was directing a production of *Long Day's Journey into Night,* scheduled for Broadway, starring his frequent collaborator, actor Brian Dennehy. Both of them had made the trek to 325 Pequot Avenue in New London many times before. This time, they were joined by the other members of the cast. "Philip Seymour Hoffman and Robert Sean Leonard and Vanessa Redgrave had never been there. I think we were in about our third week of rehearsal. We asked if could stay into the night. They opened the house for us, and we had it to ourselves. We sat at a table and read the play until about one in the morning. Vanessa, being Vanessa, could not help but get up and move around and explore the space and go up the stairway. The other actors were sort of forced to follow Vanessa around. Everybody had scripts in hand, kind of chasing Vanessa around.

The Monte Cristo Cottage in New London, Connecticut. Eugene O'Neill spent summers here as a boy and young adult, and he used it as the setting for his *Long Day's Journey into Night* and *Ah, Wilderness!* The O'Neill Center owns and operates the Cottage as a museum. Photo by A. Vincent Scarano.

"But as you can imagine, it was a turning point to be able to read that play in that house. You're really aware how small it is. You really can hear people pacing around on that second floor. The floors do creak, and the stair creaks. You get a sense of the claustrophobia of that space." Though Falls and his company found inspiration at Monte Cristo, he and designer Santo Loquasto decided not to go for a design that referred to it. "It was much more a metaphoric set rather than claustrophobic. We wanted to present a world that was sort of immersed in fog. But yeah, when you're sitting in that house at 12 o'clock at night in the summer, you really do get kinda connected with the ghosts that were in that house."

Built in the 1840s, the property was purchased by Eugene O'Neill's father, actor James O'Neill, in 1884. The name he gave it came from *The Count of Monte Cristo*, the stage adaptation of the adventure novel by Alexandre Dumas (père) about a wrongly imprisoned man who escapes from his cell to assume a new identity and avenge himself. James was enormously successful in the play—so much so that he revived it decade after decade at the expense of maintaining his talents as a Shakespearean actor. In time, that the house's name referred to an imprisoned character held its own irony. In a passage in *Long Day's Journey*, the character based on James O'Neill, James Tyrone, speaks bitterly of the prison of his success. The play also reflects the sense in which some of the O'Neills felt they were imprisoned by the house and the town. Summering in New London was James O'Neill's choice. His wife Ella had few friends there. Elder son Jamie thought of it as a hick town that kept him from the action of big-league drinking and whoring. Surrounded by misery and resentment, Eugene's feelings for the place were hardly warmer, though he had friendships with others his age and had recourse to New London's Bohemian elements at Doc Ganey's.

A form prepared for the successful 1971 Special Act of Congress naming the Monte Cristo Cottage as a National Landmark lists its owners as Mr. and Mrs. Lawrence A. White. David Hays heard a rumor that Mitchell College was interested in buying it, and he made the case that it would be more appropriate for the organization named after its former tenant to take it over. In 1974, the O'Neill Center did indeed buy the house, and more than $200,000 was secured from the state

The living room in the Monte Cristo Cottage, where Eugene O'Neill set his masterpiece, *Long Day's Journey into Night.* Photo by A. Vincent Scarano.

Sally Pavetti, Fran Pavetti, and Lois MacDonald

The Pavettis, Sally and Fran, have been key contributors to the O'Neill's success, especially in the early decades. Fran served as board secretary and successfully guided the O'Neill through its incorporation. Sally, initially a volunteer for the National Playwrights Conference, quickly found her calling as the curator of Eugene O'Neill's boyhood home—where he set Long Day's Journey into Night—*the Monte Cristo Cottage. George C. White bought the Cottage from Lawrence White (no relation) in 1974, and it was designated a National Historic Landmark by the U.S. Congress the same year.*

Sally, working alongside associate curator Lois MacDonald, oversaw the renovation of the Cottage into a museum, outfitting it as it would have appeared in 1912, the year in which Long Day's Journey *is set. Since that time, they have guided tens of thousands of visitors through the house. Every time there is a major production of O'Neill's work in New York, London, Sydney, Stockholm, St. Petersburg, or elsewhere, the director and set designer, and often the cast, make the journey to the Cottage to commune with the O'Neill family's ghosts and hear the New London foghorn.*

The O'Neill continues to own and operate the Monte Cristo Cottage as a museum and resource for the nation.

—PW

of Connecticut to rehabilitate the building. The Center continues to maintain the property, offering tours to visitors and scheduling events there.

At the time the O'Neill bought Monte Cristo, Hays and his family were often sleeping in his office at the Hammond Mansion while he ran the National Theatre of the Deaf. A solution to the Hays family's housing dilemma presented itself. Says Hays, "I designed *Long Day's Journey*. It was my first big Broadway success. Twenty years later, I moved into that very house. The room that O'Neill describes in the play was exactly there. He remembered it needle sharp. Except, unlike O'Neill's description, it was a sunny house. We lived very happily there."

Actually, "cheerful in the morning sunlight" is how O'Neill described the place in *Ah, Wilderness!* In their book, *O'Neill: Life with Monte Cristo*, Arthur and Barbara Gelb

Eugene O'Neill and his wife Carlotta Monterey at Tao House, California, ca. 1949. In 1964, Monterey gave permission to George C. White to name the Center after her late husband.

cite evidence that the same house served as the model for the homes of the families in both *Long Day's Journey* and *Ah, Wilderness!* The former play was a heightened depiction of O'Neill's memories of 1912, when he contracted tuberculosis and—between his father's decline, his mother's drug addiction, and his brother's alcoholism—the O'Neills were at their most tortured. In contrast, *Ah, Wilderness!* takes place on July 4, 1906, and the family in residence was based on the family whose life O'Neill envied, the McGinleys. The father, John McGinley, was editor of *The Day* (the New London newspaper), and O'Neill sometimes played with his sons. One of them, Arthur, once claimed, "I can identify every character in the play, including myself and my brothers."

On July 4, 2006, one hundred years to the day after the events depicted in *Ah, Wilderness!*, Joe Grifasi (head of the first summer of the NTI's Theatermakers program) supervised a celebration, during which some students put up scenes from the play. Presented in the backyard of the property, a substantial audience from New London attended, including members of the McGinley family.

George C. White chose to name his Center after Eugene O'Neill in part because he was trying to start a theater, and it seemed smart to frame it with reference to the area's most famous theatrical figure. But the connections between O'Neill and the O'Neill go beyond the name on the letterhead and the gloomy caricature of the playwright that for years graced much of its literature. (That the

Frequent National Playwrights Conference actor and director Joe Grifasi (left) with Brian Dennehy, O'Neill Center trustee and recipient of the 2004 Monte Cristo Award. Photo by T. Charles Erikson.

mustache in the caricature made it look a little bit like a skinny Hitler may have had something to do with retiring the image.)

O'Neill himself expressed ambivalence about the town and the house where he spent much of his young years. That he set plays there suggests the hold that the place had on him. He was able to confront his past in his writing. In real life, he had more trouble. The Gelbs describe the visit he made with his third and final wife, Carlotta, to New London in 1931. He intended to take her inside Monte Cristo. The Gelbs quote Carlotta's description of O'Neill's search for the house: "We drove along Pequot Avenue, and he said, 'I can't find it, I can't even see it.' In the time that Gene had been away several little houses had been built along the water, and everything was so changed he couldn't find his house at first. I was thunderstruck when I saw it, this quaint little birdcage of a house, sitting there. Somebody had bought it, and we didn't go in. Gene said, 'I shouldn't have come.' And I said, 'Well, never mind, you have come, now let's get out of here.' And he said, 'Yes, let's go away, I don't want to look at it,' and that was that."

The pain O'Neill's parents suffered witnessing the torturous paths Eugene and his brother Jamie traced was echoed in the playwright's relationships with his own children. His elder son, Eugene, Jr., achieved distinction as a classical scholar at

Yale (among other accomplishments, he coedited *The Complete Greek Drama*, a 1938 Random House anthology of all the extant classic Greek plays), but the familial curse of alcoholism and melancholy led him to commit suicide in 1950, three years before his father's death. Another son, Shane, was disowned by his father and, in 1977, having battled heroin addiction, he too committed suicide. O'Neill also disowned his daughter Oona when, at age eighteen, she married the fifty-four-year-old actor-director, Charlie Chaplin. Despite efforts on her part to reconcile, O'Neill never spoke to or communicated with her again.

In 1994, one of Charlie and Oona's children, a son named Eugene, arrived in New London. Eugene Chaplin (who was born the year his namesake died) was a sound engineer, and he was checking out the Sonalysts Sound Stages, an internationally regarded recording facility in Waterford. According to White, Chaplin happened to see a sign referring to the Eugene O'Neill family homestead. Curious about the man who was rarely mentioned when he grew up, he made the visit to Monte Cristo Cottage that his grandfather had been unable to complete. After this came a visit to the Center. The September 7, 1995, issue of *The Day* reported that Eugene Chaplin narrated a video co-produced by the Center called *Eugene O'Neill's New London* "designed to boost tourism." The article describes scenes shot in front of Monte Cristo and by the statue of Eugene O'Neill as a boy looking out to sea on City Pier. According to the article, while filming near the statue, a local man approached Chaplin and asked, "Are you here to see the local drunk?" (The statue, by Connecticut sculptor Norman Legassie, was commissioned by White in 1988. A copy sits on the terrace of Blue Gene's.)

Closure of another sort came for one of the young Eugene's antagonists, Edward Crowninshield Hammond, the railroad tycoon mentioned in Chapter 1 as having chased the future playwright off his property and having served as a model for the humiliated millionaire in *A Moon for the Misbegotten*. *The Day* reported that William O. Taylor, the grandson of Hammond, was unhappy with the upkeep of his family's graves in New London's Cedar Grove Cemetery. He wanted his family—including his grandfather—to be moved to what had been the Hammond Estate. Some years before, the O'Neill Center, needing to accommodate more people, had moved a Victorian mansion named Ironsides from a neighboring hill to its grounds, where it was renamed the White House, in honor of George's parents. Having accomplished the move, though, the Center found it didn't have enough money to finish renovations. According to *The Day*, "Taylor agreed to donate $100,000 to restore Ironsides, plus $10,000 per year for the cemetery's upkeep until his death, at

Catherine Zeta-Jones presents O'Neill trustee Michael Douglas with the 2012 Monte Cristo Award. The O'Neill annually presents the award in New York City to an artist who shares Eugene O'Neill's "pioneering spirit" and who has had a positive impact on the American theater. Photo by T. Charles Erikson.

which time interest from a $500,000 bank account would be used to maintain a family plot. Taylor and his wife wish to be buried at the [C]enter upon their own deaths." Taylor, who served for years as publisher of the *Boston Globe*, joined his grandfather there in 2011. Quoted in *The Day*, Arthur Gelb speculated on the reaction the playwright would have had to these arrangements. "O'Neill, despite the fact that he was a tragedian and often looked gloomy, had a wonderful sense of humor and irony, and this would have tickled him."

One of the ways the O'Neill Center keeps the connection with its namesake alive is its annual Monte Cristo Award, given to a person who, in Eugene O'Neill's "pioneering spirit," has had an impact on the American stage.

The first award went in 2000 to Jason Robards, whose association with the playwright began in 1956 with his career-making performance as Hickey in the off-Broadway revival of *The Iceman Cometh*, followed that year by playing Jamie in the American premiere of *Long Day's Journey into Night*. He played Jamie again in the hit 1973 revival of the sequel, *A Moon for the Misbegotten*. (He re-created these performances in a film of *Journey* and TV versions of the other plays.) Other recipients of the award include Edward Albee, Zoe Caldwell, Brian Dennehy, Michael Douglas, Arthur and Barbara Gelb, James Earl Jones, Karl Malden, Christopher Plummer, Harold Prince, Neil Simon, Kevin Spacey, Meryl Streep, Wendy Wasserstein, and August Wilson.

Perhaps the most meaningful connection to O'Neill harkens back to an early point in his life. Hearing that a group of young people dissatisfied with the theater of the day were gathering to create something not beholden to the prevailing tastes in the commercial realm, in 1916 the 27-year-old playwright journeyed to a town on the New England coast to join them. They were called the Provincetown Players. One of the founders was named George Cram Cook. More than five decades later, in another town on the New England Coast, George Cooke White would found another enterprise with a similar goal.

16. The O'Neill Today and Tomorrow

 At a ceremony on January 30, 2012, when George C. White was inducted into the Theater Hall of Fame, his name joined the list of legendary theatermakers inscribed on the walls of Broadway's Gershwin Theatre. Between this honor and the Regional Theatre Tony Award given in 2010, the O'Neill has not lacked for recent acknowledgment of its place in American theater.

Awards reflect what has been accomplished, but an organization's vitality and relevance rest not on its past but on its future.

One memorable day in 2013, in the living room of the Hammond Mansion, under the gaze of the portraits of White, Lloyd Richards, and Edith Oliver, executive director Preston Whiteway broke out champagne and, in the company of Tom Viertel, Pat Daily, and other staff, he announced that the State of Connecticut would soon make public the news that it was granting $3 million to the O'Neill Center. According to a news release from the O'Neill, the money would be used to build "seven new dormitory cottages creating living spaces for 65 artists and faculty, a laundry building, a new rehearsal hall" and to renovate "existing buildings into additional production and rehearsal space."

The physical growth, the largest in the O'Neill's history, is to support an expansion of the National Theater Institute's mission. Says Whiteway, "We're expanding

Executive director Preston Whiteway accepts the 2010 Regional Theatre Tony Award at Radio City Music Hall along with the O'Neill's six program artistic directors and board chair Tom Viertel (to the left of Whiteway). Photo by Tony Awards Productions. © WireImage.

into musical theater training with the National Music Theater Institute. With the majority of shows on Broadway being musicals, and with *Glee* and *Smash* on television, more and more when young people think of theater, they think of musicals. Certainly it's the great American theater export to the world. The O'Neill has a long history of developing new musicals, but we haven't been training for them in our educational programs. The students are clamoring to do this kind of work already. NMTI [National Music Theater Institute] is going to address this hunger. Like NTI [National Theater Institute], it's a semester-long course of total immersion. Not only will students learn to sing and dance and act, they will learn to write, compose, direct, and choreograph. They will touch on every discipline that goes into making a musical.

"This and NTI will be on parallel tracks with some overlap. One of the classes the musical theater students will be taking, for instance, will be in dramatic acting, because those skills translate well to the book scenes in musicals. And the NTI students will continue to have singing classes. The existing NTI, since Richard Digby Day's time, has been traveling to the UK and Russia to explore dramatic traditions there. The musical theater students—where else to take them but to two weeks in

(*above*) Rendering of the O'Neill's new rehearsal hall and cottages (background). The view is looking east from the Edith Oliver Theater, with Long Island Sound to the viewer's right. The new construction surrounds the existing parking lot to avoid interference with the expansive vistas of Long Island Sound to the south. Rendering by Centerbrook Architects. (*left*) Jeremy Ladyga, director of institutional development, and Jill Anderson, general manager, serve plates at the O'Neill summer barbecue, 2013. Photo by A. Vincent Scarano.

New York? So it will be a really extraordinary opportunity for an undergraduate—nineteen, twenty, twenty-one years old—to spend fourteen weeks completely absorbed in the world of the disciplines of musical theater."

The new program will serve both idealistic and practical purposes. The idealistic purpose is to meet the needs of American theater even more fully. The practical purpose, to serve the stability of the O'Neill. The income from NTI currently covers much of the cost of the summer conferences. The addition of the National Music Theater Institute, as Whiteway anticipates, will put the O'Neill on "an incredibly firm financial footing. We will not be facing the lean, hand-to-mouth times that we have had over certain periods in our history. Musical theater NTI will also allow us to build up reserves and an endowment, so that we can offer scholarships to students in a way we haven't been able to in the past."

With musical theater students in residence during the school year, there is also the possibility of putting up programs to engage the local population, which has come to be a reliable audience for the Cabaret and Performance Conference

O'Neill chair Tom Viertel with Senator Christopher Murphy (Connecticut) and his wife Cathy, 2013. Photo by A. Vincent Scarano.

(see Chapter 9). Whiteway quickly adds that "I want to be careful, though, that we stay true to mission—process, not product. Not have them geared up to put up something every Saturday night, say. The motto of NTI is something I take very seriously—'Risk. Fail. Risk Again.' That there is a safe space to fail, so that they can then get up and do it better next time."

The additional housing and rehearsal space being built will benefit programs in addition to NTI and the Music Theater Institute. The plans include building an extra cottage, so that the O'Neill can offer residencies to professional groups— companies involved in devised theater, improvisational theater groups, groups organized around clowning or mime skills—to develop new work throughout the year. The expectation is that such groups would interact with NTI and Music Theater Institute students, whether through talkbacks and workshops or involving them in projects. This idea is in part a response to seeing how valuable it has been for students in the summer Theatermakers program to have contact with professionals in the National Playwrights and Music Theater conferences.

As the O'Neill is scheduled now, there are no programs in January and May. Whiteway, Viertel, and their associates are considering how, when the increased housing becomes available, the O'Neill might use the resources during these days to the advantage of developing artists and their projects.

Whiteway comments, "I don't have all the answers of what the Center will be in the future or what sort of work it will be supporting. What I can guarantee is that it will be true to this mission of discovering, nurturing, and developing new work of every sort. What's the next page of American theater going to be, and how can the O'Neill be there to push it forward and support it?

O'Neill founder George C. White and executive director Preston Whiteway, 2013. Photo by A. Vincent Scarano.

"The O'Neill organizational model is a unique and slightly bizarre one for the American theater, but one that works for the organization—an executive director overseeing six co-equal artistic directors, each with oversight over their programs. At times, it has threatened to be like the Balkan states here, but we've managed to integrate and overlap in such a way that strengthens each program individually and forges an O'Neill identity."

Frisbee on the lawn at the O'Neill, summer 2011. Photo by A. Vincent Scarano.

Part of the concern for the O'Neill's future stems from so many other organizations having assimilated many of the O'Neill's practices and innovations (see Chapter 14). Artist and project development are being pursued by theaters, schools, and organizations at every degree of the compass. If similar experiences and opportunities are available elsewhere—even if imitation is the greatest flattery—the question arises: what makes the O'Neill stand out?

Yale's James Bundy has one answer: "There is no substitute for the impact of beauty on the artist. The transformational experience of being in the setting has incalculable power. Also, having a lot of artists in one place doing a lot of projects and in a lot of disciplines." Whiteway echoes, "When you put 200 creative minds together, to mix a metaphor, it lifts all boats."

Speaking of the National Playwrights Conference, Lee Blessing adds, "The O'Neill was the template for all of them, but I'm not sure any of them does it better than the O'Neill. It allows poor, young, on-their-uppers playwrights a chance to spend the kind of summer that only the well-to-do generally spend in Connecticut. They get a chance to interact with the level of professionals whose offices they mostly couldn't otherwise get into. It may have changed. There may be things that I like more and less about the place as it evolves, but I can't think of a better place to go with a play."

Groundbreaking for the O'Neill's campus expansion, November 13, 2013. The expansion, consisting of new residential cottages and rehearsal spaces, will accommodate a new musical theater undergraduate training program, under the auspices of NTI. Pictured, left to right, are NTI artistic director Rachel Jett, executive director Preston Whiteway, chairman Tom Viertel, Connecticut state representative Elizabeth Ritter, Connecticut state senator Andrea Stillman, and Waterford first selectman Dan Steward. Photo by A. Vincent Scarano.

Executive director Preston Whiteway introduces a play in the Amphitheater, National Playwrights Conference, 2013. Photo by A. Vincent Scarano.

What's more, with the Wendy Wasserstein Fund in place, the National Playwrights Conference is one of the few places that is accessible purely by virtue of talent. Although playwrights trained in the academy are welcome, unlike some programs, you don't need an MFA—or indeed, any schooling—to be eligible for consideration. The discovery of August Wilson speaks to the value of this principle.

"Ten years ago," says Whiteway, "a lot of people were wondering if the O'Neill's time had passed. Was it still relevant? Would it survive? While many had great affection and admiration for the place, some were thinking that perhaps the O'Neill had served its purpose. What I think we've shown in the last ten years—both by turning the place around financially and by having so much great work come through and introducing so many important new artists—[is that] it's as vital today as it was when it first made its reputation."

Bibliographic Essay

THE BULK OF THIS BOOK is derived from a hundred-odd one-on-one recorded interviews with alumni of the O'Neill Center as well as several group discussions. This original material is introduced by phrases written in the present tense, for example, "she remembers," "he explains." Material introduced by phrases written in the past tense are derived from previously published material.

Reporters at the *New York Times* and a New London paper, *The Day*, have been diligent about keeping their eyes on the developments at the Hammond Estate, and Frank Rizzo of the *Hartford Courant* has provided valuable additional material and insights. I cite them in the text when I quote from their articles. Edith Oliver and Michael Feingold wrote for the *New Yorker* and the *Village Voice*, respectively, and they saw to it that material from the conferences received appropriate attention in those publications. The quotes from Lloyd Richards are largely drawn from "Lloyd Richards: Reminiscence of a Theatre Life and Beyond" by N. Graham Nesmith in *African American Review*, 2005, volume 39, issue 3, and from The Academy of Achievement website at http://www.achievement.org/autodoc/page/ricoint-2.

Most of the stories about the old system of developing commercial productions have their sources in the numerous seminars and interviews sponsored over the years by the Dramatists Guild and in articles in Guild publications—first *The Dramatists Guild Quarterly* (which was founded and edited by the late Otis L. Guernsey, Jr.) and then its successor, *The Dramatist*. I also drew on interviews the *Paris Review* has run with playwrights over the years. Neil Simon's story about Elliot Norton's help with *The Odd Couple* is in his memoir, *Rewrites: A Memoir* (Simon and Schuster, 1996).

Some of the information about the first National Playwrights Conference in 1965—including the summary of Audrey Wood's comments—was in a promotional brochure printed by the O'Neill. As mentioned in Chapter 2, Harold Clurman's book, *The Fervent Years: The Group Theatre and the Thirties* (Harcourt Brace Jovanovich, 1945), details the history and spirit of the Group Theatre. Copies of all scripts developed at the O'Neill are housed in the Hammond Mansion, and I made regular reference to them. Information on David Pressman can be found at this website: http://www.emmytvlegends.org/blog/?p=3531.

Accounts of Lloyd Richards's involvement with *A Raisin in the Sun* were found in *You Can't Do That on Broadway!: A Raisin in the Sun and Other Theatrical Improbabilities* by Philip Rose (Limelight Editions, 2001), and in *Sidney Poitier: Man, Actor, Icon* by Aram Goudsouzian (University of North Carolina Press, 2003).

So far, the only program started by the O'Neill Center to have been the subject of a book is the National Theatre of the Deaf, showcased in *Pictures in the Air* by Stephen C. Baldwin (Gallaudet University Press, 1994).

Information about critics Ernest Schier and Dan Sullivan largely comes from interviews in *Under the Copper Beech: Conversations with American Theater Critics*, edited by Jeffrey Eric Jenkins (Foundation of the American Theatre Critics Association, 2004). Useful discussion of dramaturgs was found in *What Is Dramaturgy?* edited by Bert Cardullo (Peter Lang, 1995).

Joan Harrington, who conducted a number of interviews with August Wilson, wrote a particularly valuable chapter on his experiences at the O'Neill Center in her book *I Ain't Sorry for Nothin' I Done: August Wilson's Process of Playwriting* (Limelight Editions, 1998). She in turn referred to Dennis Watlington's article "Hurdling Fences" in the April 1989 *Vanity Fair*. Also useful was "August Wilson: An Interview" by Vera Sheppard, in the summer 1990 *National Forum*, and John Lahr's evocative profile of August Wilson, "Been Here and Gone," in the April 16, 2001, issue of the *New Yorker*.

Puppetry being primarily a visual medium, some of the most valuable resource material on the National Puppetry Conference was found on the internet. The description of *Dustbowl* is derived from a video of it at http://vimeo.com/43162271. (By the way, video of the wedding of two Puppetry Conference participants who met at the O'Neill may be seen at http://www.nytimes.com/2008/08/17/fashion/weddings/17VOWS.html?.)

Biographical material on Eugene O'Neill was largely derived from two books by Arthur and Barbara Gelb: *O'Neill* (Harper, 1962) and *O'Neill: Life with Monte Cristo* (Applause Books, 2000).

The recording of Wendy Wasserstein's speech, which was the basis of the transcript edited for inclusion in a sidebar in Chapter 12, is courtesy of the Richard and Alicia Kuranda Archive at Epic Repertory Theatre Company, New York.

Special Thanks from the O'Neill Center

Jill Anderson
Betty Beekman
Eric Brandt
The Burry Frederick Foundation
Anne and Leon Calanquin
Roger S. Christiansen
Connecticut College
Pat Daily
The Dramatists Guild of America
Bethe Dufresne
The Educational Foundation of
    America
Heidi Ettinger
Alden Ferro
Sophie Gandler
The Gladys Krieble Delmas Foundation
Barry Grove
Philip Himberg
The Horace W. Goldsmith Foundation
Phyllis Kaye

Jean Marie Keevins
Barnet Kellman and Nancy Mette
Richard Kuranda
Jeremy Ladyga
G. W. Mercier
City of New London, Connecticut
New York Library for the
    Performing Arts
Kristine Niven
Annella Preble
J Ranelli
Amanda Kay Ritchie
Brenna Ross
Jillian Ruben
A. Vincent Scarano
Oz Scott
Richard Termine
Town of Waterford, Connecticut
George C. and Betsy White
Samuel Yates

Transcribers

Martha Wade Steketee

Teresa Bayer
Ashley Cease
Meg Jones
Alexandra Keegan
Jay Koepke
Marina McClure
Melissa Nocera

Anastasia Olowin
David James Peterjohn
Sara Sugihara
Robin Vacek
Alison Valtin
Kathryn York

Index